ROCASTLE'S

CREDITS

My thanks go to the many friends who read excerpts from this novel in its early days and gave me comment and advice. Particularly I want to thank fellow sailor Michael Glanister who both edited and proof read the book, and Jo Smith who knocked into shape and typeset the final version. Any errors of fact are entirely down to me. In writing fiction one can do outrageous things. In this case I have stretched the coast of Southern England by one mile and inserted my imaginary and dysfunctional community of Duddlestone. I have wonderful boyhood memories of rural Dorset and that county is among my favourite places in all the world.

Duddlestone has as much relevance to present day Purbeck, as Brigadoon has to the Scottish Highlands. I need hardly say that not one of the characters has any relation or resemblance to anyone in the real world.

AUTHOR

Jim Morley has sailed and raced small boats all his life. He spent forty years in agriculture and forestry before changing to a career in freelance writing. He lives near Petersfield in Hampshire and sails a small family yacht on Chichester Harbour.

COVER:

The Pinnacles, between Poole Harbour and Swanage, Dorset
– photograph by John Owen Smith

ROCASTLE'S VENGEANCE

James Morley

Rocastle's Vengeance
First published 2006

Published by Benhams Books, 1 Fir Cottage, Greatham, Liss, Hampshire GU33 6BB

Typeset by John Owen Smith

ISBN 0-9548880-1-4

Printed and bound by CPI Antony Rowe Ltd, Eastbourne

CHAPTER 1

SATURDAY, JUNE 14th 1997

Five minutes ago I was at peace, enjoying this lovely June morning, and I didn't need these soldiers pointing guns at me. One of them walked to my car side window and glared, his thin pallid face looking menacing under the Military Police cap, while beads of perspiration ran down his face and neck.

'Have you an ID, sir?'

I offered the pass with my tiny photograph pasted to it.

'And when was this issued?' The voice resonated suspicion.

'Today.'

'So, this picture's supposed to be you – is it?"

The man had a point. The photo was the work of a booth in a supermarket, one of a batch taken six weeks ago.

'This pass was issued to a Captain Wilson, and you ain't 'im,' said the soldier triumphantly.

'How d'you know?' I'd had a long journey on a hot day and this was beginning to be boring.

'In the Army facial hair ain't allowed – Queen's regs.' He looked pointedly at my neatly trimmed seaman's beard.

I eyeballed him back. 'I'm a master mariner, a captain of ships, not some chinless twit in charge of a squad of woodentops.'

Inwardly I smiled. I remembered the fury of my late father, a Royal Navy captain, when a gushing woman had asked him which regiment he served in.

Ignoring the insult the guard walked a few paces muttering into his radio. He looked back at me. 'You something to do with the new harbour?'

'That's right, I was told it's down here.'

'Well, you was told wrong. Go back to the fork and turn right.'

With difficulty, I shunted the car around on the narrow strip of melting tarmac; at least the other guard was no longer pointing his gun. I drove back to the point where the ways divided and turned the cooling system to maximum. I could see now where I'd gone wrong. The road to the guard post was well maintained, while the fork to the right was built from squares of crumbling discoloured concrete. I was still annoyed; it was clear these ID cards were going to be a damn nuisance. At present the main village of New Duddlestone was connected to Old Duddlestone by a single dirt road cutting across a mile of military ranges. We had been promised a new link across private farmland, but when? That was in the hands of fate and the local planners. In the meantime, all our customers would need these stupid passes. What on earth could the government have, worth guarding, on this empty hillside?

The road ran upwards to a steep downland ridge and a narrow cutting, as if a giant had taken a bite from the landscape. At the crest of the hill I slowed my car and stopped, the unpleasant taste of the last few minutes washed away. Before me lay the sea glittering in the morning light, with high cliffs stretching away to Portland in the west and Durlstone Head and Swanage in the east. Beyond them lay the hazy loom of the distant Isle of Wight. Wheeling gulls called as they soared above the cliff face, and the scented wind buffeted against the windshield and through the open windows. Near the horizon I could see single ship, a small coaster, chugging westward.

The depression and regret that I'd lived with for months began to well up inside me. A year ago it could have been me on her bridge. Now I was unemployed, another statistic: a master's ticket in one pocket and P45 in the other. A captain with no ship, happy to take a harbour manager's post in a minor yacht marina. I clenched my fists as another black cloud began to choke me. Since my troubles these mood shifts were a daily occurrence; my normal matter-of-fact self one minute, followed by depression and despair the next. I suppose this was a consequence of my odd ancestry. What could one expect from a man with one grandfather an English admiral and the other a Russian musician? I wished I had some half-decent music to play now, but my CD collection was in storage, and all the radio could find were irritating snippets on Classic FM or old pop tracks on Radio Two. To hell with it; I put the car in gear and descended the narrow chine towards the huddle of grey houses below.

So this was Old Duddlestone, the ghost village commandeered by the navy in 1943. I had expected to see ruins, but not so. The houses in the tiny street looked to be in perfect repair. I was reminded of the strange places I had seen on my travels – Petra perhaps, or that ancient Mayan city excavated from the jungle.

The road skirted the village and turned towards the artificial harbour, the only visible relic of the Second World War. Duddlestone Harbour was an ugly utilitarian pouring of reinforced concrete and local stone. It was an impressive structure, not unlike the Cobb at

Lyme Regis, but lacking the charm. Cleverly sited and engineered, it had withstood fifty years of winter gales unscathed. It remained the one place on this coast where small craft could lie safe in all weathers. Even nearby Lulworth could be untenable in anything of a blow from the south.

Piled on the quay was a huge stack of timber and the components to launch a yacht pontoon. A completed dock was already afloat at right angles to the harbour wall. Two cars stood parked on the quay; an anonymous blue Peugeot and the other a newly registered, bright red Jaguar. The only living being in sight was a scruffy looking woman, aged around thirty, clad from head to foot in denim. I had a closer look at her as I parked the car. She might have been pretty, even desirable, if she'd taken some trouble with her lank blonde hair.

Two men emerged from a Portakabin office. One I knew and was scheduled to meet; he was Hugh Crowfoot, the managing director of United Marinas PLC.

'Good morning, Captain,'

Crowfoot was a tall, gangling man, aged late thirties, with receding brown hair. I'd sized him up at our first meeting, as an amiable but dim public school type, not likely to cause me too many problems.

'Who is that?' I asked pointing at the woman.

'She's an Australian journalist – says she's writing something about the wartime harbour.'

The woman stared at us, turned, and walked away towards the village.

'Captain,' Crowfoot continued. 'May I introduce Doctor Paul Hooder? The Doctor owns the freehold of this site and he's our main investor.'

The doctor was an impressive, if greying, middle-aged man. He might have qualified as classically handsome but for the over-flared nostrils that gave the look of one permanently offended by some unpleasant smell.

'Glad to meet you, Wilson,' he said. 'Hugh has told me about you.'

He stared rudely, taking in my navy standard sweater and my well-worn jeans. I guessed I wasn't his image of a captain.

'You understand, Wilson, we've been advised to hire a qualified ship's master as our site manager. It'll ease our way with the authorities, planners and so forth..." His eyes narrowed. 'Personally, I would have chosen someone with business background and management skills.' No doubt it wasn't his fault, but the twitching nostrils seemed to signal me as the offending odour.

'I've done my share of managing, Doctor – try me.' I stared at him.

His eyes were an unusual blue. For a moment he stared back, then shied away again while he flapped a hand at an intrusive fly.

'You see,' Crowfoot chipped in nervously. 'It was conditional on our appointing a professional, that we were allowed to operate from here as an officially recognised harbour.'

'Wilson,' the nose was twitching again. 'I've made a concession in your case, but my priority is to make the maximum return on our investment. So no flights of fancy – always remember the bottom line.'

'I'll do my best,' I replied contritely. I needed this job, the money was good, so there were bound to be pitfalls.

'Your best may not be good enough in a competitive world, but we will give you the benefit of the doubt.' The doctor shot me a tigerish grin and then turned away to face Crowfoot. 'Laura, my assistant, is around somewhere. I've instructed her to show Wilson the village – fill him in on all the historical stuff,' he glanced at his watch. 'Now I've surgery in half an hour – so duty calls.' He gave a little twittering laugh, waved to us and walked away.

I watched Crowfoot's face as the Doctor's Jaguar drove up the hill in a cloud of dust. 'You never told me about that guy,' I said.

'I know,' he was looking uneasy again. 'Hooder's a doctor with a large private practice. Apart from that, he's loaded with money from somewhere – we checked him before we went into this project.'

'I'm not complaining, but I do need to know who I'm working for. What happens if something goes wrong? And I don't like all this talk about bottom lines. You'd better understand that I will run this place to my standards. There'll be no cost cutting on safety.'

'Oh absolutely,' Crowfoot nodded vigorously. 'Look, you're working for United Marinas, but Hooder is a major shareholder; it's his money that's financing this harbour. He owns the whole shebang, but he says this is the only way he can earn an honest penny from it. But he can't push you around on day-to-day matters, and frankly, I don't think he'll try.'

Crowfoot fairly bubbled with enthusiasm as he raced me around the dock. He drooled over the proposed facilities, the onshore breeze ruffling his sheets of plans. I listened politely but I wanted to escape. The meeting with Doctor Hooder had unsettled me. I needed time to collect my thoughts and the little cluster of houses by the cliffs fascinated me. Twenty minutes later Crowfoot left with a cheery farewell from his car horn. I was alone, or was I? Twice I'd seen a man moving among the buildings of the village. I walked over for a closer look.

The little greystone cottages formed a single street. The first was only a few yards from the high tide mark. It was a tribute to the builders of these abandoned houses that they had withstood fifty years of weather and vandalism and still remained sound. The first cottage had a good oak door with traces of blue paint. I tried the handle but it was locked. The keyhole was clear and showed signs of recent oiling. The front door of the next house had been removed and was leaning against the wall. It seemed builders were working here. Inside I could see bags of cement stacked in a far corner. I walked into the gloom of the front room. It was wonderfully cool in contrast to the midsummer heat wave outside. The flagstone floor had been swept but in the middle was a pile of broken and rotting doorframes. Next to the cement pile was an open door, and through it I could see a small kitchen. The old clay sink was smashed but a gaping hole remained in the wall where once there had been a range. The back door was wide open, and a pleasant breeze filled the room with the mixed fragrance of the sea, and the scent of flowers. I looked out onto a well-tended garden bright with colour. Perched on a folding stool was a woman working at an artist's easel.

CHAPTER 2

'Hi there, welcome aboard, Captain.' It was a pleasant cultured voice, with an undertone of Dorset.

I stood gawping awkwardly. This girl, was the most attractive thing I'd seen in the place. She must be in her thirties with round features and a mass of tumbling dark brown hair. Her trim figure, and lightly tanned skin were nicely complimented by a white halter-top sundress.

'I take it you are Captain Wilson?' the dark eyes were inspecting me.

'That's right.'

'I'm Laura Tapsell. We'll be working together – I'm Paul Hooder's business manager.' She held out her hand; the grasp was firm and assured.

Suddenly I was wary. I'd had my fill of women managers and lawyers for the past six months and it must have shown. She dropped her hand and stepped back.

'Do you have a problem with me, Captain?'

My anger began to kindle. I was certain I was going to dislike this woman. I suspected that behind those inscrutable eyes she was laughing at me. Suddenly, she seemed much less attractive and she smelt of sun lotion.

'There's no problem,' I said flatly. 'I can work with anyone.'

'They say you wouldn't work with your ship's first officer.'

That was snide and below the belt but I kept my temper. 'My only concern was the efficient running of the ship. I refused to have that person aboard, not because she was a woman, but because she was a liability.'

'After she'd spent ten years at sea battling in a man's world.' The dark eyes were coldly hostile. 'Oh come on, Captain, there's not a woman on earth you'd find competent, is there?'

How little you know, lady, I thought. I could have referred her to my ex-wife's divorce lawyer. There was one supremely competent woman. Between the two of them they'd stitched me up, taken all my savings, and left me with a half share of a house I wasn't allowed to live in and a sailing yacht. I was already dossing down in the latter because I'd nowhere else to go.

I returned an icy stare. 'I also qualified for my master's ticket after ten years, but I didn't get to be first officer for another eighteen months. As for the recent problem, the company was expecting me, in the cause of political correctness, to force a crew, half of whom were Muslims, to take orders from a woman.' I glared at her and for a second the eyes flickered uncertainly. 'How d'you know about it anyway?'

'I read about it in the *Guardian*.' She was relaxed now. I guessed she'd been testing me and found the honours even. 'Paul checked up on you. Of course he thinks you're the bees knees because of it – the prat.' Suddenly her expression softened and her face broke into a friendly grin. 'Sorry, it's Paul who really pisses me off, I've no right to take it out on you, especially as we're going to be neighbours.'

'Are we?'

'That's right. This is my grandparents' house, I'm having it done up – all mod cons. United Marinas are doing the same for the one next door. It's yours if you want it – official residence for the harbour master.'

'This Paul you talk of, I assume he's that doctor fellow. I've just met him and he said someone was here to show me round.'

'That's right, he told me to keep an eye open for you. I'll show you the sights if you like.'

'Thanks.' I turned and looked seawards over the garden wall. 'Odd name, Hooder,' I mused.

'His father came from South Africa; brilliant scientist they say. Paul thinks he's brilliant himself of course. He's got a soothing manner with old ladies, but he's an arrogant bastard with everyone else.'

'Why work with him then?'

'Good money.' She grinned.

'The name Hooder doesn't sound particularly Afrikaans?'

'It's Dutch. Paul's grandfather emigrated there from Holland. His own father came to England just before the war started. He was a top government scientist.'

I walked across and looked at the easel. On it was a sheet of paper with a half-completed watercolour painting. It was good too: nicely conveying the light and shade of the old cottage and the colours of the garden borders.

'It's only a hobby,' for the first time she was looking defensive, almost shy. 'I call myself a painter, but working for Paul's my day job.'

'You've got talent,' I said and I meant it.

‘Not enough,’ she smiled, ‘but I try…’

Her words were interrupted by an unpleasant mocking laugh. I was startled and angry as I swung round to meet this intrusion. Standing in the kitchen doorway was a young man, his face twisted in an insolent leer. Laura Tapsell reacted with fury. I stood open mouthed as she swept past me and stood squaring up to this newcomer.

‘Captain, this is Steve Gulley. Look at him carefully, he’s a certified pain in the arse, and Doctor Hooder has banned him.’

The man still had a smirk on his face, but the ferocity of the woman had made him shrink back. ‘Is that so, Laura, my little love? Then you tell the Doc to come an’ throw me out…’

The voice was rich Dorset. More suitably garbed and he could have sprung from the pages of Thomas Hardy.

I looked at him with distaste. He was both tall, and grossly fat, with greasy shoulder-length hair. He wore muddy trainers, camouflage trousers and his enormous paunch bulged beneath a replica Arsenal football shirt. He smelt sweaty and he hadn’t shaved today, or probably yesterday. I’d handled his like before. Have him aboard ship, slim him down, and with a bit of discipline I’d make a seaman of him.

‘You’re the one I saw moving around these buildings while I was on the quay,’ I told him.

‘What if I were?’ he answered mockingly. ‘I got a sight more right ’ere than what you has.’

He rolled his tongue around his mouth and spat a large gob with deft accuracy three inches in front of my feet. I wasn’t standing for that.

‘D’you want this man out of here?’ I asked calmly.

‘Out!’ the man guffawed. ‘I’d like to see you try, mate – that I would. Who be this little runt, eh, Laura?’

Inwardly I sighed, how very much less complicated was life at sea compared with the turmoil on land. This day, that had started so brightly, was fast turning sour. I was still irritated from my brush with the military. Now, having arrived at my new workplace, I’d faced in turn that pompous doctor, a waspish female and finally this Neanderthal oaf. At least the psychology of the Gulleys of this world was something I understood. The way the man had backed away from the Tapsell woman was a fair indication that he was mostly bluster. Without others of his kind to spur him on he was unlikely to be too difficult.

'I'll answer the question for you,' I said.

I walked to within a foot of him and as I expected, he shied away from eye contact. 'I'm the boss man around here and I say you're going.' Then I stepped forward and kneed him in the balls.

He screamed and retched. The stench of his breath almost made me vomit: an awful mix of halitosis, stale beer and cheap fags. I grabbed him by his left arm to swing him round, but he recovered quickly. I felt the rage of the man as he took a swing at me with his other fist. As I ducked beneath his flailing arm I felt a stinging slap to the back of my head, vicious and totally unexpected. I let go of Gulley and staggered a pace backwards. A slight figure had dived between us; it was Laura Tapsell. I was caught off balance as she gave me a push that sent me sprawling. Humiliated, I looked up. She had hold of Gulley from behind and had his long locks of hair clenched in both her fists.

'You stupid, stupid men,' she screamed, her voice grittier and the Dorset accent broader. 'Like children you are.' Her tanned face had taken a tinge of red and she was breathing heavily. 'I'll not have this nonsense and you'll stop it now!' She'd released Gulley's hair and was pushing him bodily through the front door.

I climbed to my feet trying to conceal my dented pride. I didn't like this woman, but I had to admit her performance was magnificent. Gulley had left the house; I could hear him outside in the street uttering lame threats. Laura reappeared in the kitchen doorway. She was flush faced and breathing heavily and seemed preoccupied and flustered. The halter tie, that was all that secured her skimpy dress, had come undone and she was frowning as she tried to fix it.

'Allow me,' I offered.

With a rueful grin she turned her back and I took the two ends and knotted them. 'Is that too tight?'

'No, it'll do.'

'Reef knot, much safer, but you'll have to get your husband to untie it.'

'Haven't got one – he buggered off and left me a year ago.'

I wasn't altogether surprised; that unknown man had my sympathy.

'You all right?' she asked.

'I'm strong in body but sore in ego. Are you always like this, or is it midsummer madness?' I stared at her coldly.

She laughed. 'When I was a student I did some time as a nanny. I looked after three kids, all boys, aged four to eleven. I didn't stand nonsense from them and I'm not starting now.' She returned my stare, then her face relaxed. 'Come on, I'll show you round.'

Half way up the hill on the entry road, Laura pulled her car over onto the left-hand verge and stopped. 'There you are,' she said. 'That's as good a view of the bay as you'll get.'

The view was indeed spectacular and I tried to reconcile its features with the half-folded Admiralty chart on my lap. Below, I could see the harbour wall with the water inside looking reassuringly calm. All morning I'd had nagging doubts about the claims for this harbour, and I said so to Laura.

'How secure is this place in a southwest blow? I've seen similar harbour walls in Cornwall and Braye in Alderney; the wall there's twice this one and the seas come right over the top.'

'No it'll be all right, really it will,' she was adamant. 'I've known this bay all my life and I've seen it in all weathers. Look at the chart.' She leaned across me pointing. I tried to ignore the soft brown skin, and the wisp of hair that brushed against my cheek.

'See here,' she continued. 'That's the key to it – the Mixon reef to the west, and the Ledge to the east. Let's get out and I'll point them to you for real.'

She opened her door and jumped onto the short grass, startling a rabbit that scuttled into a hollow. I climbed out my side, alarmed to find a one-hundred-foot drop almost at my feet. I stood still for a moment drinking in the scene. I was beginning to like this place – the scents of downland, the warm onshore breeze, and the slap of the waves at the foot of the cliffs. Laura came round and handed me a pair of binoculars.

'Look, that's the Mixon.' She grabbed my arm and pointed at a long line of rocks stretching out parallel with the artificial wall. 'We've put a south cardinal beacon at the end, but it's only a couple of triangles welded to a metal pole. United Marinas are putting up a bigger one and that'll be lit at night.'

I nodded, I was beginning to get the picture. 'So that reef takes the first shock from the west?'

'That's right. In my grandfather's day that was good enough to protect the boats in high winds, though they hauled them ashore most days. The Navy built the wall and afterwards they operated in all weathers.'

'OK – what if it comes on to blow south or east?'

'Then we're protected by the other reef, the Ledge.' She was pointing to a similar line of rocks to the east. These were two thirds covered by sea. I calculated there was still an hour until high water.

'Do those rocks cover right over?' I asked her.

'Never completely, and I know it's not easy to pick out from seawards; but we've thought of that already.' She seemed pleased with herself. 'We've put two leading beacons on the shoreline – black and yellow striped triangle, in line with a red and white disc…'

'Ball is the correct term,' I said stiffly.

'Well, double ones to you too, Captain,' she grinned.

We were back at the dock standing beside my parked car. Throughout the journey Laura Tapsell had been giving me sideways glances and she was clearly irritated. I guessed that she had been expecting me to probe and had already rehearsed a dozen devastating put-downs. One thing I did give way on. She had offered no explanation for the antics of the man Gulley. I had retaliated by feigning a lack of interest, but it wouldn't do. It seemed the man was trespassing, and he might claim I had assaulted him.

'You haven't told me who the "incredible hulk" is?'

'Yes I have – he's Steven Gulley.'

'Not good enough, tell me some more – this concerns business. I don't want a character like that mooching around and upsetting our customers.'

She half turned and looked towards the cliffs. 'I expect he's still around somewhere.'

'He can't frighten you surely, not after the way you dealt with him just now?' I was being provocative, but I needed answers.

'Frightened of Steve, good God no!' Her tone of astonished derision was genuine enough.

'OK, who is he and what's biting him?'

She didn't answer at once; she had turned towards the sea and was shading her eyes against the midday sun. The breeze was fluttering her hair and pressing the flimsy dress against her slim figure.

'Trouble is,' she said at last, 'I've got divided loyalties. In a way I sympathise with his attitude, but not the way he expresses it.'

'So, he's got a chip on his shoulder about something?'

'You could say he think he owns this place, and in a way morally he does.'

'Mrs Tapsell, you're talking in riddles. Please can you come to the point?'

'Aye-aye, Captain, sir,' she grinned sardonically.

Despite myself I was laughing as well. 'Sorry, First Officer, force of habit – carry on.'

'This village, Old Duddlestone, belonged to the big estate. But the estate never charged the fishing families rent; not money anyway. There was an unwritten understanding that the families had possession, in exchange for fresh fish and the use of boats when they were needed. It was like that for generations, but when the war came, the Government commandeered the village and moved the families out.'

'Hooder said you were to give me the historical background.'

She laughed. 'More fool him. He thinks I'm going to give you his version.'

'Which is?'

'Never mind, I'd rather deal in facts.' She shook her mane of hair back over her shoulders. 'The agreement said that when the Government had finished with the requisitioned land, they had to offer it back to the original owners at the original price.'

'How come Hooder?'

'All right, give me a chance to finish,' she cut me short with a displeased grimace. 'In 1945, Paul's father, Professor Pieter Hooder, bought the rights to this land from the estate. Unfortunately, both the landowner and the regular manager were away in the forces. A land management company was running the place, and it seems Hooder senior offered them the kind of money you don't refuse.'

'Was this common knowledge?'

'No way! It came as a bombshell six months ago. You see I don't think any of us were seriously going to rebuild the fishing community. That was dead and gone, only a few memories and fading photos. But we do feel cheated, all of us – Rocastles, Gulleys, Stonemans…'

'And Tapsells?' I asked.

She rounded on me, her face showing her annoyance. 'Tapsell's my ex-husband. He comes from bloody Birmingham and he should stay there.'

And he'd be well advised to, I thought.

'My people are Rocastles,' she said. 'But we're all related – Steve's a sort of cousin.'

'How do you fit into all this – which side are you on?'

'Paul had me head-hunted. I was working for the National Trust when his agent came and offered me this job at double what I was earning.'

'So you looked after number one.' It was my turn to be nasty.

She was smiling. 'No, I've got a clear conscience. Look, we've got to adapt. There's very little employment here, and with the Army cutting back, it's going to get worse. Most of our youngsters have the sea in their blood, a lot of them go yacht crewing in Poole. This marina could be a lifeline for the whole community. It's just a few thickheads, like Steve and his father, who can't see it.'

'So the Doctor's hired you to pacify the natives?'

'Perhaps he also heard I was good at my job, just like he heard you were good at yours, Captain,' she hit back triumphantly.

I was watching the corner of the portakabin. For a split second I'd caught a movement there; a small head was peeping round the side. Laura broke into a happy laugh,

'Hi Tommy, you can come out – we've both seen you.'

Round the corner came a small boy, dressed in grubby shorts and an even grubbier T-shirt. His hair was cropped short in the current style. He was, I supposed, about ten years old.

'Not at school, Tommy?' asked Laura.

'It's Saturday,' the boy answered, looking her full in the eye.

Well done, Tommy, I thought. For the first time Laura Tapsell looked disconcerted.

'It always pays to know what day it is,' I remarked airily.

She was smiling again. 'Meet my nephew, Tommy Stoneman.' Tommy shuffled his feet and regarded me warily.

Laura continued, 'Tommy, this is Captain Wilson. You weren't trying to burgle his office, I hope?'

'I never.' Tommy looked outraged at the suggestion.

Laura laughed. 'Tommy, the Captain here's going to take charge of the harbour. He's a really hard captain and he'll be watching you.' She turned back to me. 'By the way, do you want temporary accommodation in New Duddlestone? It'll be weeks before your house here's ready.'

I shook my head. 'No thanks, I'm sailing my boat round tomorrow morning and I'll live aboard her for the time being.'

Laura showed me inside the office. I was pleased to find how well it was equipped. The place consisted of an outer reception area for the marina and an inner office with my name on the door.

'They reconnected the power last week,' she said, 'and we're installing the VHF, ship-to-shore, on Monday.'

'I'm impressed,' I said and I meant it.

We came outside again and I looked around for Tommy; I was not surprised that he had vanished. For the first time I took in the vast area of concrete that lay a little way from the end of the concrete wall.

Weeds were growing in the many cracks, and anywhere else with enough soil to root.

'That's a left-over from the war, I suppose?' I pointed at it.

'Yes, it was the Navy base. Paul wanted to build a yuppie village here – all fake fisherman's cottages. The planners wouldn't wear it though – quite right too.'

'What sort of base was it?' I asked. I didn't know why something was disturbing me.

'You mean in the war? They had MTBs here, motor torpedo boats. All this area was huts and workshops.'

'How much do you know about them?'

'Not much, it's way before my time, and anyway I'm against war.' She stared defiantly at me.

'Not half as much as the poor sods who had no choice but fight. Your generation suffers serious delusion if you think otherwise.' I returned the glare and then let my expression soften. 'Tell me what you know please, I've my own reasons for asking.'

'I only know they had a whole flotilla of boats here.'

'You wouldn't know the number of that flotilla?'

She looked puzzled. 'You mean the number of boats?'

'No, the unit number. You know, the Fifth Flotilla, or the Twentieth – that sort of thing.'

'Yes, I do know that. They had a reunion here during the D-Day commemoration, and they're having another in a week or two, I think.'

'Tell me, was it the "Double Six", you know – Sixty Sixth?'

'That's right, how did you guess?'

I didn't answer, I was musing on the smallness of the world and the strange workings of fate.

'Do you know the name of the Flotilla commander?'

'Yes, it was Wilson – same as you.'

'He was my father.'

CHAPTER 3

The following day, Sunday, I sailed *Stormgoose* the twenty-five miles from Poole to Old Duddlestone. The relationship between professsional seamen and yachtsmen is akin to that between farmers and ramblers. There is a mutual, polite, but suspicious, stand off. People who belong to both camps are regarded as oddballs.

I had been brought up with small sailing boats since the age of six. Sailing was a release from the pressures of big ship handling, a return to the real world of my forebears – the world of Ezeikiel Wilson, master's mate, who had sailed the world with Admiral Anson. Generations of Wilsons had followed him culminating in Captain James Wilson, VC, RN, my late father. It was typical of my ignorance of the man that until yesterday I hadn't known that Old Duddlestone, then part of Portland Command, had been the base of the "Double Six" Flotilla: the home port from which my father had sailed on the eve of his great battle.

To the public, Wilson VC, was a swashbuckler, a latter day Drake. The old man had done nothing to disabuse this image. He could bore for hours about Sixty-Six and their famous clash with the German E-Boats. Then one day, when I was ten years old, he had taken his shotgun, walked into the little wood beside our house and blown his head off. I'd heard the shot and come running, the first to discover the awful bloody wreckage of a proud and enigmatic man.

With the west-going tide under her, *Stormgoose* made short work of the passage to Old Duddlestone. With Swanage on our starboard beam, I settled down for the last leg of the trip. *Stormgoose* is a Hunter 27, a modern design, popular with weekend sailors and racers alike. I had bought her from the builders as a kit. Just a hull and deck bonded together, and a huge pile of boxes and crates, fixtures and fittings. The whole lot had been lowered by crane into the back garden of our house in Cowplain, witnessed by a gallery of startled neighbours.

The house was empty; my daughter Emma was at medical school and I'd just returned from my last voyage to the news that my wife had run off with her boss. I had plunged into the building of my yacht with a zeal such as I had not felt since childhood. I became a perfectionist. All my fury at my wife's betrayal, all the resentment towards my late employers, was channelled into my boat. I would make her the best-equipped little ship on the water. That first summer I had sailed her to all my favourite South Coast haunts. The boat had been my refuge from the world of bickering lawyers and divorce hearings. I had sailed these mini-voyages alone. I had found peace and solace in the backwaters of Langstone, Newtown Creek and finally Poole. It was here in late September that my daughter Emma had joined me and we'd made our first cross-Channel run. We'd sailed to Cherbourg and St Vaast, and back via St Peter's Port and Alderney. Poor Emma: her life torn apart by her parents failure.

The day after our return we'd moored alongside the quay at Poole. Another yachtsman had called out to us from the dockside; we invited him aboard for a beer. He settled for a mug of coffee, then stated his business. He was Hugh Crowfoot and he had been searching the South Coast for weeks on the lookout for *Stormgoose*. He knew of me by reputation and he had a job to offer. That was history. Today I was five miles off the Purbeck shore sailing to take up my new responsibility.

The wind was increasing, to at least twenty knots. I pulled down a second reef and then turned my gaze to the shore looking for a landmark. I had kept well out to sea to avoid the rough water off St Alban's Head. *Stormgoose* was lurching uneasily in the confused water. The wind had shifted south, making Duddlestone a lee shore, just about the worst conditions for entering a strange harbour. At least I would gain first hand experience of this place and its approaches. I took a back bearing on St Alban's Head and then stared at the long line of cliffs, trying to recognise something. We would have to install a "day mark", some prominent object on the skyline to mark the harbour. It was almost impossible to identify things at this distance; a few miles further west and we would be in the danger zone of the military ranges. Then I saw it, the cut in the downs that I'd driven through the day before, that little bite above the village. I took a quick bearing, three hundred and fifty degrees, very nearly due north; a perfect line for the run in. But with the wind driving us towards this lee shore it could become exciting.

For a start the wind was fighting the tidal stream, a condition that bred an uneven, confused sea. *Stormgoose* lurched and pitched horribly; already I was feeling a twinge of seasickness. I pushed the thought to the back of my mind and concentrated on what I was doing. There would be very little danger if only one knew what to look for, the trouble was I only had my sketch plan of the harbour and a note on the leading marks.

I left the steering to the autohelm and scanned the shoreline through binoculars. I could see the harbour wall now, and the village beyond. I had only to hold my present course until I found the leading marks, then line them up, and come on in safe and sound to the shelter of the harbour. By my calculations, I should be able to see the two beacons by now, but they seemed to have vanished. I was puzzled more than worried as I searched the shoreline. Then I saw them, not where I had expected, but they were there: a black and white triangle on a pole with a second red and white mark in front. The sea was a nasty lumpy swell, but nothing dangerous. If these conditions were normal, then I could sell Duddlestone to the sailing public as a safe refuge.

We were closing the land fast. I couldn't see the half-submerged rocks of the Ledge but the wall was clear enough, looming high above me to port. The harbour stretched ahead smooth and empty. This was easy; just line up the beacons and in we go. It seemed I wasn't the only craft around. A tiny boat was buffeting towards me, its lone occupant waving like a madman. I focussed the binoculars.

It was a grey inflatable dinghy with an outboard motor. It was less than fifty metres away, pounding through the waves, lifting and crashing down in sheets of spray. The seas were steeper and rougher now and the little craft was clearly struggling. At that moment I saw the helmsman stand up. He let go his tiller and waved frantically. The inflatable spun through a hundred and eighty degrees. The man tried to recover his balance before, arms flailing, he toppled over into the water. The dinghy sped away from him, turning in ever more erratic circles.

Now I had an emergency on my hands. Whoever this lunatic was I must reach him before the vicious undertow sucked him to his death. Even the strongest swimmer would have problems out here. I let slip the main halyard and groped with the sail, pulling it down on the boom. I hadn't time to tidy the thing, it would have to take its chance. I pressed the starter button of the diesel; the motor fired into life instantly. I knew it would, but it was a relief all the same. I wished I had a crew to point me to the man in the water, but somehow I kept him in view. He was in bad trouble, twice his head had vanished. I pushed the throttle wide open, and took *Stormgoose* in a circle that would take me up to the casualty with the yacht head to wind. I needed to be quick, but at the same time, I dare not surge up to the man at speed. I could as easily kill him that way as rescue him. I pulled a coiled mooring line from the locker and released the little life-float ready to throw. I hoped I wouldn't need this; I wanted to bring the boat right up to the man and haul him aboard; delay could be fatal.

Now I could see him in the water and his struggling was definitely feebler. I steered to pass him as close as possible on the port side. I was much nearer now; I could see his head almost under the bows. I think he instinctively struck out towards the yacht with his last reserves of strength. I pushed the tiller to port as I saw his clutching hand grasping at *Stormgoose's* smooth topsides. I slammed the engine in neutral and dropped the loop of line into his hands. He caught it and I heaved. Though he was clutching the end of the line his strength had gone. He was too heavy for me to haul aboard, and he had neither the will nor the energy to help himself. I knew now that this man would likely die unless I did something decisive.

I secured the line, then raced to the stern and flipped down the folding swimming ladder. I looked back along the side. He'd managed to slip the wide bowline loop under one armpit while clinging to the main part with both hands. I seized the line, released it from the cleat and began to slide him towards the stern. *Stormgoose* was rolling wildly, the line kept slackening and tightening and the sloping stern was rising and falling in the waves like a pile driver. If part of the underside, or the ladder, struck him he'd be just as dead as if he'd drowned. In retrospect, I think I must have found a rush of adrenaline born of desperation. I braced my legs and hauled on the line with everything I had. The body jerked round the stern of the yacht, the hands inches from the ladder.

'Climb,' I yelled. 'I've got you! Try and climb!'

He looked desperately cold and weak but he kept his head. He grasped the ladder with one hand, and hung on as *Stormgoose* pitched her bows down and momentarily lifted the body clear of the sea. As the stern sank again I saw him bend his waist, place his feet on the lower rung of the ladder, and slowly and painfully lurch the four steps to the stern rail. I dropped the line, grabbed him under the armpits and all but threw him over the rail and into the cockpit.

He retched and vomited a mouthful of seawater. He was trying to say something, mouthing the words even as he retched.

'You're OK now,' I shouted. 'Take it easy.'

'You gotta' turn round…' he gasped. 'Leading marks… they're in the wrong place. You're going on the rocks!'

I looked wildly around. We were still in line with the beacons but dangerously near the shore. And there were rocks – submerged rocks very close and I could see the waves breaking on them not twenty yards away.

'Quick,' he was shouting. 'The leading beacons. They're a trap. I saw two of the local goons move 'em… first thing this morning.'

I hardly heard the words of my new passenger. I was staring, mesmerised, by the rock that had emerged not six feet from the yacht's port side. I could see it clearly in every grisly detail; a green slimy lump of wave-polished stone. Self-preservation screamed: push the throttle wide open and get the hell out! Inner sense told me that the side thrust of a full speed propeller would pull our stern straight onto the rock. My heart pounded as I placed the lever to half speed. Seconds more and we'd be done for. Very slowly we were pulling clear of the rock. I could see a little black-headed gull sunning himself on its summit, oblivious to the drama being played out a few feet away. As the gap opened I shoved the throttle to full-ahead. Amidst a cloud of exhaust smoke *Stormgoose* lifted and slammed her way towards the horizon and safety. By now I was trembling – my mouth was dry and I felt dizzy.

I sat down gulping deep breaths of lovely secure sea air.

'Thanks, mate.' It was my rescued companion. He was sitting opposite me shivering convulsively but, apart from that, surprisingly unfazed.

'Introductions later,' I said. 'Get below, there's spare clothing and blankets in the bunk locker, starboard, that's right hand side.'

He nodded and climbed down into the cabin.

'When I think it's safe, we'll stop and talk.' I called after him.

Three miles offshore I hoisted sail and set the yacht to sail herself, without attention, and going nowhere in particular. The man I'd rescued was back on deck dressed in some of my spare clothing, all a size too big for him. He was short and stocky, with flat features and curly black hair and his speech, such as I'd heard, had a familiar twang.

'Right, I'm going to phone the police and report those vandals. I assume the man Gulley was involved?'

'Yeah, fat bozo – Arsenal shirt.' My passenger pulled an expression of deep distaste and spat in the sea.

'You a Scouser?' I asked.

'Sure,' he looked pleased. 'It usually takes one to know one.'

'Can't help you there. I was born in Surrey; different culture altogether.'

‘I know – you’re Peter Wilson and you were born at Elstead near Farnham – March twenty third, nineteen forty seven.’

I was startled and mildly irritated. I owed this guy for saving my ship, but he was a cocky little sod. ‘How come you know so much about me?

He saw my expression and laughed. ‘I’m Brian Byrne, I’m a journalist – freelance crime writer. I’ve done work for…’ he named a Sunday broadsheet.

‘Pleased to meet you, Mr Byrne, but I haven’t committed a crime and don’t intend to – so why this interest in me?’

Byrne looked contrite. ‘I was hoping you would help my research that’s all. I’m writing a book about the Duddlestones.’

‘Can’t be a lot of crime in New Duddlestone. Only petty thieving and a few drunken squaddies from the camp.’

‘No, I’m talking about past history. I’m investigating the Duddlestone murders, in 1946 – you must’ve heard of them?’

‘Not that I’m aware of.’ This wasn’t true; Byrne’s words had aroused a distant blurred memory. I was experiencing an unpleasant moment of *déjà-vu*. I couldn’t think why and I didn’t like it.

‘Did your father never mention them?’

‘For God’s sake man,’ I snapped. ‘Half an hour ago you were as good as dead – give it a rest.’

‘Sure, sure,’ he grinned. ‘I guess I would’ve been a dead’un but for you – thanks again, mate.’

I had no intention of trying the Duddlestone entrance again. I turned *Stormgoose* around and made the return trip to Poole. Byrne seemed to have some notion of sailing, and I was able to hand the helm to him while I used my mobile phone. The police were suspicious. They seemed unaware that there was now a yacht harbour at Old Duddlestone and I think they suspected a hoax. Irritated, I made a direct radio call to the Coastguard and reported the vandalism.

I think Byrne enjoyed the return trip, as I would have done on any normal occasion. I do not like my plans being messed about, and today’s experience had scared me. Destruction of navigational marks is a serious offence; it can be construed as deliberate wrecking. My deepest wish was to grab hold of that slob Gulley and impale him on one of the leading marks he’d tampered with. However as harbour master, I had the full weight of the law behind me, and with any luck, Gulley would be on his way to a spell in jail.

Byrne said little. I guessed he was too astute a professional to ask more questions about my father. In my turn I felt embarrassed. I had revealed too much of my inner feelings. This journalist would know he had touched a raw nerve. He would note the fact and he would work on it. I had been racking my brains to remember where I'd heard of these Duddlestone murders and why mention of them was having such a disturbing effect on me. Who'd been murdered, when, and by whom, I had no idea. I only knew that somewhere in my subconscious I had information that I could not retrieve.

It was late afternoon before we picked up our mooring at Poole. There followed a dreary hour-and-a-half in the police station. Byrne's press credentials carried a lot more weight with the interviewing officer than anything I might say. The journalist cut a strange figure in his outsize clothes, but the police seemed to have heard of him and I was surprised at the respect they showed him. We made our statements, there were further calls to the coastguard, and at last we were released, with a promise that a squad car would be sent forthwith to bring in Mr Gulley for an interview.

'Turn right here,' said Byrne.

He touched my elbow and pointed to a narrow unmade track: a sign board said, *Ashwood.* For fifty yards we bumped along an appalling road surface. At the end was a stone cottage set in a little orchard. The scene intrigued me. It was so very like the fantasy retirement cottage that I dreamt of during my years at sea. Beside the house was a garage with a car, a new Rover, parked in front.

'These people have been helping me with my book,' Byrne remarked. 'I lodge here as well.'

I think his intention had been to invite me in but at that moment the front door opened, and a woman came out; it was Laura Tapsell. Even from this distance I couldn't miss the mutual hostility. As Laura left the house, Byrne passed her; each ignored the other. Laura stopped, stared, and strode towards me. I was struck by the way this woman used such eloquent body language. She didn't need to speak; I could see she was incandescent with rage and it was all directed at me.

CHAPTER 4

'Well!' Laura Tapsell almost spat the word as she thrust her face at me through the car window. 'Well?'

'Well what?' I replied wearily. I was desperately tired and not in the mood for female tantrums.

'What's that little creep doing in your car?'

'I was giving him a lift home. As he saved my boat today, I think that's the least I could do.' I glared back at her. I was pretty angry myself by now and I let her know it.

She took the full force of my glance and recoiled breathing heavily. 'How could he have saved your boat – what's happened? I thought you were sailing round today. Your yacht's not in the dock – I've looked – you realise there's a full scale alert going?'

'Alert?'

'That's right. The Army have found one of their inflatables drifting two miles out. There's a panic on. They've sent for the helicopter from Portland.'

I mentally kicked myself for not anticipating this. 'What size inflatable?'

'Eight foot long Avon, plus outboard motor.'

'All right, I get the picture. That's almost certainly the one Byrne used to reach me.' Briefly I told her what had happened, while I rang the coastguard again.

'OK,' I said with relief. 'They're recalling the helicopter. The Army have already confirmed that they lent the boat to Byrne yesterday.'

'Was it really Steve who moved the beacons?' She was quieter now and sounded worried.

'Byrne saw him and whatever you say, he risked his life to warn me. He could've drowned.'

'What a pity,' she said sarcastically.

'What's wrong with Byrne? He's a bit nosy, but personally I like him.'

'He's an insensitive little bastard!'

'Why?'

'He wants to make a fortune with his book and he doesn't mind how much misery he makes on the way.'

'Hadn't you better explain?'

'All right, but can you give me a lift? I walked here and it's getting late.'

'You can have a lift to anywhere you like if you'll kindly tell me what the hell is going on.'

Laura opened the passenger door and dropped her slim form into the seat. She was dressed for walking. Yesterday's minimal frock had given way to jeans and a denim jacket, while her muddy walking boots were doing no favours to my carpets.

'How much has Byrne told you?' she asked.

'Practically nothing. He asked me if I'd ever heard of a Duddlestone murderer. I told him no. Then he asked me something about my father and that riled because it's bloody sensitive.'

'Good,' for a brief moment she smiled. 'Well, the incidents here happened fifty years ago and, as you put it, they're still bloody sensitive. This is something we never talk about. Something we really thought people were beginning to forget. Then Mr Brian-bloody-Byrne, comes crashing in like a herd of elephants…'

'He can't be a whole herd,' I laughed at the illusion. 'He's only a half-pint little reporter.'

'You can laugh, it doesn't affect you; or maybe it does. Paul's been telling me all about your father.'

Instantly I was defensive and bristling. 'Do you mean Hooder – what's he been saying?'

'Now perhaps you'll understand, that what happened here fifty years ago is just as sensitive to us as your father blowing himself away is to you.' She glared at me. 'Yes, they remember your father all too well in this village.'

'And what the hell does that mean?'

'No more than that. It seems he was quite a guy.'

I sighed, 'Point taken. Now, where do you want me to drive you?'

'Tell you what,' she said. 'I'm fed up with my sister's cooking – I'll buy you a meal at the "Gooleys".

'Where?'

'Sorry, that's what we call our pub, everybody does. It's really the De Gullait Arms – French,' she spelt the name. 'There's a real bit of local history for you. De Gullait was the family that owned everything in these parts and they lost the lot in the English Civil War. That's where you get the name Gulley. Steve is the last of a noble line, though you wouldn't think it to look at him.' Suddenly she paused in mid-flow. 'What will the police do?' Momentarily her tone had softened.

‘If I choose to prosecute him, he could go to prison.’

‘Oh,’ she sounded worried. ‘Do you really want that to happen?’

‘He deliberately tried to wreck my boat. That used to be a hanging offence.’

‘Don’t say that,’ she snapped. ‘Oh sorry, but that ties in with what we were talking about before. Hanging’s an emotive word in Duddlestone. The one we had here was enough.’

We drove the rest of the way in silence. I’d never been to this village before, and I looked around with interest. New Duddlestone is three miles from Old Duddlestone harbour. At that time there was no direct connection except for the wartime military road half a mile to the west. This larger village seemed a pretty little place of traditional-stone houses set in a fold in the hills. In some ways it looked a twin of nearby Corfe Castle, but with one difference – an irrational gut feeling I know – but to me New Duddlestone had the aura of an unhappy ship.

None of this could apply to the De Gullait Arms. The “Gooleys” was a rambling building of Purbeck stone with several smaller annexes. This being the tourist season, the car park behind the pub was already half full. I stood and looked up at the encircling downs that brooded over this little cluster of houses. It was evening now and the hills were beginning to shut out the light. This must be a cold shadowy place in winter, I mused. I shaded my eyes against the orange globe of the sun and, as it slid behind the ridge, I saw the figure of a man, silhouetted against the skyline, standing on the highest point of the hill. He must have been half a mile away, but he seemed to dominate the scene. Then, slowly he vanished into a copse of wind stunted trees.

‘Look, there’s someone up by that wood,’ I pointed.

‘Only a visitor – hundreds of them this time of year.’ Laura was making a play of being bored, but I knew that she was edgy about something.

‘I don’t think so,’ I replied. ‘It was Byrne.’

‘Don’t be bloody stupid. How can you possibly know?’

Of course I couldn’t, but I was right, I knew it, and there was something else. Laura knew it too and she was rattled.

As we passed through the pub door the tensions of the day began to ebb away; for the first time I realised how hungry I was. The aroma from the kitchen was enticing; I was painfully aware I hadn’t eaten a thing since a snatched breakfast on the boat. The main bar was dimly lit, but it had a mellow atmosphere with a pleasant rumble of conversation and the clink of glasses. I liked this place with its obvious feel for tradition – no piped music and no gaming machines. The only intrusion from the outside world was a solitary television with the sound turned low. It showed Prime Minister Blair striding purposefully through the door of Number Ten. We were only a few weeks on from the May election and the seismic shift in the nation's government that had emerged. I sighed, such things hardly bothered one at sea, even if they intruded in a place like this.

Laura touched me on the arm. 'If you want the answers to your questions you'd better ask Harry. He was here when it happened.' She led the way to the bar.

'Harry,' she said, 'Peter here's our new harbour master. Peter, meet Harry Broadenham.' She was grinning happily as she nodded to the man behind the bar.

'Mr Wilson, it's a pleasure and an honour.' It was a firm hand that gripped mine. I looked into clear blue eyes and features weathered by some seventy years. 'Yes, it's a pleasure to meet you, Captain, and your drink is on the house.'

Although I didn't know this man from Adam, his face had broken into a grin of pure delight. I accepted my pint happily and glanced at Laura, who looked mildly embarrassed.

'Hold on a tick while I get someone to take over here,' said Harry. 'Then I'll show you something.'

He shot through a door like a rabbit into a burrow. I looked questioningly at Laura but her face was inscrutable. The other customers were staring at the TV screen, now showing pictures of a mournful looking Princess of Wales.

A minute later Harry returned on our side of the bar. 'Follow me, Mr Wilson, and tell me what you think of this.'

He led the way to another room and pointed to the far wall; staring at me was a portrait of my father.

'My Captain,' Harry's quiet voice cut through my reverie. 'One of the doctors painted that picture. It was when your father was in hospital after the fight. He was the first out of that place – discharged himself against orders.'

I stared at him. 'You mean you were there – fighting the E Boats – that night?'

Harry's expression changed, the old face showed a flicker of pain. 'Yes, I was there, and I lived to tell the tale, which is more than two hundred other poor buggers did.'

That was true: of the fourteen torpedo boats in battle that night, eleven had been lost: five British and six German, with only twenty survivors. One of them had been my father, indestructible in war, only to die, depressed and vulnerable in peacetime. And this Harry; it seemed that by some miracle he'd survived as well.

'We call this the "Double Six" bar.' His outstretched hand pointed around the room. Other photographs filled the wall space, along with a tattered White Ensign, and a row of empty shell cases lovingly burnished.

'War,' Laura grumbled, 'men!'

'Now, Laura, that is where you're wrong. See here.' Harry pointed to a framed newspaper photograph.

It was a picture of men in the sea, clinging to an old style life raft. Men, faces blackened with oil, hanging on when hope had all but gone, then pictured for posterity at the miraculous moment of rescue.

Harry pointed at the picture. 'That fellow there, Hans is his name. He saved my life, tenacious little sod – strength of ten. He held me on that raft for the last three hours. I'd have been a goner but for him.' There was a break in his voice. 'Laura, Hans had no reason to help me – know why?' The question was rhetorical. I had already guessed the answer. 'Because Hans was a German, a Kraut. So don't ever say I glorify war. War's bloody pointless and that moment brought it home to me.'

'But you still fought.' said Laura.

'Sometimes you have to fight, young lady, because the alternative is too awful to contemplate.'

Laura and I sat at a table in the "Double Six" bar, while Harry waited on us himself. I'm not sure what special instructions went to the kitchen, but the food was exquisite, beyond anything I had ever tasted in a country pub. Harry intrigued me. He was an alert little man who moved with the ease of one thirty years younger. The Guillait's wine list was a revelation. Harry produced a fine claret which we preceded with a local English white wine. In the midst of this, Laura had unfrozen and became surprisingly good company.

'Look,' she said, 'we're going to be working together, so will you stop calling me Mrs Tapsell. From now on it's Laura and Peter.'

And may the best man win, I thought.

The evening passed quickly. Harry brought a second bottle of claret and then a velvet-textured brandy. He sat with us for a while and plied me with stories of my father. Vividly he told of the moment my father had taken the wheel from a dying coxswain. With a sinking ship and all ammunition spent, father had deliberately steered to ram and sink his last adversary. I was moved by the way that Harry revered his captain. Odd, too, when one remembered that my father's act of reckless madness, in the final moments of the battle, had so nearly killed them both.

We left the pub at ten thirty. I was worried; I knew I'd drunk too much, as opposed to Laura who had only sipped her wine. I was certainly above the legal limit, and my only home was my yacht in Poole, ten miles away.

'Does Harry let rooms?' I asked Laura. 'If not I'll have to phone for a taxi.'

'No you won't. I'm still fit to drive. Give me the keys, I'll see if my brother can put you up.'

Something was teasing me. 'Laura, Byrne isn't the only journalist interested in Double Six.' I told her about the scruffy looking woman I'd seen yesterday on the dock.

'Her name's Jo something. She's an Oz – I think her father was in the Navy at Duddlestone. I wouldn't trust her any more than I would Byrne.'

This time I sat in the passenger seat determined not to fall asleep. Laura drove at a cracking pace through the village. I noticed for the first time that New Duddlestone was a community of two halves. The picturesque stone houses gave way to a large, featureless council estate and, a little further on, a development of upmarket private houses. Laura turned sharp right, down a long winding lane sunk between high banks and overhanging hedgerows. Then we were turning up a concrete ramp and into a farmyard. I emerged from the car stiffly and looked around, taking in the sounds and smells of a substantial livestock farm. In the failing light I could just make out the shapes of dairy cows in the field beyond a huge open barn stacked high with deliciously scented bales of new hay.

'Here we are,' Laura jerked my elbow, 'Honeycritch Farm. I'm staying here until my place at the harbour's ready. Come in and meet the Rocastle clan.'

The kitchen of Honeycritch Farm dominated the ground floor. It was a place to put a visitor instantly at ease: warm and brightly lit, with a long refectory table down the middle. An Aga and a second electric range were stationed against the far wall. At the table sat a middle-aged woman busy knitting. Her needles, wool and paper patterns lay spread before her on the table. Facing her was a much younger woman and, I must admit, I noticed her first. She had round sun-tanned face, with dark hair tied back in a ponytail.

'This is Peter, the new boss at the harbour,' said Laura.

The dark girl smiled a greeting. 'My son said he'd met you.'

'That's Tommy,' Laura explained. 'Remember, the kid outside your office yesterday?'

'The one who told you what day it was?' I laughed.

'Mother,' Laura addressed the older woman. 'Peter lives in a little boat moored at Hamworthy. He's got himself half-pissed at the Gooleys, and he can't drive home. I've offered him a bed here – OK?'

'Hello, Peter,' the older woman turned round to have a good look at me. 'Of course, you're very welcome.'

I could see the likeness between her and her daughters. Not the voice though: that had the cadence of the Welsh valleys.

The dark girl seemed to have read my thoughts. 'Mother's from Carmarthen, she can still speak the real lingo, can't you Mam?'

'I should say so,' said Laura. 'You should hear her and Timmy Hughes the shepherd, rabbiting away.'

'Ignore her, Peter,' said Mother. 'Our Laura is a force of nature – don't let her grind you down.'

'No chance, Mrs Rocastle.'

'And this is my other girl, Carol.'

'Hi, Peter.' The dark girl had a soft Dorset accent and round dark eyes.

'Where are Ian and Trish?' asked Laura. 'That's my brother and his wife,' she said to me, 'they run the farm.'

'They're still carting hay bales,' Carol replied.

'You might as well know what Peter was up to today,' said Laura. Her voice was grim but she winked at me. 'Quite a hero, he rescued a man from the sea.'

'Really?' Carol looked impressed.

'Now hear the bad news. It was that bloody bugger, Byrne.'

'Hey, that's an alliteration,' Carol giggled. 'Sorry, I teach English and I notice these things.'

'And what was Mr Byrne doing in the sea?' asked Mother casually without looking up from her knitting.

I explained the events of that morning, and then for good measure I looked Laura in the eye. 'It was Byrne up on the hill just now – you know it was.'

'He's always up there,' she said sulkily.

'I only dropped him off twenty minutes before – how did he get up there in the time?'

'There's a footpath at the back of "Ashwood". It's only a few minutes from there.'

'Peter,' said Carol. 'If you rescued the man it won't make you everyone's favourite around here.'

'Can I ask what's wrong with him? If I'm going to work here I think I ought to know.'

I looked around the room. These women were offering me hospitality. I didn't want to abuse it, but I had to have an explanation.

Laura ignored me and addressed her mother and sister. 'First, I think you should know that Peter here, is the son of that Captain Wilson, the one from the wartime Navy base.'

'Really,' said Mother. 'He was quite a character I've been told.'

'In more ways than one,' Carol laughed.

'Basic facts,' Laura began. 'Fifty years ago a cousin of ours, called Arthur Rocastle, murdered a girl here; but when he was tried he got off…'

'No, not so, he was acquitted because he was innocent!' Carol broke in; I was surprised how flushed and angry she'd become.

'Yes, dear,' said her mother soothingly. 'But the police must have thought he'd done it, or he'd never have been tried.'

'Rubbish, I've read the court transcript. It never even reached the jury. The Crown offered no evidence and the judge ordered an acquittal.' Carol turned an angry face to her sister. The room had become very tense.

'All right,' said Laura, 'have it your own way, but don't start sounding off in public…'

'Don't you dictate what I can or can't say – stroppy bitch!'

Carol was standing glowering at her sister. I was too fascinated to feel embarrassed. These women were clearly different sides of the same coin.

'Will you remember your manners, both of you.' Their mother had joined the ring now. 'You'll not make an exhibition in front of a guest. Mr Wilson, please forgive us. My girls can be wilful some-times.'

Suddenly Carol was smiling and the tension relaxed. 'Wilful, that sounds like we're in a Jane Austen novel.'

'More's the pity you're not. In those days there'd be a father, with a strong arm and a good stick.'

'Ooo, politically incorrect,' Carol laughed. 'Sorry, Peter, we must be a bit of a culture shock.'

I grinned and made no comment.

'You'd better finish the story,' said mother.

'Yes,' Laura's face puckered as she weighed her words. 'Yes, after Arthur was freed he made one mistake. He came back here. That was in July 1946. He'd had a clear warning to stay away, which he ignored. A few days later he had visitors. They took him out in the night and hanged him from a tree.'

CHAPTER 5

'Let's go out there and I'll show you what happened.' I put the engine in gear and pointed *Stormgoose* towards the harbour entrance.

I had sailed my boat from Poole on Monday morning and finally docked in Old Duddlestone at two o'clock. We had all assembled at the harbour that afternoon, twenty-four hours since my last brush with the Duddlestone rocks. My companions now were Laura Tapsell, a uniformed police constable and Brian Byrne. The policeman's face already had a tinge of green as we hit the first of the swell. I watched the shoreline slide past as I took some bearings with my hand compass. Now clear of the harbour wall, I slowed the engine, so that the ship just stemmed the wind and tide.

I pointed to the shore. 'Those are the proper beacons, bearing zero zero five degrees or just about true north. All I can say is I looked for them yesterday, and they definitely weren't there.'

The policeman nodded without enthusiasm and stared at his carefully polished shoes.

'Right,' I continued. 'When I found them they were on a bearing of something like, zero-six five – over in that corner.' I pointed. 'So I was on a course straight into that submerged ledge. OK, I was at fault. I was entering a strange harbour for the first time, and I should have used more sense.'

When I'd moored alongside the pontoon at midday, I'd found Laura and this copper already waiting. Laura was showing him the restored beacons with an ill-concealed glee. Moreover, I could now see, even from a distance, that these were substantial metal shapes mounted on steel scaffold poles. At that moment Brian had arrived.

Laura had torn into the man. 'That's him,' she said to the policeman. 'He made up the whole story – charge him for wasting police time.' She swung round on me. 'Took you in well and proper didn't he?'

'I only know that the marks were not there yesterday. Mr Byrne nearly drowned coming to warn me, so I think you should take us seriously.' My tone was a severe as I could make it, but I was baffled and worried. It was then that I suggested this re-enactment.

Feeling even more angry and depressed I docked *Stormgoose* once more. Brian Byrne was unmoved, sticking to his story, Laura was infuriatingly smug, and the seasick copper was relieved to be on dry land. We walked round the rocky shore to the beacons. It was true nobody was going to move them in a hurry; it would have taken a concrete breaker and a crane.

'When was it you saw these posts being dismantled?' the constable asked Byrne.

'I never said that. I saw them putting the beacons up again over there.' Byrne pointed.

This was beginning to be embarrassing. Luckily the policeman, who was no fool, had begun to examine the beacons. He spotted a narrow strip of ragged material, flying like a flag from the top triangle. With impressive agility, Brian had shinned up the pole and brought it down; it was a fragment of an army camouflage net. It had been a clever trick and deadly.

Laura was furious. She was unwilling to accept that Byrne was right but, like me, she was worried about the implications for the harbour. We walked over the ground but found nothing, except a small pile of rocks on the shoreline at the place where I had seen the beacons from the sea.

Our police constable departed with his report. Brian had followed, leaving Laura and me in the harbour office. The portakabin was stuffy even with the windows open and the fans going. Outside the building the contractors were fitting out the fuel dock. This floating pontoon with a fuel pump was a vital facility, but it was bringing with it a problem. I wasn't going to spend my time pulling a diesel pump and I couldn't see Laura doing so; it would muck up her designer sun frock. We needed an extra hand and speedily.

'Here's all the applications and their CVs,' she said, handing me a file. 'I've been doing some weeding out already.' She leant over me, and I took in the waft of scent and sun lotion. 'This one's been done at Chichester – stealing VHF sets.' She pointed to a name. 'The next one's reference is a bit ambiguous for my taste, and that girl is a scrubber – known for it.'

'That only leaves two,' I said looking at the list. 'Crikey, is that really the man's name – Milo Tracic?'

'Yep, he's Australian, a dinghy sailor and he's good – wins trophies on the race circuit.'

'Sounds promising, when can I interview him?'

'Tomorrow I expect – his work permit's running out, so he's

pretty keen to land the job.'

'What about the other man?'

'I don't know a thing about him; he's in Scotland at the moment.'

'OK, I'll meet Mr Tracic here and we'll see what he's made of.'

Both Laura and the construction gang had departed. Old Duddlestone had returned to its normal peace. I walked again along the foreshore following the line we'd taken a few hours before. I looked back to the harbour wall. It was just on low tide, and the stone quay towered over the little bay, just as it had in my father's time. I looked back to *Stormgoose,* my own little ship, and my home for the present. Here was I, Harbour Master, and for the moment, sole inhabitant. At least that man Gulley would not be able to try another wrecking. I was in a dilemma about Gulley. The police had warned us that Brian Byrne's identification from several hundred yards might not be enough to secure a conviction. Laura had been adamant against pressing charges and Roger Crowfoot, at United Marinas, had been in a tizzy about bad publicity. I would probably have to let the matter drop. No doubt there would be another day and another place where I could settle scores with Mr Gulley.

I reached the spot where I had seen the false beacons. The cliff at this point was nothing like so steep as the one to the west of the village. It was more of a hillside, with a narrow defile running down it from the top: a chine it would be called in the local dialect. I began to walk up this path. Within ten yards I saw, two pieces of timber jutting out from behind a boulder. I pulled one onto the track and found a freshly cut ash pole with a brightly painted wooden triangle nailed to one end. I had found my false beacons, and very clever they were too. Half the size of the real ones, but enough to fool a newcomer to the harbour. I finally had my proof; not enough perhaps to convict Gulley, but concrete evidence that there had been a wrecking attempt.

I decided to walk on up the chine to the top of the cliff. I was exploring now and I wanted to see this view of the harbour. A sedentary life at sea had made me more unfit than I realised, and this humid evening made the going hard. I remembered that we were less than a week away from the twenty-first, the longest day. I was sweating and breathing heavily as I rounded a corner; there, leaning on a rock beside the track, was a shiny new mountain bike. Sitting on the rock was the bike's owner; Laura's nephew, Tommy. He didn't move but stared at me suspiciously.

'Hello,' I said.

'Hello, Mister – I've been watching you.'

'Have you now. D'you do a lot of watching?'

'Sometimes.'

'Tell me, Tommy,' I smiled, I hoped reassuringly. 'Were you here yesterday morning?'

'No,'

'You heard what happened?'

'Yeah, Auntie Laura said Steve tried to wreck your yacht.'

'Tommy, did you tell Steve Gulley I was going to sail here?'

'Might've,' he was squirming now.

I remembered from years past that guilty feeling when confronted by adult authority. It had been troubling me all day that Tommy was the only person outside the harbour management, who knew I was sailing yesterday.

'Do you realise that if my boat had sunk I could have been drowned? I glared at him.

'I didn't know they were going to do it. Steve told me to listen.' The little chap's face was reddened and mournful; tears wetted his cheeks. 'Steve said he'd smash my bike if I didn't listen to what you was saying…' Tommy looked utterly miserable, frightened and contrite all in one.

I grinned at him, he was so obviously telling the truth, and that alone was a weight off my mind.

'All right, Tommy, another time think before you get pushed around by people like that.'

'You won't tell Auntie Laura?' This prospect seemed to worry him.

'Behave yourself in future and she need never know.'

'They were talking about you.' The tears had vanished; he was looking at me with interest.

'Who's they?'

'All of 'em, after you'd gone.'

He must mean the Rocastle family.

'Yeah, they were all talking about you,' he repeated solemnly.

'Really,' I replied cautiously.

'Auntie Laura says you're a pompous tosser.' He nodded sagely. 'But my mum – she likes you.'

'They should put a padlock on your tongue, young man,' I grinned ruefully at him.

'They said you've been asking questions about that Margaret.'

'Who?'

'The one that was murdered – long time ago in the olden days.'

Now I understood. 'I gather they still can't agree who did it?'

'That's right,' the boy was alert now. 'My mates at school say that my uncle was a murderer – but my mum says he didn't do it, and he's never my uncle – just a sort of cousin.'

'Either way, I'm told he was murdered himself?'

'That's right, they strung him up in Tollands Copse.'

'Who did?'

'Nobody knows for sure. That Brian's trying to find out.'

I shook my head. 'It must be ancient history by now. Quite likely the people are dead.'

'Brian says there's plenty around who know – like your Dad.'

'Who?' I snapped at him and he was frightened; his lower lip drooped and he began to blink.

'Sorry Tommy, I didn't mean to yell at you. Go on, what have you been told?'

'That Margaret, who was strangled, she was a slag. Brian says she was going with all the sailors. He says pinning it on Arthur was a cover-up. He says the Navy done it, and your Dad knows who.'

So that was why Byrne was probing me about my father. Well whatever the old man had heard and seen it had died with him. It was disconcerting though. My father's loyalty to his men was total, but would it stretch to concealing a murder? I couldn't say; but passing the blame to an innocent scapegoat? No, the old man would never have condoned that in a thousand years.

I turned back to Tommy. The lad was staring at me in an odd way. 'My father died thirty years ago. Mr Byrne knows that, so he'll have to talk to someone else.'

'My dad's in Australia,' said Tommy. 'He never sent nothing for my birthday, not even a card.'

'Perhaps it went astray.'

'No way, he doesn't give a shit for Mum and me. Mum says he's got another girlfriend.' The childish voice relayed this adult statement as if it was the most natural thing in the world.

'Your mum's a teacher?'

'That's right.'

'What d'you want to be?'

'Footballer.'

'It's a hard life – very few make it big.'

'My dad's stopped sending my mum's money.' Tommy looked

mournful again. 'We used to live in Wareham, but our house got reprocessed.'

'You mean repossessed?'

'Yeah, that's why we're staying with Trish and Ian. Mum can't get the money cos' Dad's in Australia, but now the CIA's after 'im.'

'I think you mean the CSA.'

'I dunno – s'pect so.'

Poor Tommy, I thought. Like my Emma, another casualty in our disintegrating society.

'Gotta go now,' he said suddenly. 'We got pizza for tea. See yer!'

I watched as he pedalled furiously up the hill. Near the top he gave up, dismounted, wheeled his bike over the brow and vanished.

CHAPTER 6

I have never had much time for ghosts. My former wife will jump at her own shadow, and our daughter isn't much better. I am prey to a number of seaborn superstitions, but not ghosts. What I do have is a feel for places that I can't define or explain with any logic. I've said before that New Duddlestone had the feel of an unhappy ship. It was a charming village, filled no doubt with charming people, but something about the place already made me feel uncomfortable. It was a gut feeling; don't ask me to explain. I can only report that my instincts were to be proved all too accurate in the weeks to come.

By contrast, deserted Old Duddlestone had a warmth and benign feel that seemed to radiate from the very rock from which it was built. If the ghosts of the old fishermen were still around, they certainly didn't resent my presence. It's lucky I feel this way because that night my good sense was tried to the limit.

I had taken a walk around the village as the last of the daylight faded. At this time of year it is still twilight at ten o'clock. I walked until I came to the furthest building, almost under the cliff. It looked like a village hall, but it was probably a chapel. It appeared a stark gloomy pile and its door was locked. Fifty yards further and I came to the base of the cliff. Like all its kind it wasn't as white, nor as perpendicular, as it appeared from the sea. It wasn't the cliff that interested me; I was intrigued by a ramshackle structure that I hadn't noticed before. A concrete archway, jutting out from the cliff, with a roof of iron girders and worn corrugated sheeting. In the archway was a pair of heavy steel doors. I guessed this place to have been a torpedo and ammunition store, tunnelled deep into the rock; one more relic of my father and his "Double Six" flotilla.

I walked back to the dock and stopped by the cottage that was to be mine. Again I felt the warmth of the place; the perfect symmetry of the plain little dwelling. I was glad this was to be my home, and I knew I would be happy here. I was not overjoyed to be living next to Laura who, apparently, was determined to dislike me. "Pompous tosser", Tommy had said she called me. I had one consolation; it seemed the rest of her family liked me. I was glad of that because these Rocastles counted for something in this place, and I needed all the friends I could find. I boarded *Stormgoose*, went below and cooked myself a meal. For the first time in eight months I felt completely at peace with myself and the world.

What was that light? I sat up on my bunk, alert, sleep banished. The clock said two thirty in the morning; still a couple of hours until dawn. A narrow beam of light shone through the cabin window and diffused dimly on the unwashed dishes by the galley sink. I looked out of the window; a dazzling pinpoint of light shone back at me, fixed somewhere on the far shore of the bay. I pulled on my jeans and shoes and went to investigate.

On deck I took a quick compass bearing. The light was still there and close to the proper position of the entry beacons. If this was friend Gulley again I was ready for him. I walked as quietly as I could past the quay, over the slipway and onto the rocky foreshore. The tide was flooding fast with less than one hour until high-water. The light still shone, though at a different angle. It was less intense and seemed to alternate, first dazzling and then slowly fading. There seemed no rhyme or reason until I guessed the cause; a little miasma of dawn mist was spreading across the water. I stood still and listened. Out to sea I could hear waves breaking on the rocky ledges. Here, in the shelter of the harbour, the sea was glassy although I could hear the ripple of the flooding tide as the water soaked into the rocks and fissures.

Then I heard voices. I froze on the spot, ears straining. The sounds came from inland, somewhere high above me. One voice loud with natural authority; for a brief second I caught a snatch of speech. 'Check your respirators…' then nothing. A few indistinct burblings followed by silence. I turned round to seek out my light, but it too had gone.

Now I could hear another sound – powerful ship's engines, not far away and growing louder. Incredibly, a large vessel was steering straight into the harbour. I ran up the slope and climbed onto a little rocky ledge. Curse the mist, I could see nothing as the thump of the motors and the swirl of the prop wash came closer. I could hear a change of note in the engines and my experience told me that she was slowing and stemming the tide before laying alongside our own dock. Whoever this late arrival was he knew these waters well.

I was too far away to judge what was happening, but I could hear another engine beginning to hum, a much smaller engine attached to what I was fairly certain was a pump. I stood listening but I could make nothing of it. It was time for me to don my official hat and go and investigate. I had hardly reached the half way point to the dock when the pump ceased and I heard the ship's main engines fire and heard the unmistakable sounds of a large craft reversing off the quay.

Curiosity was now replaced by annoyance, after all I was the Harbour Master. I didn't want to over-dramatise, but this vessel was acting illegally. She was entering a controlled harbour at night with not a single regulation light showing. I ran the remaining distance to the dock and dived down to my cabin. I recovered the key to the office and sprinted to it. I staggered over the threshold and switched on the harbour control radio.

For five minutes I blasted the airwaves, politely at first, and then with increasing irritation. There was no response. I ran onto the quayside carrying binoculars and stared into the darkness and mist; I'd need a high-tech imager to see anything. I heard the craft slow down, before the engines roared as the helmsman turned the ship and made for the open sea. Her wash reached the pontoon, lifting and tilting it, before slapping and sighing along the shoreline. Two minutes later the sounds had faded and the scene was tranquillity again. Far away in the east the sky was lighting; soon the sun would be over the horizon – dawn and a new day.

I returned to my bunk and tried to sleep. For an hour it was hopeless, then I must have dropped off. Out of a jumble of dreams I had suddenly returned to childhood. I was in a darkened room alone. Through the wall I could hear my mother shouting. Every word was distinct, as she yelled in her guttural East European accent.

'Murder, so many dead, all murdered! You think you are such a brave man with your big medal – so why you not do something? To you they will listen.'

I was awake again, forcing myself from sleep, anxious only to escape the nightmare. I focussed on the cabin clock: it was six o'clock and broad daylight. I pulled myself deeper into the sleeping bag; suddenly I felt cold. The dream, if it was such, had the clarity of a video recording. I'd read about "recovered memory syndrome" and heard of the uncertainties and emotional havoc it could cause. With a sigh I climbed from my bunk and staggered moodily on deck. It was a perfect morning. The sun was well up and beginning to warm the day. A light breeze rippled the surface of the harbour. I walked to *Stormgoose's* stern and dropped the swimming ladder. Then I pulled off my shirt and briefs and dived naked into the sea.

Laura drove up to the office at eight o'clock, so I made her a cup of coffee. She told me Milo Tracic would appear for interview at ten-thirty.

'Last night there was a big power vessel nosing around in here.' I watched her face. For just a second I detected a flicker of something. Then she went deadpan.

'You don't say,' she replied. 'Must be the ghost ship – there's lots of stories they tell in the village.'

'Bullshit, I don't buy ghosts and even if I did I wouldn't buy ghostly prop wash. That ship was solid enough.' I looked her in the eye. 'Any ideas?'

'Sorry, none.'

I laughed. 'Perhaps it was the Flying Dutchman, looking for his life partner.'

'No takers.'

'You're heartless. By the way, yesterday your nephew Tommy was over there by the shore.'

'He's always there, specially since Ian gave him that bike.'

'He told me about his father.'

'Oh, don't talk to me about that arsehole. He's even worse than my ex.'

'I'm divorced myself and I don't feel charitable towards the other party either.'

She looked at me with renewed interest. 'I did wonder. The others were asking about you the other night.'

'Tell me about these stories.'

'What stories?'

'Ghost ship, you said.'

She smiled and shook her head. 'I wasn't really serious. There is a sunk ship a mile or so out but there won't be any ghosts. Your father's boats rescued everyone. There's one old legend, but that's in the Armada time, way before any phantom power boats.'

'I heard something last night and you'd better believe it.' Why the hell did this woman irritate me so?

'All right, cool it. It so happens in this case I do believe you.'

Not good enough, I thought. She knows something – if it's on the level why doesn't she say?

I forced an eye contact. 'I didn't see this ship, but I heard enough. I would say she was a high power, light displacement craft of around sixty to seventy feet.'

'A ghostly MTB, Second World War?' she joked.

'Now you're just being bloody stupid. That ship was real. It made a wash that lifted the pontoon six inches. I wish you would take this seriously.'

'I can't do anything. If you think it was something dodgy you'd better phone the police.'

'I'll certainly inform the coastguard but honestly, I'm asking you because you know the way things are here.'

'I think you're overstating my role. I'm a bit of an outcast with some people.'

'Why?'

'I've already explained. I work for Paul Hooder and for United Marinas; for you as well I suppose. Some of the people would say I'm betraying my heritage.'

'All right, you can tell me this. Why do the army keep a guard post just over the hill here – what on earth is there to guard?'

'Oh, I can tell you about that,' she seemed relieved to change the subject. 'Back in the war, your father's time, there was a research establishment. Top secret, to do with chemical warfare. Paul's father, Pieter Hooder was the director. The whole place was demolished and sealed up in 1946. A lot of it was underground you see. For some reason they've never removed the guard. You can't get within half a mile of the place. But there's nothing there; we regard it as a bit of a joke.'

'What a waste of resources – it's crazy.'

'It's all covered by the Official Secrets Act. Paul says there may once have been some residual contamination, but that's all long gone.'

'The less said about this the better. It's publicity we can do without. Christ, does Byrne know?'

'Yes, to give him his due, he's a good journalist. He soon sussed out the chemical warfare lab.' Laura gave me another unsettling stare. 'Look, if you're going to manage here, you'd better know the whole story.'

'It would be helpful.'

'I was going to tell you the other night, then Carol put her oar in.'

'Yes, you got as far as the murder, then I thought I was going to have to drag the pair of you apart before there was another.'

'Carol's soft in the head. Can't believe wrong in anybody. She likes you by the way. You've made quite a hit there.'

'I gratified to hear it. Now tell me all.'

'Around the time Arthur Rocastle killed the girl, there was an accident at the lab. Nobody, literally nobody, who worked there that day has ever been seen again. But the government still pretends it never happened. The families have never been told officially that their people are dead.'

'Were they all scientists?'

'No, there were several local people. That Margaret, the one Arthur murdered, she used to work there. She looked after some of their animals.' Her voice hardened. 'They kept them in cages underground. Chimps and monkeys – cruel bastards. Serve them right if they did gas themselves. Perhaps there is a God.'

'But Margaret was already dead before this?'

'Yes, Arthur killed her two days before the accident in the lab.'

I didn't know what to make of any of this. 'It would seem to me that this government cover-up would be a better story for Byrne than the murder in your family. Either way it's a hell of a long time ago. Neither of us was born then.'

'It's not as easy as that. Now the silly little sod is claiming the two incidents are connected. He says he's going to call his book, "Poison Village".'

'How d'you know all this? You don't even talk to the man.'

'You know the house where Byrne lodges, "Ashwood"?'

'I saw you there yesterday, when I gave you a lift.'

'I went there because I thought Byrne was out of the way. That's why I gave you a bit of the verbals when you showed up with him – sorry about that.'

'Don't worry – finish your story.'

'Byrne lodges with Arthur's younger sister, my cousin Ivy. Ivy's an airbrain, but she's married to a solicitor, who's an outsider and another silly old fart. They say they're going to clear Arthur's name.'

'What's wrong with that – suppose he was innocent?' Now I'd said the wrong thing.

'Don't you start giving me that,' she shouted. 'You're an outsider like all the others.'

'Others?'

'Yes the others. Look, we belong here. We know he did it. Our local police thought he did it. Then he gets off on some technicality.' Laura's face had reddened.

She was angry, but it was the anger of uncertainty. I had seen prejudice enough times; the sort of racial and religious hate, instilled into very young children by ignorant adults. I was seeing something like that in her now.

'Laura, I guess you're very loyal to your roots? This place is important to you – all its legends and traditions. You know what I mean?'

She gave me a cold look, stood up and left the room, pushing rudely past a man who had been standing outside the office. He was dressed in green overalls and had an expression of baffled annoyance. He explained to me that he was the driver of the lorry booked to fill our new diesel holding tank.

'I can't fill it when the bloody thing's full to the brim already.'

'But that can't be right; the tank was only installed yesterday and it was empty last night.'

'Well, another supplier must've filled it,' he grumbled. 'Now I'll have to take all this lot back to the depot.'

Another supplier? Yes, a large vessel with a fuel pump. I went in search of Laura. I found her in her cottage and I didn't waste words as I told her again what I'd heard last night.

'Now, you tell me what's going on.'

'I'm sorry,' she replied. 'But I really know no more than you, and if someone wants to give us a full tank of fuel…well, I don't look gift horses in the mouth.' She was unbearably smug and I knew she was lying.

CHAPTER 7

Last night's dream was troubling me more than any of the earlier happenings. There would be logical explanations for the voice, the light and the ship, but not the dream. Most disquieting was the way it seemed to fit so naturally with this Duddlestone mystery. Of course, I might well be putting two and two together and making sixteen. If my mother's words were part of a recalled event, they probably had nothing to do with Duddlestone. Mother had lost her entire family in the Holocaust, and that tragedy, as well as my father's suicide, still cast a shadow over her life. For that reason alone, I wouldn't tell her about my dream; or at least not yet.

I was released from my brooding by a shout from Laura. I could see her through the window on the edge of the quay pointing at something. Speeding through the harbour entrance was a tiny racing dinghy. I recognised her as a *Contender* class; an extreme single-handed racing design. I could see her helmsman riding on the end of his trapeze wire with an athletic nonchalance I envied. The dinghy sailed onto the slipway and the man pulled her clear of the waterline. He lowered the sail, pulled off his buoyancy aid and then strode towards us. We saw a tanned, dark-haired, six footer; barefoot, dressed in a wetsuit topped by purple lycra shorts and a lurid Hawaiian shirt.

'G'day, I'm looking for the harbour master,' he was grinning cheerfully. 'I'd say you're the man – right?'

'Quite right.'

'Great, I'm Milo, but my mates call me Mick. Before you ask, the name's Croatian. My Dad's what we used to call a "reffo", but I'm all Aussie and proud of it.' The voice was resonant of waterfront Sydney.

I held out my hand. 'Pleased to meet you, Mick, and for what it's worth, my Mum's a "reffo" too.'

We interviewed Milo, or Mick, informally, standing on the quay. Mick explained that he had been working for a local boat builder but had lost his job when the firm went into receivership. He'd just set up home with a new girlfriend in Poole and he needed to renew his work permit. This sounded to me a mite like expediency. Not so, replied Mick. Sailing was his life. He lived for dinghy racing, a sport for which he had won two major trophies. He wanted to start a club at

Old Duddlestone; they could race unrestricted on the open sea, away from the congestion of Poole or the Solent.

'I could make this place a top racetrack. Bring in all the big names – make you guys a lot of bucks.'

I was sceptical, but I liked his style. We took him on.

'What about transport,' I asked. 'You can't always arrive by sea.'

'No probs, gotta motor bike.'

Mick set to work with a will. His arrival coincided with our first visiting yachts. He helped them dock and topped up their fuel with our new pump. Whatever its origin, I was relieved to find that the tank was full of pristine white commercial diesel.

The construction gang had launched another pontoon and promised it would be ready for tomorrow. At six o'clock, Laura gave Mick and me a lift back to Poole; Mick to give the good news to his girl, and me to recover my car from Hamworthy.

As we crossed the strip of military land we passed three army trucks, pulled over on the edge, near the point where the roads divided. I could see two lines of men being briefed by an officer; next to them was some sort of earth moving machinery.

'This is new,' Laura grunted. 'I hope they're not going to start regular manoeuvres on this end. The Brigadier's been co-operative up to now.'

I gave Laura a good start for the return trip; I had my own plans for this evening and I didn't want her around. I reached the turning for "Ashwood" and once again, bumped up the rough unmade road. I was looking for Brian Byrne who had told me he lodged here. I knew nothing of the householders, who Byrne claimed were helping him with his book, nor had I the first idea why Laura should be visiting here. I hadn't asked because I assumed I'd have a dusty answer.

It really was the most delightful cottage. I suppose it had once been the home of a gamekeeper or a shepherd, but I could see that it had been tastefully modernised and lovingly maintained. I noticed two cars parked outside; the same Rover I had seen before and a BMW with last year's plates. I parked my car clear of these others and walked to the front door. Before I could ring the bell it opened and I came face to face with a woman. She was a greying, middle - aged, middle-class housewife, a complete stereotype: well-dressed in country style and exuding an air of unshakeable self-confidence. The universal village stalwart; whether it was the Mother's Union, WI, or the local Conservatives, she would be there.

'Hello,' she beamed at me. 'You're Captain Wilson. I saw you bring Brian home on Sunday – come on in. You know I can just remember your late father. I was only a very little girl then, but he was such a hero for all of us,' she paused to draw breath. 'Have you come to see Brian? He said you would, sooner or later. He's going to clear poor Arthur's name, you know.' I was swept into the house, my head buzzing, on this irresistible wave of chatter.

'Put a sock in it, Ivy and bring the good Captain in here.' A cheerful voice bellowed from a door off the tiny hallway.

The room was dark, but light streamed in through a pair of French windows overlooking a colourful walled garden ablaze with shrubs and roses. Two men were in the room. One was Byrne and the other a tall balding character, looking slightly incongruous in tennis kit and white socks.

'I'm Stanley Bowler,' he said holding out his hand.

I took it gladly; I had a feeling I was going to like Mr and Mrs Bowler.

'Stan's a solicitor,' said Byrne. 'He's the man who called me here in the first place.'

Mr Bowler waved me to a seat in a well-worn armchair, while he perched on the sofa opposite. I sized this man up as a steady profess-sional but also, thank goodness, the first wholly sane person I had met in Duddlestone.

'Captain,' he had a lawyer's stare. 'How much do you know about our local history?'

'Only the little I've dragged out of my work colleague.'

'Meaning Laura Tapsell?'

'Exactly.'

'Excuse me, but you sound a little wary of that lady?'

I laughed. 'She's all right really. I've known worse.'

'Very tactfully put, Captain. In certain matters Laura has the rationale of one who believes the Earth to be flat.'

'Arthur Rocastle was my brother,' Ivy Bowler could no longer contain her indignation. 'He never touched Margaret Gulley. He was such a gentle boy and with that foot, how could he have run all that way? And what about the nine people, yes, *nine* eyewitnesses, who saw him in Swanage.' She was becoming flushed and tearful.

'Hold on Ivy.' Mr Bowler stifled his wife's torrent. 'I doubt the Captain's heard any of this. He looks understandably baffled.' He stood up. 'I say, I rather fancy a drink – what's yours, Captain?'

'I'm driving,' I said, 'but I think I could get away with a cold lager. And please forget all the Captain stuff – I'm Peter.'

'And we're Stan and Ivy. If you please, my dear, cold beer and refreshments all round.'

Ivy bustled out of the room and Stan turned back to me. 'As Brian told you, I'm a solicitor – I run a practice with our son in Poole. When I came to these parts and married Ivy, the Arthur Rocastle case was taboo, for two reasons.' Stan moved to a leather armchair and sat down. 'Reason One: Ivy was very attached to her elder brother. The whole thing was a terrible trauma. I think you ought to know that Arthur was abducted from this house. Ivy wasn't here at the time, thank God.' Stan stopped for a moment. We could hear his wife bustling away in the kitchen.

'Reason Two: New Duddlestone was a closed community. The police received no local co-operation in finding Arthur's killers. The whole place closed ranks against the outside world.'

'Typical tribal reaction,' said Byrne.

Stan nodded in agreement. 'And not an iota of justification. The charges that Arthur faced were nonsense. When it came to trial the judge ordered an acquittal, then he publicly rebuked the police and prosecution. It's something almost without precedent then or since.'

'What's my father's connection with all this?' I looked at Byrne.

'I thought we might be coming to that,' Byrne half smiled. 'What have you been told already?'

'A source told me that you thought my father might know the identity of the real murderer of the girl Gulley. Yesterday I would have said rubbish; now I'm not so sure. I'd like to hear your take on all this.'

'All right,' said Byrne. 'My researches, which have been as thorough as I've been allowed, lead me to believe that your father, among others, witnessed a disaster at the research lab under Weavers Down. I believe that he was pressured to keep his mouth shut.'

'I doubt that,' I said. 'They would have found that very difficult.'

'I know, your father was not the sort of man to conceal the truth if it was morally repugnant to do so.'

'Certainly not.'

'In fact your father made quite an impression.'

'How do you know all this?' I was annoyed, suspecting he was playing with me to inflate his ego.

'Sorry Peter,' he smiled. 'I'm an investigator so I've an advantage over you. Last year I met a man with an uneasy conscience. I know this is going to sound corny, but you'd be surprised how often it happens.'

'Look,' I said. 'Tell me what you know. If it's honest research I promise I won't take offence.'

'When I started the Duddlestone project, I began by writing letters to all the national newspapers asking for witnesses. I didn't get a great response at first, but I had one good call. There was this man in a hospice near Scarborough. Apparently the guy had had a visit from MI5. Ironically, he hadn't read my letter, he'd never even heard of me. But the goons said that if he talked to me, his wife would lose his service pension when he died.'

'I take it this was official pressure?' I wasn't surprised.

'Definitely, though in this case a brilliant example of how to put the ball in your own goal. My man knew the threats were empty bullshit, but it made him mad. He only had a week or so to live and he knew it. So he sent for me and I came running.'

'I can imagine.'

'What he told me was this, so please, Peter, hang on to your cool. In 1946, this guy was a Navy Intelligence officer, based at Portland. He was ordered to visit your old man and tell him that the Admiral was aware of his private life.'

'OK, 'nuff said.' I understood fully.

'He told your father that the Admiral was inclined to use his blind eye because of your father's outstanding war record, but he might not be able to defend him if your father disclosed the truth of the events at Duddlestone.'

'Jesus, what happened next?'

'Your Dad smacked my witness on the nose. Made himself open to a court martial for that alone.'

God, yes, I could imagine the scene. Not only was the old man's pride wounded; after two years of accumulated resentment he was probably ready for an explosion. Mother had told me some of it. The hundreds of little deceptions they'd had to make to conceal their engagement and keep this happy innocent little secret from the ears of authority. Father understood, if mother could not, the overbearing nastiness of Establishment prejudice. How he had broken every convention by falling in love with a girl from the lower ranks and worse, much worse, a foreigner and a Jew.

Byrne was watching me digest this. 'What happened then?' I asked.

'My source, who seems to have been a decent guy, didn't mention the punch. He just reported a negative. Then it seems they gave your father the full treatment. He had a visit from Whitehall wizards, specially trained. Appealed to his sense of duty and patriotism, and then waved the Official Secrets Act.'

'They should've done that in the first place, blackmail would've been like a red rag to a bull.'

'So it seems,' Byrne nodded. 'Did he ever talk about it in your hearing?'

'I think he might've done, once.' I was trying to find a way to introduce my dream sequence. 'I've a sort of sub-conscious memory. Look, this may be complete balls, but the other night I think I remembered something from early childhood. My mother was shouting at my father, something about mass murder, not just a single killing, rather as if there'd been a serial killer around. She seemed to think Dad could've done something to stop it.'

'There were only two murders as far as we know, but we think there could've been a dozen or more killed when the research lab blew up.'

'Laura told me about that. She said there's a complete blackout on information. Relatives still don't know what happened to their people.'

'That's about the size of it.' Byrne was staring at me again. 'Peter, in the interests of truth, would you care to tell me why your father died the way he did?'

I didn't react with anger; such self-indulgence wouldn't do. Laura was wrong, Byrne wasn't a sneaky journalist out to make a quick buck. The man had integrity and a cause he believed in.

'He'd been depressed,' I said. 'General opinion is that he couldn't take civilian life.'

'That's the general opinion – what's yours?'

'He didn't have to leave the service, but they told him on the quiet that if he married my mother, he'd never be an admiral.'

'Because your mother had been a national of a country under Soviet control?'

'That's their mealy-mouthed version, yes.'

In those days an admiral was required to have a "Navy wife", one of a horrific breed, now happily almost extinct. Equipped with a posh accent, Laura Tapsell would have made a splendid Navy wife. An exotic East European girl, like mother, would have been the squarest of pegs in the roundest of holes.

'Could there have been more to it than that?' Byrne was clearly unconvinced. 'Your father was doing well with his business. He was happily married – he thought the world of you.'

This man was slowly stripping away my defences; well so be it. 'No,' I heard myself reply, 'you're right, something happened. Whatever it was it came out of the blue and the man's whole character changed.' I looked him in the eye. 'Brian, help me to find the truth.'

I followed Brian Byrne up the steep track. We'd emerged from the shadow of a tangle of thorn bushes and now we were in the evening sunshine on the crest of the down. On either side of the tractor way sheep nibbled the turf behind wire mesh stock fences. Below us the village of New Duddlestone lay spread at our feet. I could just see the garden of Ashwood Cottage, from where we'd started this climb twenty minutes ago. Already I was gasping for breath although Brian seemed unaffected.

'Not much further now, about a hundred and fifty yards and we're there.' Ahead of us was the same windswept copse of stunted trees that I'd seen from the pub two evenings ago.

'You were up here on Sunday,' I gasped. 'Not long after I dropped you at the Bowler's.'

'I went straight up here. I wanted some space to think. How d'you know anyway?'

'I was with Laura – I saw you against the skyline.'

'They say sailors have sharp eyesight.'

He walked to the edge of the trees. They were a poor collection of windblown ash and field maple, interspersed with more thorn.

'This is Tollands Copse,' Brian walked on into the trees and kicked a wide and very rotten stump. 'This was the oak tree; they've cut it down long since. Whether superstition or guilt complex, I couldn't say.'

'It was fifty years ago,' I said. 'Does it matter any more?'

'There's no statute of limitations on murder.'

'But fifty years! Anyone involved will be old now, or dead more likely.'

'Makes no difference. Look, that night six men – there may have been more but I can name six – a gang of fit, strong men dragged a crippled, mentally backward boy up here and hanged him.' Byrne's voice was cold and expressionless. 'I don't know how many of them are alive, but those that are, I'll hunt down and I'll see they live out their time behind bars. Any that's dead won't rest easy, because I'll let the world know who they are and what they did.'

I drove back to Old Duddlestone and my floating home, in a thoughtful mood. I had developed a new respect for Brian Byrne. This professional crime writer was something more than another Fleet Street hack. Every decent person wants the law to work and see true justice done, but to Byrne it was his life, an obsession; for that reason Arthur Rocastle had become a talisman. Before I left Ashwood Cottage, Brian had thrust a bulky envelope into my hands. 'Read what's in there,' he said. 'There's photocopies of everything: the killing of Margaret Gulley, the court at Winchester, and then the second murder, the lynching.'

I turned the envelope around in my hands as I lay in my bunk that evening. Then I yawned and threw it across onto the chart table unopened. I couldn't share Brian's obsession with Arthur's fate; my quest lay with my father. I desperately wanted to know if these events had a connection with his death. In the morning I might have a clearer purpose, but tomorrow could take care of itself. That night I slept undisturbed by dreams, nor strange lights and bumps in the night.

I awoke to a bright cloudless sky; it was eight o'clock. I put my head out of the hatch in time to see a motorbike speeding down the hill into the village. I dressed quickly and climbed onto the dock, my dignity intact.

'Sorry I'm late, Chief,' said Mick pulling off his helmet. 'Had a bit of trouble wi' the pongos.'

'I thought Laura fixed you a pass?'

'She did, all stamped and official. Didn't make a difference. They stopped me at the camp and they must've radioed ahead 'cos another lot pulled me, just over the hill there. Had a bit of a run in with one.'

'Why?'

'The bastard made a racist dig about my name. Seems some of 'em been in Bosnia."

'We don't want to antagonise them.'

'Yeah, I know.'

Mick went away grumbling about the military. I assumed they had taken against him on the strength of his appearance and the motorbike. The sooner we had our own entrance road the better.

For the rest of the day I was too busy to think about Duddlestone, Arthur Rocastle's murder, or even my father's past troubles. The work on the harbour was going splendidly. We now had a fourth pontoon in place and, by evening, we'd seen the arrival of our first two permanent berth holders: one motor cruiser and a thirty-foot sailing yacht. Mick was an inspiration and it was clear our new arrivals liked his laid-back style. I had not the slightest doubt we'd made the right decision taking him aboard.

By nightfall the place was deserted. Mick had gone home to his girl in Poole, Laura had vanished somewhere and once again I had the place to myself. It was time for me to cook a meal and catch some sleep. I felt restless, and for the first time in weeks I found myself craving company. I climbed down into the harbour dory, a flat-bottomed motor launch with the words "Harbour Master" painted boldly along her topsides. I enjoyed the feel of sitting there, listening to the rumbling of the pontoons against their mooring piles and the distant wash of the seas outside.

Returning aboard *Stormgoose* I couldn't sleep. I was haunted by memories of ships I'd sailed in, the men and the places we'd known together. I thought of my daughter, Emma. If only for her sake couldn't I have made a better go of my life? Could I have held my marriage together for a few more years? What would have been the point? Rhona when all was said and done was a mistake. The daughter of close friends, we'd almost been forced together by our respective families. The marriage had been a bumpy ride from the beginning. Contrary to accepted wisdom, my absences at sea had probably kept us together long after we should have parted amicably. Rhona's betrayal had outraged my pride, but deep down I knew her to be a stupid woman and I was glad she had gone. Of course it begged the point; why was I always thrown together with such bloody awful women? Not just my wife, and now Laura, but that ghastly female the shipping company had tried to impose on me. I'd made a stand on principle and it had got me the sack; probably I'd never command at sea again. I rolled over on my bunk engulfed in self-pity.

Something had woken me. I looked at my watch: it was two thirty in the morning. I must have been sleeping better than I'd expected. A second later I was sitting up all slumber gone. That bloody light again; it was burning on the far shore in exactly the same place. Half a minute later I was on deck, dressed and staring across the harbour. Then I heard it, the slow drum of heavy engines coming from seaward. I raced along the quay and jumped into the dory, half-winding myself as I slipped full length on the bottom boards. I scrambled to my feet and stood listening. Tonight I could see no fog, just a glimmer of light from the new moon. As the minutes passed my night vision improved. Now at last I could see something: a bow wave. A massive dark shape was coming in, passing the end of the harbour wall. I slipped the dory's mooring lines and turned the starter key; the big outboard motor roared into life drowning out all other sound. From now on I'd be reliant on my eyes and my judgement.

I opened the throttle and sped towards the centre of the harbour. I concentrated on the area at the end of the big wall. Yes, there she was, moving slowly as before, not a light showing. I slowed the dory and waited. I wanted to know what this intruder was up to before I made a challenge. She was close now, moving at no more than a couple of knots. It was unlikely that her helmsman could see me, and provided he didn't run me down, that was fine by me. The vessel, distorted by darkness seemed to fill the entire bay. She was a seventy foot *Omega,* one of a line of luxury motor yachts, built in Britain mainly for the American and Arab markets.

I glanced at the shoreline, but the white light had vanished. The *Omega* was starting to make her turn, exactly as she had done the other night. Once again her bows were facing me. If I was going to do anything about this incident, I had to do it in the next three minutes. I set the dory on a course to intercept the ship in mid harbour. She was beginning to pick up speed. I pushed my throttle open to keep station. If my memory served me right, these yachts had a stern bathing platform, where tanned lovelies draped themselves in the Mediterranean sun. I lined up my approach as carefully as possible. The big yacht was moving faster than I'd expected. Had they seen me? We'll have to impose a speed limit was the daft thought that flashed through my head. She'd passed me now and I was tagging on in her wake some fifteen yards astern. I must make my move or be left behind. I opened the throttle wide – the gap was closing then, bang! My boat stopped dead in the water as if clutched by a gigantic fist. I had been standing with my hand on the tiny steering wheel. The next second I was flat on the floorboards, shaken, winded and in pain, while simultaneously the motor had cut out. I heard the larger vessel's engines roar as her throttles were pushed wide open. Her wake hit the dory and for a few horrified seconds I thought we would capsize. Then the seas subsided, the engines faded and I struggled, angry and mortified, to my feet.

It didn't take long to discover what had happened. My engine had stopped when my fall had activated the emergency kill-cord, wound around my wrist. Worse still the engine had torn clean off its fixings snapping the fuel line. Now it was several feet below the surface held by a safety wire, and beyond that I could see a line wrapped around the propeller stretching away below the surface like an anchor cable. My little launch, of which I was so proud, was caught like a pig by the tail with its engine drowned and useless. I rummaged in the bow locker for an anchor buoy. I tied a line to the top of the motor, heaved it half way aboard and disentangled the line from around the propeller. The buoy would secure this rogue cable for tonight and leave it marked. Tomorrow I would have to raise it before any more damage was done. The plastic propeller was ruined, the engine mount had twisted and the ignition and fuel systems were full of seawater. There was no point in trying to restart the motor. I fished out the emergency pair of oars and rowed slowly and painfully back to the jetty. I was angry and my chest still hurt from my tumble.

I secured the dory and staggered back to bed. I fell asleep and never heard another sound that night.

CHAPTER 8

The next morning, as soon as it was light enough, I examined the dory. I could see at a glance that, seawater apart, the outboard motor was a write-off. The force with which we had hit the cable had been enough to twist the drive shaft a few centimetres out of true. One of our visiting yachtsmen came over and confirmed to me that the motor would never run again. Until I could drive to Poole for a replacement, I was reduced to paddling around. I told the man what had happened. He remembered that he had heard engines.

Laura was uncommunicative and surly that morning, which suited me fine. We had three visiting yachts and a score of letters, emails, and faxes, all enquiring about permanent berths. The whole project was beginning to look promising. It was late morning when Dr Hooder honoured us with a visit. I saw him from the office window talking to Mick. One didn't need a lesson in body language to sense Hooder's disapproval.

'That man's an Australian.' The doctor sounded as if he was diagnosing an unpleasant disease.

'What's wrong with Australians?' I was annoyed. 'Mick's a fine sailor and our customers like him.'

'My dear Wilson, two hundred years ago we sent, at huge expense to the tax payer, our criminal low life to the other side of the earth. The understanding was that they would not come back here.'

This statement was so preposterous that I wondered if the Doctor was making a heavy-handed joke. Seemingly not, he appeared completely serious.

'Well Mick's not a criminal. He's an ambitious young man and he's staying here as long as I can keep him.' I replied coldly.

Laura who was crouched over a computer screen looked up and winked.

'As you wish,' he nodded. 'Wilson, a word in private please,'

I waved him towards the inner office. Laura followed us and shut the door.

'Very well, Laura, you may remain.'

'That's because I wouldn't bloody go anyway and he knows it.' She looked me full in the face with a mischievous smile. My word, she was a good looking girl.

'On the contrary, dear lady, I need your business skills. We will discuss cash flow. What's our break-even point?'

Laura produced a spread sheet and a hand-written summary.

The doctor studied the figures. 'What are our prospects of achieving this?'

'We've had thirty-three definite bookings and we've only been open a week.'

'There you are, Wilson. Laura has management skills – learn from her.' His nostrils twitched as he looked at me. 'I understand from your boatman that you have destroyed a valuable engine. How did that happen?'

With great restraint I told him.

'I'm sure you were being most conscientious in your duties but I must remind you again. The bottom line is what counts – remember that and you will do well.'

Hooder changed the subject. 'You will have noticed an increase in military activity.'

'Yes, there's soldiers all over the place,' said Laura, 'and I followed two huge great concrete mixer lorries. What's going on?'

'Apparently a vent shaft in one of my late father's tunnels has collapsed.'

'You mean the germ warfare place?' I didn't like the sound of this.

'All right, Wilson.' The doctor laughed. 'No cause for alarm. There is no material in there that could possibly be harmful.'

'So he says,' growled Laura.

'And germ warfare is an incorrect definition. The Establishment was concerned with counter-measures only.'

'Big deal,' said Laura. 'What about all those animals they poisoned?'

'Sacrifice for the greater good. I have a scientific training – I understand the priorities.'

'Bollocks,' Laura glowered at him.

'It didn't do much good for the people who worked there, or so I've been hearing.' I stared at Hooder. 'What really happened?'

'It was before my time. My father was away in London. Such a tragedy – he lost three years' research.'

Twelve people dead, without including Margaret Gulley and Arthur Rocastle, and that was all the man could think of. I abandoned further questions as a waste of time. I was relieved when shortly afterwards the doctor left.

'I can't make head nor tail of that fellow. Is he real? Surely nobody could be as pompous as that.'

'He doesn't intimidate me,' she said. 'I wish I knew what he sees in this place.'

'How so?'

'Well his line of country is private medicine – rich women. The older ones he charms rigid and takes their money. The younger ones he passes to some mate of his who lifts their tits and restructures their bums.'

I glanced at Laura and smiled inwardly. Her body was impressive – certainly no restructuring needed.

'I gather he inherited this place from his father,' I said.

'That's right – they paid a lot of money for it, one hell of a lot more than they'll ever have back from this harbour. Did they want the place for the beauty of the landscape?'

'Possibly.' I didn't know where this was leading.

'Like hell – no way, there's a hidden agenda somewhere only I can't see it.'

The rest of the day went smoothly enough. Then, just after five o'clock, I had a surprise. Walking along the dock was Carol, Laura's sister. Laura went out to meet her and I watched the two in earnest conversation. Then they both walked into the office.

'So this is where it happens,' said Carol.

I grinned at her and waved her to a chair. 'Have a cup of coffee, I'm about to take a break.'

'Thanks, no sugar.'

I watched her out of the corner of my eye as I boiled the kettle. She was dressed in a pair of blue shorts, white trainers and a sleeveless white T-shirt. Her hair, which I had last seen in a ponytail, had been set free and swirled around her shoulders. She looked stunning. What on earth had possessed her husband to run away to Australia?

'How's Tommy?' I asked.

'He's over there watching the builders,' she smiled and pointed.

I could see the boy now, watching intensely as a JCB gouged a hole in the roadside.

Laura shuffled a pile of papers into her briefcase and closed the lid with a snap. 'You two can gossip all you like, I'm off.' With that she left. We watched her car as it sped away.

'She never even waited for her coffee,' I grumbled.

'I expect she thinks I'm spying on her,' said Carol.

'You're not, are you?'

'No I'm not!' she swung round to face me. I met her eyes and was struck once again by how round and dark they were.

'Sorry,' I sighed contritely. 'This place is all contradictions and your sister is one of them. Why does she dislike me?'

Carol looked surprised for a second by my bluntness. 'I don't think she does really,' she paused and then seemed to make up her mind. 'Laura's very suspicious of … oh, let's say she doesn't like establishment males.'

'Christ, is that what she calls me?'

'Well, you are a sea captain from a Navy background. All that patriotic warlike thing. I don't like that either.' Those eyes were fixed on mine, questioning.

'So I suppose you both think I'm kicking my heels here hoping every day for another war.'

I was annoyed and I knew the sarcasm had bitten home. Her eyes flickered and her lower lip drooped. I couldn't help smiling, the expression was so like Tommy the other evening.

'No, of course I don't think that,' she paused, clearly uncertain how to go on. 'I don't think that, but Laura does.'

I'd met this attitude before, always from well-educated women who ought to know better. 'Neither of you knows the first thing about me.' I looked at her coldly.

'I know, I'm sorry. Can we talk about something else?'

'In a minute.' I handed her a cup of coffee. 'First you listen to me. If, God forbid, there was a war, I'd be in the Merchant Service, and that means being a sitting duck for every enemy plane and submarine, with no chance whatever of hitting back. Also, I am not an uncultured fascist oaf, thank you. My maternal grandfather was the composer Vladmir Panov, so I like music and surprise, surprise, I can actually read books.'

'Oh God,' she laughed. 'I have put my foot in it, but please, don't judge me by my sister.'

Certainly I would never do that. The two women were alike in some ways and utterly different in others. Of the two, I definitely preferred Carol. Like me, she had survived a bad marriage, but unlike me she seemed without that poisonous sense of grievance. However, I was not prepared to let the matter drop.

'What is it that makes your sister the way she is? I don't think I've ever met such an abrasive person, and I've known a few in my job.' I wondered if I'd gone too far but Carol seemed amused.

'How can I put this,' she hesitated. 'Well, Laura may be anti-war but she's been fighting one for most of her life.'

'You mean women's rights and all that?'

'No, not so simple. Laura is the eldest of we three and the cleverest. There was good money in farming thirty years ago so my parents sent Laura to a posh girls' school. She was a target for snooty bitches including some of the teachers – you know, fisherman's granddaughter – speaking broadest Dorset.'

'She doesn't speak it now,' I said, 'only traces of it when she's cross.'

'Oh yes, she soon put a plum in her mouth and that antagonised her friends back here in the village. Anyway, in the end she made it all the way to Cambridge where she met that twit Lawrence Tapsell.'

'Her husband?'

'That's him – not a wise choice.'

'How so?'

'Gorgeous hunk, brilliant in bed...' Carol sniggered, 'but useless with money and bone idle.'

'OK, I get the picture. She thinks all men are like that – the idle and feckless bit I mean.'

Carol only smiled and shook her head.

'Drink your coffee,' I said, ' and I'll show you round.'

Mick was standing on the end of the new pontoon. He was holding a large object that he had just removed from the deck of his own dinghy. Here was the buoy I had set on the stray cable last night. The harbour dory was useless without an engine so Mick had taken his sailing boat and quartered the harbour looking for this marker. Until now there had been no sign of it.

'What's that?' asked Tommy.

Mick handed the float to me and I examined it minutely. It was the same anchor buoy but the line attaching it to the cable had been deliberately cut.

'That's happened since yesterday,' said Mick. 'Saw it on the far shoreline. Someone's been back after you fixed it – divers I guess and...' He broke off and looked warily at my companions.

'Possibly,' I grunted, 'it's certainly suspicious – maybe it's time I reported this.' I switched my gaze to Carol, caught her eye and held it. 'D'you know what goes on in this harbour?'

There was just a flicker of doubt in her eyes. 'No, I don't come here very often.' Her face became deadpan.

'But you young man,' I swung round on Tommy. 'Your Aunt

Laura says you're always here, so what do you know about it?'

The boy's mobile face went through a dozen changes in as many seconds. He didn't need to say anything. I knew that he knew the answers, that he was burning to tell me, but he was frightened to do so. I let the matter drop. I liked the pair of them. I found I liked them very much. Along with Stan and Ivy Bowler, these two were the only people I felt wholly comfortable with in this odd place, and I was not out to pick a quarrel with them. I would reserve that for Laura Tapsell first thing tomorrow morning.

'Hello, no car?' I was standing outside the office ready to say my farewells.

'We came along the green lane on our bikes,' Carol explained.

'That would be the track where I met Tommy the other day?' It made sense. I had looked at the ordnance map and had been surprised how close we were to Honeycritch Farm. In fact the green lane was to be upgraded as our new entry road.

'That's right,' said Carol. 'We left our bikes at the top of the chine. Tommy can ride down but I don't fancy it.'

'I'll walk the first part with you, if that's all right.' It was odd, but I didn't want to part company with her just yet.

It took a little over ten minutes to walk to the chine; the same little defile that ran up the sloping cliff.

'Would you like to walk to the top with us?' Carol asked. 'It's not as steep as it looks.'

The pathway had eroded with time and was partially blocked with bushes. There were signs that it might once have been in regular use. I asked Carol.

'Yes, this was the old road into Duddlestone village. Horse and cart transported everything in those days. They had an old tractor to pull the boats out and a fish van in New Duddlestone. Everything else was horsepower or manpower.

'Laura says it's your grandparents' house she's doing up?'

'Yes, but it's still a couple of weeks from ready.' She laughed. 'Laura can't wait to escape from Honeycritch.'

The climb was steep enough, despite Carol's assurances. We both ceased conversation to save breath. Tommy, with the energy of youth, ran ahead. We reached the summit and I turned to admire the view. Below lay the harbour with the great wall and our new docking pontoons. *Stormgoose* and the other yachts seemed like toys. A lovely cooling breeze came from the sea with a scent of grass, heather and wild flowers.

'I never feel too comfortable here,' said Carol. She was sitting down on the short turf hugging her knees.

'Why's that?' I was surprised. To me the scene was idyllic.

'This is the place,' she hesitated; for a second there was an expression of real anguish on her face that startled me.

'What place?' I looked at her, but she avoided my eye.

I felt embarrassed. She seemed lost in some inner reverie; some private hell. 'What place, Carol? Please tell me.'

'It was here. It's where they found Margaret Gulley's body. It's where she was raped and murdered.'

CHAPTER 9

The next morning I drove to Poole, to buy a replacement for the dory's smashed outboard. Needing a stronger vehicle than my car, I had borrowed a Land Rover from Laura's brother Ian. The journey was not a pleasant one. The vehicle suited my purpose, but it was old and battered, and it stank of livestock.

The engine dealer offered me a derisory part exchange for the wrecked outboard, which in the end I accepted. I needed that new motor and it wasn't me picking up the tab. The salesman called a young employee to wheel the trolley with the new engine. I walked ahead pausing, to glance over the crowded marina. It was a well-organised, functional place but very expensive, and it lacked charm; Old Duddlestone was more attractive on every score.

One yacht stood out. She had an entire pontoon to herself and she dwarfed the other craft like a tower block in a suburban road. She was a seventy-foot *Omega*, identical to the ship that entered my harbour at night. I was excited, there couldn't be more than half a dozen of these exotic craft in the UK. I hurried back to the Land Rover. The boy with the trolley was staring mournfully at the heavy engine and it was starting to rain. It was one of those deceptive low-pressure systems that occasionally drift up from the continent. A hot haze that deepens and slowly turns to warm, windless, rain; wonderful for gardeners, but frustrating for sailors.

'Come on,' I said. Between us, we sweated and heaved the twentyhorsepower monster into the back of the Land Rover.

'That's Mr Rocastle's wagon, i'nnit?' commented my helper.

'That's right – how did you know?'

'I does 'is garden sometimes, and Mrs Stoneman, she were my teacher.'

'Carol Stoneman?'

'S'right.' The boy was a weedy youngster, with a shaved head and apparently terminal acne. His Dorset accent was the broadest I'd so far encountered.

'What's your name?'

'Daryl Gulley.'

He froze as he caught my angry stare.

'What connection are you with Steve Gulley?' I snapped.

'I don't have nuthin' to do wi' him.' Daryl looked indignant.

'You must be related?'

'His dad's my uncle, but we don't 'ave nuthin' to do with 'em. Them's wasters, and anyways they're Duddlestone, we lives in Langton.'

Langton Matravers, the village a mile or two down the road to Swanage, was hardly the ends of the earth.

'But you're still related.'

'We'm all related around here.'

That was probably half the trouble with Duddlstone, I mused. The lad stared defiantly at me. Clearly he had heard about the incident with the beacons.

I changed the subject. 'Tell me,' I asked casually. 'Who owns that *Omega*?'

'She's the *Perzy Phone*, Mr Eriksen's boat.'

'What was that name?' I made him spell it.

'Ah, you mean, *Persephone*,' I laughed. 'She was queen of the underworld, as I remember.'

Daryl looked blank. He was even more on the defensive now and I wondered why. 'Do you know where this Mr Eriksen lives?' I asked as casually as I could.

'London mostly, though they say as he's gotta' place up Shaftesbury way.' Daryl looked at the ground, for some reason he was unwilling to meet my eye.

Grey seas, grey skies and a swirling blanket of rain enveloped Old Duddlestone. The windscreen wipers on the Land Rover squeaked and a leak in the roof spat a steady drip of water on my left shoulder. Mick helped me unload the motor. We clamped it onto the stern of the now repaired dory and reconnected the controls. The boat was pulled up the slipway and in an hour or so the incoming tide would float her off again.

'Is Laura around?' I asked.

'Yeah, she's up the street – in that new house of hers.'

Two builder's trucks stood parked in the street. For a few minutes I forgot Laura. The men had started work on the first cottage, the one I was to occupy. As United Marinas were paying for the work I could hardly demand anything too elaborate. I was happy with the plans the foreman showed me; I only hoped they would finish soon and I could move in before the autumn gales.

I found Laura next door. I was impressed with what had been achieved with this house in the last few days. The doors had been fitted and the walls re-plastered. Electricians were renewing the wiring, and packing cases containing a modern kitchen were stacked in the front room.

'A couple more days,' said Laura, with a happy grin. 'Just forty-eight hours and I move in.'

'Won't you miss your family?'

'Will I hell!'

'Laura,' I was serious now. 'Do you know a man called Eriksen?'

'Why do you want to know?' She was suddenly cold and withdrawn.

'In the marina at Poole I saw an *Omega* class motor yacht. I was told the owner was someone called Eriksen.' I stared at Laura; her face was inscrutable.

I continued. 'It was an *Omega* that I saw nosing around here at night and I'm sure it was the same one that wouldn't acknowledge my radio calls. I doubt there's two such craft on the South Coast. That's why I need to trace this Eriksen and talk to him.'

'I would have thought,' Laura's tone was icy, 'I would have thought that your purpose here is to build a profitable yacht harbour. If I was you I'd confine my activities to that.'

I concealed my annoyance and stared her out. 'You know something, don't you?'

She turned her back on me and stumped off up the stairs. It was a most eloquent and seductive rear that disappeared from view. I turned around and walked back into the rain-swept street. As I did so I saw a figure flit stealthily away from the open door. It was a woman and I recognised her instantly. She wore the same shabby denim but this time she walked barefoot and silent. Here was that alleged Australian journalist and I knew that she had been listening.

'Can I help you?' I asked.

The woman ignored me and tripped away up the street towards the cliffs.

I was far more intrigued than annoyed. Returning to my office I made a mental note to ask Byrne if he knew anything about this nosy-parker. My present concern was with Mr Eriksen. Whatever he was up to, he wasn't going to buy me with one measly tank of diesel fuel. I reached for the shelf with the local phone books. I guessed the spelling of Eriksen to be Scandinavian. The boy Gulley had said the man lived near Shaftesbury. I found the relevant book and sat down at Laura's desk. Sure enough there was an Eriksen: Greatham Manor

Farm, Fontwell Magna. I dialled the number. An answerphone told me that Mr and Mrs Eriksen were not in residence until June the twenty third. Matters concerning the estate should be directed to the Farm Manager.

I looked up the number for Stan and Ivy Bowler. Ivy answered and I asked for Brian Byrne. She told me Brian had gone to London but should be back by five that evening. I said I would ring him then. Through the window I could see Laura advancing in a purposeful manner. I quickly restored the phone books to the shelf and retreated to my inner sanctum.

In the end it was Byrne who rang me, not on the marina phone but on my mobile. I could see Laura watching me closely. Casually I remarked that I would find a better signal at the end of the quay – she made no attempt to follow me.

'I was told you were in London,' I said to Byrne.

'Got back ten minutes ago,' he replied. 'If you want to talk I'll be around tonight. How say we meet at the Gullait Arms – about seven.'

Byrne was in the saloon bar of the Gullait Arms; he was cradling a pint of beer and talking to an elderly couple sitting on a leather settee by the empty fireplace. I counted some twenty other assorted persons in the bar, most of whom I guessed to be locals. They showed no hostility to Brian, he seemed to be generally accepted, giving the lie to Laura's supposition. Harry was serving behind the bar. He waved to me, but he seemed to be engrossed in conversation with a wizened little man perched on a barstool. He looked at least eighty, although his clothes were modern and stylish. He had his back to me throughout, which meant I could stare at him rather longer than good manners allowed. His thick hair was bleached white, not by artificial means, but by age, wind and weather. His hands around his beer glass were almost skeletal. The wrinkled skin was tanned like dark leather, as was his neck and such of the face as I could see. Something seemed strangely compelling about this man. Something that told me that he, too, had spent his lifetime at sea.

Brian bought me a beer and ushered me to a corner table. 'I've spent the day in London,' he said. 'I've been following up something in the Public Records Office.'

'Concerning Duddlestone?'

'Of course, but not the murders. I've been researching the germ warfare lab and the Navy base.'

'Any luck?'

'I can't unearth a thing about the lab,' he sighed. 'The official mind has gone blank. Apparently the place never existed.'

'But it did, Hooder's father ran it and the military still mount a guard there.'

'I know that, you know that, and so do they.'

'Who's they?'

'Bureaucrats whose minds function on the Orwellian principle that the truth is "What we say it is". I don't know who they think they're kidding.' Byrne took a long pull at his beer. 'They're the same people who tried to make out that the Bletchley Park code breaking operation never existed.'

He was right, of course. I had had some contacts with the official mind myself. Brian was looking at me in an odd way. It was as if he needed to say something and was trying to phrase the words tactfully.

'What I really wanted to tell you is this,' he paused. 'I went to the Public Records Office because I wanted files on your father's Sixty Six flotilla.'

'So?'

'The files are closed. No access until the year 2046.'

'That's strange – is this usual?'

'I would say it's absolutely unique. It means closure for one hundred years. In other words there is something hidden that is so mega-embarrassing that they don't want anyone alive, then or now, to know about it – ever.'

'Brian, for Christ's sake, Sixty-Six was an elite unit. There's nothing secret about them, there's miles of stuff in print already and my father wrote an account of the big battle.'

'I know, all that's in the public domain. They've put a secrecy block on everything after May 1945.'

'But that's when the war ended.'

'Exactly,' Brian sat back grinning. 'Now I wonder why?'

I wondered why as well, but at that moment I was hungry. I was about to suggest that we ordered when all hell broke loose.

A hubbub of angry shouts had broken out in the main bar. With surprising agility for his age Harry raced through the door. Brian and I followed.

The public bar was crowded and reeked of beer and cigarette smoke. In the centre of the room was the bulky figure of Steve Gulley. He stood in an aggressive posture, fists clenched; facing him was Mick Tracic. In the few hours since I had last seen him, Mick had transformed. He was smartly dressed, well groomed and clearly not looking for trouble. He stood facing Gulley, hands by his sides. Clinging to his right arm, wide-eyed and frightened, was a pretty fair-haired girl.

Harry crossed the bar in three strides and caught Gulley by the arm. It was amusing to see the great oaf flinch at the grasp of this septuagenarian.

'You,' said Harry. 'Out of here! You've been warned before. Now you're banned.'

'No you don't. You ain't banning no Gulley from the pub as bears his name.' An elderly man had pushed his way to the front. 'You get yer hands off of my boy, or I'll smack you one, Harry.'

Harry seemed unruffled despite the fact that the other man, although of similar age, was twice Harry's weight and had all the makings of an awkward case. If, as it appeared, he and Steve were father and son, I'd rather tackle the son any day.

'Sharon,' Harry spoke quietly to the barmaid. 'Ring the police. We may need some help here.'

'No!,' it was Brian Byrne, standing beside me. 'No, not yet, Harry. Let 'em have their say.'

'All right,' said Harry. 'Come on then, Roy – you've got sixty seconds.'

'It's Hooder and that Wilson. They're giving our jobs to outsiders – like this fuckin' foreigner!' Steve Gulley bellowed across the room, while jabbing his finger at Mick.

'That's right,' said the elder Gulley. 'I were born in the ole village. Us has got a right to it, and that Hooder be stealing it an' givin' it to foreigners.'

I wasn't standing for this. 'What qualifications do you have to work in a yacht harbour?' I asked coldly. 'And why should I take on someone who's done his best to wreck my boat?' I stared hard at Steve and saw the shot hit home. The man reddened, and I was gratified to hear a mutter of agreement spread round the room.

The elder Gulley swivelled round glaring. 'So, you be Wilson.' He was breathing heavily with perspiration pouring down his face. Like his son he was unshaven, though his head was rounder, grey-haired and balding.

'I'm Peter Wilson. Who are you?'

'So, you wanna' be knowin' who I be?' The tone was mocking, and his whole posture spelt deep malevolence. 'I know who you be. I know'd your father. Topped 'imself, didn't 'e. Have summat on his conscience did 'e?'

'Not half what's on your conscience, Roy Gulley. You're a murderer, a cold-blooded murderer.' It was Brian Byrne, quiet but intense, his Liverpool accent vivid, his voice cold as ice.

A hint of a smile was on Byrne's face, but it was a bleak remorseless expression. Even in the stifling heat of the room I felt a chill.

'Justice,' said Byrne. 'Justice for an innocent crippled boy, whose murderers are still unpunished…'

'Innocent! Innocent, my arse.' Roy Gulley had pushed his way through the spectators and was now face to face with Byrne. 'He raped my sister, then 'e strangled 'er. So, if your fuckin' courts don't give us justice, we shows 'em our justice. Too right we 'anged 'im. Yer, we 'anged 'im, and 'e ung slow…'

'Shut up! Shut up, you bloody fool!' This was a new voice, a voice ringing with authority. A well educated voice with just the scintilla of an accent. It was the little troll man I'd seen talking to Harry. I felt him brush past me to stand in front of Roy Gulley. He couldn't have been an inch over five foot but he had a presence that made Roy step back. Something was teasing my memory; somewhere, sometime long ago, I'd seen this little man before and heard his voice.

The whole company stood silent and tense. I could hear a clock ticking in a nearby room and a dog barking somewhere in the village. All eyes were on Roy and the little troll, as I named him. The latter stood flushed and angry, staring at Roy who had taken a step backwards. Some of his bluster had faded but he still looked surly and defiant.

'Yaah, Magnus, what's biting you?' Roy sneered. 'It don't matter what Byrne says, or Wilson. Nobody 'ere 'eard nothin'.' He looked around challenging.

'I heard everything you said – every word,' said a quiet female voice that I knew. I turned round to see her in the shadows by the door; it was Carol Stoneman. So intense had been the scene in the middle of the room that I'd missed her.

Roy swung round open mouthed, but his son Steve broke into a raucous laugh. 'Oh yeah, Carol, you stupid cow. You won't grass on your own kind. Look at yer, all lah-di-dah teacher. Well you ain't nuthin'. You're a Duddlestone fishy like the rest o' us.' Steve glanced round the bar, this time there was a rumble of agreement. I looked at Carol, she made no reply but her face was a picture of misery and there were tears on her cheeks. I flashed a quick supportive smile.

My temper was kindling. I had meant to keep out of these local feuds, but what the hell. 'I also heard every word spoken.' I turned towards the two Gulleys.

'You keep out of this, Wilson!' snapped the troll. He sounded overbearingly self-confident as if he was giving orders to an underling. I wasn't standing for that.

I turned on him. 'I don't know who the hell you are, little fellow, but you don't order me around – see!' I glowered down at him.

He glowered back, and then suddenly he smiled. 'You sound just like your father.'

'Don't worry about 'im,' said Roy. 'He won't do nuthin'. His old daddy were in the shit as deep as any 'o us. When it comes to it, you'll worry about the family honour, won't you, Mister?' He jeered at me.

'Right, that's it,' said Harry, and for the first time he was really angry. 'Out you go. I won't hear Captain Wilson or his son defamed – understood?'

Roy laughed unpleasantly. 'You 'eard what I said, Harry – we ain't going nowhere.' The chips were down with a vengeance now. The pair of them were staring at Harry, calling his bluff.

'Mr Broadenham?' It was Mick, in the intervening furore I had forgotten him. 'Mr Broadenham, you want these jokers out?' His laconic Australian drawl was completely relaxed. He could have been asking if the windows needed opening.

'I'm requesting the two gentlemen to leave,' said Harry. 'If they don't I'll have to send for the police, and I'd much rather not.'

'Sure,' said Mick. 'Right, you heard what the man said, and he said – out!'

Mick must have been ready. He'd hardly finished as Steve Gulley took a mighty swing at him. Mick's girlfriend screamed as he ducked, caught the flailing arm, and tipped the luckless Gulley to the floor. He followed the action with a deft kick in the place it hurts most. Steve doubled up in silent agony. As I'd suspected, the older Gulley was made of sterner stuff. I guessed that in earlier years Roy had been an accomplished brawler. For a second he caught Mick off balance and the younger man almost fell. Then Roy himself stumbled. Mick, recovering with amazing speed, caught the old man from behind. Grabbing him by his collar, and the seat of his trousers, he lifted Roy bodily and projected him through the open door into the street.

My instincts told me we were now in real trouble. I moved closer to Mick while glancing quickly around; I needn't have worried. There followed a startled buzz, that turned to a swelling roar of laughter. I crossed the floor to where Mick was looking down at Steve. 'Come on,' I said, 'that's enough – let's get out.' I hustled Mick into the street. Roy Gulley had vanished.

I was not pleased about this episode. I caught Mick's eye. 'Look, this isn't bloody Sydney dockland.'

'Too right – you can say that again. You Poms have no idea how to conduct a good pub fight. Frightened you'll spill your G and T's.'

'All right, well done for the way you sorted things, but don't make a habit of it. I know you were properly provoked by that Gulley fellow, but just remember who you are and what your position here is.'

'Sure,' he grinned, 'I'll remember.'

Mick's girlfriend was glaring angrily. 'You're a show-off and you've spoilt our evening.'

I left it at that. I reckoned the poor man was in enough trouble for one night. I went back into the pub. Byrne was still standing where he'd been all along.

'What was all that about?' I asked bluntly.

'I think we've just raised the stakes,' he said. 'Roy's their weak link and they know it.'

'He's one of your lynch mob by the way he talked.'

'Yeah, one of three still living in these parts, but Roy's the one who'll break.' Brian Byrne had a satisfied glint in his eye. 'God, just give me time – another couple of weeks and I'll crack this.'

'Who's that little squirt who tried to order me off?' The memory still rankled. 'He seemed to know my father.'

'I dunno' for certain who he is, but I've seen him around. I gather he's one of your father's old matelots.'

'Tell me more!' I snapped. 'I didn't like what was said just now.'

Brian glanced around. There was no one within earshot apart from Carol who was standing beside me. Harry was behind the bar, but the little troll man had vanished.

'Don't worry,' said Brian. 'Your father knew nothing about the killings at the time.'

'I should think not.'

He was staring at me and I didn't care for the expression on his face. 'Yes, but there is a thing called, "accessory after …".' Abruptly he turned and walked out into the night.

'Peter, can we talk?' it was Carol.

‘Certainly, but not in here.’ I nodded towards the door and followed her outside.

‘Have you got your car?’ she asked.

‘Yes, it’s round the back.’

‘Give me a lift to the farm and we’ll talk there.’

‘Where’s your motor – you were never going to walk home?’

I looked at Carol; her black dress and strappy sandals were not the attire for walking country lanes.

‘Laura’s taken Tommy swimming. She was calling in here if you didn’t turn up.’

‘How did you know I might be here?’

‘Harry said you would.’

‘It seems nothing’s secret in this place.’

‘Not much – except old murders.’

‘All right, let’s go, I want to know some more about those murders myself.’

The light was beginning to fade as we reached Honeycritch Farm. I remembered that this midnight was summer solstice – the shortest night. I decided I liked this place. It had a happy feel that seemed to distance itself from the sinister air of the village. Indoors we had the kitchen to ourselves. Suddenly I felt hungry. I remembered the meal that Brian Byrne had promised but never delivered. Carol started to make coffee.

‘I couldn’t have a slice of toast, could I?’ I asked tentatively.

‘Of course – you’ve not eaten?’

I explained, and Carol set about making omelettes. ‘Lucky for you I’m an old-fashioned girl,’ she laughed. ‘Laura would’ve pointed you to the stove and told you to get on with it.’

‘I can imagine.’

She put the plate in front of me, then sat down opposite. ‘I suppose you thought it was fun,’ she said.

‘Eh?’

‘That stupid fight in the pub; I hated it. I can see why poor Arthur was killed. Men – it’s just under the surface with all of you.’

‘Oh come on, I thought you were different from your sister. All men are rapists – that’s her line isn’t it?’

‘Not so: that’s sexually repressed American feminism. Actually Laura’s rather keen on sex – so watch out,’ she giggled.

‘Thanks for the warning, but I think I’m fairly safe.’ I laughed in return. It was impossible to be angry with this girl for long. ‘Now tell me,' I looked her in the eyes, 'why do you feel so strongly about Arthur Rocastle?'

She hesitated. 'Arthur was a reject, his face didn't fit, and they killed him for it.'

'Who rejected him?'

'His own peer group. I think what happened was a nasty piece of primeval savagery.'

'Explain, I don't see what you're getting at.'

'I'm a teacher. I've witnessed similar things, and sometimes I've been able to stop it. Arthur was born disabled, some sort of club foot. He could walk, but not far, so he was rejected for military service. Secondly, he wasn't all that bright. His school classified him a "moron". I've seen an entry on a report they made at the time of the trial.'

'Was he – a moron that is?'

'No, of course not. He was probably mildly dyslexic, maybe a case of Aspergers, but neither condition was recognised in those days.'

'But he must have left school by then?'

'Of course, he was nineteen when he died. He was working for the War Agricultural Committee; that was the local body that ran the farming effort for the war.'

'What was his work?'

'Anything going. Tractor driving, fencing, rabbit clearance, all sorts.'

'So, what went wrong?'

'He was isolated. The village lads despised him because he wasn't in the forces. The local girls rejected him and anyway, there were too many of your father's sailors around.'

I was beginning to get the picture. 'In those circumstances couldn't he have killed out of spite? You know – hitting back at the world?'

'That's a fair point, Peter but it's not valid. I've discovered a lot about Arthur, and, as I've said, I'm a teacher. I've had a lot of kids pass through my hands. I don't think he was spiteful, and he certainly wasn't violent.'

'I've heard the girl was raped.'

'So the police charges said, but Peter, rapists are motivated by hate rather than lust, and Arthur didn't hate Margaret. Anyway, if he'd wanted sex with her he could have paid for it. She was that sort, I'm afraid.'

'So I've been told. Laura says Margaret worked at the germ warfare place – looking after the animals.'

'Yes, that's right.'

A car was pulling into the yard, its headlights lighting the kitchen through the uncurtained window.

'What made the police so certain it was Arthur?'

Carol didn't answer, or rather she never had a chance. Footsteps, then voices, sounded the other side of the door, and Tommy burst into the room followed by Laura. Tommy caught sight of me and retreated into shyness. Laura stood in the doorway, looking me over with an expression I didn't care for.

She ignored me and addressed Carol. 'I called in at the "Gooleys", but they told me you'd gone. What the hell happened tonight?'

'Roy Gulley was sounding off and he and Steve got thrown out.'

'Harry threw them out?' Laura sounded incredulous.

'Actually,' I said. 'It was Mick Tracic on behalf of Harry. I ticked him off afterwards, you know, good name of the harbour and all that. But it was a brilliant performance all the same. He's a good lad is Mick – I'm glad he's on our side.'

'And what was Roy sounding off about?' Laura asked heavily.

'Roy had two pints too many,' said Carol, 'and would you believe it – he admitted killing Arthur, all in front of Brian Byrne.'

'Oh shit! Any outsiders in the place?'

'Only Peter and the Australian. Everyone else was village or connected.'

'Thank God for that.'

'Oh really.' Carol had stood up, her big eyes glinting dangerously. 'Actually, it was me that sparked the real trouble, because I told the Gulleys I'd heard what they said, and I implied they couldn't rely on me to keep my mouth shut.'

'Oh you stupid bitch!' Laura hurled her shoulder bag onto the table. 'It's your big talk isn't it. You don't really mean it?' I was surprised how genuinely worried Laura looked.

'I meant it at the time.' Carol's face was a picture of unhappiness, much as it had been in the pub. 'All right, I shan't be running to the police, but if they come to me and ask for a statement, they'll get one. I'm sorry Laura, but I've had it up to here with all this deceit.'

CHAPTER 10

For ten minutes the sisters hurled abuse at each other with a fury that took my breath away. Being an only child, and never having had a sibling, perhaps I didn't understand. Tommy seemed to think this routine. Ignoring the uproar, he settled down at the table and began to leaf through a football paper.

I was certain there was more to this disagreement than a difference over Arthur Rocastle. Whatever injustice he had suffered, it was all a long time ago. Why should Carol treat the issue as if her own life depended on it? Laura's attitude was even harder to understand. She was an educated, intelligent woman, and yet she sided with ignorant and murderous vigilantes. It was so wholly out of character that there could be only one explanation. Laura was a deeply-troubled woman, and, despite her bluster and self-confidence, she was frightened. Frightened of the truth? There was something about the weird chemistry of this family that I didn't understand, and when all was said it was none of my business.

As on the previous occasion the quarrel ended abruptly. I can't remember what was said; possibly both stopped yelling from sheer exhaustion. Laura flounced upstairs and Carol began cooking a supper for Tommy. I decided to go, but as I made my move Tommy looked up from his paper.

'Say, Mr Wilson. You said you'd take me sailing?' He looked at me eagerly.

'That depends on your mum,' I replied. 'Tell you what; I'll take you both, first day you're free.'

All the memories of this extraordinary evening were running through my head as I reached the turning through the army camp. I've already mentioned the problem of the ID passes. Unlike the officious guard on the downs, the regular military had been indifferent to our comings and goings. Apart from Mick on his first day, we'd been ignored. Nobody had asked to see my pass; even our visitors had been cheerfully waved through. Tonight I found a pole barrier lowered across the road. A guard appeared followed by an officer, a young lieutenant. He was friendly and apologetic.

'Commanding officer's orders, sir,' he said. 'You're required to drive straight through to your own property without stopping.'

I was baffled. ‘I never do stop. I just want to go home.’

‘I understand that, sir, but I was ordered to give you that instruction anyway.’

‘May I know what’s going on?’

He pulled a rueful face. ‘Officially not, but as the whole world will know tomorrow, we might as well tell you now.’ He stood up and pointed towards the downs. ‘Did you know there was once an MOD research facility up there?’

‘Yes, I’ve been told a little; wasn’t it mostly underground?’

‘That’s the problem. Part of the old tunnelling has collapsed and we’re told there could be toxic agents on the loose.’

‘Hell no!’ So much for Paul Hooder and his assurances. ‘How long has this been going on?’

‘Investigating team’s been here about a week. It’s only a precaution. We’ve got to be two hundred percent careful or we’ll have a whole shower of politicians and environmentalists down our throats.’

I grinned; the metaphor tickled my imagination.

The lieutenant signalled to the guard who raised the barrier. I set off along the two miles to the point where the roads divided and the right hand forked towards the guard post. I was not surprised to see two army trucks and a dozen soldiers milling around. An NCO waved me on, his arms flailing like an animated toy. I reached the crest of the hill and crossed the line into my own domain. Below me the harbour lay bathed in moonlight. My driver-side window was down and, as always, I breathed in the scent of downland herb and grass, mixed with sea ozone. Somehow I couldn’t believe in toxic poisons here.

I parked the car in my usual place on the quay. In front of me was the office and it slowly dawned on me that something was different. The moonlight was reflecting on only half of the first window. I strode across; the lower pane was smashed. Broken glass was littering the ground in front. Damn: the only people around were two couples, both visiting yacht crews. Sober middle-class citizens, I couldn’t see either as vandals. I pulled out my key and walked to the door. I didn’t need it; the door swung open at a push. Inside was chaos.

I turned on the light and went straight to the radio equipment. Incredibly it was still there and so was the windspeed indicator and the barometer. Every valuable item was in its proper place; even the petty cash was untouched. Elsewhere all was mayhem. Every drawer had been pulled open and all our files strewn on the floor. I walked through into my private office. The desk drawers were out and papers scattered around. The computer screen was alive. I looked at it and shook my head. It showed United Marinas data base with yacht details and addresses of all their berth holders in the UK. What possible use this information could be to anyone else I couldn't begin to surmise. I was surprised to see two coffee cups on my desk when I was certain we had washed and put the crockery away. I touched the electric kettle; it was still warm. Bloody cheek, the intruders must have made themselves at home while they searched for whatever. I had to face the fact that this could be the work of someone on the site. I checked the details of both our overnight visitors. One was in our database; a doctor, his wife and six year old kid: it couldn't be them. The other boat was what we would call a trawler-yacht, a motor vessel built in the style of a small commercial fishing boat. Her owner had been elderly and bluntly spoken; a self-made businessman type, and a bit of a rough-diamond. He'd paid his dues in cash, and announced his intention of sailing for Plymouth in the morning.

It was time I rang the police. The woman's voice answering sounded detached and uninterested, but she promised a patrol car would call within an hour. It was time for me to do some investigating myself. I checked the clock: it said ten thirty. I went out and looked along the second pontoon. The sailing yacht with the medical couple was still there; the trawler yacht had gone. I walked down to our remaining visitor and wondered if I should wake her crew. I decided no; I wasn't going to advertise our troubles before I had to. What of the missing boat? She had paid her dues, so there was no reason why her skipper shouldn't leave any time he wished. If I remembered correctly the yacht was *Marietta* and her owner was one George Dunlass. I had no idea where he lived; we didn't ask for addresses.

I looked up the road; no sign of the police. I had left the office exactly as I'd found it. I could see neither sight nor trace of the intruders. I wondered if I should ring Laura but decided not to. She was already in a foul temper and would be more inclined to shoot the messenger. No, Laura could wait until morning and I would deal with the police, if and when they turned up. In the meantime I would board *Stormgoose* and make a cup of tea. Then I stopped, my ears and eyes straining towards the quay. I'd heard a noise near the office, only a slight scraping sound, but on this still night it echoed like a gunshot.

I ran along the pontoon and up the sloping ramp that connected it with the stone quay. The office stood in front of me, a dark silhouette against the quarter moon. To the right was the gear store, a simple wooden garage in which we stored ropes and oars; perhaps after tonight I should lock it. Again I stopped and listened. All my senses were alert. I knew someone was nearby, I wasn't sure where, but… there, the same noise but closer, only yards away. A scraping noise and with it the glint of moon on metal. Somebody was opening the gear shed door; somebody who had been hiding in there the whole time. A dark figure had tiptoed into the open. I could see the shape of him, but it was too dark for recognition. A man, or was it a boy; girl even? I had been psyching myself to confront an older thug, but this was a youngster. One of Steve Gulley's cronies? Very likely, but I would be stupid to assume he was as docile as his leader.

'Stop there!' I didn't need to shout. My life at sea had taught me to menace my voice when needed. 'Stand still and face me.'

I'd clearly shaken him, he froze like a statue. I moved fast while I still held the initiative. I ran at him as hard and fast as I could. I wanted to grab him before he had second thoughts. In retrospect that was pretty daft of me, because I never saw the second man who came out of the night and shoulder charged me over the edge into the water.

The cold water numbed me before I surfaced spitting out oily sea. I was disorientated; I couldn't see anything and my eyes stung and would not focus. I was on the edge of panic as I tried to kick off my tightly laced deck shoes. I tried to swim and found I could and that the water was warmer now the first shock had gone. I knew I mustn't yell and splash. If someone up there wanted me dead, I'd better act dead. I caught a glimpse of the moon and the outline of a jetty. In desperation I swam towards a pontoon that was clearly moving. No, it was me that was moving. I was caught in the grip of the ebbing tide; the four-knot stream in the harbour entrance would carry me out to sea and beyond hope if I didn't catch hold of something fast. Then, thank God, above me loomed the huge bulk of a yacht. Relief, then near panic again. The stream was carrying me straight between the pontoon and the yacht. She was a *Westerly Konsort*, a boat with high topsides. I could only hope to duck under the pontoon to avoid being trapped between hull and dock. Her bows looked vast in the darkness above. I scraped my fingers on the slime below the waterline and then something seized me around the neck. Lashing out with both arms I forgot everything as I screamed wildly. I found I was in the grip of a rope, a slack centre warp drooping down from above. It was careless of her crew to have left it but for me it was a life saver. I heard a clattering from within the hull, then a clear voice from the air above – an authoritative voice telling me to stay calm. Out of the darkness dangled a rope ladder. Arms reached down and helped me, gasping and exhausted, to reach the deck.

Now I felt foolish. Harbour masters should not have to be pulled from their own docks. My rescuers asked no questions, nor did they give me much chance for explanations. With no concessions to my dignity, they pulled off all my clothes and pushed me into the yacht's tiny shower. It's true my teeth were chattering but more from shock than cold. It was ironic that it was my turn to be snatched from the sea, the second rescue in a week. The warm shower was welcome though, and I found I was able to think sensibly again.

My protests ignored, I was pulled from the shower compartment and towelled down like a three-year-old. Then my rescuers, the visiting doctor and his wife, took my temperature, listened to my breathing and finally watched me down a mug of sweet tea. Satisfied, the doctor allowed me on deck to meet the police who were now gathering on the pontoon. I felt embarrassed and short on dignity, dressed only in a towel robe. The two officers seemed not to notice; I supposed that nothing much surprises them these days. Ten minutes earlier they had arrived and found the office in the same state I'd left it, with no sign of the intruders. I told them what had happened and how I'd come to be in the sea. My rescuers supported my story. They'd heard a splash and then my cries beside their boat. I took the two police officers back to the scene of the attack. One of them pointed his torch around but it was a waste of time; my assailant and his companion had long since fled. I showed them the open shed door where I'd seen the first man emerge. Then I pointed to the direction from which my attacker had sprung. I surmised that he must have been lurking in one of the two portable toilets, sited between the office and the store. A police constable peered in the first, the one with a female logo: no trace of anyone. He pulled open the men's side, stiffened and jumped back with a grunt. Sitting on the toilet seat was a large man. None of us had time to feel embarrassed. As the door opened, the body rolled gently forward and fell to the ground with a thud. It remained there unmoving.

I've had some shocks and surprises in my time, but this one shattered me. The policeman shone his torch while his colleague examined the body. He felt for a pulse and then shook his head. Between the two of them they rolled the body face upwards. One of them felt the pulse again and then stood up.

‘Whoever he is, he’s a goner,’ he said.

‘Can you identify him?’ the other copper asked me.

‘Yes, but I’ve only seen him once, and that was earlier this evening.’

‘Give us a name.’

‘He’s Roy Gulley.’

CHAPTER 11

'Heart failure.' The doctor dusted his trousers and stood up. 'That's my view, but of course it's up to your people to make the official post-mortem.'

'Natural causes?' asked the police constable.

'I should think so, he looks a heart case; elderly and obese. He should have stayed at home.'

We all looked at each other, there was a distinct lightening of the mood. The policeman draped a cloth over the bulky form of the late Roy Gulley.

His colleague looked at me. 'In your opinion, was this man involved in the burglary?'

'I can't think of any other reason for him being here, and he had a grievance against us. I heard him shouting the odds earlier this evening.'

'He wasn't alone – you say someone pushed you in the water?'

'I only saw two people tonight and I couldn't name either. One was a young lad, I think, possibly a girl, but the one who shoved me over the edge was a big guy, fast and fit.'

'Any idea who they are?'

'There's a whole tribe of them in Duddlestone. They're all related and they've a vendetta against our venture here.'

'Three persons,' the copper began to write on his note pad. 'Breaking and entering – assault.'

'It was a bit more than assault,' I interjected. 'He bloody near drowned me.'

The police departed leaving instructions for us to touch nothing until their forensic team had finished. I was dazed, baffled and out of my depth. I still felt cold and I had an overwhelming wish to lie down and sleep. I felt no remorse for the man Gulley. He had been a dirty, foul-mouthed lout, and if I was to believe Byrne and Carol, he was an un-convicted murderer. If he'd over-stretched his heart vandalising our office, then maybe there was some justice somewhere. That, at this moment, was as far as I could think. With the tension relieved, I felt very weary and I was trembling violently. The doctor and his wife saw me. They led me to my boat and my bunk. Then they injected me with something, I'm not sure what, I wasn't in a state to resist.

After that I remembered nothing until the following morning.

'Do you know what time this is?' Someone was pummelling me and none too gently. I opened my eyes to find Laura standing glaring down at me.

'And you can sod off,' I replied rolling over in my bunk again.

'Oh charming,' she laughed. 'Well you can get up – we've visitors.'

'What visitors?' I sat up as the events of last night flooded back into my consciousness.

'Police, they're all over the place and they want statements.'

'Oh, God.' I slid stiffly out of my bunk. 'What have you heard about last night?'

'Not a lot. Somebody trashed our office and the law say it's Roy Gulley.'

'You know we found him dead?'

'Yes, I've heard and I'm not surprised. He's had a couple of heart attacks already. Wouldn't listen to the medics – stuffed himself with beer and fags and lived on greasy chips.'

'Was he another of your relations?'

'Yes, second cousin, but that's nothing here.'

I could believe that. What had I done to land myself among these backward, moronic, inbred bumpkins? Not all of them of course. There were exceptions. I remembered Byrne's friend Ivy Bowler; though by all accounts her elder brother, Arthur Rocastle, had been several pence short of a pound.

I chased Laura off the ship while I changed into formal Harbour Master's gear: properly pressed trousers and my old merchant service blue jacket. Then my friend the doctor appeared. I had expected him to have taken the east-bound tide and have been long gone. He seemed rather shocked at the suggestion. I was, he said, still his patient. He made me sit down once more while my temperature was taken and pulse sounded. He was right of course and I knew that but for his help last night I could have been in bad trouble.

The police were in the office. They had just finished dusting for fingerprints and taking photographs. An ambulance had, thankfully, removed the dead body. Laura was grumbling in the background, wanting to start tidying the chaos.

One of the police was examining the broken windowpane. 'Now that is odd,' he said.

'Why?' I asked.

'Broken glass is all on the ground outside, but we've found splinters of glass in the dead man's hair – back of the head. Seems almost certain he collapsed in here and fell against the window.'

'How come he's in the toilets?'

'No doubt your intruders couldn't think of anywhere else to hide him.'

This made me think. 'The man couldn't have been less than fifteen stone. There must be more than one of them and bloody strong with it.'

These were a different team of police from the two last night. Today we had two plainclothes men, a photographer and a uniformed police constable whom I knew. He was the same man who suffered a seasick trip in *Stormgoose*.

The leader of the team was a shifty little man in an ill-fitting blue suit. When I arrived, he produced his ID and told us he was a detective sergeant from Poole. We all sat down and I made a second statement. By now I had composed my memories in an orderly way, with only one flaw. Try as I might I couldn't give a useable description of either my assailant or the young boy or girl I had seen by the gear store. The first had come at me with the speed of an athlete and the physique of a charging bull. The other had been in shadow.

The second CID man wrote all this down on an official form in ponderous longhand. He handed it across to me and I signed. The sergeant locked the paper away in his brief case. 'Very well, sir. Our police surgeon confirms the death of Roy Gulley to be natural causes. This man was known to us as a petty criminal, and it seems he was living on the edge with his medical condition. It looks like he died on the job – nuff said.'

I nodded feeling much relieved.

'Now, sir,' the sergeant continued. 'You say you saw this man alive last night – in the pub that is?'

'Yes, in the De Gullait Arms, that's the pub in New Duddlestone.'

'Can you put a time to this?'

'Yes, it was about eight o'clock, give or take ten minutes. I last saw him go through the door forcibly. The landlord had him thrown out.'

'That wouldn't have done his heart much good.'

'I don't suppose so. He'd been shouting and blustering before that as well.'

'Who else saw this?'

'The whole pub did, about two dozen customers. You'd better talk to Harry Broadenham, the landlord.'

'Will do,' the copper wrote a note in his book. 'I understand from this lady,' he pointed at Laura, 'that nothing's missing from these premises, despite the damage and forcible entry.'

'Is that so?' I looked at her.

'I can't see a thing missing,' she replied. 'All the equipment's here and the petty cash. They've made a hell of a mess of our files though and someone's accessed the computer.'

'Anything confidential?'

'No, all our programmes are data bases, and the emails are just routine stuff. No interest to anybody outside the boat business.'

'I must say that's odd,' replied the sergeant. 'Knowing old Roy I'd have expected your petty cash to have walked, and your radio gear.'

'Maybe the others panicked when Roy collapsed,' I said.

'Or maybe they didn't expect you back so soon. Have you thought of that?' said Laura.

'Who knew you'd be off the site that evening?' asked the sergeant.

I thought hard. This was something that hadn't occurred to me, and I didn't like it. 'I had an appointment to meet a man at the pub. But, there's no way anyone would have known that. Anyway, Roy Gulley and his son didn't expect me to be there; Roy didn't even know who I was until he was told. That was when he turned nasty. You see we've had trouble with these people already. You know about them moving our entry beacons?'

'That was Steve Gulley,' confirmed the local constable.

'Motive?' asked the sergeant.

'Pure malice,' I said. 'Some of the locals are against our development here.'

The sergeant grunted. 'Nothing personal, but I hate Duddlestone!'

'Why?' I was startled by his outburst.

'It's their attitude,' he began to gather up his case and coat. 'You know, I've worked in some rough neighbourhoods, inner cities – really hard. You get used to them clamming up; looking sideways at you and the like.' He looked across to his colleagues who all nodded in agreement. 'But this place, Christ they're worse than anywhere I've ever been…'

'For what it's worth,' I said, 'last night in the pub Roy Gulley admitted to being one of the lynch mob fifty years ago.' I looked long and hard at Laura; her face was expressionless.

As the police team climbed into their car the sergeant spoke to me. 'Mr Wilson, I understand you have a family connection with Duddlestone?'

'What do you mean?' I was instantly on the defensive.

'Through your father, there's a picture of him in the pub, I've seen it. The resemblance between the two of you is striking, if I may say so.'

'That was all a long time ago,' I said. 'He's been dead for years.'

'So I understand.' He fixed me with a penetrating stare. 'Yes, so I understand.'

'We're leaving now. You should be all right but I'd like you to see your own GP.' It was my rescuer, the doctor.

'My doctor's near Portsmouth. I haven't signed up with one here.'

'Then it's time you did. I suggest you go today and see Doctor Baker in Swanage – he's an old colleague of mine so you can mention my name.'

Something was worrying me. 'Did the police ask if you'd seen a car? I mean how did those thieves get here?'

'The police asked us that, but we couldn't tell them anything. We heard your car drive down the road but we never took much notice.'

'If they were already here they must have come in a vehicle of some sort.' My mind was racing now. If the intruders never left the site by car then logically that vehicle must still be here.

I thanked my rescuers once more and helped them with their mooring lines. Minutes later they were motoring out through the harbour entrance.

The office had returned to normal. Laura and Mick between them had cleaned up and confirmed the amazing fact that nothing was missing.

'I'll slip over to the village and get one of the builders to fix this window.' Laura examined the empty frame. 'You coming? My house is nearly ready.'

'Yes, all right. I want to check if they left their car among the buildings.'

'I think the police have already done that, but there may be places that they've missed.'

Laura set off at a brisk pace along the quay and into the village street. 'I'm all set to move in here in a couple of days.' She looked around happily. 'They'll be working on your place next week,' she added. 'You don't realise what this means to me. My own space, and a million miles from my bloody sister and that lousy hole.'

'What's wrong with Carol?'

'I've told you. She's soft in the head, always has been, and you'd better watch out.'

'Why?'

'Because she goes all drippy whenever your name is mentioned. Come on in and I'll show you where my studio is going to be.'

Eventually I left Laura to luxuriate in her new home while I hunted up the street for signs of a strange vehicle. I found nothing: no tyre marks on the soft ground, no sign that something might have been concealed. I looked towards the cliffs and the entrance to the old ammunition store. It was then that I saw her, that odd Australian girl, the alleged journalist.

'You!,' I yelled with my best captain's bellow. 'Stop right there.'

She spun round and stared back at me. A more ragged looking female it would be hard to envisage. With her stringy blonde hair, tattered jeans and denim top she could have passed for a drug-sodden dosser. The fact that she could well be just that alarmed me even more. I strode towards her but she wasn't waiting for me. She turned and took off at a loping run along the shoreline and I did not intend to compromise my dignity by running after her. This, I resolved, was one for Mick to deal with. He would have firm instructions to corner his fellow countrywoman and extract either an explanation or deliver a firm warning off.

I walked grumpily back towards the quay, then I had an idea. I went back to my car and drove out up the road and onto the military land.

Unlike last night there was not a soldier in sight. Disappointed, I drove the whole route until I reached the main camp checkpoint. Once again it was unmanned, but it was here that I had a stroke of luck. Striding self-importantly down the road came the same young officer I'd spoken to last night. I stopped and called out.

'Hi, Mr Wilson, what cheer?' He was a nice lad, though typical public school and Sandhurst.

'Please,' I said. 'Can you help me? Last night – how many vehicles passed through to Old Duddlestone before me?'

'Not sure,' he looked puzzled. 'Any reason for wanting to know?'

'Several. You see when I got to the other end I found intruders in my office and some bugger pushed me into the dock. Have the police been here?'

'So that's what it's all about. Someone was hurt?'

'He's dead.'

'What happened – not one of your people?'

'No, he was from New Duddlestone and definitely up to no good.'

'Not death by foul play?'

'No, heart attack.'

'Come into the guard room and I'll check the record.'

Inside the building the young officer made a call on an internal phone. He looked at me and shook his head. 'That's a puzzler. They say no civilian vehicle passed this post before you. I was on duty from twenty hundred until midnight, and definitely nothing went through except yourself, our trucks, and a police car. I take it that was the one you called.'

I took a quick decision. I liked this lad and I owed him an explanation. 'We have a problem,' I said. 'The man who died was in the pub in New Duddlestone between eight and nine o'clock, or twenty one hundred, if you like. I saw him there myself.'

'They must have walked in along the footpath from Honeycritch. I know it because I ride a bit – hoping to go hunting this winter.'

'How long have you been here – do you know the area well?' I was beginning to look at this guy in a new light.

'I've known it for years. My aunt and uncle live in the village. I passed out of Sandhurst last year, and it's pure chance my first posting is here.'

'Are you enjoying it?'

'Up to a point. I've got a great bunch of lads in my troop, but things can be a bit boring for us in camp. We're a long way from the bright lights.' He held out his hand. 'Awfully sorry, I haven't introduced myself, rotten bad manners. I'm Alistair Pickering – Lieutenant of course.'

'And destined for great things I'm sure. Glad to meet you, Alistair.'

'Actually,' he said, 'you've already met my uncle – he mentioned you. He said your father won the VC. Is that a fact?'

'Yes it's true, but who is your uncle – is he the solicitor?'

He nodded. 'Stanley Bowler.'

Ivy Rocastle's husband and Brian Byrne's friend. Duddlestone was indeed a small world.

CHAPTER 12

'I take it you've met Brian Byrne?'

'The newspaper man? Yes, I know him, he's been around the camp asking questions.'

'What about?'

'The germ warfare place, but he was wasting his time. We can't tell him anything, it's top security classification – we don't know any more than you do.' Alistair shrugged.

We were sitting in the corner of a pub in Swanage. The place was noisy and smoky with a background of chatter, while the music system belted out a UB 40 tape. We wanted to talk in confidence so it suited us.

My new confidant had been going off duty when I found him. He had changed into civvies, and I'd taken him for a meal and a beer.

'Stan's my mother's elder brother,' he explained. 'But Arthur's killing was a taboo subject. It was just something I knew never to mention. I saw her sobbing over his photograph once.'

'She talked about him when I visited them,' I said. 'Couldn't stop her – no inhibitions now.'

'Everything changed when Brian Byrne arrived. She's convinced he'll clear Arthur's name.'

'What's you're opinion?' I asked.

'I'm certain he never touched that girl, but he was up to something – that's what Ivy still won't swallow.'

'What makes you think he was up to something?'

'As I figure it, he didn't kill the girl but he knew who did and there's more. The way Ivy talks makes me think that Arthur knew some secret that was unhealthy. He wasn't that bright and he may not have realised the implications.'

'What sort of secret, can you be more specific?'

'No, but Ivy says he tried to tell her something. Sorry, Mr Wilson but I can't elaborate, it'd be disloyal.'

'OK, understood.' I knew better than to push too hard. I guessed young Alistair had opinions to offer but he was not one to gossip with family secrets.

'I'll tell you this much,' he continued. 'I've been coming to these parts on visits ever since I was a kid, and there's something about Duddlestone that gets to you…' He frowned and began to tap a finger in time to the music.

'I think I know what you mean,' I said. 'I visited New Duddlestone for the first time the other day. I got the feel of an unhappy ship – you know, a sort of ambience. It's odd because, as I say, I'd never been there before and hardly knew a soul.'

His face was positively beaming. 'You sense it too. You see my mother always says I'm far too romantic and perceptive to be a soldier. I don't agree: in war, feel for a place could be vital.'

'What I call gut feeling,' I said. 'I've needed it a few times at sea in my career.'

'I can imagine. Anyway, this is my take on Duddlestone. Fifty years ago something happened here and it's left a legacy of fear that poisons the whole community. They are scared witless of something, and it's not just the villagers. Take our masters, the Ministry of Defence. They're as jumpy as shit about that germ lab, and we reckon there's some other hidden agenda that nobody knows about, except it all dates back to 1946. Before my parents had even met. It's not just my view; we talked about it in the mess one night. Had some fun dreaming up conspiracy theories. It was all light-hearted – just passing the time, but somebody must have been listening. Two days later some slimy little Intelligence Major turns up and warns us not to discuss anything connected to events here in 1946 – waved the Official Secrets Act. Our Brigadier went ballistic when he heard, but even he advised us to be careful – hinted about our promotion prospects. For God's sake, fifty years ago – it's crazy.'

'Was it only the germ lab they were warning you off?'

'No, it was everything, including Duddlestone and the bloody Navy. Sorry, didn't mean that, but there's a hell of a lot being hidden. Much more than some bastard raping and killing a prostitute.'

I remembered what Brian Byrne had said about 1946 and my father's flotilla. Records closed for one hundred years.

I looked at Alistair. 'I also have a family interest in Duddlestone. Did anyone tell you who commanded the navy base in 1946?'

'Stan told me – it was your father.'

At four o'clock I delivered Alistair back to his quarters. I asked him to stay in touch and promised to take him sailing. As I turned the car round to head back to the harbour my mobile phone rang.

'Skipper, it's Mick. There's a bird here says she's your daughter.'

'My daughter – you mean Emma?' I couldn't take this in for a moment.

‘Sure, that’s what she said her name was. Didn’t know you was married?’

‘I’m not any more – once was enough.’ I replied grimly. Why did Australians always have to be so bloody blunt and to the point? ‘OK, Mick. Keep her there, I’ll be with you in ten minutes.’

I was feeling guilty. In the morass of problems here I had forgotten that Emma was waiting for the results of her medical finals. I wasn’t sure if this arrival out of the blue was a good or bad omen. Suddenly it didn’t matter, it was good to see her again. To listen to her chatter and know there was one person in the world who cared. Nothing the po-faced Duddlestonians might do could change that. I felt lighter at heart as I crested the hill and sped down to the harbour.

Emma ran across the quay and flung her arms around me planting a wet kiss on my cheek. She looked suntanned and fit, with long unruly locks of dark hair fluttering in the breeze. There was a young chap with her, standing sheepishly in the background. ‘Dad,’ she said, ‘this is Simon.’

I shook hands with Simon. Emma ran through boyfriends at the rate of five or six a year. This one seemed a pleasant enough lad. He was taller than me, with sharp features and slightly receding hair. His handshake was firm and his grin friendly enough.

‘Simon is a doctor,’ said Emma. ‘In fact Dad, we’re both doctors.’

It was my turn to hug her. She had passed her finals; tears were shed as the words poured out. After years of toil and study she had reached her goal. There would be a gruelling time ahead as a junior hospital doctor but that was tomorrow. Today was for celebration. My little girl was something in the world and, by reflection, my personal life was no longer a complete disaster.

Laura rose to the occasion. From somewhere she produced two bottles of pseudo-Champagne and a clutch of wineglasses. Three visiting yacht crews joined us with more bottles, and we ended the evening with an impromptu barbecue on the quay. I had assumed that Emma had arrived by road. No, she explained. Simon had a boat and she was crewing for him during a two months break following the end of school in May. Proudly the two of them showed me their yacht, an elderly *Vega* class boat. I was pleased and relieved to find the vessel was well-maintained and properly equipped. Emma explained that they would like to berth the yacht permanently here in Duddlestone. I explained that such a choice would not come cheap. I wondered how that would square with a junior doctor's pay. This didn't seem to bother them. Simon went into the office with Laura and wrote a cheque for the full amount.

Brian Byrne appeared at eight o'clock that evening. It was clear by the expression on his face that he hadn't come to help us celebrate. He beckoned me aside, so I invited him into the office. Laura scowled at us but did not follow.

'I think you'd better know,' he said, 'that the police will be back. Roy Gulley never died from a heart attack. He was poisoned.'

'Come off it, our doctor said heart attack – he was certain.'

'Sure Roy had one all right but that's not the half of it. Police pathologist found a poison in his stomach and bloodstream. That's what triggered off the heart attack but it would've killed him anyway.'

'How do you know all this?'

'It's my business to know people who'll talk to me off the record.'

'What was this poison?'

'They told me the Latin name but it didn't mean a thing. In simple terms Roy took a strong dose from the juice of minced up yew tree.'

'Yew tree?'

'That's what I said. Traditional remedy for mother-in-law in these parts. Christ, if the witch doctors are active we'd all better watch our backs.'

Next day the police returned in force, led by an inspector and accompanied by men and women in white overalls and gloves. These repeated the fingerprint dusting and took more pictures of our office and the now empty portaloo. We were going to have some disastrous publicity as a result of this business. I felt the police could have been a little more contrite. Not only had our premises been vandalised; I had narrowly survived a murderous assault and I was pretty bloody angry. If the police and these forensic people had to rip the place to pieces, they should have done so before Laura swept away the evidence. I didn't hide my chagrin as I put this to the Inspector.

'I hear what you say, sir, but we're very stretched at the moment. It's the holiday season – more petty crime than we can cope with. The paper work alone…' he grimaced.

'This is hardly petty, though I can't weep too many tears for the dead man.'

The Inspector looked defensive. 'Yes, sir, I agree, but by your own admission nothing was stolen. The doctor on the scene diagnosed heart failure and that seemed logical, in view of what we know about the deceased.'

'But, for God's sake, I was assaulted. I could've drowned!'

'Yes, sir, and I promise we will pursue our enquiries with vigour.' Suddenly the man relaxed and became more human. 'We'll do our damnedest to get a result, I promise,' he sighed. 'But remember this is Duddlestone and that means we'll have to be patient – the bastards will close ranks. We'll meet a complete lack of co-operation from all sides. Just have to wait and listen out for whispers. That's where you can help – you and Mrs Tapsell.'

'How?'

'Listen, and tell your employees to keep their mouths shut and their ears open.'

Ten minutes later the police packed their equipment and left. The Inspector formally requested that Laura, Mick and me report to Poole police station that afternoon. They would need our fingerprints for elimination and they would like, he remarked ominously, to run through a few routine details.

'Daddy, please … please?' Emma was looking up at me, head tilted to one side, with soulful eyes, and that pleading half smile. Behind her stood Simon. He looked embarrassed as well he should. My daughter's transparent attempt to wheedle her way around my good nature would have fooled no one.

'Please, Daddy, please?'

My car stood exactly where I'd left it last night.

I glanced over her head at Simon. 'You insured?'

'Oh yes,' he replied eagerly, 'fully-comp, and clean license.' He hesitated. 'Or nearly.'

'What's that mean?'

'I had a motorbike. It was two years ago – got done for speeding.'

'Where, and how fast?'

He shuffled uneasily, looked at Emma, and then at the ground. 'Was doing ninety eight on the M6.'

I nearly gave the game away by laughing. Emma knew, and I knew, that I was putty in her hands but I wasn't in a hurry to let any potential son-in-law into the secret. I stood in a posture of deep thought, while subjecting him to one of my captain's withering glares. I watched him squirm, before I let my face break into a friendly grin. I tossed him the car keys.

‘One condition.’ I said. ‘This afternoon you two will have to take charge here while the rest of us are in Poole.’

I wrote them a note for the Army guard post and they departed in my car on a quest for stores and spare parts. Laura had just returned from inspecting her cottage. With a cheerful grin she told me it was nearly ready.

‘I’m having a housewarming,’ she said, ‘and I’d like you to come as well. What d’you say?’

‘I’d be honoured.’

‘That’s fixed then. Tuesday evening eight o’clock.’ She smiled obviously pleased.

I began to warm to her a little, though I couldn’t fathom the contradictions of the woman.

‘Why do the police want us?’ she asked.

‘Fresh lot of statements,’ I replied. ‘Hardly surprising now it’s murder and attempted murder.’

Laura shook her head. ‘That’s a bit over the top isn’t it?’

‘Oh really,’ suddenly she was riling me again. ‘Are you suggesting Roy Gulley committed suicide?’

‘He could’ve done.’

I fixed her with an icy stare. ‘You belong to this backward hole. Who would’ve mixed a witches brew enough to kill a man?’

‘Why should I know?’

‘Oh, don’t you bloody fence with me. You’re part of the conspiracy of silence. Even if you did know you’d bloody close ranks with the rest of your bumpkins. Thank God your sister’s got some sense.’

‘Now that’s where you’re wrong,’ she hadn’t taken the least bit of offence. ‘Not only about Carol, she’s as daft as they come. No, if I catch the slightest hint of who harmed Roy, then most certainly I’ll tell the police. Do me a favour, I’m not a complete moron.’

‘That’s how they classified Arthur Rocastle – moron?’

‘That was a very long time ago, before either of us was born, and after all he was a murderer.’

The interviews with the police were something of an anticlimax. Laura grumbled, while a subdued Mick arrived clutching his work permit. We had our fingerprints taken, making us all feel guilty although we knew it was a matter of form. Then we had to repeat everything we’d said before, at which point my mind went blank, and I couldn’t remember the precise time that I’d been pushed into the water. Eventually they let us all go; we having promised not to leave the district for forty-eight hours.

I stood by the waterside, enjoying the sunshine and the fresh air. The police had been friendly, if formal, but we were all mightily relieved to be out of that place. I shaded my eyes, staring across the wide expanse of Poole Harbour, looking for *Persephone,* the *Omega* class yacht owned by the mysterious Eriksen. She was there, moored against the same pontoon as the other day. Even though the marina was a quarter of a mile away her bulk was unmistakable.

'That's her,' I said to Laura. 'The one that keeps nosing into our harbour at night.'

'It just looks like a big yacht to me,' she said. 'I think you imagine things.'

'I didn't imagine that yacht. I saw her, she was an *Omega,* I doubt there's another like her on this coast.' My temper was rising. 'Who is Eriksen?' Laura made no reply as she turned on her heel and walked back to the car park.

Emma and Simon were enjoying their stint as harbour managers. When we returned we found them busy, welcoming a whole clutch of visiting yachts. By dusk we had twenty berthed, including Simon's *Vega.* I was about to suggest to Laura that she could go home when we saw the lights of another incoming vessel. We went down to meet her. She was the same trawler yacht, *Marrieta*, that sailed not long before the break-in and the death of Roy Gulley. Apparently her owner had changed his plans but his arrival was fortuitous. Here were some people who might have seen something, anything, that could shine a little light on the mystery.

I'd met Mr and Mrs George Dunlass when they arrived two days ago. George was a broad-shouldered stocky little man, obviously fit and strong despite his age which must have been at least seventy. I put him down as an archetypal self-made businessman of the kind who is happiest dealing with a suitcase of "readies". Mrs Rita Dunlass was dyed-blonde and fortyish, with a laugh that would have challenged a hyena. George had a red, cherubic face, but for all that he had seemed a surly fellow. I asked him what had gone wrong with his intended voyage.

'Business,' he grunted.

'That's right,' Rita gushed. 'Spoilt our bloody holiday as usual. Mister Dunlass is an entrepreneur, aren't you George?'

George grunted again.

'Got three businesses, he has, and he's a JP and a master of the

Masons, aren't you George?'

'Put a sock in it, Rit, that last's a secret…'

Rita interrupted with another shriek of laughter.

There was something familiar in the lilt of the man's speech.

'You're from these parts originally?' I asked.

He swung round on me and his look and tone were hostile. 'What d'you know about it?'

'Sorry, no offence meant,' I replied contritely.

'Nor taken,' said Rita cheerfully. 'You're right though. Mister Dunlass is a Dorset man, born and bred, aren't you George? Not me though – I'm an Essex girl. Yeah, the real thing.'

I would never have guessed, I thought morosely. George said nothing but he was definitely not pleased. We all went into the office. Laura was still there making out receipts for the night's berthing fees.

Something was wrong with Laura. The same inherent instinct that I had mentioned to Alistair was active now, ringing noisy alarm bells. She spoke not a word to either of the Dunlasses and made no attempt to give them her usual sales patter. Yet this was the first time she'd met them. When their yacht had first arrived, I'd dealt with George myself. Laura had been off the site at a meeting with Paul Hooder. Now something was wrong; I had not spent ten years in command of polyglot ship's crews without picking up a thing or two. I knew all about guilty glances and snide sideways looks. I knew that my instinct was right. Laura said not a word, but I caught the expression in her face and the twist of her eyes as she looked furtively at me and then back to the man sitting opposite. At that moment I would have betted any money you liked that Laura and George Dunlass had met before and that they had something to say out of earshot of me.

Mick was hovering by the door obviously trying to catch my eye. I went outside and he followed me onto the dock.

'What's up?' I asked.

'The Oz bird – you wanted me to have a word?'

I remembered the scruffy Australian journalist. 'Right, what's she up to?'

'Her name's Jolene. Says her granddad was here in World War Two and she writing stuff for the Sydney Morning Herald.'

'You sound doubtful.' I said.

'It didn't quite add up – for a start she don't know a thing about Sydney – I reckon she's never seen the place. I set a trap and caught her out twice. The accent's not right for a start – I'd say she comes from the Territory.'

‘The where?’

‘Northern Territory – Darwin – that part of the world, a thousand miles from Sydney. I’m Aussie by birth but I’ve never been to the Territory.’

The complexities of all this were beyond me. ‘You’re on about accents – all you people sound the same to me.’

‘Not so– Oz is a big country, a real mixed ethnic bag. You’ve got almost as many speech variants as your country. That’s not what’s bugging me. If she works for The Herald she’d know every bloody district and street. I doubt she’s ever been in Sydney in her life.’

‘OK, Mick. Keep an eye out for her and report back to me.’

CHAPTER 13

Laura had gone home but I had waited to see if any more craft would come in from the sea to join us. Our entrance was still unlit and I hoped no one would be so foolish as to try a night visit. Except for Mr Eriksen of course. I very much wanted a word with that gentleman. I wished to put a face to his name and hear his explanation. I had spoken to Mr and Mrs Dunlass and warned them that the police would need to talk with them. I suggested, with as much authority as I could muster, that they report to the law voluntarily.

'I don't need no lectures, mate,' George replied. 'I knows the form.' Rita pulled a face but said nothing.

The next morning I rose early. It was a beautiful morning; I can use no other adjective. The early mist was clearing, the sky was blue and a gentle breeze was rippling the water. It was so peaceful and so still, with only the sound of the sea washing on the rocky ledges outside the harbour.

At seven o'clock Mick rode in on his motorbike and at eight Laura arrived. She was unusually cheerful as she hustled into the office dressed once more in her revealing sundress. By this time some of our visitors were stirring. I hope they were impressed by our efficiency. Everything would have been perfect, had I not had this awful sense of foreboding. Already the more squeamish of our customers were avoiding the portaloos. Where else they were relieving themselves I didn't care to speculate. We had a total ban on pumping waste into the harbour and our primitive toilets were the only alternative. I suspected that any minute the police would be back and the facts of the murder would be common knowledge. Gloomily I switched on the radio and tuned it to the local station. A full news bulletin and no mention of Duddlestone.

By this time I was too busy to care; I was absorbed in my job, helping visitors to unmoor and sail, negotiating with the foreman of the harbour construction firm, handling the lines for a fresh batch of arrivals and signing cheques for Laura in the office. At last things began to quieten. Laura departed to bully the builders at her cottage and I had the office to myself. I went into my inner sanctum and at my own expense put a call through to my mother in South Africa. If my calculations were right she should be making breakfast.

Grant Bowker, my step-father, answered and I heard his cheerful bellow calling mother somewhere outside the house.

'Six weeks since you last write,' her familiar voice shouted down the line. Such is the miracle of modern technology that she could have been speaking from the next village. 'Six weeks, and now this. I do not understand.'

'I wanted to talk to you that's all, and you don't have to yell. I can hear you perfectly.'

'From England you are speaking?'

'Of course. I just wanted a chat.' I tried to sound aggrieved.

She was not taken in for a moment. 'What is it you want? Has something terrible happened?' Her East European vowels were rising to an operatic crescendo.

'Mother, will you shut up and listen! This call is costing me a bloody fortune.'

'Ah, now you sound just like your father.'

'That's interesting, you're the second person to say that to me in two days.'

'Who was this?'

'Never mind, I want to talk about my new job. I run a yacht harbour and I bet you won't guess where?'

'Why should I guess. I know nothing of English yacht harbours.'

'You'll know this one. It's Old Duddlestone.'

There was a gasp followed by five seconds of silence. Then I heard a distinct intake of breath. 'Peter, you would not be making cruel jokes with your old mother?'

'No, I'm not, and don't you dare come the dear old yiddisha-mama with me. Why should I be joking? I'm telling you I manage the harbour at Old Duddlestone and I know there's a family connection. That's why I'm ringing you.'

'I know,' I heard her sigh. Russian Estonians have an eloquent way of sighing. 'Peter, I wish you had not told me this. That is a most evil place.'

'No it's not. It's a delightful place but the people are barking mad, or a lot of them are.'

'Mad and also bad. Is there one Stoneman and some brothers called Gulley?'

'I know a girl, surname Stoneman – Carol Stoneman. She's very nice.'

'Why is this girl so nice? I do not like the way you say that. I would not like you to be involved with one of that name.'

‘For a start, Stoneman’s her husband’s name. He walked out on her and they’re divorced. Last I heard he was in Australia and I don’t know why I’m telling you all this...’ My temper was becoming prickly, almost as if I was a stroppy teenager again.

‘I see,’ she sighed. ‘You are in love with this girl. What did you say her first name was?’

‘Her name’s Carol and I’m not in love with her or anyone else. By the way her maiden name was Rocastle.’

‘Good, that is better. Would they be the family that used to run the farm with the cows.’

‘Honeycritch Farm, yes it’s still there.’

‘That is much better. I remember them as good people,’ she paused. ‘I think they are good people, but Peter, a warning.’

‘Yes?’

‘Be careful, be very careful, do not ask them how they came by the money that paid for their farm.’

‘Come on, I’m not likely to. It’s none of my business.’

‘Now you sound like your father again.’

That evening I climbed to the top of the cliffs following the same track I had walked with Carol and Tommy. I half hoped I might meet them again but there was no one there. I sat for a while gazing down on my little domain and watching the seagulls drifting on the thermal currents. It was so peaceful, it was very hard to reconcile that this had been the scene of a vile crime. I walked on a little further, looking for the green lane that was to be our new entrance road. I found it in a sheltered valley where the trees began. A rutted tractor way led into a wood of mature ash and beech. These trees were healthier and taller than the stunted copse on the downs – the scene of the Rocastle lynching. My mother had told me very little, and I was beginning to regret my impulsive call to her. Face to face, I believed I could have wheedled from her everything she knew. It would have been painful and possibly cruel. It seemed that Old Duddlestone held only bad memories for her. ‘Terrible things were done in that place,’ mother had been crying as she shouted down the telephone. ‘Terrible crimes, but Peter, remember your father was a great man, a wonderful man, and he was like a god in that village.’ She broke down sobbing. I felt shocked and appalled at the trauma I had induced. I wanted to hold her in my arms and comfort her; ask forgiveness for awaking her demons. Now I knew why Old Duddlestone was never mentioned within the family circle, why my father’s connection with this place had come as a total surprise.

Through the window I had seen Laura striding towards the office. Tactfully I tried to console my distraught mother on another continent.

'Peter,' suddenly her voice was almost calm. 'Peter, I will pray for you. I think there is some awful fate that has pulled you to that place. It killed so many people and it killed your father. See that it does not destroy you.'

My mind in a turmoil, I was hardly conscious of walking, but I had reached the far end of the copse. The track stretched ahead, running in a straight line through fields of ripening corn and grass, with gulls wheeling overhead, and butterflies flitting among the grass heads. The pastureland on my right was crowded with black and white milking cows. I watched them for a while as they munched contentedly behind a strand of electrified wire. Across the landscape drifted a wholly unexpected sound: a train whistle – a steam engine, awaking a host of childhood memories. As I don't believe in either ghosts or time warps, I assumed there must be a logical explanation.

On the far side of this field was a stone house and a range of modern farm buildings. I knew this was Honeycritch Farm, the property of the Rocastles.

Carol was in the garden sitting at a table with a sun umbrella above it. In front of her was a pile of paper weighed down by a flat stone.

She flashed a welcoming smile. 'Mock exams,' she explained. 'I'm correcting English Lit.'

'Do they pay you overtime?'

'Like hell they do – no chance.'

'Never mind, my job's always been twenty four hours round the clock,' I laughed. 'Anyway you people get the longest holiday breaks of anyone, except politicians.'

'Could be we need them,' she smiled again. 'I'm going to make a pot of tea. Will you join me?'

I carried the tea tray back into the garden. There was a scent of roses and a blaze of bright colour from the shrubs and borders. A little sundial sat in the middle of the newly mown lawn. 'Is this your work?' I asked.

'Sorry no, this is all Mum's doing. She spends hours out here. Trish, my sister-in-law helps a bit, but she's always busy on the farm and my brother is hopeless.'

'Why hopeless?'

'In the garden I mean,' she giggled. 'Farmers are hopeless at gardening. Too small a scale for them, I guess.'

Carol sat back in her chair and stretched her legs. They were nice legs, I noticed covertly; well tanned with genuine sun and not lotion from a bottle.

'Laura's gone to Swanage,' she yawned. 'It's her yoga class night. It wasn't her you've come to see?'

'Christ no.' I was immediately embarrassed by my own vehemence. 'I'm sorry, that was rude,' I added contritely.

'No it wasn't. You expressed your emotions and very understandably too.' A piece of paper fluttered away in the evening breeze. I retrieved it and put it under the stone weight.

'Thanks,' she said. 'As for Laura, you know what they called her at the National Trust when she worked there?'

'No,' I grinned, 'but I fancy I'm about to learn.'

'In the office they called her, "Colonel Wild Thing".'

'*Wild thing, you make my heart sing.*' I trilled the first line of the song, and gave up, laughing.

'Hey, that sounded good. Of course you told me your background was musical.'

'My grandfather was Viktor Panov, the composer. That's on my mum's side of course. They were all musicians, real ones. I'm only an amateur.'

'I think I've heard that name, but I can't say I'm familiar with any of his work.' That was tactfully put.

'My mother's the only one on that side still living. Stalin purged Viktor and his work was banned. The Nazis caught the rest of the family in Estonia. They were part Jewish, so…'

'Oh no, oh Peter, I'm sorry.' Her distress was real.

'You know, I used to cry myself to sleep as a kid thinking about it but I don't have hang ups now. Anyway Viktor's been rediscovered, he's quite fashionable again.'

We sat in silence for some minutes. I sipped my tea and munched a chocolate biscuit. I was looking to change the subject and I had questions of my own.

Carol anticipated me. 'Is it true the police say Roy was poisoned?' She stared at me with those expressive dark eyes.

This was unexpected. 'How did you hear this – from Laura?'

'No, it was in the shop just now. The whole village is talking.'

I bet they are, I thought.

'Somebody poisoned him with yew tree leaves,' I said. 'The

police think it was in a cup of tea. It's a deadly poison; my daughter told me the proper name but I can't remember. Seems it causes heart failure in seconds.'

'Well I didn't do it,' she said. 'But don't expect me to feel sorry.'

'You heard him in the pub when Byrne accused him. He as good as admitted he'd been one of the lynch mob.'

'We all knew that anyway,' her voice was hard. 'But this is the first time it's been aired in the open.'

'Well he's up before a higher judge now. Byrne says there's others still alive.'

'There's at least four. It was the "Brotherhood".'

'That sounds melodramatic to me. Are you saying we've some sort of mafia in this place?'

She laughed. 'Good God, no. The Brotherhood was the fishermen's committee. They had eight boats in the harbour. The Brotherhood met once a month. They were the eight skippers plus one or two others, like the guy who maintained the engines and the family who acted as middlemen in the market. They decided who fished which bit of sea and anchored the pots.' She thought for a moment. 'It wasn't meant to be sinister; in fact it was rather sweet, communal spirit – true socialism in action.'

'And did it work in practice?'

'Very well, so I'm told. Mind you they wouldn't get away with it today. It was men only, the proceedings were secret, a man could be disbarred if he discussed them with his wife.'

'Are you telling me these were the people who lynched Arthur?'

'Yes I am, but that was after the war, and it's true the Brotherhood had degenerated into a sort of drinking club. The fishing was gone; the men who weren't in the forces had local jobs but they maintained the Brotherhood. It was a sort of stupid male bonding and it got out of hand.'

'That explains why you always close ranks and won't talk to the police. My old mother's got a point when she says this place stinks.'

'Don't include me in that.' There was a little frisson of anger in her voice. 'And another thing, it may have been men from the Brotherhood, but who put them up to it, and why?'

I looked at her and shrugged.

'Brian says he gave you the transcripts of Arthur's trial,' she looked at me with a cool stare. 'Have you read them?'

Of course I hadn't. I'd stuck them in the chart drawer on *Stormgoose* and there they had remained. Prevarication was a waste of time. I admitted I'd been too busy.

'You see,' I told her, 'until yesterday I'd only been concerned with my father's role.'

'And now you're worried?'

'No, of course not. It's nothing to do with me.' I replied with a little too much asperity and I knew I hadn't fooled her.

'I would like you to read those papers. Read them and tell me what you think.'

Carol left her schoolwork, and walked with me as far as the top of the cliff. Once again came the old style train sounds echoing across the fields. 'It's the Swanage preserved railway,' Carol replied to my query. 'Tommy loves it – we've travelled the whole line several times.'

'Where's young Tommy?' I asked.

'He's helping his uncle with the sheep dipping,' she waved a hand in the general direction of the downs. 'Peter, how about this sailing trip you promised him? He keeps asking when we're going.'

'How about next Sunday if the weather's nice. I'll make my daughter and her young man take charge of the harbour, so we can make a whole day of it.'

I watched Carol walk back towards Honeycritch Farm. She turned as she entered the trees and waved. I sat on the turf at the edge of the cliff and pulled out my mobile phone. I had been waiting for a moment of privacy away from the office and I had written down the number I needed. I called the home of Mr and Mrs Bowler.

'Stan, this is Peter Wilson. I've a job for you, professional assignment, but maximum discretion.'

'That sounds exiting,' he laughed, 'but I'm not sure I'm your man. Most of our work is property – dull as ditch water.'

'No, it's property I'm interested in. Stan could you do an official search for me. I want to know when the Rocastle family bought Honeycritch Farm, and if possible what they paid for it?'

There was a pause the other end followed by a dry cough. 'I've already extracted that information for Brian. He's beaten you to it by a month. I've been half-expecting you to ask me but I suspect you know the answers already.' There was something very odd about Stan's tone.

'No I don't. I'm asking you to search because of a chance remark I heard this evening.'

'Then you will need to hang onto your cool, as they say. Honeycritch Farm was purchased from the Purbeck Downs Estate, in October 1946, by Captain James Wilson, VC, RN. In December 1946 he made a deed of gift transferring it to Mr Rubin Ernest Rocastle, the sitting tenant.'

CHAPTER 14

I started my seagoing career thirty years ago and my first ship was a tanker, plying from Southampton to Bahrain. Our captain was a man with a lifetime's experience, there was hardly a port in the world he had not seen. He had sailed in every class of ship, even square-rigged sailing vessels. He was one of the kindest and gentlest men I have ever met. Almost everything I know about the sea and its lore I learnt from him. We were all deeply fond of the old man, although sometimes he would drive us mad. He was an insomniac, who suffered long periods when he never slept. He would refuse to take his proper rest and would haunt the bridge night after night. This irritated the watch keepers who felt it was a slight on their competence. It made we humbler deck hands mildly paranoid, with the feeling we were being watched. Years later, the captain's wife let me into the secret. She explained about her husband's "visitations". The Captain had spent three and a half years as a wartime captive of the Japanese. He had survived well physically, but the mental scars remained, invisible to the outside world but never far beneath the surface. His visitations went beyond the normal experience of a nightmare. They were as real as if he had been transported back to Hell in some time machine. I knew exactly what this meant because I too have my visitations, and that evening in Old Duddlestone harbour I knew instinctively I was due for a bad one that night.

It is a warm day in Surrey and the heather and pines smell sweet. My mother has been mowing the lawn and the grass trimmings smell good too. The lawn looks as smooth as a cricket pitch with its long striped lines. I float my little balsa model glider across the grass and into the lilac bush. I am two days short of ten years old.

I have heard my father's car roll up the drive, which surprises me because this is Wednesday, normally his London day. Perhaps he has some news of the boat. He has decided to buy a sailing cruiser. I am thrilled, although mother is dubious. She cares little for the sea and can never understand the attraction. The previous evening he and I had pored over the small ads in the yachting press. It is one of the few times that my father has unbent enough to descend to my level. For an hour we are both small boys, excited carefree dreamers.

The single shot in the wood has startled the songbirds and sent a rabbit scuttling into the borders. I wonder who could be shooting. Our garden fringes on army training land; perhaps I can witness a mock battle. I run into the wood and there I see it. Lying on the ground is an odd elongated bundle. It is a smart suit, with legs and shoes. It looks like a man, but this man has no head; just a bloody mess with bits of hair and brains stuck to the gorse and heather around it. I know this is my father but I cannot react. I have this eerie feeling that I am watching myself watching the grisly tableau. The gun is a twelve-bore, my father's own favourite, his Holland & Holland. It lies soaking in congealing blood as speculative flies begin to gather. There is a piece of string knotted tightly around one trigger. It is a perfect seaman's knot, a little clove-hitch.

I am in reality again, lying curled up on the bunk in the cabin of my little boat. I am shivering and I know I am about to sob and wail, the tears flowing down my face, just as they did that day as I awoke from the numbness. Amidst the uproar in the adult world, no one had noticed me for over an hour. It should have become easier as the years pass but it doesn't. The visitations are less frequent, but when they come they are worse. The demons gather, un-exorcised and meaner than ever. Already I am waiting for the repeat performance, the first of many this night.

'You been on the piss or something – you look awful?' Laura looked at me, her head tilted to one side.

'I am suffering the cares of office,' I replied. 'This is my first land-based job and I seem to be making a mess of it.'

I hadn't slept a wink that night. I had finally got up to find a cold grey overcast morning.

'Midsummer solstice just gone,' I remarked nastily. 'I suppose your bloody village has a dozen rituals. Is it human sacrifice tonight, or just biting the heads off chickens? And how was your yoga class?'

'I hope you're not suggesting a connection,' she laughed. 'You've been talking to Carol. I know, she told me. Anyway who says you're making a mess of things – I don't. I think you've done bloody well considering everything.'

'How many boats sailed when they heard about the murder?'

'Five altogether, but they'll be back. Curiosity will draw them.' She stared at me again. 'For God's sake, man, what's got into you. Go and have a shave and get rid of that awful beard. You look like an escapee from the doss house.'

Laura was right, I did look a mess. I walked back to *Stormgoose* and fetched a change of clothes. Back in my private office I took a shower in the cramped little cubicle. I felt better and certainly I smelt better. Somewhere there was a rumble of heavy diesel engines. I ran outside to look. Two removal vans were backing gingerly up the village street. Laura was already walking briskly towards them. I ran to catch her up.

'That's my furniture,' she said. 'With a bit of luck I'll have moved in by evening. Could you watch the phone for half an hour while I sort things?'

'Of course, but I didn't know your place was ready.'

'It's ready enough. I'll finish off the odd bit of decorating myself.' She swung round to face me. 'I'm having my house-warming tomorrow night – seven thirty. You'll come won't you?' Her smile was so friendly and open that I almost reversed my view of her. Almost, but not quite. I suspected she was up to something, but what? I had no idea.

'The honour's mine,' I said.

Mick and I managed the harbour without Laura. Emma appeared at a loose end, so I put her to answering the phone. She told me Simon was working on their boat's engine and was better left alone. The furniture lorries departed at midday and Laura returned with an air of satisfaction. I left them to it. I was fed up with my home cooking and I fancied a bar lunch at the Gullait Arms.

The sun had broken through the cloud layer and it was another glorious hot day. I was glad to leave the heat of the morning outside and walk into the relative cool of the main bar. Most of the customers were holidaymakers. The distinction between these visitors and the locals was clear enough. I had a quick look round, but failed to recognise any of the people from the other night. I ordered my meal, steak and salad, and asked the bar girl to bring it to the Double Six room. I carried my pint of beer into the latter and found a quiet corner table. There was a buzz of conversation from the other clientele: a couple with two children and a pair of travelling salesmen. I could see no sign of Harry, which was a pity, because he was the man I needed to talk to.

I stood up and began to study the pictures on the wall. Apart from the pen and ink drawing of my father, I counted a dozen other pictures, including the sea rescue shots I had seen before. These varied from photographs of MTBs cruising in formation at thirty knots, to formal pictures of ship's companies and individual snapshots. I stood up and walked across the room to examine these, especially one group picture that intrigued me. It showed a miscellaneous group of Navy lads, all grinning happily. I counted eleven of them; their scruffy sweaters and unkempt appearance would have made the average naval disciplinarian blow a fuse. I guessed that MTB flotillas had a different ethos, and that a free and easy atmosphere belied a tight discipline and a strong group loyalty.

'Those were the foreign lads,' it was Harry speaking. So intent had I been on the picture that I hadn't noticed him enter the room. 'We got them together for that shot. There's six different nationalities there.'

'How come, Harry?'

'An MTB flotilla was a combat unit, in daily contact with the enemy. That's what attracted those lads. They were refugees who wanted to fight with us – Poles, Dutch, Greeks, Spanish Republicans, Norwegians. They were all good seamen but very committed: they had scores to settle.'

Norwegians. That gave me an idea. I swung round to face him. 'Eriksen's a Norwegian name. Was he one of them?'

Good, my shot had hit home. Harry looked shiftily around and then seemed to make up his mind. 'Yes,' he said quietly. 'He remembers you from your father's funeral.'

'I can't say I remember him.' I felt exultant.

Harry was looking troubled. 'I've got to go back to the bar, we're just getting busy. Look, you're food's coming now – I'll talk to you later.' He scuttled away, rather too furtively for my liking. I would let him stew for the moment. Patience was needed in prising out the darker secrets of Duddlestone; that was something I was fast beginning to learn.

It was Sharon the barmaid who served my lunch. I was hungry and the fare looked good. I smiled my thanks.

'Mr Wilson,' she whispered excitedly as she set the table. 'You know the other night; when old Roy snuffed it?'

'I was there, although snuffed it isn't the term I would use. You've heard the police think foul play?'

'Her face suffused with ill-concealed glee. 'They've been all over the village and in here. We've had detectives, plain clothes like – wanted to know where I went after work.'

'I take it you've an alibi,' I grinned.

‘Oh yeah, they can’t touch me. When my shift here ended, my boyfriend picked me up, and we went clubbing over Bournemouth.’

‘Well, Sharon, I’m glad to hear it. Any ideas yourself what happened?’

‘Might have, but that’d be telling wouldn’t it?’ Her girlish confidences had vanished. She was all frost now. The Inspector had it right; Duddlestone would close ranks against the outside world.

I returned to the harbour to find two newspaper reporters and their photographer pestering everyone in sight. They wanted first-hand accounts of the death of Roy Gulley. Mercifully they seemed to have heard nothing about my fall into the dock. I had no comment to make and referred them to the police, who would be holding a press conference anyway.

They remained unimpressed. Did I know that Roy Gulley was suspected of being one of the Duddlestone lynch mob? Yes, I was aware of that, but it was long dead history and didn’t interest me.

They tried another tack. Did I know that Arthur Rocastle’s sister, Mrs Bowler, was launching a campaign to reopen the old murder inquiry? Did I know that Brian Byrne was writing a full page article in next Sunday’s press and that the local MP was going to ask questions in Parliament?

I told them bluntly, that I neither knew nor cared, which probably sounded rather callous. Then one of them, a little squirt with a posh accent, asked me what my father’s involvement had been in these events? I felt tempted to pick him up bodily and heave him into the harbour. I had to forego that pleasure; I knew better than to make a complete idiot of myself, and put my job in jeopardy. I must be mellowing with age. Then Laura, who had witnessed the confrontation from a distance, came storming in. With icy hauteur she ordered them off the site, which was annoying in one sense. Standing on the fringe of the group was that dishevelled Australian girl. She was an oddball whose face didn’t seem to fit with the other hacks. If she persisted in hanging around our premises she would have to offer a genuine explanation or be banned.

CHAPTER 15

'Laura's invited you and Simon to her housewarming tonight. How about it?'

Emma frowned. 'We were thinking of sailing on this afternoon's tide.'

'Only thinking?'

'Well yes, it depends on whether Simon's happy with the engine. He's still got a filter change to do.'

'I'd like you to come – you'd be doing me a favour.'

'For heaven's sake, why?' she giggled. 'You want us to protect you from that woman?'

I smiled. 'No, I don't think that'll be necessary, but I've a serious point. Did you know that your grandfather Wilson commanded here in the war?'

Emma made a face. 'Yes, so I gather, what of it?'

I knew I was on tricky family ground. Emma had always shied away from talk of her famous sailor grandfather, although she was immensely proud of her descent from Great Grandfather Panov. However this was Duddlestone, and Wilson VC had to be confronted. His footprints seemed to be all over this place, accompanied by something distinctly murky about the old man's past. I needed to know the truth, and the whole of it, for my own peace of mind.

'Emma, love, I've been hearing things about my father. I never knew this was the place he commanded, I always thought his boats were based at Portland.' I knew I was deviating from the point. Duddlestone had been an integral part of Portland base, and anyway such semantics would leave Emma cold.

'Dad, are you trying to tell me that Grandad was never the great hero we've all been led to believe, because I never thought he was. He gets himself snarled up in some failed business deal, and then blows himself away leaving you and poor Gran to face the consequences. I don't call that heroic.' She stared me eye to eye defiantly.

It was a familiar defiance. Emma, I thought, whether you like it or not, there's something of the old man in you too; in both of us.

'We don't know for certain why he did it,' I said. 'But he was a brave man in war, that's certain, you can't take that away from him. I need to know why he killed himself, and your Grandmother thinks it all traces back to something that happened here.'

'What's this got to do with Laura's party?'

'I want moral support and, more important, I want you both to size the people up. Ask them about the past, be tactful and act naive as you can.'

'I get it,' she looked at me sardonically now. 'Simon to play the medical student twit, and me the dumb bimbo?'

'Well, you said it, not me.' I grinned at her.

'OK Dad, it might be a bit of fun, and we're not ones to turn down a party.'

Midday came again and I was tempted by the thought of a good lunch at the pub and another opportunity to corner Harry. As I reached for my jacket, I saw through the window the arrival of a noisy and rather worse-for-wear Lotus 7 sports car. From it stepped my friend Alistair Pickering, dressed once more in his civvies. He stood on the dockside looking lost, so I went outside and waved to him.

'Hi, Mr Wilson, I hoped I'd catch you, I've news.' He sounded excited.

'Good news, I hope?'

'In a way, yes. The MOD have decided to come clean about the old research lab.'

'Really?'

'That's it, they couldn't keep the lid on it any more, not after the rumours about it collapsing.'

'I take it the risk is sorted. I mean there's none of your people checking passes today?'

'No, in the end it was a false alarm. There was no tunnel collapse; only a chalk fall in one of the old ventilator shafts.'

'Is it safe – no escaped poisons?'

'No, it all tested AOK; they're taking the press up there this afternoon. If I get us passes, how would you like to tag on?'

'I say, have you ever read Tolkien?' Alistair was pointing across the flat acreage of grassland to the steep face of the hill, labelled on the ordnance map as Weavers Down.

I shook my head. 'Odd question. Actually I never quite got my head around Tolkien but my daughter's potty about him – why?

He laughed. 'As I said before, my mother says I'm too imaginative for a soldier, but that's what this place reminds me of – the gates of Moria. The entrance to the dark mines that the Company passed through – very sinister. You see, nobody knows what's down there, except an awful lot of bodies.'

I followed his outstretched hand. In front of us was a hard standing: about an acre of very weedy concrete. A short path led into what must once have been a quarry. It ended in a grassy mound.

'That's the entrance into the old tunnels. Under that earth bank there's concrete. They sealed the whole place up so tight even a spider wouldn't get in or out.'

I wondered. 'Do you know what the place is built of down there. Does anyone know if it'll really collapse?'

'No, it's hard rock, that's the one thing they told us. It's so strong it'd survive a nuclear. Apparently they filled the ventilation shafts with loose chalk and it's that that keeps subsiding.'

I looked back up the hill. 'These must be the press boys.'

A collection of cars and a minibus had parked on the grass verge just beyond the guard post. Two uniformed army officers and an assortment of civilians were stumbling down the track. They halted a few yards away. Alistair and I moved diffidently to the back of the crowd. Nobody took the slightest notice of us; all eyes were on the two army men and an elderly and dour looking civilian in a grey suit. The latter had detached himself a short distance behind the other two and was scanning the crowd suspiciously.

'The army guy on the left is our adjutant,' Alistair whispered. 'The other one's our press spokesman. I don't know who that miserable looking git with them is – spook for a guess.'

The army press man picked up a loud hailer. There was a wail of noisy feedback as he fiddled with it. 'Your attention please. Welcome to Duddlestone Number One Exclusion Zone.'

At four o'clock I said goodbye to Alistair and drove back to Old Duddlestone. The afternoon had been something of an anticlimax. The official spokesman had been a master of the obscure. None of us had been allowed within five hundred yards of the derelict research tunnels. The journalists had thrown a barrage of questions, which the officials had either blocked or refused to answer. Everyone was given a printed leaflet with a mass of data. Apparently, on-site readings proved that there was no radioactivity, chemicals, bacteria or any other nastiness. The army men had kept a wary eye on the unsavoury looking civilian. His expression had remained deadpan throughout. I saw Brian Byrne on the fringe of the crowd, though he asked no questions.

I arrived back at the harbour in time to relieve Mick and Laura. She was off to make the final touches to her party and Mick had been pressed into helping. I found my private inner office had been invaded, or rather my daughter had hi-jacked the shower compartment. She was standing wrapped in an enormous towel with another one draped around her head like a turban. She had left a trail of damp across the floor and a pile of filthy laundry. Naturally I grumbled.

'It's no good,' she said. 'If we're coming to this do, we've got to be clean, hygienic and dressed for the occasion. Another thing, if you want customers here, you'll need a proper shower block.'

'I suppose you've left some water for me?' I glared at her.

'Plenty of water, but you'll have to wait for it to heat up, and Simon's next in anyway.'

I left her to it. There are some battles I can never win. I went across to *Stormgoose* to dig out a suitable rig for the Harbour Master to wear at a social gathering.

Mrs Rocastle, Laura's mother, was helping her daughter lay out food for the evening. I had expected Carol to be present as well and felt a tinge of disappointment to find her missing.

'She's staying in to keep an eye on Tommy,' Mrs Rocastle explained.

Laura's cottage had indeed been reborn. I would hardly have recognised it from the shell of a dwelling I had seen on my first day. The rooms were all decorated in plain white. I did not care much for Laura's taste in furnishings, apart from some nice pieces like the old Welsh dresser that sat against one wall of the living room. Mostly, the house was filled with minimalist artefacts in tubing and glass. The interesting object, to me, was a large upright piano made of dark-stained wood.

'That's my grandmother's,' said Laura. 'She used to play the hymns on it in the chapel up the street.'

I lifted the lid to see a row of yellowing ivory keys. 'May I?'

I pulled a stool to the keyboard, sat down, and ran off a couple of scales. The thing was catastrophically out of tune. There was a nasty clash of semitones in the base, and the top C was a dumb wooden rattle.

'You can play that thing?' Laura looked almost stunned.

'Get a tuner in and I can.'

'It sounded all right to me,' she grunted. 'You can give us a rendition later on.'

'That depends on how much booze I've been given, and it won't be hymns. If your grandma strikes you down from beyond the grave, don't blame me.'

Mick Tracic was down on the quay directing the car park. Soon the guests were arriving; among the first was Dr Hooder. My heart sank as he homed in on me.

'That man who died … Gulley wasn't it? It can't possibly be murder,' he remarked.

'Someone fixed him a cup full of tea laced with alkaloid taxus, that's fatal within a minute.' It was Emma, she had come into the room unnoticed and had sidled up to me, wineglass in hand. She looked stunning in a white off-the-shoulder dress with tiny silver-gilt straps. Simon was beside her, also smartly dressed in pressed slacks and a blazer with a yacht club tie.

Hooder swung round, nostrils flared, staring down at this slip of a girl who had dared to challenge him. 'Madam, I am a doctor. You shouldn't voice opinions on matters that you do not understand.'

'That's where you're wrong, matey,' said Simon. 'Emma is a doctor. What's more, when she was at St Thomas's her tutor was Professor Lytton, and what he doesn't know about toxicology…' Simon never finished. Hooder had turned on his heel and stalked away.

'Whatever did you say?' Laura had witnessed the exchange.

'Nothing to do with me,' I said. 'He had a medical disagreement with these two.'

Emma was spluttering with laughter. 'It wasn't that so much. Did you see the man's face when Simon called him, "matey"?'

'Who is this professor you mentioned?' I asked.

'That was a wind-up,' said Simon. 'Lytton's an expert in forensic medicine, he's written books on it.'

'He taught us,' Emma explained, 'but not specifically about poisons. Mentioning him rattled that bloke's cage though. Who is he?'

'Paul Hooder, he owns the land here,' Laura sniffed. 'He's supposed to be a doctor, but I'd call him a third rate quack.'

'He's got no bloody manners,' said Simon, 'but that doesn't make him a bad doctor.' I noticed he was staring at Laura.

I could hardly take my eyes off her myself. She had dressed herself in the tightest figure hugging fashion jeans I had ever seen. Every contour and dimple was displayed like a second skin. It was a figure to outshine any alleged super-model. These jeans were topped by a floppy, diaphanous shirt through which it was just possible to see, pair of very shapely breasts. The ensemble was in perfect taste, but intensely erotic.

A little man, whom I had already seen on the fringes, had caught my attention. I was feeling uneasy myself. I am not a good social mixer and I knew hardly anyone here. I marched up to the stranger and held out my hand. 'I'm Peter, I run the harbour.'

'Charlie Mortimer, I'm the dinosaur man.' He shook hands with a sunny smile. Inwardly I groaned; was this another species of Duddlestone nutter?

'Palaeontologist – Southampton University. We're working the old quarries on Weavers Down.'

'Searching for dinosaurs?' I looked around for rescue; none was forthcoming.

'That's right, there were some remains found in 1939, then the war came and the whole area was out of bounds. We've just been allowed back and we're very excited.'

I tried to show some interest, but already Laura was bearing down on me. With her were a couple whom I had met briefly before. I recognised Ian and Tricia Rocastle, Laura's brother and his wife.

'Here you are,' said Laura. 'My brother Ian, principal farmer of the village, Chairman of the Parish Council and Master of the Old Duddlestone Fisherman's Brotherhood.'

'Your sister, Carol, told me about this brotherhood,' I said cooly.

'Oh, God,' Laura snorted.

'She told me about them in the old days. She called it socialism in practice.'

'I'm no socialist,' Ian grimaced. 'O' course there's no fishing left now. We're a charity organisation these days – we raise money for Children in Need.' Ian's Dorset accent was more pronounced than either of his sisters.

'Don't be fooled, Peter,' said Tricia. 'The Brotherhood are an all male drinking club.' I was amused that she, by contrast, spoke with the cut glass accent of one who had been to some very posh school.

I have to say I liked Ian. He was a stocky, round-faced man aged around forty. He seemed to walk through life with a happy grin and a supreme air of self-confidence.

'By the way,' I remarked, 'I'm told that my father was friendly with a man called Rubin Ernest Rocastle.'

I detected a tension in the group. I caught Laura and Ian exchanging glances. 'You mean Ernie Rocastle,' she said. 'He was our granddad.'

'Was he the one who lived in this house?' I knew I had worried her. I decided to rattle her some more. 'If he was a fisherman how did he come to be a farmer?'

'The opportunity came to take the tenancy, so he took it,' Laura said icily. 'Look Peter, I've guests to see to – haven't time to gossip with you.' She walked away.

'It's true, about your father,' said Tricia. She looked puzzled as if she knew something was wrong. 'We've some photos of him in an album at home and he was an honorary member of the Brotherhood. He signed the roll.'

I didn't question further. I had learned a little and in the fullness of time I would discover more.

A strident whistle sounded through the room bringing all conversation to a stop. Mick was standing in the kitchen doorway. His head was covered with a red bandanna and he wore a striped butcher's apron over his awful Hawaiian shirt, knee length baggy shorts and flipflops. 'Come on folks, out in the garden. The barbie's alight – dinner is served.'

In the end it was a good party. The food was excellent, the wine flowed. Mick took over the bar and brewed some evil concoction he called, "surfer's punch". Laura had borrowed an enormous stereo system. There was nobody here to complain about noise, so we all boogied uninhibited, in the garden and out in the street, while the disco music bounced off the cliffs above in surreal echoes.

At one o'clock in the morning, we who had survived the evening were gathered indoors.

Without warning Laura pointed at me. 'Peter is going to play the piano.'

'Am I?'

'Yes, go on.' She lifted the lid of the keyboard, stepped back, and gave me a none too gentle shove.

I was not happy with this development. I hadn't practised for weeks, months more likely, and my own piano was in a furniture store in Portsmouth. I caught Laura's eye and something clicked. I was being set up for public humiliation. Well, sod you, I thought. I have played for my supper the world over, in bars, pubs, and seaman's missions, so this was not a new experience.

I sat down and rattled off Scott Joplin's, "The Entertainer", followed by "Mapleleaf Rag". Then I switched periods and played my versions of "Yesterday" and "You Were Always On My Mind". I didn't care by now whether I had an appreciative audience, I was in my stride. I made a terrible hash of some Oscar Peterson jazz improvisation and quickly switched to Mozart. It was time for my very own party piece. I was playing out my personal fantasy as I launched into the second movement of the Shostakovich piano concerto in F; that lovely lyrical allegro, which was one of my mother's favourites. Music that stirred deep ancestral memories. In my imagination I could see the attentive audience and the orchestra arranged on my left. I watched for the conductor's down beat.

I finished and sat back. The room was in total silence and I was drenched in sweat. Suddenly I felt sick. I knew I had been showing off. I had probably made an utter idiot of myself, apart from insulting great music, on this ex-Methodist relic of an instrument.

The hush probably lasted for seconds only, but to me, it seemed for ever. Then there was a huge cheer followed by applause, somebody clapped me on the back as the room spun around me and then slowly refocused.

'I'll give you a hand,' I said.

Laura was looking round her trim new home, which by now was littered with empty glasses, plates of half-eaten canapés and all the usual debris of an adult party. At least there were no broken cigarette butts. Laura's draconian no-smoking rule had driven the habitual puffers into the street. The last guests had left, leaving just the two of us, Old Duddlestone's only permanent residents.

'Mick hasn't tried to ride home on that motorbike?' Laura looked concerned.

'No, that dinosaur man's giving him and his girl a lift. Who is he anyway?'

'Charlie? He's what he claims to be – an academic with a taste for bones.' She began to clatter the plates together. 'He and I were at Cambridge together, and his girlfriend Babs is a mate of mine.'

'Which was Babs?'

'She wasn't here tonight – only Charlie.'

'I'm afraid I didn't know who half the people were. They didn't strike me as Duddlestone types.'

She swung round on me. 'I'm not sure what you mean by that but they were mostly my old crowd from the National Trust and some others from my misspent past.' She turned back to the sink. 'Come on, I thought you were supposed to be helping. Run some hot water and come back here for the glasses.'

Gradually the pile of dirty plates began to diminish as Laura scrubbed each one with venom and handed it to me to dry.

'Where did you learn to play the piano like that?'

'At home, from the age of five or so. We're a musical family; my mother's Russian, she'd been a professional violinist before the war.'

'You're full of surprises, Peter. I'd never have guessed.'

'I'm sorry if I don't conform to my stereotype,' I replied acidly.

'I'm not,' she laughed. 'You've suddenly become interesting. My sister seems to have got something right for once.'

'What's that supposed to mean?'

'All right, don't go all uptight on me – sit down.' She pointed me to one of her avant-garde chairs. It may have sounded like a request, but I took it as an order.

Very quietly she walked round behind me and began to massage my neck muscles. 'Christ, you are tense – relax man.' Slowly she began to work with her fingertips. It was strangely pleasant and I did begin to relax as ordered. I felt languid and at peace as my antagonism vanished.

'Who taught you this?' I asked.

'At my yoga club – it's an additional part of the discipline.'

'It's certainly effective. You're not conforming to your stereotype either.'

'Which means you rate me as a bossy harridan.'

'Something of the sort.'

'That's at least honest.' She let go of my neck. 'Come on we can't do any more down here. Let's have sex.'

'What!' I wasn't sure I was hearing right.

'Oh, don't go all coy. We're both free – let's try my bed. We'll be the first couple to screw in Old Duddlestone since the Navy moved out.

CHAPTER 16

I had been invited to, "have sex". There was no hypocrisy, no talk of "making love". I was caught in a carefully laid snare. Suddenly I was very aware that I hadn't had a woman for six months, and that is far too long for a normal, healthy, heterosexual man. Celibacy had seemed less of a burden than it might have been. I had been so consumed by hatred and self-pity that I had become near to being a misogynist. All this was forgotten. My eyes were blurred, my face was burning; I felt myself aroused. All my senses were focused on hot smouldering lust and with it an awful loss of dignity. I was a proud man being half-seduced, half-raped, by his female assistant. With an enigmatic smile Laura had released the belt around those figure hugging jeans and did a little shimmy as they slipped to the floor. Without a word being spoken, she had signalled me to slip off her flimsy blouse. Then, naked in my arms, I had carried her up the short flight of stairs to the lovely soft bed she had prepared for us in the room above.

No "love" was made that night, only five hours of delicious, guiltless, sexual pleasure. I can think of other similar encounters around the world: Maria the Filipina girl, Felicity in Buenos Aires, Anna in Copenhagen and half a dozen others in as many ports of the world. I was surprised to find these same skills from a girl in a remote village in Southern England.

I lost count of the number of frenzied couplings we made, followed by short intervals of sleep. At six o'clock we started again, this time in the shower. I had staggered back to bed and then Laura, laughing with delight, had hurled herself on me. Straddling my limbs she had dragged me deep inside her one final time.

I awoke to broad daylight outside the bedroom window. I didn't want to move. I lay there perfectly relaxed and replete, as I let my eyes scan around. Laura was sitting cross legged, still naked, at the edge of the bed. On her knees was what looked like a flat piece of board. She was staring at me in an odd way, a pencil clamped between her lips.

'What are you doing?' I asked sleepily.

'Nothing, just keep still for a moment.'

I shut my eyes and drifted away into a pleasing languor. I could vaguely hear some scratching noises.

'OK, that'll do – want to have a look?' Laura had slid her feet to the floor and was now standing beside me. 'Come over here, the light's better.' By the window she pushed the object into my hands.

It was sketchpad with a picture. To be precise it was a life drawing of a naked man lying on a…

'Hey, that's me. I say that's a bit off…' I was indignant.

'I've done three others – quick pencil sketches, but you kept rolling around.'

'Bloody cheek!' I was doing my best to be annoyed.

'I'm an artist. It's not often I get a free model to practice on. Better model than the art classes. They're all fat bastards – no muscle – and the blokes have tiny cocks.'

I tried to be angry but it was no good. I had been stripped, not only of my clothing, but of my last shred of dignity.

'I don't know what you're so worried about,' she said. 'I've blurred the facial features, not even Carol will recognise this.'

'You're not going to show it to her?' I was suddenly suspicious and on the defensive.

'Peter, I think you should understand that tonight was a one off. It was fantastic and I enjoyed every minute.'

'Me too,' I interjected rather lamely.

'But,' she continued, 'that's got to be the end of it. We had a good time and I'll take some good memories.'

In a way she was making it easy for me. There was not the slightest chance of us forming a relationship. I no longer disliked her but I was no closer to understanding this woman than I was on the day we met.

'I've never told you about Larry Tapsell, my husband?' We were sitting on the bed next to each other as she leant against me, her fingers ruffling through my hair.

'You told me he was in Birmingham.'

'Did I? Well I'm not sure where he is now but Brum's his home town. I can't really blame him, I'm not cut out for marriage, the split was my fault. The long and short of it is, I like my own company, I don't make relationships with anyone, and I don't want to.'

'Your sister warned me you enjoyed sex.'

'Oh did she really?' Laura laughed softly as she rested her head on my chest. 'Carol's different – her ex-husband is a rat.'

'Why did he push off and leave her like that – I simply don't understand it. It sounds like a cliché, but Carol's a nice girl, she's clever and kind, a sweet nature if you like.'

'The reverse of me, eh?' Laura ran her wet tongue along my shoulder

'I never said you weren't clever.'

'No, but I'm not really very nice. My poor dear sister can't win against me. If she wants something I need to have a taste first.'

'I don't get you?'

Laura gripped my upper arm and squeezed. I winced as her nails almost broke the skin. 'Peter,' she spoke slowly and clearly almost in my ear. 'Carol is different, she needs a man, a real man, and Tommy needs a father. In the last few weeks, Carol's fallen for a certain man in a big way. Despite everything and all our differences, I'm fond of the stupid girl – I don't want her hurt.'

'Why are you telling me this?'

'Because this man Carol is besotted with is you. So from now on I'm going to be all sisterly honour.'

I made sure I was well clear of that house before Mick arrived for work. He had no transport after last night but I guessed he would still make it here on time. I was right; an army Land Rover appeared on the dot of nine o'clock, driven by my friend Alistair Pickering, and sitting beside him was Mick.

'Your Australian chappie turned up at the gate on foot. He wanted to walk the last mile, but we don't allow that, so I took pity.'

'Thanks, Alistair,' I replied. 'Got time for a coffee?'

'Sorry, no can do, duty calls – thanks all the same.' He gazed round at the scene. 'Some of our lads are into sailing. There's talk of moving one of the army boats to this harbour. Would that be on?'

'I'm sure we'd be delighted.'

He moved to climb into his vehicle. 'I say, have the police found anything? You know about the other night?' He was diffident, almost as if he expected me to jump down his throat.

'No, we haven't been told a thing.'

'We have now.' It was Laura who interrupted me. She had just emerged from the office and I hadn't noticed her. 'The police have been on the phone, they're on their way back to talk to us.' Laura was her normal self. Her attitude to me was the same as any other morning. There was not a hint that our relationship had changed through the fun and games in the night.

Fortunately we were kept busy. A steady stream of visiting yachts began to enter the harbour. With the wind dropping, several families had decided to give the trip westward a miss and try our harbour instead. By midday we had sixteen extra craft berthed in our marina. I left Mick to cope with this influx, because by half past ten, the police had arrived.

Our visitor was Detective Inspector Channing, the same investigating officer as before. 'Mr Wilson, I would like to run over your statement.'

This was boring. I had to repeat everything I had said two days ago. I had no new evidence to add, although the facts were now clearer in my mind.

'The thing that troubles me,' I said, 'is will they try again? It looks as if somebody wants me dead.'

'No sir, we don't think so. We believe you came back too early and they panicked. Then they ran fast and left the evidence of the poison behind.'

'The tea cups?' said Laura.

'Exactly. We took them away for finger-printing, then forensics became suspicious about the cause of death and they analysed the contents. One cup was untouched, perfectly innocent tea leaves – it was the other one they'd contaminated.'

'Why access our computer?' asked Laura.

'As yet we couldn't say. It's the same with the tea cups – no prints, everyone was wearing surgical gloves.'

'What about DNA?' asked Laura.

'The lab people are trying that, but they're not sure the safe cup was ever drunk from.'

That was a lot of help. It seems the police were getting nowhere. I looked at Laura. 'You must have some idea what's behind this – you're Duddlestone born?'

'Sorry, Peter, but if anyone's in the know, they won't talk in front of me.'

'Why not, you're a Rocastle. You're as deep in the secrets here as anyone.'

'I'm not deep in any secrets. The people you have in mind think I've sold out by working for Paul Hooder. I've told you this already.'

'All right,' said the Inspector. 'Perhaps you can help me with another inquiry. Owing to outside pressures, our Chief Constable has been compelled to reopen the Arthur Rocastle and Margaret Gulley, murder cases of 1946.'

Laura groaned. 'That was fifty years ago.'

'There's no limitation of time in the case of murder.'

Laura frowned. 'It was eighteen years before I was even thought of. I can't help you and I'm not sure I want to. You call it murder but we call it justice. Unorthodox justice but Arthur Rocastle was a murderer and a rapist.'

'I don't see how you can make that judgement, Mrs Tapsell. Have you ever read the record of the trial at Winchester?'

'No, and I don't want to. Some senile old judge let him off. Told him not to be a naughty boy and do it again.' Her tone was withering in its contempt.

'Well, I have read the trial report, the whole record verbatim.' Inspector Channing's voice was coldly hostile. 'As a police officer, I am satisfied that Arthur Rocastle was an innocent man. In fact it baffles me how any police force could have thought they had a case.'

The barometer had climbed overnight and with it more glorious weather. A gentle early morning breeze was blowing from inland. Now Emma and Simon were preparing to sail. Simon was cheerful enough, but Emma seemed distant and grumpy.

'We're going west, making for Brixham,' said Simon.

'Keep well south of Portland,' I advised. Of course he knew that perfectly well.

He nodded. 'There was a big gin palace nosing around last night.'

This brought me back into the real world with a bump.

'When was this?' I asked. 'I never heard a thing.'

'Of course you didn't. You were with that whore!' Emma snapped. She turned her back on me and stormed down below into the cabin.

I was stunned. In the excitement of last night I had forgotten I was so close to home. My embarrassment was not lessened by the smirk on Simon's face. 'Don't worry about it,' he whispered. 'She'll have forgotten in a week or so,'

'I doubt it,' I muttered. 'Was it so bloody obvious?'

'No, just your bad luck. Em went for a walk and she heard your lady moaning and groaning.'

'Simon,' I was desperate to put my explanation to him before Emma emerged. 'I think I've been set up. There's nothing between me and that woman.'

'Yeah, sure if you say so.' His face puckered. 'Useful looking bird, that Laura, but frankly we don't like her.'

'Tell me about this motor yacht?' I wanted to change the subject, and anyway I needed to know.

'Never saw her properly – wasn't showing lights, but she was a big'un.'

'What time?'

'Three fifteen, it was still dark.'

I found Laura at her desk. 'Come in here a minute, please?' I indicated my inner office. She followed and I shut the door.

She looked at me with a puzzled expression. She was suddenly confronted with a wholly different Peter Wilson.

'You deceitful little bitch. You set me up last night. You deliberately set me up so that Eriksen could make another smuggling drop in my harbour! Give me one good reason why I shouldn't fire you on the spot and call in the police.'

CHAPTER 17

Laura froze and then stepped back as if I'd hit her. The blank look on her face, turned to shock, that kindled into blazing anger. I knew at once that I was wrong. Hers was an anger born of false accusation and real hurt.

'That's a lie! How could you say a thing like that?' She was white faced under her suntan, and she spoke very quietly, with none of her accustomed verve. I had clearly hurt her but my pride drove me to bluster.

'What else am I expected to think?' I shouted.

'I don't throw myself at any man,' she yelled. 'I'm not a bloody trollop. I slept with you because I fancied you. I thought it would be fun, do us both good – round off a nice evening.' Incredibly there were tears on her face, and her eyes were reproachful.

I sat down and buried my face in my hands; for the first time in this job I was at my wits end. There was movement in the next room, and to my relief, Mick put his head round the door.

'Poobah's just pulled up in his motor. Thought I'd better warn you.'

'Who did you say?'

'Dr Poobah – Hooder. My name for 'im. Strewth, Pete, I thought Poms like that went out with World War Two.'

'I think they did,' I managed a smile. 'Actually the good doctor's a South African.'

'Is he now? – that figures. I can just see 'im using the whip on the black fellahs.' Mick looked philosophical. If he had heard my slanging match with Laura, he was being unusually tactful.

'Tell the doctor I'll meet him on the quay. I can handle him better out there.'

Mick left; I looked at Laura. I needed to put things right now. 'Sorry,' I said contritely. 'I shouldn't have yelled at you like that. I think I'm becoming paranoid. It's not your fault, this place is getting to me.'

Her usual composure had returned. 'Come and have a bite to eat in my place, midday, and we'll try and clear the air.' I doubted if I was forgiven but at least we had a truce.

Outside on the quay Laura tore at Hooder. The man was obviously the recipient of most of the anger she had intended for me.

'Paul, why the hell did you stalk out of my party last night and without so much as a by-you-leave?'

The doctor withdrew a pace backwards. 'I had another engagement. I am very busy but I paid my respects to your new house. I don't know what else you expected?' He turned away from her and began to speak to me.

Laura wasn't having that. 'You were rude to my guests, you bastard. You can bloody well apologise.'

The Doctor raised his eyebrows, he had fixed her with that irritating sniffing expression. 'Really Laura, you are making too much of this. Some woman was impertinent to me. I felt it was better I leave.' He paused for a full three seconds. I could feel Laura seething. 'However, if it will please you, most certainly I apologise.'

I thought it better I intervene. I could see Emma walking along the pontoon towards the quay. I wanted to wave her off on her voyage without further ill feeling. The last thing I needed was a full-scale confrontation between her and these two.

'Doctor,' I said' 'how can I help you?'

He held out a sheet of paper. 'Today I have received permission from the Ministry of Defence to access the former navy ammunition bunker. I thought, knowing your connections, it might interest you.'

'That'll be those doors into the cliff?'

'Yes.'

'You want to look now?'

'Yes, I have man waiting up there.'

I glanced at Laura. She seemed to be smouldering in some private world of her own.

'OK,' I said to Hooder. 'I can spare half an hour. Let's go.'

Hooder led the way briskly along the street; Laura stayed behind. I could see Emma walking up the sloping ramp from the pontoon. If she was bent on a face-to-face with Laura there was nothing I could do about it.

A battered Ford Transit van was parked outside the gloomy abandoned chapel. Standing by it was a man in mechanic's overalls. I can only describe him on first appearance as crumpled. He was probably in his mid-forties, and his features were heavily lined and morose. At his feet was a disc cutter, the sort powered by a two-stroke petrol engine.

'This,' said the doctor, 'is Jake Stoneman. He's going to do the business for us.'

‘Hello,’ I said, ‘you related to Carol Stoneman?’

‘No,’ he said bluntly. Clearly I had made a tactless start. ‘She’s my cousin’s ex.’

‘Jake’s my general factotum,’ said Hooder.

‘I does his garden – fixes his cars,’ said Jake. It seemed Mr Stoneman was a man of few words.

The doors of the magazine were made of heavy-duty corrugated iron with traces of their original paint still visible. They were semi-sliding doors made of hinged sections that folded back concertina fashion. They were in halves, fastened in the middle by two heavy-duty padlocks. Both were rusty and evidently hadn’t been touched in years. Jake had donned a facemask and an eye visor. He pulled the cord of his disc cutter and the machine whirred into life. The air was filled with the smell of hot abrasive disc and showers of sparks. Jake put down the cutter and heaved on the doors. There was no movement. As I expected they were seized solid.

‘Shall I cut a hole?’ he asked.

‘Yes,’ said Hooder testily.

It took two minutes to hack a hole in the old iron covering big enough for us to squeeze through.

‘Captain,’ the doctor addressed me. ‘I think you should have the honour of entering first.’

I half climbed through the gap. ‘It’s no good,’ I said. ‘I can’t see a thing.’

‘I’ll get some torches,’ said Stoneman.

He handed me a battery lantern through the gap, and then climbed through himself; Hooder followed.

Already my eyes were beginning to adjust to the semi-darkness within this cavern. I found enough illumination, through the newly cut hole, to show that this place was a great deal larger than I had expected and that its walls were substantial looking rock.

‘Purbeck stone,’ said Hooder, shining a torch at the roof. ‘Nothing could touch this place in war, not even a direct hit. My father’s laboratories were exactly the same.

‘It must have been one hell of an operation to mine this lot.’ I mused.

‘This was the first job they did. They blasted their way in and used the spoil to build the harbour. It was lucky that the rock here is like this.’

‘Why’s that?’

‘A few miles on and it’s oil-bearing shale. Not safe for an

ammunition store, let alone a scientific lab.' I noticed a change in Hooder. He was speaking quietly with none of his usual prickly pomposity. He had transformed and become a normal intelligent person, alert and interested in what he was seeing. I wondered if there was a second persona to this man. Could it be possible that his usual demeanour was an act?

I walked ahead, shining the lantern as I went. The place was a labyrinth, with side tunnels branching off the main level, which must have been twenty feet high. These minor tunnels were smaller and rounded, rather like those of the London tube system. The main level stretched ahead and from above came tiny pinpoints of light.

'Ventilation shafts,' Hooder explained.

'I thought all the vents had been blocked.'

'No, only the ones over the laboratory.'

'Couldn't someone fall down these?'

'No, they've concrete security caps with grilles. Very well built – last a hundred years.' He seemed very sure on this point.

The cavern appeared to be completely empty. My light shone on a number of brick-built bays and the remains of notices, black with white stencil lettering. *No 1. Torpedo Store*, read one, accompanied by a skull-and-cross-bones and a No Smoking sign.

'I wonder how they handled this stuff?' I said.

'Had a couple o' tractors and low loader-trailers,' said Stoneman.

I shone my lamp into the far right hand side of the main area. There, to my surprise, was a mint condition Nissen Hut with a chimney leading through the wall into the outside world. Intrigued, I walked across and tried the door. It opened with a push and an unpleasant rasp of unoiled hinges. The place comprised two rooms, both empty. I guessed one was the store chief's office, and the second part a rest room. This latter contained two objects; a mouldering dartboard and the remains of an old "Tortoise", coal stove. Holes in the wall indicated that there had once been some sort of cooker and a sink. A further door led into a urinal, the bowl still in place and next to it a latrine, with an overhead cistern and a rusty dangling pull chain. Somewhat lacking in privacy, I thought. I was about to turn round when something caught my eye. My lamp revealed writing on the wall and a crude and blatantly pornographic cartoon. The writing was two doggerel verses.

Georgie did his little shimmy
And now he's up before the Jimmy.

I smiled. The *Jimmy*, in this context, would have been the First Lieutenant. This officer was the second-in-command of the base. Basically, his function was to see that the whole flotilla ran like a well-oiled machine and that the Navy's beloved standards were upheld. Not an enviable task with a wild polyglot crowd like Flotilla Sixty Six. Georgie had probably overstayed his shore leave and had been carried back to base drunk. I shone my torch on the second couplet.

Double six have done their bit
Now Churchill's dropped us in the Shit
So when as next we goes to sea
We'll take a little liberty

God alone knew what that meant. Obscure, and rather cryptic, for a normal seaman's grouse.

I was pleased to be out in the sunlight again. That munitions cave was a depressing place and it had unsettled me. I knew I was walking on ground that had been my father's, a part of his life of which I knew nothing. Stoneman had asked me if I wanted the main doors opened. I could see no useful purpose for this gloomy cave in my scheme of things. Instead, I asked him to make a wicket door in the hole we had entered and to put a lock on it.

It was interesting to see Hooder return to normal the moment we surfaced into fresh air. 'Wonderful commercial possibilities,' he boomed. 'We can make a museum – Second World War theme show.'

Simon must have had a talk with Emma. Her attitude to me was much more like her usual self. I was more relieved by this than I can say. Emma was all I had in the world, or rather the only thing in my life that mattered. She and Simon sailed at twelve thirty, ideally timed to catch the west going tide round Portland Bill.

'We're going to Brixham,' Emma told me. 'Then we'll sail back next week and leave the boat here.'

All was quiet by one o'clock. I left Mick in charge of the office and walked up the village street to find Laura. I knew this alleged lunch break was going to be difficult. It had been grossly insulting of me to accuse her of an ulterior motive for last night and she had every justification for being furious. I had blundered my way into a very tight corner and charm alone was never going to work with this lady.

Laura was in her garden. She had set up a picnic table with a sunshade. She waved me to a chair, and without saying a word, vanished indoors. I remembered this little patch of light and shade from the day I had first met her. In days gone by it must have been a vegetable patch; a few yards of imported topsoil protected from the salt wind by a stone wall. That Laura was a gifted gardener was clear. This little square was a delight; a tiny lawn surrounded by borders and sweet smelling shrubs. I wished I knew the names; years at sea had left a gap in my education that needed mending.

She reappeared carrying a laden tray. 'Orange juice for you,' she said. 'Too much booze is your problem. I assume that's what made you a bear with a sore head this morning.' She set a plate of sandwiches in front of me. 'Now, what's all this about smugglers in the harbour last night?'

CHAPTER 18

At least I now knew who Eriksen was. For the first time Laura had been willing to talk, although when it came to the point, she knew very little. She suggested I see Harry at the pub which was what I had intended doing anyway. However before seeing him I had a better idea.

'I hope we trust each other now,' said Laura.

'I hope so too, but trust is two way. Why, in the first place, did you hold out on me about Eriksen? Why should I trust you? What else are you concealing from me?'

I thought I might have roused her ire again, but she only smiled sweetly. 'I promise there's nothing concerning the harbour that I haven't told you.'

'Maybe, but you know things about my father and 1946.'

Now she was annoyed. 'How can I know anything about your father? I wasn't even born then. They used to talk at home about him. It was always Commander Wilson, but you say he was a Captain?'

'An MTB flotilla was a commander's post. He was made captain later and given a shore job, but it didn't last. He seems to have left the Navy under a cloud and my mother says it all stems from this bloody village.'

'Peter, aren't you being a bit obsessive? All these people are dead and gone. I could suggest you get yourself a life.'

'In the pub, the other night, just before Roy Gulley was killed...' I paused and glared at her.

'I wasn't there, but I've heard of nothing else from Carol for days,' she interrupted.

'Just before Roy Gulley was killed, he admitted taking part in the murder of Arthur Rocastle, and then he said to me, "your father was as deep in the shit as any of us", or words to that effect. Now do you understand?'

'Well you can rest easy. Your father had no direct connection with any of it. Not the murders anyway.'

'Why are you so certain that Arthur Rocastle was a killer? You heard what that copper, Channing, had to say?'

She was no longer angry. I saw something in her face and eyes that disturbed me. It was a look of intense anguish. For a few seconds the abrasive self-confident Laura was no more.

'Peter, I'm the oldest of three and Carol is the baby. Fourteen years ago I accidentally discovered something I wasn't supposed to.' Incredibly, Laura was weeping, shaking convulsively, clutching her head in her hands. It was so uncharacteristic that I could not believe what I was seeing. I was horrified and deeply embarrassed.

I pulled a large handkerchief from my pocket. 'Here, take this, it's clean. I haven't used it.' I admit I am not adept at soothing tearful females and certainly not this one. My instinct was to run, but not yet; I guessed was about to discover something.

'Sorry Peter, I shouldn't do this, it's not me.' She forced a smile.

'I'm not going to pry,' I said, 'but if it would help to talk…'

'No I can't, not about this.' She sniffed. 'Carol doesn't know, she must never know. She's not like me, I have no illusions about the human race. Sorry, I don't suppose I'm making sense.'

'Are you saying that Carol is too immature to be told some family secret. If so I think you're wrong.'

She shook her head. 'Peter, this is for your ears only, you are not to repeat it to Brian Byrne. I want you to promise that on your word of honour.'

'You have it. If you take me on trust, there's no way I will talk to anyone.'

'Good, I appreciate that.' She sat for a moment staring ahead, inscrutable. 'I know Arthur didn't kill Margaret; I'm not completely thick. Her killer was never caught. Those men shouldn't have killed Arthur; I don't condone lynching. That's all I'm prepared to tell you and I've said more than I should.'

'Laura, either he was the killer or he wasn't. You're talking contradictions. If he didn't kill Margaret, someone else did?'

'Arthur died,' her voice was barely audible. 'Margaret's murderer was never brought to justice, and now he never can be.'

'Because Duddlestone will protect him come what may?' I was scathing.

She shook her head. 'No, Duddlestone will keep its secrets because the truth would destroy all of us – maybe you as well.'

Harry let me into the De Gullait Arms, via the back entrance, that led directly into his living quarters.

'I've a visitor,' he said. 'You've met him before.' He pointed to the man sitting drinking a cup of coffee. It was the "troll", the one I'd so named on the night of the brawl in the bar.

Upon leaving Laura, I had had gone straight to my office and put a call through to my mother. Once more she filled the airwaves with high drama that I could have done without, but I did learn a little – not much, but enough to make up my mind. I made a second call, this time to Harry.

'So you are Eriksen,' I addressed the troll. 'I gather you served under my father. I've been warned about a Norwegian.'

'Who warned you?' The little man had a pleasant voice and no discernible foreign accent.

'My mother. I've spoken to her on the phone today. She remembers a Norwegian called Eriksen and she says he was trouble.'

This was a slight exaggeration. Mother had said nothing of the sort, though she did remember a Sub Lieutenant Eriksen. She hadn't voiced an opinion, only a lengthy silence and that tongue clicking sound that I knew was a sign of disapproval.

'Your mother is still alive?'

'Yes, very much so.'

'Ah,' the little man smiled. 'The lovely Irena. We envied your father. I think we were all a little in love with her.'

I was momentarily speechless. The notion of Mother, now arthritic and over seventy as a femme fatale, took a leap of imagination I couldn't cope with.

'Some of us went to their wedding,' said Eriksen. 'It wasn't done as we would have liked.'

'Why not?'

'It was in a grubby little registry office in Bournemouth. All low key – no guard of honour – you know, officers in full dress, crossed swords.'

I could understand. This had been more than a wedding, it was an act of defiance to the Navy establishment.

I tried to explain. 'They were both in the Service. A Royal Navy commander wasn't supposed to marry a junior-rate Wren.'

'We know all about that,' said Harry. 'It's what turned your old man against the Navy.'

'Led to him founding his own navy,' Eriksen laughed, but Harry did not. I caught a frisson of displeasure as he glanced at the other.

Once again my alarm bells were ringing. 'I'm afraid you've lost me,' I said.

'Yes,' Eriksen was staring at me in a way I didn't like. 'The trouble is, none of us knows how much you've been told.'

‘That is something you’ll have to work out for yourselves,’ I said. Suddenly, I had the feeling of a poker player with a half-decent hand. I knew I had these two old codgers worried.

I changed the subject. ‘Laura says you two play smugglers. She says it’s nothing serious – just putting two fingers to authority. She says you’re a couple of geriatrics who’ve never stopped being small boys. However, importing untaxed white diesel fuel is another matter. So what was all that about?’

Eriksen roared with laughter. ‘I dispute geriatric, but I don’t deny the other bit.’ Again he looked me in the eye. ‘There has always been smuggling on this coast. What we do is what you might call a historical re-enactment. Giving the harbour master a little gift is all part of the tradition.’

‘It’s not part of my tradition. What happens if Customs want to inspect my fuel bills?’

‘That’s hardly likely.’

I had to admit that was true, but it was still an unwanted gift that I could have managed without.

Eriksen continued. ‘It is not Mrs Tapsell’s opinion that concerns me. We have been wondering if your arrival here is really such a coincidence.’

Good, I thought, you’re worried. ‘Look, my wife left me, my company fired me. I was willing to take any job offered and it just so happened, one was offered here.’

‘By Paul Hooder?’ Eriksen lifted an eyebrow.

‘No, I was head-hunted by United Marinas. Hooder’s an important share holder, but he didn’t recruit me.’

‘Coincidence, and yet more coincidence,’ said Eriksen.

‘Rubbish. Before last week, I didn’t even know this was the Double Six base. I always assumed it was in the main harbour at Portland.’

Harry and Eriksen exchanged glances. ‘All right,’ said the latter. ‘You know, you really are very like your father, and for that reason alone we believe you.’

‘I don’t give a sod if you believe me or not. Why shouldn’t you anyway – what could I have to hide?’

‘Who knows?’ said Eriksen. ‘We all have a few secrets hidden.’

‘Exactly, like this game of smugglers. I do not like being made a monkey of so that little charade will stop. You will tell me now what is in this illicit cargo that you’re so keen not to be found with?’

‘Well, I’m not a terrorist and I deplore drugs and you’d better believe that.' The little man glared at me. 'There is nothing illicit. I go to Cherbourg and buy legitimate goods for my own use and for that of my friends. I drop these goods in sealed containers and they are recovered by our friends in the military. The fuel was straight from my main tank.'

'So, Laura's right, little boy's games.'

'Maybe, but what harm is done? Harry and I gain a few cases of good wine, and there's some nice Belgian beer for the sergeant's mess.'

'Tell me this, if *Persephone* is your boat, you never paid for her by smuggling a few crates of lager.'

'Your right there,' said Harry. 'Magnus owns the yard that built her.'

I was staggered. 'You own Omega Yachts?'

'I'm the majority shareholder, but it's only a sideline.'

'Christ, what's your mainline?'

'The holiday industry. I'm the chairman of Engel Nordsk Dampskipsselskap…'

I was aware of my mouth sagging open. I felt my face flush with anger. 'You,' I half stood, 'you're the fucking bastard that fired me.'

'Really?' he looked surprised.

'Does the name *Northern Defender* mean anything?'

Eriksen's face puckered. 'Yes, container ship – out of Southampton on the South American run.' He looked at me intently. 'I do remember some trouble among her crew.'

'Eight months ago I was her master. I was forced to take a first officer I didn't want. The fact that she was a woman is material only in so far as you wanted me to foist her on a Muslim crew. I am a victim of fucking political correctness and I resent it. If you're the bloody chairman, why did you refuse to see me?'

My fury, simmering for months, was not eased by the patronising smile on Eriksen's face; but for his age I would have hit him.

'For a start,' he said. 'I am not the chairman of the cargo carrying side of the line. The man you are talking about is my brother-in-law, Jens Anderssen.'

I tried to re focus. 'Come to think of it, the name was Anderssen.' I was not to be deterred. 'What do you do then?'

'As I said, I'm in the holiday trade. My division of the company does cruises.' He smiled. 'You should go on one, Captain. Every time I've seen you, I form the impression that you are a little overstressed.'

'I am not bloody stressed.' I was seething, and this irritating little bugger was still smirking.

'Of course not – of course not,' he replied soothingly.

Words fail me in trying to recall my state of mind. Life wasn't like this; these coincidences were so unlikely, as to be plain silly. I should be in some surreal dream from which I could awake if I wanted.

'May I be the first to apologise,' Eriksen spoke quietly. 'I do recall the board meeting when we discussed the *Northern Defender*. You see, Wilson is a not unusual name. I never connected you with my old captain. Please understand I revered your father, we all did; we would have followed him anywhere. Had I known who you were, I would have intervened and we might have acted differently.'

'I suppose so.' I was on the defensive. Eriksen was a difficult man to quarrel with.

'I think we did feel we were behaving shabbily,' he shrugged. 'In Scandinavia it is not a good thing to cross the feminist lobby.'

I left the pub at five fifteen. Eriksen, or Magnus as I had agreed to call him, had been reasonable. In fact he had no choice but accept my ultimatum. From now on, smuggling activities in Old Duddlestone harbour would cease.

Solving this mystery hadn't really helped. Duddlestone contained a dozen other conundrums, and disquietingly they all seemed connected to Captain James Wilson, VC, RN.

That evening I cooked myself a three-course supper in *Stormgoose's* galley. Then I poured myself half a tumbler of scotch, put Schubert on the stereo system and settled down to read the Arthur Rocastle dossier. These papers, that Brian Byrne had given me, had been sitting unread in the chart table drawer. I hadn't touched them: I hadn't wanted to because truthfully I was frightened of what I might find.

The first photocopy was a trial report from Winchester Crown Court, November 1946. It was the era of capital punishment. The prospect of a good hanging gave press and public a ghoulish appetite for murder trials. In these days it would be sex scandals in high places.

COURT SENSATION
ROCASTLE ACQUITTED ON ORDERS OF THE JUDGE
PUBLIC REBUKE FOR PROSECUTION

Apparently the prosecution's case had been so flimsy that they had thrown in the towel in the first half-hour and offered "no evidence".

Mr Justice Venner-Harris had delivered a blistering rebuke to the prosecuting counsel, in which he encompassed the popular press and, unusually for those times, the police. It was a devastating piece of old-world oratory that must have blown its targets into oblivion. I wished I had been there to hear it.

ACQUITTED MURDER SUSPECT FOUND HANGED
POLICE CLOSE DORSET VILLAGE

This was the first item in a bulging file of photocopied newspaper clippings. It told me nothing that I had not already heard from Byrne. The police had suspected foul play. They had swamped the village for a fortnight and questioned over one hundred people. The press had speculated about "early arrests". Then the reports had gradually fizzled out. Towards the end, I found a clipping that made me sit up and take notice. It was a statement by the Navy authorities at Old Duddlestone Harbour. It told of the Navy's "comprehensive investigation" among its own personnel. "The Navy is satisfied that there is no involvement by any member of His Majesty's Service in the tragic events that have occurred in New Duddlestone". The spokesman was one Lieutenant Eriksen.

At the bottom of the envelope was a photograph. It was a group of men, mostly middle-aged and elderly. The picture was mounted on a piece of stiff card and on this was written, *War Ag workers. Rabbit clearance party. September 1945. Committee Supervisor. E. Rocastle Esq.*

The names of the group had been carefully inked in on the photo itself. Mr Rocastle was a stout man, wearing a bowler hat, breeches and a black waistcoat. So this was Laura, Carol and Ian's grandfather. More important to me; my father had given him Honeycritch Farm.

In the picture was one solitary youth, Arthur Rocastle. I had already guessed this and I hardly needed the neatly written name against his figure. There was nothing distinctive about him, just a very ordinary teenage boy, dressed in shabby farm clothes and wearing a flat cap. He stared back at the camera with an oddly enigmatic expression. In his right hand was what appeared to be a gallon tin of paint, and over his left shoulder was a long stick with, of all things, a large tablespoon bound to the top with tape.

I pushed the papers back in the envelope and returned it to the drawer. I had survived an eventful twenty-four hours. What I needed was a full night's sleep; tomorrow was another day. Somewhere my mobile phone was ringing. I groped under my jacket, and among the discarded items on my bunk I found the wretched thing, glared at it, and then answered.

'Peter, sorry to trouble you so late, but I think there's something you should know.' It was Stanley Bowler.

'Hello Stan, another five minutes and I'd have been dreaming.'

'I've just come from the police station in Poole. There's been an arrest. The police are questioning Steve Gulley for the murder of his father.'

CHAPTER 19

Now it was Sunday morning, the day I was committed to taking Carol Stoneman and her boy sailing. The weather was perfect: warm with clear skies and a gentle southwesterly breeze. Despite this, I fervently wished I could put off the trip for at least a month.

The night with Laura troubled me; by God I was going to pay for that. What an idiot, to allow myself to fall for a torrid one-night stand with a woman I didn't much like and, worse, a close work colleague. I was supposed to be a responsible middle-aged man, working in a responsible management post. I had behaved like some young sea apprentice relieving himself into the first available whore. No doubt half Duddlestone knew of my misspent night and the other half would learn about it tomorrow. Worse, much worse, my behaviour had offended my daughter.

At least the minds of the village gossips were, for now, wholly concentrated by the arrest of Steve Gulley. That slob revolted me. What form of dehumanised scum would kill their own father? It wasn't as if the killing was some spur of the moment brawl. No, Gulley had murdered his father in cold blood. He had mixed a deadly poison and watched him die. Seconds later he had tried to drown me. I had not the slightest doubt that the man who had pushed me over the dock wall was Gulley. He must have been consumed by frenzy because I would not have expected the man to have the speed and fitness that my attacker had shown.

Unbelievably, Laura had returned to her state of denial. 'No, Peter, you don't know what you're talking about. Steve loved his dad.' Her expression was soft, almost wistful. 'I know he's a waster; Roy and he were two of a kind, but I grew up with Steve and all the other kids in the village. Whoever killed Roy, it wasn't Steve.'

'In this case,' I said, 'I prefer to back the judgement of the police.'

Tommy came running along the pontoon and I helped him over the rail; his mother followed carrying a small sports bag. 'I've brought some extra clothes in case it turns cold,' she said.

That was sensible, and I was pleased she had remembered. There may be a heat wave ashore but temperature on the water is always a few degrees colder. I fetched an old lifejacket of Emma's and fitted it on Tommy, along with a safety line.

‘Stay in the cockpit at all times,’ I told him. ‘If I want you to help me up forward, then you clip on that safety line.’

‘Why?’

‘Then if you fall over the side you stay with the ship. Your mother doesn’t want to lose you.’

I started the engine and headed for the open sea. As we cleared the harbour wall I felt my spirits lift. I had cut the link with the shore. For a few hours I could forget Duddlestone. I could be an ordinary humdrum yachtsman, taking a remarkably pretty girl for a jaunt on a sunny summer’s day.

‘Where shall we sail to?’ I asked.

‘Can we go to Lulworth Cove?’ asked Carol.

‘Of course, it was the place I had in mind, and it’ll be an adventure for me too – I’ve never been in there.’

Lulworth lies a few miles to the west of Duddlestone, but the wind had swung a further ten degrees; we were going to have to work our way against it. I explained to the others about beating to windward.

‘We make our way along in a series of zigzags,’ I said.

‘I know,’ said Tommy. ‘Our granddad’s boats used to do that – then they got engines put in.’

‘Who wants engines?’ I laughed. ‘Stink boats we call those. Sailing’s much more fun and ten times the skill.’

Lulworth is a natural feature; a little circle of water scooped out of the cliffs. An easy anchorage to enter on a day like this, but dangerous with a strong wind from the south.

‘What about the firing range?’ Carol asked.

‘No shooting today, I rang up and checked.’ Behind the downs was an artillery range. Rogue shots had been known to clear the hills and fall in the sea.

Carol was steering, concentrating on the wind indicator at the masthead. She wore white shorts and her long legs were even more tanned than the other day. She had even painted her toenails a striking shade of purple. She sat, hand on the tiller, with a set expression, the tip of her tongue poked between her teeth; the whole effect was wonderfully erotic. I deliberately expunged any such thoughts and set about looking at the chart. I found a buoy marking a wreck about a mile from where we were, and I wanted to spot it.

‘Mind how you go,’ I said. ‘Your jib’s flapping – ease off a bit.’

‘Sorry,’ she grinned and shook her head.

‘Don’t worry, you’re doing fine,’ I reassured her. ‘Tell me about that wreck – what’s down there?’

'Lots of lobsters, the boats come from Poole and Weymouth to catch them.' She was thinking about fishing of course. Lobsters tended to breed around shipwrecks.

'How long has there been a wreck there?'

'It went down at the end of the war.'

'Really, was it a Navy ship?' I was becoming interested.

'No, it was a cargo carrying ship; American – she hit a mine and sank. One of the Duddlestone MTBs took off the crew.'

'Big ship, d'you know? I'm interested because that's my trade?'

'Harry says she was a "Liberty ship". Does that help?'

'They were mass-produced in the States – hundreds of them. I'm told they were pretty basic, although I never sailed in one. Say, what's the matter?'

'Peter, do you have to talk about war? It's such a lovely day.'

I met her eyes and smiled ruefully. 'Sorry, I'm an unreconstructed male warmonger – you've warned me about that before.'

She smiled back. 'They say you played the piano brilliantly the other night.'

'Who's they?' Suddenly I didn't want to talk about, "the other night".

'Everyone, I wish I'd been there but I couldn't, not that night.'

The talk was heading down a path I didn't need. Luckily Carol's concentration had lapsed to the point where the ship was sailing well off the wind and away from our planned destination. I called Tommy from the cabin, where he was exploring, and let him have a go on the helm.

Half an hour later we were there; in sight of Lulworth Cove. I could see the dip in the downs and below it the little cluster of houses.

'Sails down, it's engine from now on.' I started to roll up the jib.

'Can't we sail in?' Carol asked.

'No good, I haven't been in here before, and I'm told the wind's flukey – all over the place in the entrance. We've got to watch out for rocks.'

'Rocks?' Tommy gasped. He looked part apprehensive, and part excited.

'There's a line of them on the westward side. Nothing to worry about, we're going in bang down the middle of the fairway.'

Stormgoose motored sedately through the narrow entrance. Before us the still waters of the cove opened up. I put the engine in neutral and gave the tiller to Carol. I went to the bows and lowered the anchor gently to the bottom, which I could just see through the clear water. 'OK, put her in reverse,' I called. Carol moved the gear lever as told. 'Now open the throttle and try to steer a straight line backwards.' We were using our propeller in reverse to dig in the anchor. We were only here for a picnic, but I liked to do the proper drill.

'I can't,' Carol squeaked and let go of the tiller. The force of the propeller wash against the rudder had jerked it from her hands.

'Sorry,' I called. 'I should have warned you. You can put the gear in neutral now.'

I took a quick transit with a bush on the skyline. All secure, we were safely anchored. I went back to the cockpit and switched off the motor.

I said nothing. I wanted the others to experience one of the most magical moments that life can deliver. The moment when a small boat swings to her anchor, in a new setting, at the end of a voyage. It really didn't matter if that voyage had been a little more than six miles. The magic is always the same and it never fails. We could hear the sounds of the ship, the bubbling of the water against her hull and the sounds on shore – a car descending the road to the village, children's voices, high pitched, excited and happy.

I made a check of the time. Just right, slack water at low tide. 'Who's for a swim before lunch?'

I lowered the stern ladder, the same one that had rescued Brian Byrne. This time we could use it for its real purpose. I dived in and swam round the ship and climbed aboard again.

'OK, you two can go now – I'll stay here and watch. Don't swim more than twenty feet from the ship.'

Tommy jumped in feet first and swam vigorously up and down. Carol lowered herself slowly down the ladder and gingerly put a toe in the water. I admired her turquoise, figure hugging swimsuit. Apart from a slight trace of former baby bulge, her body was more than a match for her sister's. With a grimace she let go and slid into the water.

We ate our lunch in the cockpit. I had filled the ship's cold-box with all the goodies I remembered from the days when my daughter was ten years old. I put up a little folding table with a white cloth, and spread out the platefuls of crisps, buttered rolls, sauce bottles, cakes and sweet biscuits. I screwed the mini-barbecue to the stern rail and we grilled sausages under the burning sun. It could easily have been the Mediterranean or the Caribbean. Carol had lathered a grumbling Tommy with high-factor sunscreen while I rigged our cockpit awning over the boom. We relaxed, almost, but not quite. I could not forget the troubles of Duddlestone a few miles away on the map, but still a different world, and my guilty conscience was becoming active. I could not forget that I had deceived Carol, by sleeping with her sister.

It should have been our perfect moment to ignite a relationship, but I could only feel this glass barrier between us, and I didn't know how to demolish it. Suddenly I hated Duddlestone. I hated its petty conspiracies and deceits, its ancient feuds and its odious people. Above all, I hated Laura Tapsell who, in a fit of spite against her own sister, had played on my weakness. I believed she had set out to satisfy her own lust and at the same time humiliate me; and by God she had succeeded. And I hated my own father. I was thinking the unthinkable, emotions were boiling to the surface; emotions I had suppressed almost all my life. Why had he killed himself? What right did he have to inflict such trauma on my childhood? What right had he to ruin my mother's life, when she had already suffered enough tragedy? On one thing I was resolved. I was not leaving Old Duddlestone until I had found the answers.

'Peter … Peter, wake up.' I opened my eyes. Carol sitting opposite, was looking at me with an odd lopsided smile.

'Sorry,' I said, 'I was miles away.'

'I was asking if we could use the dinghy?'

'I don't see why not. I'll blow it up.'

The little inflatable dinghy lay lifeless on the cabin top. I fetched the foot pump and began to fill the boat with air.

'Fancy a run ashore?' I asked.

'Yes please,' said Carol. 'We've been here loads of times, but never from the sea. It'll be something for Tommy to tell his friends.'

I dropped the dinghy over the side, climbed in and fitted its tiny outboard motor. It took us three minutes to reach the landing place. I pulled the dinghy above the high water mark and we all three walked up the sloping village street. We did the things that an everyday tripping family would do. We looked at the boats on the shore and bought ice creams from the beach café. Finally, we walked to the top of the hill to look proudly at our ship anchored so tranquilly far below us. It was mid afternoon and we needed to be moving.

We returned to the dinghy in silence, or at least Carol and I did; Tommy ran on ahead. I was feeling utterly miserable. I felt as if something wonderful should have happened. Now the opportunity was passing and would be unlikely to recur. Within hours, Carol would hear about my night with her sister; nothing was secret in

Duddlestone. Failing that Laura would tell her, if only to relish her sister's hurt.

Carol had stopped walking, and was looking at me with that odd smile. Then I told her. I told her the whole story of the house warming party and its aftermath. It hurt; I watched the impact go home and felt wretched. I had spoilt her happy day out, but what else could I do?

Carol had clenched her hands. She stood blinking in the sunlight before she answered. 'That bitch, that evil bitch – thinks she can have any man…' She spoke quietly, her eyes on Tommy a few yards down the hill.

Suddenly I felt a new resolve. 'Carol, Laura doesn't always have to win.'

'She thinks she can have any man. She always thinks she's better than me.' Her eyes flashed. 'But I'm the one who has a son.'

CHAPTER 20

I am not sure if Tommy noticed the change in atmosphere. Probably he did, but kept the knowledge to himself. I imagine he had long learned to insulate himself from the turbulent adult world. In other circumstances our return trip would have been a delight. The sun was warm and a sea breeze had set in from the south. *Stormgoose* revelled in it. I let Carol take the helm while I hoisted the full size Genoa jib. Now the little yacht's racing pedigree began to show. At one point the speed indicator in the cockpit clocked up ten knots, as we gently surfed on some of the larger waves. Tommy yelled in delight and I think Carol took some memories with her. It would have been the perfect conclusion to what should have been a perfect day. I glanced at Carol surreptitiously. She was very quiet, speaking hardly a word throughout. I had expected anger and animosity, knowing I deserved nothing else. Her attitude was different and difficult to describe. She had the look of one whose life had been a series of disappointments. What a good pair we were, Carol and I, two of life's natural born losers.

We were now within sight of Old Duddlestone. I suppressed my gloomy thoughts as I turned to the business of lowering sail and motoring into the harbour.

Thank goodness Laura was not there. Mick was anxious to be home. He had no idea where Laura was; she had left in her car an hour ago. At least that avoided a public dockside cat fight between the two sisters. I walked with Carol to her car. I noticed it was a battered ten-year-old Astra, a contrast to Laura's smart new Peugeot. The difference seemed to symbolise the pair of them.

Carol smiled, mumbled some formal words of thanks and drove away. I felt an awful emptiness; an overwhelming sense of what might have been.

I did my duty and made a quick round of the visiting boats. Everybody seemed content. I felt envious of the happy family crews sitting down to a quiet evening meal and a good night's sleep. I slumped down at my office desk and buried my head in my hands. For a few minutes I was tempted. Despite my resolution this day, I was tempted to run, to send my resignation to United Marinas and then sail away and never see this place again. I noticed the little light on my answerphone was winking. For want of anything else to do I pressed the play-button.

'Peter, this is Stanley Bowler and the time is one thirty. Could you ring me at your convenience. I need to talk to you with respect to the Steven Gulley case. My firm has been asked to act for the defence. I feel you could help define some of the facts.'

Oh did he indeed? I was fairly sure I didn't want to talk to Bowler about Steve Gulley. I cared only that the murderous thug receive the longest stretch in HM prison that the law could contrive. Defence solicitor Stan could go to hell as far as I was concerned. I picked up a book from the desk and hurled it across the room. It thudded with a metallic clunk against the filing cabinet and fell shattered to the floor. I walked across and picked it up. My only copy of the almanac and tide tables ruined. This was plain stupid. I stumped outside and went for a walk.

It was half past four and the midsummer sun was still beating down. I was walking in a daze, hardly caring where I went. Waking from my reverie I found myself at the top of the chine looking towards Honeycritch Farm. I could visualise Carol's face. Perhaps I was beginning to see what an attractive face it was; soft round features and melting dark eyes. It was a trusting face, and it seemed that the trust had been too many times betrayed.

Abruptly I turned from the path and struck away to the left, uphill and towards the summit of the downs. It was a hot sweaty climb and I felt in the mood for it. Sheep grazed on the slopes and the grass was dry and cropped short. Little tufts of wool clung to the thorn bushes, though the sheep newly-shorn looked uncomfortable and rather comic. Rabbit holes were visible under the bushes and some of their inhabitants scuttled away as I approached. I reached the crest and took a breather. I could no longer see the harbour but I had a stunning clear view, all the way to Portland in the west, and east across the sea to the faraway shape of the Needles and the Isle of Wight. I knew I was near the spot where we intended to set up a harbour day mark.

An object about fifty yards in front puzzled me. It was a mushroom, a very large mushroom. This one was no product of the fairies, it was modern, a metre in height and made of pre-cast concrete. It stood on four legs between which were fixed cast iron metal grilles. These were aged and rusty, but substantial, and they were held in place with heavy hexagonal bolts. So well built was this structure that it had been left unfenced, and the sheep had grazed right to the edge of the concrete plinth on which it was set. For a moment I was baffled, then I remembered; the ventilation shafts above the Navy ammunition store. I looked around and saw a second one, and a third and two more all in a line across the pasture. They stopped at a point where the next dip in the downs occurred. That was logical because I knew it to be the gap through which our existing entry road passed. I walked along the line examining each in turn, and then I had a surprise. Another group of similar mushrooms extended on the flat land the other side of the dip. I looked back over where I had been. The last of these mushrooms must be a good half a mile from the entrance in the cliff face. This could only mean the network of tunnels under the hill was vast; far larger than anything I had envisaged. I wondered if it was safe to explore and what it might reveal.

I was about to turn round and walk back to the harbour when I noticed a vehicle, a Land Rover; not one of the fancy new breed but a workmanlike long-wheelbase model. I wondered who this might be. In two brisk walking minutes I had reached it. The Land Rover was almost new, very shiny and had inscribed on its door: *Southampton University Palaeontology Survey*. It was parked on the edge of a hollow, some two hundred yards in length though rather less in width. Within it I could hear a scraping noise; the sound of a hand shovel and the clink of metal on hard rock. I walked to the entrance and looked in. Ten yards away was a slim girl with tangled blonde hair. She was on her knees scraping the ground with a trowel. Her elbows were stained with dirt and a film of dust covered her body, which was naked, apart from the skimpiest bikini I had seen away from the beaches of Rio. This bizarre vision of loveliness had me temporarily rooted to the spot. The girl must have heard me because she put down the trowel and turned to look.

'Hi, you must be Peter Wilson, I'm Babs.'

I made an effort to remember my manners and stop blatantly ogling. 'Yes I am. How did you know?'

'Laura pointed you out the other day – outside the pub in New Duddlestone.'

'I never saw you.'

'We were passing in the car. Laura said you looked in an evil temper.'

'Oh, did she.' I was not pleased.

'Don't take it to heart. I'm sure you weren't – that's just Laura.'

'OK, understood. Now, Babs, what's going on here?'

'We're reviving the work abandoned in 1939. The initial reports were very promising.' She stood up and looked around. 'I say Charlie!' she yelled. 'Over here – we've a visitor.'

Charlie appeared round a corner. I recognised him as the dinosaur man from Laura's party. This time he was dressed in nothing more than a sun hat and a pair of floppy shorts.

'Peter isn't it? Welcome to our dig. She here,' he indicated Babs, 'is Doctor Barbara Stent, my partner in life and my boss in academe.'

'Very pleased to meet you,' I said. 'Have you found any dinosaurs?'

'Not yet,' said Charlie, 'but the signs are here. All this area was linked to the Isle of Wight in those times.'

'What times are we talking about?'

'Oh, seventy million years ago, give or take a millennium or two.'

'That's when they all died?'

'We think so, but the precise reason is still conjecture.'

'Is this military land?' I asked.

'Was until six months ago. It's part of the property Doctor Hooder bought. You know him I suppose?'

'I'm afraid I do. He owns the harbour.'

'He's been to see us twice,' said Charlie. 'He's only interested in the commercial possibilities.'

'What Charlie means is that Hooder wants our research to make him a few quick bucks,' said Babs.

'I can believe that,' I said. 'He probably wants you to create Jurassic Park and me to run it. No thank you.'

I looked down into the hollow. It was much deeper than I had first thought. It contained a couple of stone structures that were certainly not Jurassic. The nearest was an odd little building, made of stone slabs, that reminded me of a Scottish Pict dwelling. On level ground at the bottom of the working stood a proper building. Its roof had long since gone but the rest of it had weathered well.

'What used to happen here?' I asked.

'Stone quarry,' said Charlie. 'Down there's below our work line. Won't be any remains.'

'What are the buildings?'

'The big one housed a steam engine at one period – drove a conveyor and some sort of stone crusher.'

'And the little diddy house?'

'Shelter for the workers to brew up. All the quarries round here have those.' Babs had picked up a small bath towel and was beginning to wipe the dust and sweat from her shapely form. The sight was making me feel uncomfortable. I looked at my watch, it was nearly half past five. It was time I headed to home and duty. I said my farewells and was invited to come again.

'I don't suppose you get too many visitors up here?' I remarked.

'Apart from Hooder,' said Babs, 'and that Jolene.'

'Who is she?'

'Scruffy Australian hippy type – been hanging around for weeks. She comes up here sometimes.'

'I know her,' I replied. 'My boatman, Mick, is an Aussie and he reckons she's a fraud.'

'And there's that young kid,' said Charlie. 'Got a little mountain bike.'

I was hot and dusty and looking forward to a shower. My walk had done some good, although I still felt miserable about my parting with Carol. I saw a car parked by the office. My spirits sank, it was Stan Bowler's Rover. The man himself was standing outside admiring the view.

'Did you get my message?' he asked.

Stan is not the kind of person one can easily quarrel with, but I was determined to resist. 'I got it and the answer is, no.'

Stan fished in his pocket and pulled out a pipe. He filled it from a round tobacco tin and lit it. A plume of smoke drifted away on the breeze. The smell was pungent but not unpleasant.

'Would you care to tell me why?' he asked.

'Simple, you're the defence solicitor. OK, you've a job to do, but don't expect my help. I want Gulley put away.'

'Why?'

'Why? For God's sake he killed his father and then he had a bloody good try at killing me!'

Stan nodded and inhaled deeply from his pipe. 'Sounds to me, Peter, as if you've gone native.'

'What does that mean?'

'Spoken like a true Duddlestonian. You remind me of Laura.'

'Oh come on…'

'No, you listen.' Stan Bowler swung round to face me. 'You want to believe that Steve Gulley killed his father, because that would be a neat and tidy solution. You're not interested in facts. You're only interested in what you find convenient to believe.'

'It's got to be true.'

'Why has it got to be true?'

'Because the police say so. They must have something pretty conclusive to charge him.'

'Just like Arthur Rocastle,' he spoke very quietly but with a force I couldn't ignore. 'And by the way, my client is being held for questioning. The decision to charge him has not been made.'

'I understood he was definitely charged and the case was all sewn up. Laura came up with some nonsense of course.'

'What was that?'

'Oh something about Gulley being fond of his father. I didn't take much notice.'

'Perhaps you should have.' Stan's tone had not altered.

I looked him in the eye. 'Do you know something I don't?'

'Having spoken to my client at length, I am certain he is not guilty. The police have no conclusive evidence to link him to the crime scene apart from one article of clothing.'

'Then he was there – end of story.'

'Certainly the jacket was there, but it was a warm night and nobody recollects seeing him wearing or carrying it.'

'Where was this jacket – I never saw it.'

'It was hanging on a nail in your gear store.'

I felt an awful sinking feeling. My first instinct was to keep quiet, but I couldn't do that, it wouldn't be right. 'There was a jacket hanging up as you say, but it'd been there all along. I didn't know whose it was, it could have been there for weeks.'

'Good, I hoped it would be something like that.'

'I suppose you'll want me to tell the police?' I said heavily. 'But it doesn't mean I think Gulley's innocent – there'll be other evidence.'

'Peter, I want you to recall very carefully the timing of each of your movements that evening…'

'Don't you even try and suggest I did it,' I said. 'I've witnesses for almost every quarter of an hour.'

'I know, that's the whole point.'

'Sorry, I don't follow.'

Stan's face flickered into just the suspicion of a smile. 'I can't tell you any more, the police might suggest collusion if I did.'

'Come to the point. What do you want from me?'

'We've an appointment at Poole police station tomorrow morning at half past ten. I want you to be there to answer a few questions put by Inspector Channing, but in my presence.'

‘Morning’s my busiest time.’

‘Justice waits for no man, and the police want this matter settled.’

‘All right, I’ll do it, but I need to be back here before midday. You tell them that.’

It was the third time in a month that I’d had to visit this police station; each time had been as a consequence of a Gulley. By the time I arrived at the reception desk I had lost all feeling of charity. Despite anything Stan Bowler might say, I wanted Gulley convicted and put away for life. I would answer whatever fool questions the police wanted to ask but that would be that.

Stan was already there and looked relieved to see me. ‘Glad you came,’ he said. ‘Much better to put the record straight now than have to answer the same questions in open court.’

Inspector Channing had the look of one who had had a sleepless night and an indigestible breakfast. He spent ten minutes making a timetable of my movements on the night of the murder. That my answers failed to please him was obvious. Conversely, Stan looked increasingly smug.

‘Bloody Duddlestone,’ the Inspector muttered as his colleague switched off the tape recorder. ‘We’ll have your statement typed. You can read it and we’d like your signature.’

I agreed, and anyway I had told them all this before. The whole exercise seemed pointless. Now came the surprise.

‘Mr Bowler,’ said Channing. ‘I think we’ll have your client next.’

‘Can Captain Wilson remain?’

‘It’s a bit irregular. All right, yes.’

A short interval passed before a PC appeared escorting Steve Gulley. Steve had visibly changed, it seemed almost as if he had shrunk. He was haggard and even more unshaven than usual. The arrogance was gone. He seemed neither frightened nor defiant, just defeated and listless. A flicker on his face registered as he saw me; the expression faded to a sullen blank. The PC pressed the record button and the Inspector logged the interview time.

‘Steven Gulley, may I remind you that you are still under caution. Think very carefully before you answer. On the night in question, what time did you leave the De Gullait Arms?’

‘I didn’t leave. I was assaulted by that fucking Aussie psycho. Why ain’t you charging ’im?’

‘I’ve told you already,’ said Channing wearily. ‘If you want to make a complaint, go ahead. Now answer.’

‘It were eight thirty, or round abouts of.’

‘What did you do then?’

‘I stays outside and watches.’

‘What happened?’

Gulley glared at me. ‘’Im there comes out wi’ that Carol. Yeah everyone knows as she fancies ’im.’

‘Keep to the point,’ Channing snapped.

‘They gets in ’is car…’

‘Who gets in what car? – be precise please.’

‘I mean Carol gets in Wilson’s car and they drives off.’

‘What did you do then?’

‘I takes me bike and I follows ’em. I knew as they was going to Honeycritch. Heard ’em say so.’

‘Why did you follow them?’

Gulley’s face puckered. ‘Dunno, I was uptight, wanted to get at ’im,’ he jabbed a finger at me. ‘I knows things about ’is Dad. Reckoned I might get back at ’im for what happened in the pub.’

‘All right, you were hoping for a confrontation?’

‘Yeah, my Dad knew things about them Rocastles and Wilson’s old Dad.’

‘Never mind that. What time did you arrive at Honeycritch Farm?’

‘It were nine o’clock. I sees ’em through the window in the kitchen. Carol were doin’ a fry up for ’im –very cosy like.’ Gulley sneered. ‘Then that Laura drives up in ’er posh car,’ his tone had changed to active hatred. ‘She goes in with the little nipper, Tom. Then I ’ears ’em ranting and shouting.’

‘Who was shouting?’

‘Them two bitches. Bitches, and witches, if you asks me.’

‘I’m not asking you. Stick to the questions. What was the next thing that happened?’

‘Mr Wilson comes out and ’e drives off.’

‘Time?’

‘It were just after ten. I could see it on their clock in the kitchen.’

Channing stared long and hard. A subdued Gulley avoided his eye. ‘Print up the statement and get him to sign it.’ He sighed. ‘Steven Gulley, you are released on police bail. You will report here daily before twelve noon.’

If Steve was relieved he didn’t show it. ‘Are you goin’ to get who done it?’

‘My only mission in life at this moment is to catch the person or persons who killed your father.' For the first time Channing looked almost benevolent. 'But you, Steve, are still holding out on me. Think about it. Loyalty to your Dad should count more than loyalty to your so called mates and that bloody village.'

Steve Gulley left the room and the Inspector began to gather up papers.

I was still not happy. 'Look,' I said urgently, 'there's something wrong. The Rocastle kitchen clock is fast. I left the house well before ten. That soldier, Alistair Pickering, clocked me through the guard post at ten past ten. It took me at least a quarter of an hour to drive there from Honeycritch.'

'No good, Captain. Gulley only had his push-bike. There's no way he could have reached Old Duddlestone by your route in much less than forty five minutes, even if he was an Olympic runner.'

'There's Ian Rocastle's testimony as well,' said Stan. 'Ian was sorting sheep in pens, right beside the Duddlestone bridleway. That's the short cut to the harbour. He says no person or vehicle passed him at that time.'

'Can you trust him?' I was worried. 'I like the man, but he's deep in Duddlestone's secrets. He's the master of their "Brotherhood".'

'That doesn't mean a thing,' said Channing. 'Also his wife was with him. Mrs Teresa Rocastle happens to be the daughter of the Lord Lieutenant, and he's a friend of my Chief Constable.'

I finally had to admit defeat. 'Bloody disappointment but…'

Stan intervened. 'I find nothing disappointing in an innocent man walking free.'

I didn't reply. I still had my doubts but obviously this wasn't the time. 'How did Roy Gulley get there? The army says no one drove up their road before me. Ian says nobody went down his track. Anyway Roy wasn't in a fit state to walk, and there were two others at the marina, I saw them.'

'Yes, I know all this,' said Channing wearily. 'I don't like it any more than you do. This isn't police work – it's bloody Agatha Christie.'

Laura was in the harbour office. I told her what had happened.

'That's good,' she said. 'I told you Steve would never harm his father.' She gave me a hard long look. 'Why have you upset Carol, you pig?'

'I didn't want to upset her. I thought it best I clear the air.'

‘You did that all right. You know, last night she hit me – first time ever…’ Laura looked almost pleased.

‘Frankly, I don’t blame her. You’ve probably had it coming for years.’

‘If so, the worm really did turn this time. She went bonkers. Told me I was trying to steal you from under her nose.’

‘In your dreams, woman. Now can we get on with some work?’

‘Sure,’ Laura grinned. ‘By the way, while you were out there was a phone call for you. A rather strident foreign sounding woman –says she’s your mother.’

‘What! Why didn’t you tell me straight away?’

‘I was going to, but you burst in here with all that stuff about Steve, and I’ve only just remembered.’

‘What did she say? Is she ringing back?’

‘I gather she was overseas somewhere?’

‘Yes, South Africa.’

‘Anyway she said to tell you she had a ticket for Heathrow, arriving Wednesday morning, ten o’clock.’

CHAPTER 21

Four times that evening I rang my mother's number in the Cape. Each time there was neither reply nor recorded message. I could think of no reason why she should want to make a long, wearisome and expensive trip to England; let alone to visit a place that had such powerful and unhappy memories. She had given me no details of her journey. No airline name or flight number. Did she want to stay in Duddlestone? I couldn't put her up, although no doubt I could find a hotel in Poole or Swanage. Maybe this was just a holiday trip, a stopover in London, before travelling on to Estonia. I doubted this last idea. Mother had always been adamant that she would never return to Estonia, Russia, or any place east of the Denmark Sound. Suddenly I felt guilty. It was self-centred and selfish of me to see her arrival as an inconvenience. It would be good to see her again and hear news of my step-father and the vineyard. We could talk music, and maybe play some together like the old days.

More important, mother knew about Duddlestone. She knew about my father's incredible land deal with the Rocastles. I guessed she knew many, possibly most, of the secrets of my father's time here. Yes, it would be good to see her again.

Morning saw the arrival of our boat-hoist, or rather a lorry load of steel girders and hydraulic rams.

We had barely finished unloading this gear when another vehicle drove up. It was a Land Rover towing a large RIB, or rigid inflatable boat. The three young men with it hung diffidently around while I signed the lorry driver's ticket. At last I was able to give them my attention.

'We're the Joint Services Sub-Aqua Club and I'm Keith,' said the spokesman. He was a broadly-built young man, with red hair, freckled face and a northern accent. 'We were wondering if we could operate from your quay?'

'I don't see why not,' I said. 'What would you be up to?'

'We want to dive on the wreck out there. It's shallow water and a well-preserved ship – brilliant training ground.'

I was wary. 'Have you permission? It's not a war grave is it?'

'No definitely not. She hit a mine, sank very gracefully, they say – everyone saved.'

'This one would be the Liberty ship?'

'Yes, she had a cargo of motorbikes. The war had ended as well – bloody waste.' Keith shook his head sadly.

I thought long and hard. 'OK, if you can produce your diving certificates and official permission to operate, we'll let you berth here. You'll have to exempt us from liability if you dive within the harbour.'

Keith glanced at his companions. They were all of the same stamp; typical young soldiers or marines. 'Is there somewhere we could store our boat?'

'We haven't started building facilities yet.' I thought for a moment. 'But there is an old wartime torpedo store. It's tunnelled into the cliff up the street. I've been in there, it's cool and dry. You can take a look if you like.'

Mr and Mrs Dunlass were back. *Marietta* had docked at four o'clock. Rita Dunlass had breezed into the office to pay the harbour fees.

'We left the boat in Poole while Mr Dunlass attended his business,' she explained. 'Now we're starting our holiday again.' Ignoring me she turned to Laura and said in a conspiratorial whisper. 'Tell Carol we've had a letter from Jim.'

This time the garrulous Rita had put her foot in it. I saw Laura stiffen, glance nervously at me, and then glare savagely at Rita who put her hand to her mouth. She left without another word, leaving a trail of expensive perfume. Laura was looking sideways at me waiting for a reaction. I stood up and went outside. I wasn't ready for a confrontation but my suspicions were confirmed. George Dunlass had the accent of a local man and Laura had pretended not to know him.

I was about to shut up shop for the day when the sub-aqua boys returned to the slipway in the RIB. I gave them a hand to winch it onto their trailer, and watched as they towed it up the street to park outside the old ammunition store.

'You can't put her in there tonight,' I told them. 'The door's still seized up, but you can have a look inside and see what you think.'

I unlocked the little wicket door we had fitted. The sun was low in the western sky and there was very little light.

'I'll get our spotlight from the truck,' Keith offered. He was back in a trice with a massive halogen battery lantern. It lit the cavern with a dazzling white glare. I could see details of the roof which I had missed before. A little pile of broken chalk and fine dust had fallen from one of the vent shafts. In the roof hung heavy duty electric lamps that looked as good as new. On the wall was an ancient fuse box. I swung the cut-off lever over but nothing happened. Keith pointed the lamp to the far end of the tunnel. There were five smaller branch tunnels and, for the first time, I could read the faded black and white notice boards bolted to the arches.

No 1. Navy gunnery store.
No 2. Army small arms / anti-tank.
No 3. Army armoured.
No 4. Communications way. DRA & medical.
No 5. Army .303 ammunition.

'What's all this lot mean, skipper?' asked Keith.

'War relics,' I said, 'but there's a lot more to this place than I thought. All this army stuff in a Navy base?'

'I'll hazard a guess,' said one of the other lads.

'Go ahead.'

'I've been reading about Old Duddlestone. Sure, the navy had their boats here, but just before D-Day there was a flotilla of landing craft. The whole place was jammed with them, and they had two full-size ships alongside the quay.'

'Dave's our historian,' Keith grinned. 'Say, skipper, can we have a look around?'

'Sure, be my guest.'

The storage tunnels were empty. Everything had been removed apart from a few wooden pallets and similar rubbish. We all commented on how dry the atmosphere was. A cardboard box lay at the far end of one bay. It was still in mint condition. *Cigarettes – three hundred packs. US Govt Property,* read the message on the side. Needless to say its contents had gone.

Tunnel 4. *Communications. DRE and medical,* was different. It was tube-like, about seven foot high, with a rough cement floor and it seemed endless. It was bare apart from a heavy electric conduit in the roof. At intervals we could see glass encased light fittings. Useless, but not needed now we had Keith's massive spotlight. Had it not been for the airshafts in the roof I would have turned back. I wasn't prepared to risk our health with foul air. With the passage hewn from the hard rock there was no danger of a roof fall. We decided to press onward.

The gradient had been rising for some time. I calculated we must be well under the hill by now. I remembered from my walk up top, that the ventilation cowls stretched in a line a long way beyond even this point. I could see another shaft in front of us. This time the light filtering from above was much brighter. I stood underneath the opening in the roof and looked up. Now the concrete cowl was visible and less than thirty feet above us. The gradient had levelled but still the tunnel stretched ahead. We were totally reliant on Keith's light beam and I couldn't see the next shaft. We walked on another hundred yards and then we heard it. Above us was a noise; a slow rumble of sound, part drumming, part drone. It passed and all was still again.

'Heavy motor overhead,' said Dave 'We're under the road.'

'Good God.' I suddenly realised we must have walked well over a quarter of mile and we still hadn't reached the end.

I couldn't make head nor tail of this place. The tunnel seemed an excursion to nowhere: a pointless claustrophobic nightmare, with neither end nor purpose.

'Do you lads want to go on?' I asked dubiously.

'You bet,' grinned Keith and his companions nodded enthusiastically.

'All right,' I said. I had no choice but to agree, Keith had the only lamp. It was easy for these boys, but I was a sailor and I was beginning to crave the open air.

As it happened we reached the end five minutes later. The tunnel finished in a room about ten feet square. Set against the left-hand wall was an iron staircase leading to another gallery above. I tested the first two steps, but like everything else the atmosphere seemed to have left it in perfect preservation. We climbed to the top, I counted twelve steps. Ahead of us was a blank wall of rendered cement. This plastering had been a careless job. We could see where a section of it had fallen the day it was laid. Underneath was a wall of very substantial concrete blocks. So that was that. Keith was shining his lamp on the ground by the top of the steps. He reached down and picked up something.

'Nothing more here,' said Keith. 'Lets go.'

With a relief I cannot properly describe, I stood in sunlight again and breathed like a newly freed prisoner.

'Tell you one thing, skipper,' said Keith. 'We're not the first up there since the war.' He passed me an object held between his fingers. It was a standard black fibre-tip pen. 'Found that on the floor, top of the stairs. It's modern and the ink in it's still good.'

'Are you sure it's not one of ours?'

'No, it was at the top of those steps before we went up there. Saw it in my light as we climbed.'

At last a phone call from my mother. 'What are you playing at – what's going on?' I asked.

'Nothing happens. I am coming to visit you at Duddlestone. I have an invitation.'

'What invitation?'

'The annual reunion of the Flotilla Sixty Six Association. I am an honorary vice-president. Did you not know that?'

'No I didn't.'

'Well I am. They send me newsletters.'

'But why this sudden nostalgia for the war? Every time I tried to talk about it you used to bite my head off.'

'Peter, many bad things happened at that place. Perhaps there is some hidden purpose in this. If so, I think I should be with you.'

'Of course there isn't. I told you I took the first job I was offered.'

'Peter, I am not arguing with you. Next Friday I shall attend this reunion. It will be interesting – most interesting. The pirate crew assembled again, but no Captain Hook.'

CHAPTER 22

The arrivals area at Heathrow terminal was crowded with American and Japanese tourists. Mother's flight had already touched down; somewhere ahead of me she would be passing through customs. I strained my eyes searching the colourful throng; then I saw her. She stood out from the crowd, as she always had, walking with that purposeful limp. I ran to her and we embraced. I hadn't seen her for nearly two years. I released her and stood back while we stared at each other. Mother never seemed to age, she had looked the same ever since she passed fifty. No, she hadn't aged, only shrivelled a little under the southern sun.

'Well, what are we waiting for?' she said. 'Take me to Duddle-stone.'

We collected her luggage, just one suitcase and a plastic shopping bag. I carried them to the car, while she limped cheerfully along beside me, chattering all the while. With her second husband she had made a new life for herself in the Cape. After ten years of hard work they had made a success of it. Latterly, my career in shipping had taken me to South America, and I had not seen mother since a brief flying visit eighteen months ago. It had been an idyllic short respite because the troubles with my wife and the shipping company were already beginning to loom on the horizon.

We had cleared the London traffic and were cruising down the M3. Mother had settled herself comfortably and was admiring the scenery.

'Right,' I said. 'What's this really all about?'

'About,' she almost sang the word. 'I wanted to see you. You and Emma – tell me all.'

Briefly I gave her the family news. How Emma had passed her exams and about her new boyfriend and their yacht. I gave her the latest news I had about my ex-wife Rhona.'

'Oh never mind her,' Mother was scornful. 'Tell me about the girl Stoneman.'

'I can't, there's nothing to tell.'

'That I do not believe. When I speak to you the other day there is a note in your voice. You are in love with that girl. I will have no arguments.'

'Well, if so it's all over now.'

Mother was not having that. 'Such nonsense, wait until I speak to her myself…'

'Mother please!' I was becoming thoroughly alarmed. 'Look, we've enough problems in Duddlestone at the moment without you stirring things.'

She nodded eloquently 'Always there is trouble in Duddlestone – what is new? As for stirring things, well, that is what I have come here to do.'

'What!' I could hardly believe what I was hearing.

'Indeed, had you not gone to that place I think I would have let the secrets die with me. But you are there now – so I have decided.'

'Decided what?'

'I am the avenging angel. I will put things to rights that should have been done years ago. Or, as your father would have said, I will put a bomb under this reunion.' She folded her arms and lapsed into a stubborn silence.

I knew it would be a waste of time for me to probe further. Could Mother really have the key to these mysteries? If I was patient I might also learn it all.

I changed the subject. 'We shall have to find you somewhere to stay.'

'I shall stay at the inn, the Gullait it is called. I understand it is run by Chief Petty Officer Broadenham. I have already booked my room.'

'The hell you have.' I was surprised. 'It seems I'm the last person to be told what you're up to.'

'No, there is no secret. Mr Broadenham wrote offering rooms for the occasion. I remember him from the old days. He was a man your father relied on, so it is natural I stay at his hotel.'

'Yes, that's true, and he said he remembered you. I'm told he was a survivor of the big battle.'

'The battle of Portland, they called it. You're father's finest hour, but what a price to pay. Only four men lived from his boat. Your father of course, Harry Broadenham, Sammy Thompson and the captain of Boat 251 – the Norwegian, and his name was…'

'It wasn't Eriksen?' I turned so sharply to stare at her, that my car did a wobble, attracting an angry horn blast.

'Yes, Lieutenant Eriksen. Your father was flotilla commander, but Lieutenant Eriksen was the boat captain. They were all mad.'

I hadn't realised what a key role Eriksen must have had in these events. This was the trouble; I had never wanted to enter my father's world. Some inner fear had stopped me even reading about his feats. I knew there had been this one-to-one contest, between Double Six and the elite E Boat flotilla. There had been amazing gallantry on both sides. The boats had manoeuvred and counter manoeuvred for four hours. Neither commander had turned and withdrawn, although it might have been a prudent choice for either. These were wooden boats loaded down with fuel and ammunition. A single well placed shot could make any of them an instant flaming pyre. Not only could but did. In the end only one British and two German had limped home. Twelve hours later, the twenty survivors had been found clinging to a handful of life rafts. Two hundred and eighteen men from both navies had been lost. My father had returned a hero. The King had pinned the Victoria Cross on him, and at a later ceremony General Eisenhower had awarded him a top American gong. It was said that the destruction of the German force had potentially saved thousands of lives in the forthcoming D-Day operation.

Harry had dropped everything when Mother appeared in the Guillaits. He himself had insisted on carrying her suitcase upstairs to the prepared room. Mother had been treated very much as if she was still the captain's lady. Harry had set a table for us in the Double Six bar, and after we had eaten he came and sat with us for a while. Mother and he reminisced about the old days completely ignoring me. I found their talk with its in-jokes and personalities rather tiresome. I listened, hoping to pick up some hint of the sinister side to Duddlestone, but there was nothing of the sort. After a while I excused myself as, quite truthfully, I had to return to work. I told Mother I would be along later to show her the harbour. I was rather looking forward to taking her round. Also this might be the moment for her to tell me her secrets. Did she really know the truth about Arthur Rocastle? I suspected she also knew the other deeper mysteries rooted in Duddlestone and those mysteries concerned my father.

The Sub-Aquas were back. Somehow they had managed to open the big doors of the ammunition store. 'Brute force, a bit of science and a lot of WD-40,' said Dave.

'We've made one trip to the wreck,' said Keith. 'She's a beauty, in fantastic nick. Best training site I've ever seen.'

'Something a bit strange about her too,' said Dave. 'bit of a mystery.'

'How so?' I was wary of that word. Duddlestone was making me neurotic, I thought wryly.

'Can't really say at the moment,' said Keith, 'but we're bringing our underwater cameras next time. We'll show you the video, first chance we have.'

'That's great,' I replied. It looked as if I was in for a session of murky amateur filming. As a professional seaman, I couldn't share these people's enthusiasm for wrecks.

The harbour was filling up nicely and our meagre facilities were at full stretch. Every pontoon space was taken by visiting craft. To make more space I had to detach my *Stormgoose* from her berth and anchor her elsewhere in the harbour. Not that that was a problem, with plenty of deep water throughout the cove. Harry had confirmed that, prior to D Day, they had brought in full size ships alongside the quay.

Hooder was back again. He surveyed his empire with a mixture of satisfaction and contempt. The sight of the great British holiday-maker was clearly not to his personal taste, but he was mollified when Laura produced the burgeoning cash flow figures. As another group of yelling kids ran past him, the doctor had clearly had enough.

I watched the red Jaguar speed away up the hill; once again I wondered at this strange individual. I did not believe any man, in this day and age, could be as unbearably stiff and pompous. There had been several occasions when the mask had slipped, enough to reveal a shrewd and almost normal personality. So, how much was the stage act and how much the real man?

Thank goodness the builders were beginning work on the new toilet and shower block. It should be in commission by the end of the summer. United Marinas were advertising franchises for a new boat yard and a restaurant. Several business people had already shown an interest, including our friend, George Dunlass. Personally I didn't trust that man one inch. Something was false about him, just as there was with Hooder. Neither man was exactly what he seemed, and both left a bad taste. In George's case I had a suspicion that he was some sort of superior villain. Clearly Laura knew more of his background than she was prepared to tell me. I wondered if Laura knew that her brother owed his farm to my Father. Mother knew the answer to that one, and she was not leaving Duddlestone before she had enlightened me. That mystery was only part of a larger puzzle – one piece in a great jigsaw of deceit. I felt a sudden wave of sympathy for that police sergeant, the one who had told me he hated Duddlestone.

Mother was sitting in the bar of the De Gullait Arms sipping a large gin and tonic. She had the look of one who was already an accepted part of the scene. Harry was behind the bar cleaning glasses. From the background came a pleasant hum of conversation from the usual mix of locals and visitors.

'Are we ready?' I asked.

'When I've finished my drink,' she replied firmly. 'Remember, I am so old and not to be hurried.'

'You off to see the harbour?' asked Harry.

'That is so. My son will take me to see where his father won the war.' She grinned and added, 'with a little bit of help from his friends.'

'You'll find it changed from the old days,' said Harry. 'You know, it's like swords into ploughshares. War base to leisure facility. I just hope your boy doesn't hog all the trade.'

I laughed. 'Harry, we'll put up a big notice. "Don't leave here without a beer at the Gullaits". And I can do that with a clear conscience.' Indeed, Harry ran a tight ship. His pub had as good food and service as any similar place I'd been in.

'When's your reunion?' I asked.

'This weekend, Saturday through Sunday,' said Harry. 'We've over thirty who say they're coming, and that includes our four survivors of the Portland battle, and two Jerries.'

'Germans?' I assumed veteran's organisations were, by nature, wary of their late foes. I said so to Harry.

'Yes, I know, but this one was a clean fight. They were real navy men, just like us. Lot of respect both ways. It's not like they were SS. I've told you already about little Hans who saved my life?'

'Yes, you showed me the photograph.'

'He died two years ago. Several of us went to the funeral in Bremen. They were all nice folk, his family. Drove out the last bit of spite.' He sighed, picked up another glass and polished it vigorously. 'Yes, we've two Krauts coming, and they'll be welcome.'

'There you are Mum, what d'you think?' I had stopped the car at the top of the hill and once again we were looking down on the harbour and quay at Old Duddlestone.

'But Peter, it's all gone.' Mother was peering down at the view. 'Where are the buildings? Your father's office, the engineers' shops, the quarters, the Wrens' hut?'

'It's just weedy concrete now. Everything's gone from your

time.'

'Of course,' she sighed. 'Though it seems like yesterday. Now all those little boats...'

'They're my livelihood,' I said huffily. I turned and caught her eye. 'Why was Arthur Rocastle murdered, and did father know?'

I saw her stiffen. I had deliberately caught her unawares. I knew that my mother was impulsive by nature. She could be stubborn as a mule in defence of a secret. This would be my best chance of making her confide in me.

She thought long and hard. I could sense her making a decision. This time she was not to be hurried into anything she might later regret.

'Come on, you'll have to tell me sometime,' I said. 'I'm committed to this harbour now. It's not fair on me to hold secrets.'

'It was all about a girl called Margaret Gulley,' she said at last.

'Yes, I know that; she was raped and murdered. General view is that it was one of the matelots from the base.'

'No, that is not the whole story. Things are not as they seem.'

'What happened?'

'It was the day before she was killed. She was on the cliffs, somewhere not far from where we are now. She wasn't supposed to be there. The area had been closed. The crews had been sent on leave, all but a few trusted men.' She was mumbling now, her usual stridency vanished.

'Mother, please go on. You'll have to tell me everything now.'

'Not everything,' she caught hold of my arm. 'Not everything. I am not ready yet.' The drama was beginning to return in her voice.

'All right, tell me about Margaret?'

'She was a very silly girl. She saw something from the cliff top, something she was not meant to see. Then she fetched Arthur. He was on the hill; doing his job catching rabbits.' Suddenly, to my horror, Mother was crying.

I felt guilty, I had deliberately awakened another trauma from a person for whom life had been a series of traumas. I loved her, I hated what I was doing to her, but I had to know.

Very gently I asked. 'Can you tell me what they saw?'

Suddenly she was angry. 'It was a harbour. What would you expect them to see?'

'Ships obviously, but you said something else; something they weren't meant to see.'

'Yes, and then they both had to die.' She stared straight ahead inscrutable. I knew that was all the information I was going to win from her today.

'Come on,' I said as I started the car. 'Let's go down to the harbour and I'll show you around.'

'Laura,' I said, 'I'd like you to meet my mother, Elena Bowker, although she was Wilson last time she was here.'

Laura stood up, flashed a welcoming smile, and shook hands.

Mother looked her up and down. 'So, you are a Rocastle?'

'That's right,' Laura looked defensive, as if she was not sure what was coming next.

Mother nodded, but she was friendly enough and genuinely interested. 'I remember a Mr Rocastle, he was a fisherman and a farmer. He was a good friend of my late husband.'

'He was my grandfather,' said Laura. 'Ernest Rocastle.'

'That is so, Ernest Rocastle, the Master of the Brotherhood. My husband used to have a joke, "the importance of being Ernest".'

Laura laughed with pure delight. 'That's Grandpa' – he was a pompous, self-important old sod.'

Mother looked mildly shocked. I guessed Laura's outspokenness was a surprise. 'He always seemed such a nice gentleman.'

'Of course he was,' Laura was conciliatory. 'He died when I was six, so I don't remember him so well, but we were all fond of him…' Her voice tailed off as if something was troubling her.

I smiled inwardly. The notion of Laura being fond of anyone was not something that would have occurred to me.

'So,' Mother continued. 'If Ernest was your grandfather, who is your father?'

'John Rocastle,' said Laura. 'I'm the eldest of three.'

'Ah John, the boy with the sheep dogs. How is he?'

'He died fourteen years ago, of cancer,' said Laura.

'Ah, that is so sad.' Mother was unembarrassed and genuinely sorry, or was she? There was something that only I could detect. Mother, like Laura, was not wholly easy with mention of Ernest and John.

Mother, after her tantalising revelation about Arthur Rocastle, had sunk into a sullen silence that had lasted the whole five minutes of our journey down to the quay. I knew her too well to probe further. I tried a dozen theories as to who or what Arthur and Margaret had seen from the cliff top. Eventually I gave up. I could think of nothing that could be so damning as to inspire a murder. Besides which, Margaret had been raped, and Arthur had died some months after the event. Unless, and I was speculating wildly now, unless Margaret had witnessed something deadly of which Arthur was too stupid to see the significance.

Having paid our respects to Laura, I took Mother on a tour of the site. 'It all seems much bigger than I remember,' was her only comment. 'Maybe it's because of all these little yachts. In my time there were your father's boats and the landing craft.'

'Harry said they had big ships in here sometimes,' I added.

We walked on, and she pointed to where the various buildings had stood. She laughed bitterly as she recalled how she had to change from a Wren's uniform to civilian clothes before she could be a guest in the wardroom; the officer's mess in Navy terms. Father was risking the opprobrium of the admiral by even bringing her here.

We walked back to the car. I was going to be busy for the rest of the evening, and Mother preferred to return to the hotel. We drove up the entry road to the brow of the hill. 'There's a lot of talk of a government research laboratory buried under this hill,' I remarked. 'Do you know anything about it?'

'I remember nothing,' she replied coldly. I had lost her again. Something had made her withdraw into herself.

'I just wondered,' I said. 'It's interesting, because the man who ran it was a Professor Hooder, and it's his son who owns the land here.'

'Hooder had a son?' She was interested now.

'That's right, Doctor Paul Hooder, medical doctor in this case, and I warn you, a real prize bore.'

We drove on across the army land to the main guard post. Here I had a surprise. Standing on the roadside was Lieutenant Pickering. I stopped the car and he came over. I introduced him to Mother and asked him how things were.

'There's a bit of news actually – I'm glad I caught you,' he said.

'What's up?'

'We've had the police here. The regular ones and our Red Caps. It's about the murder down at your place.'

'Really?'

'One of our civilian drivers is on the carpet. Apparently, that evening, he gave a lift to three unauthorised persons in his truck. Took them nearly all the way to Old Duddlestone.'

‘I thought no vehicle passed through that evening. You told me that yourself. That’s why the police are baffled.’ I was not pleased.

Pickering looked embarrassed, as well he might. ‘We had four of our own trucks taking emergency equipment up to the old chemical lab. We didn’t count them.’

‘Who were these illicit hitch hikers?’ I asked.

‘I’m told the guy they’re interrogating says he didn’t know them.’

‘That’s hardly likely?’

‘I suppose he doesn’t want to incriminate himself. He’s already been suspended from duty pending an inquiry.’

‘Who is this driver?’

‘He’s a local Duddlestone man, Reg Stoneman.’

The early-evening drinkers were beginning to fill the De Gullait Arms. Mother went to her room to change for dinner. I went to the bar and ordered a half-pint of the local draught bitter. I looked around. I could see three women sitting at a table in the shadow of the far end of the room; one of them was Carol. I decided on the spot that I would avoid a meeting. If I was quick, I could take myself and my glass out into the garden at the back of the pub. I was too late. Carol looked up and saw me. There was nothing for it but to walk over and be polite.

‘Hello,’ I said. ‘How’s Tommy.’

‘He’s fine,’ she didn’t elaborate, nor did she say whether the lad had enjoyed the sailing. She turned to her companions; I guessed that they were fellow teachers and I was right. She introduced them to me adding in a pointed tone. ‘This is Peter from the harbour. He’s my sister’s new boyfriend. They’ve moved into one of the old cottages down there.’

I couldn’t contradict her without an embarrassing scene. I think her friends were puzzled. I think they suspected something was not quite right. In the end I mumbled a few words and walked miserably back to the bar. At that moment my hatred for Laura hit a new height.

I walked into the evening air and tried to take stock. How on earth could I convince Carol that I had been a victim of events, not the heartless seducer of her sister. Hell no, Carol knew Laura too well to believe that. Mother had told me I was in love with Carol. She said she could deduce this from the tone in my voice. That of course had to be outrageous nonsense. People fell in love in women’s romantic fiction. Rhona and I had been brought together by pushy friends. In a way we had gone through with it because we were soft-hearted, and didn't want to let people down. When Rhona left me she had written a letter telling me she had no animosity, but with her new partner she had discovered LOVE. She had spelt it in capital letters. Well good luck to her; to both of them.

Had I discovered love? Certainly in Carol I had found a girl I was instantly at ease with. She was interesting, the things she had to say to me were interesting. I liked her voice, her soft brown eyes and round sun tanned face. Yes, I longed to make love with her, in the real sense; not just as a form of words for physical lust. Carol was devoted to her son. The child was the one good thing she had to show for her first unhappy marriage. I liked the lad and I think he liked me. I was deeply fond of my daughter Emma and proud of what she had achieved in her short life. Suddenly I had this feeling that I had missed out by not having a son. A boy to teach sailing, to take to football matches, or go for long walks and bike rides. To tell him manly stories of the sea and his forbears who had sailed its oceans. Fantasy, I thought gloomily; I might have a hole in my life, but it was arrogant of me to expect Carol and her son to fill it just like that.

As I rounded the corner into the car park, I was jolted from my daydream. 'Hey, you lot get off my car!' I was furious.

A group of dishevelled youths were looking in the windows of my car and one of them was sitting with his feet on the ground, his fat backside on the front of the bonnet. I had expected them to make off at high speed; instead they stood their ground staring at me. To many people their stance would seem intimidating. Well, they didn't frighten me. I had spent half a lifetime whipping into shape crews of recalcitrant teenagers; the surly dross of a dozen nations and five continents.

The four by my car were a typical bunch. They wore floppy jeans Nike trainers, and two of them had their baseball caps inverted back to front. I had thought one of them was vaguely familiar, and then I put a name to his face. He was Daryl Gulley, the young lad who worked in the chandler's shop in Poole, the one who had helped me load my new motor and identified Eriksen's *Persephone.*

'Right,' I snapped. 'What's going on? Any damage to my car and I'll call the law.' I saw them glance at each other guiltily.

'We never touched your motor, Mr Wilson. We wanted to see you.' Daryl seemed to be acting as a nervous spokesman.

'Really, I'm not sure I want to see you. Tell me what this is about.'

‘Please Mister,’ pleaded another of them. To my surprise I saw this one was a girl; her thin white face peered at me from under the peak of her baseball cap. ‘Please, Mister, Steve wants to talk to you.’

‘You don’t mean Steve Gulley?’ I reacted angrily. ‘I don’t want to see him, and he’d be well advised to keep clear of me.’

‘Please, Mr Wilson,’ Daryl chipped in. ‘Steve wants to talk to you. He says you’re the only one he trusts. Steve knows things, but he can’t go to the Bill – anyways they wouldn’t listen.’ He stared at me pleading.

‘Where is Steve now?’ I glared at each of them in turn. All four shrank nervously.

‘He’s at ’ome,’ said the girl.

‘Where exactly is home?’

‘Laurel Close, ain’t far – just round the corner, like.’

‘Is it near enough to walk, or do I take the car?’

‘T’other end o’ the village,’ said Daryl. ‘Take the car.’

Suddenly I was interested. The police had told me that they thought Steve was withholding evidence. If he was willing to talk to me I had better listen.

‘All right.’ I triggered the central locking and told them to get in. They did so, two in the back, with Daryl climbing into the passenger side.

Daryl directed me onto the Wareham road, the exit from the village. Just before the last house he told me to turn left. It was the council estate that I had noticed a dozen times before. It was bigger than I had realised, with two streets. Leading off one of them was Laurel Close: a dead end with eight houses. These were all brick-built, semi-detached, dwellings of the 1940–50 period. The street was jammed with cars and wheel bins. Eventually I found a parking spot and managed to slide into it.

‘In ’ere,’ said Daryl.

He led me round the side of one of the houses. It was shabby compared with most of the other dwellings. The garden was unkempt and littered with beer and soft-drink cans. Paint was peeling off the back door, and its frosted glass panel had been broken and mended with a cardboard square. A dishevelled grey cat was licking the contents of a smashed milk bottle. Daryl pushed open the door and with a jerk of his head indicated me to follow. The room was a kitchen and the most unhygienic cooking space I had ever seen. The sink was piled high with unwashed dishes, the electric cooker was filthy, the walls were layered with dirt and the ceiling had traces of mould. A sugar bowl on the table was a resting place for dead flies. Slumped in an armchair by the stove sat the corpulent figure of Steve Gulley. He looked up when he saw me and for half a second seemed pleased. I stared back at him. My contempt for this lout was tempered by some compassion. He had lost his father to a murderer. This father had been a useless layabout and, it seemed certain, a onetime murderer himself. In such a household a growing child would have stood very little chance. I had never inquired about Steve's mother. It seemed she was dead, or more likely had fled this dysfunctional household. Now this wretched young man was alone in a world that despised him.

'Well, Steve, here I am. What is it you have to tell me?'

'Hooder,' Steve replied. 'I reckon's it was 'im what pushed you in the water, and 'e killed my Dad.'

I felt a profound disappointment. This was nonsense. Steve's personal trauma had merged with his grievances against Hooder. If this was all he had to tell me, I was wasting my time.

'Tell you summat else,' Steve continued. 'Dr Hooder's a fido-pill.'

'A what – you've lost me.'

'A sex pervert, fancies kids 'e does. You ask Kylie 'ere.' Steve jabbed a finger at the anorexic looking girl.

CHAPTER 23

My incredulity turned swiftly to unease. I had never thought of the doctor in connection with sex. I never wondered whether he had a wife, or even a mistress. I had never speculated whether he was heterosexual, or gay, as we must now say. I had automatically assumed the good doctor to be immune from all human weakness, excepting money of course.

I gave Kylie an icy stare. She was an untidy little waif, very pale, and thin. Her clothing was identical with that of the boys, which is why I had at first placed her in the wrong gender.

'What d'you know about all this?' I said at last.

''Cos he tried it on with me, that's why.'

'Look,' I said, 'I know none of you like this man, but you'd better be careful. If you start making wild accusations against a respected local doctor, you are going to be in big trouble.'

'No,' Steve intervened. 'Kylie ain't going to shout the odds all round the village – she's got some sense. We want to tell you, Mr Wilson.' He paused. 'Look, we'm all sorry what we did at the ol' harbour, moving the poles like; we didn't know you then. But we needs to tell someone what goes on 'ere, and you'll listen – we trusts you.'

I was in a quandary. I had come to this place hoping to learn more about Roy Gulley. Now I was being enmeshed in something I'd rather not hear about.

'Kylie.' I caught the child's eye and held it. She stared back unblinking. 'Please tell me exactly what happened.'

'Dr Hooder came up to me and offered me two hundred quid. Just like that.'

'Where was this?'

'In the street, near 'is place in Boscombe.'

'Did he specify what for?'

'No, that's why I wouldn't play. Two hundred's lot of money, and I don't do sado or nuthin' kinky.' She stared back at me as innocently as if she'd been describing a trip to the cinema.

'Jesus,' I muttered. This little moppet must be on the game. 'How old are you?'

'Fifteen,' she said, 'but I'll be sixteen come November.'

Oh God, get me out of here, I thought. I clutched at straws. 'Are you sure he wasn't just wanting you to do an errand? I mean he's very rich, money means little to him.'

'Oh do me a favour, Mister.' Kylie's scorn was withering. 'I knows when someone wants my body.'

I looked around the gathering. 'Do any of you know of other kids who've been approached or molested?'

There was silence, while they looked at each other. 'Not by Hooder,' said Steve. 'A lot of it goes on, there's pervs everywhere these days. But Hooder went to Kylie. It's like he knew she'm a slag.'

'Don't call me that.' The girl had turned to Steve in a fury.

'Why not,' he said mockingly. 'Course you'm a slag, like your mum and your gran.' He turned back to me. 'Yeah, her gran were my Auntie Margaret, the one who got murdered. The one they topped Arthur for.'

This was another surprise. 'I never knew she had a child. I was told she was a teenager?'

'Naah,' said Kylie contemptuously. 'She had my mum when she were seventeen. One o' them matelots got her up the duff.'

Yes, I thought. I could well imagine they might.

I drove straight back to Old Duddlestone and went in search of Laura. She was in her cottage cooking supper.

'We're in trouble,' I said. 'Big trouble!'

'Have you eaten yet?' she said.

'No.'

'Right, sit down and calm down. Whatever's happened you'll feel more rational on a full stomach.' She waved me to a chair by the kitchen table.

The cleanliness and order in this house made a total contrast to the nightmare filth in Laurel Close. Laura was right of course; I was starving and my news could wait.

She plumped a plate of lasagne in front of me; the smell alone was mouth watering. I cleared the portion in three minutes. Laura refilled my plate.

'OK,' she said. 'What's biting you?'

I countered with a question of my own. 'Is it true Margaret Gulley had a baby sometime before she was murdered?'

'Yes, that's right – Alice. Why d'you ask?'

'Tell you in a minute. I gather this Alice has a daughter?'

'She's got four, plus three sons and umpteen grandchildren. She's a Gulley. That tribe breed like rabbits.'

'I've just been told that one of her daughters is on the game – sells herself in Bournemouth.'

'More than likely I should think,' Laura laughed. 'Am I supposed to be shocked?'

'You should be. She's only fifteen, and one of her clients is your Doctor Hooder.'

'Oh come off it, Peter. Who ever told you that?' Laura was gaping at me with disbelief.

'The kid told me so herself.' I told Laura exactly what I'd learned from the girl. 'The point is, Laura, she's telling the truth.'

'That Kylie is a compulsive liar,' said Laura.

I waved aside her objections. 'That's obvious, she's the type who finds lying natural and the truth painful. That's why I believed her.'

'You're a jolly sailor. I bet you know all about brothels,' she remarked acidly.

'No comment,' I replied. 'Now, you said we should look at this rationally. What do you know about Hooder's sex life?'

'He hasn't got one. The only woman around him is that weird secretary.' She thought for a moment. 'I've never thought about it before, but the fact is, I know almost nothing about him.'

'But you work for him?'

'Yes, but that's all. His private world is a closed book and I've never been allowed near it.'

'Well, it appears he has a sex life and not a normal one. Christ, Laura, I thought just about everything that could go wrong with this job had already happened. Now I discover the major shareholder of our company uses child prostitutes. Not only that, a Duddlestone girl as well.'

'OK, point taken,' said Laura. 'I agree this could be serious. I think a course of damage limitation is in order.' She paused. 'Tell you what I'll do. I'll corner Kylie tomorrow and beat the truth out of her.'

'And then?'

'I personally will tackle Paul. I will slaughter him, stuff him, and hang him out to dry. By the time I'm through with him he'll wish he'd never been born.'

I finally went to bed that night, deeply troubled. Too much history was coming back to haunt the present. I was very conscious of being an outsider in this odd place where everyone knew more than me. No, this was paranoia. I lay on my bunk and began to sum up.

Fifty years ago, in the aftermath of World War Two, something dramatic had happened here. Twelve people, at least, had died in the experimental lab. How and why was still a complete mystery. According to Mother, Arthur and Margaret had seen something so compromising it had led to their deaths. Mother was being less than fair to me, probably she thought she was being protective. She knew that my father was directly involved in something that was less than honourable. Harry at the pub knew, and so did Eriksen. I had not forgotten Eriksen's furious public reaction to Roy Gulley's admission of guilt. Within an hour or so Roy was dead; poisoned in an unpleasant and not easily detected manner. Killed, moreover, by someone who wanted me out of the way. I had been attacked and pushed into the harbour by a total stranger. The memory was so vivid, I could recall every second. I shut my eyes and strove to make a description of my assailant. He was large, he moved fast but he was silent. A young man, I assumed, very fit but faceless. I should have concentrated on this before, instead of convincing myself the attacker was Steve Gulley.

The police insisted that the attack was coincidental. As they saw it, I had blundered onto the scene at the wrong moment. I didn't think so. I believed this man knew exactly who I was and was using an opportune moment to be rid of me. Suddenly I was glad my boat was no longer tied to the dockside but was now anchored in the open harbour. I slid off my bunk and found the canister containing distress signals. I opened it and removed two rocket flares. In an emergency they would project a red flare to several hundred feet. They could also make a nasty mess of anyone on the receiving end at close quarters. At the very least I had the means to draw the attention of the whole harbour. Beside the rockets I laid out my heaviest boat hook.

I knew from past experience that this was going to be a long night; a non-sleeping night. What was I to do about Hooder? For the time being I had managed to pass the buck to Laura. I had never liked Hooder, but until now that hadn't mattered.

Paedophilia was a vice very much in the news these days. I am tolerant by nature. Aboard ship, I have protected individual homo-sexuals, nursed a withdrawing heroin addict and handled a deluded schizophrenic. There is nothing much about the human condition that surprises me. But the sexual molesting of children is another matter. Like the majority of people the notion fills me with particular disgust. In Hooder's case I had no proof; only the unsubstantiated word of a child prostitute. I accepted that the wretched Kylie was probably immune to psychological damage. Supposing Hooder became emboldened? Sooner or later he might try to satisfy his lusts on someone more innocent and vulnerable. The ego of the man might make him think he was above the law. If Laura and I were to turn him over to the police, it would probably destroy our fledgling harbour and cost us our jobs. Well so be it, we didn't really have a choice. I wondered for the hundredth time whether I would be better out of this. It had been an ill wind that had sent me here in the first place. Eventually I did sleep, but it was an uneasy, broken slumber. I kept seeing pictures of Hooder, red faced and angry. The scene faded, and refocused as my harbour filled with sinister ships all anchored motionless under a black sky. I saw the face of Carol, with that wounded expression, hurt and resentful.

A new day had brought out the whingers: those, thankfully a minority, who objected to our ten pound berthing fee. Why, they grumbled, should they pay anything to a harbour that had no shoreside facilities? Where were the showers – why only rudimentary toilets? I kept my fingers crossed, hoping these people were unaware that there had been a corpse in these same toilets.

Mick Tracic had been a tower of strength. He had also shown talents we had never expected. He had built an exhibition in the main office, with diagrams he had drawn himself along with a photo-montage. George and Rita Dunlass were back in their *Marietta.* They were almost becoming regulars. I didn't much care for George. He was one of those abruptly-spoken, deadpan-faced individuals, who never show a flicker of emotion. I watched him very carefully, particularly when he spoke to Laura. I wondered why they kept up this silly charade in my presence. The man was clearly not what he pretended. The garrulous Rita had blown his cover in front of me two days earlier. They had had a letter from, "Jim", Rita had said. Whoever Jim was, mention of him had disconcerted Laura.

Now came a new distraction: vehicles parking on the quay outside my window. There, standing beside his car, was Brian Byrne; behind him was a large transit van. On its side were the words, *Channel 9 Television.* With Byrne were two men and a woman. One sturdy-looking fellow had a large video camera balanced on his shoulder, another carried a directional microphone. The woman strutted ahead, self importantly, holding a clipboard.

I was unaware of having invited this circus, and I was not pleased.

I went outside and fixed Byrne with a hostile stare. The girl I recognised. I had never seen her in the flesh before, but she was Tabitha Long, TV presenter and interviewer. I didn't like her much on the screen, but I knew enough about her to realise I must watch my step. Tabitha's self-proclaimed attitude to any male interviewee was: "who is this bastard and why is he lying?". If ever there was a case for the return of the ducking stool and the shrew's bridle, she was it. I decided attack was the best form of defence.

'This is private property,' I said coldly. 'I must ask you to leave at once.'

'Who the hell are you?' Tabitha snapped.

'I'm Peter Wilson, and I'm the harbour manager.'

'I see, you're the local "jobsworth".'

I looked her up and down. Her immaculate black business suit seemed at odds with the surroundings. 'Madam, I am responsible for the comfort and happiness of the users of this harbour. Everyone here is enjoying a well-deserved holiday. I cannot allow you to operate without permission.'

'Bollocks,' she replied.

'Peter, are you having a problem with this mob?' It was Mick. He looked a formidable sight, muscular and bronzed. With him were the three lads of the Joint Services Sub-Aqua Club. 'Would you like me and the boys to sort it?' he asked. The sub-aquas looked startled.

'Do you know who I am?' asked Tabitha.

'Jeez,' Mick turned towards me laughing. 'Memory loss – this babe doesn't know who she is. No, sorry, darlin' – never seen you in my life.'

Keith caught Micks's elbow. 'It's Tabitha Long.'

'Never heard of her.'

Brian Byrne, who had been standing motionless throughout, gave a cough. 'Mick, Ms Long is a leading personality on our TV.'

'So what,' said Mick. 'If she's not invited she can sod off. That's what the boss said.'

'Not quite in those words.' I thought I had better be conciliatory. Mick had clearly got under Tabitha's skin. 'Please, all of you. I think it would be much better if you rang United Marinas, who run this project. I'll give you the number. Clear it with them, and I'm sure we'll be happy to co-operate.' I gave Tabitha a friendly smile and Brian a surreptitious wink. 'By the way, may I ask what all this is about?'

'Channel Nine are making a documentary on the Duddlestone

murders, and the events of 1946,' said Brian. 'I'm hired as technical and historical adviser.'

'Not much left here from those days,' I said. 'But clear it with the company, and I'm sure it'll be OK.'

'Did you get a wrap on that?' Tabitha spoke brusquely to the cameraman.'

'No, I wasn't filming.' He spoke with a Scots accent and sounded bored.

'Christ man, no tape!' Tabitha had suddenly turned apoplectic. 'That Australian thug threatened me.'

The TV crew plus Tabitha climbed into their van. The woman was not lacking in courage. Her fury seemed to stem from Mick's daring to challenge her. Indeed the man hadn't even recognised her. I smiled; with a bit of luck this would be a bad day for Ms Long.

I caught Byrne. 'Brian, a word please.'

He followed me into my inner sanctum. I waved him to a chair. 'Thanks for nothing,' I said. 'Are you responsible for bringing that offensive cow here?'

He grinned. 'Sorry, Peter, I need this film to be made and that means I have to take Tabitha. Not my choice, Channel Nine insisted – no Tabitha no film.'

'Why are they bothering. It all happened years ago?'

'Just let it die?' He gave me a hard look. 'Peter you're sounding like a Duddlestonian.'

'That's what Stanley Bowler said to me the other day. He told me I was going native.'

'No, not yet you haven't.' He looked around. 'Where's Laura?'

I didn't answer at once. I needed to reach a decision pretty quickly. 'She's gone to beat the daylights out of Paul Hooder.' Then I told him everything I'd heard from the girl, Kylie.

'Oh shit, I can see why you don't want Tabitha Twitchit nosing around.'

'Doesn't make any difference. Laura and I both agree; if we find Hooder is a danger to children, then we'll turn him in. You can have first pick with the story.'

He sat thoughtful for a full half minute. 'It's odd, Hooder of all people.'

'I don't know, he could be just the type.'

'Peter,' he said, 'a word of warning.'

'That sounds ominous,' I said lightly.

'Look, Tabitha's dug up something about your late father. Does the name Bobby Fuller ring any bells?'

'Definitely no.'

'Bobby Fuller was a spiv, wide boy, black marketer, whatever you like to call it, but in 1946, he was paymaster and captain's secretary with Sixty Six Flotilla.'

'So?'

'According to Tabitha, this Fuller was arrested in 1957, suspected of laundering a very large sum of money, the origins of which are still unknown. Apparently, quantities of this same money had been circulating ever since 1947.'

'What exactly do you mean by laundering?'

'Bobby changed a large sum, I don't know the precise figure, from United States dollar notes into legitimate Sterling bank accounts. Most of the notes were American wartime payroll.'

'What happened?'

'Bobby Fuller was released on police bail. Two days later he died in a knife fight in an East End pub. Very convenient for somebody.'

'Why was he released?'

'Not enough evidence to charge him with anything illegal. Actually the retired copper we talked to said Bobby was scared witless of something – didn't really want to be released.'

'Another murder?'

'More than likely; this was the heyday of the East End gangs. Nobody would talk, so it all died with Bobby.'

'What about the account holders?'

'Police couldn't prove a thing. There was nothing to indicate a crime had been committed. The Americans weren't interested; they had no record of their money being stolen. The notes were part of a consignment supposed lost to enemy action.' Byrne was looking troubled; I had never seen him like this before. 'They never got to interview the man who held the largest account, and anyway the money had all been moved somewhere offshore – no trace. He died, and the whole trail went cold.'

'Who was this man that died?' I asked. I had an awful premonition. I think I knew the words of Byrne's reply before he spoke.

'Sorry Peter, I really am. But the account was held by a Surrey businessman, Captain James Wilson.'

CHAPTER 24

Laura was back. I was busy refuelling a yacht from our diesel pump, but I could see her on the quay looking down. She gestured impatiently in my direction, and I acknowledged with a wave. Even from a distance she looked taut and angry; her body language was distinct. It was another half-hour before I could return to my office. Laura looked hot and flustered, far from her usual self. I guessed her visit to Hooder had not been a success.

'That bastard!' she said. 'I don't believe it.'

'What happened?' I glanced through the door into the main room. It was all right, there were no eavesdroppers.

'I saw him in his clinic. He'd just finished surgery. I came straight out with it. Told him what Kylie said to you.'

'And he denied it of course.'

'No, he did not.' Laura flushed angrily. 'He went all pompous. Said he wanted to examine the girl for legitimate medical purposes.'

'Oh did he.' Despite everything, I laughed.

'I don't think it's funny,' she glared at me. 'Anyway, what possible legitimate purpose; that's what I asked him.'

'I can guess,' I said. 'In the old days there were village lords who used to summon young girls to their beds. When challenged, they would claim that they only wanted to examine the victims to see if they were being properly fed.'

'That sounds like Hooder,' Laura conceded. 'He told me it was a medical matter that was too technical for me to understand.'

'What did you do then?'

'I gave him a few choice words and stormed out. That creepy woman secretary of his was in the next room and I reckon she'd been listening.'

'What do we do now?'

'I've been to see my brother, Ian. He's a magistrate and I wanted his advice.'

'That was good thinking. What did he say?'

'He told me there wasn't enough proof to convict. Apparently, Kylie's twice been up before the juvenile court for soliciting, and she's been in care of the social services, on and off, since she was twelve. Since she a proven liar, the court would not act without good corroboration.'

'Do you think she's telling the truth?'

'Yes, I do, but she could still have the wrong end of the stick.'

'Damn,' I looked at Laura despondently. 'I'm afraid we've plunged into this without thinking properly. Now we've alerted Hooder, and he's going to be extra careful. It'll be embarrassing too…'

'Why?'

'Because we've still got to work with him. As I see it, he daren't sack you and he can't touch me, because I'm paid by United Marinas, but it all makes for an unpleasant atmosphere.'

'Bugger the atmosphere. I hope he'll be that ashamed, he'll keep out of our way.'

So that was that. It was a very unpleasant position for both of us. I was not prepared to let the matter rest. I would be watching Hooder very carefully, and I guessed Laura would be listening to the undercurrents of Duddlestone. It was deep in those undercurrents that my own problems lay.

'Laura,' I said, 'there's a television crew working in the village. They're investigating the 1946 murders.'

'That's Byrne's doing,' she muttered.

'I know that,' I said. 'But they've discovered something about my father. It's disturbing because it seems to tarnish his image.'

'I thought his daring deeds were set in stone.'

'Nothing to do with what happened at sea. My father was a buccaneer by instinct. He was embittered by the way the Navy treated him. He may have been involved in something outside the law. I'm sure my mother knows, but she won't talk.' I looked at Laura. I was almost pleading. 'Do you have the slightest scrap of information that could help?'

'What could I know, I wasn't even born then?' She was being evasive. I knew the signs so well by now, and this time I was in no mood to give in.

'Laura, this is very important to me. I'm not a complete idiot, and I'm not paranoid. It seems that everyone in this place knows something about those days. Steve Gulley says he knows things about my father – his very words – and other people drop hints. Then there's that sour-faced guy, George Dunlass. It's bloody obvious that you know him, so why not admit it and explain. I'm fed up with you playing games with me. Just like you've messed up things between me and Carol…'

Laura looked at me, and the flicker of a smile crossed her face.

'So now we come to the crunch. It's Carol that all this is about?'

'No it isn't. What do you know about my father, and what's his connection with what went on here?'

'You really don't know?'

'Only what I've told you.'

'All right,' she smiled. 'After the big invasion, you know…'

'D-Day?'

'That's right. After the war moved to Germany there was nobody left for Double Six to fight. It seems your father was most put out because the Navy wouldn't send the flotilla to where the fighting was going on. They were left to stew here. I'd have thought they'd be pleased.'

'Not my father, he'd want to be where the action was. He was like that – a professional.'

'More fool him and the rest of them – bloody men.' Laura grimaced.

'For God's sake try playing another record. Now tell me the rest.'

'Smuggling,' she said. 'There's a tradition here in Old Duddlestone. Some of the flotilla men were locals. They had old contacts in the French fishing ports.' Laura looked at me and shook her head. 'Frankly that's all I know.'

This was probably true, in part at least. Post war, all the armed services had been involved in smuggling. The Air Force, with the most opportunity, had turned it into big business. But in my father's case there was talk of money laundering.

'What did the French supply them with?' I asked.

'I've no idea. Probably wine or brandy; they were the traditional trade.' She thought for a moment. 'Yes, there was pornography. Apparently the French printed loads of it. There was a man in the flotilla who had connections and he sold it.'

'His name wouldn't have been Fuller?'

'I've no idea. That's not a Duddlestone name.'

Mother wasn't in the pub. Harry said she'd taken a taxi into Bournemouth. She wanted to buy a new outfit for tomorrow's reunion. I looked around the bar. Sitting in a corner was Brian Byrne and the Channel Nine TV team. My first instinct was to ignore them. My better judgement took over. I needed to know how much Tabitha Long had discovered about my father. I walked across; ignoring Tabitha, I greeted Brian.

'God help us, it's Captain Jobsworth,' said Tabitha.

'Sit down Peter,' said Brian, 'what are you drinking?'

'Accepting a drink from a journalist could be dangerous,' I said. 'What's the catch?'

'None, remember I still owe you.' He turned to Tabitha. 'Couple of weeks back, Peter here saved my life.'

'Literally or metaphorically?' Tabitha asked languidly.

'Saved me for real, from drowning.'

'Indeed, I hope posterity will be grateful, Captain er…?'

'Wilson,' I corrected her and waited.

'Really, there's a coincidence.' she raised an eyebrow.

'I know,' said Brian. 'Peter's the son of Captain Wilson VC.'

'Good God, man,' Tabitha snapped. 'Why didn't you tell me that yesterday? What sort of researcher are you?'

Brian sighed wearily. 'I'm not your bloody researcher. I'm collaborating with you because it's probably in our mutual interest.'

Tabitha switched her hostility to me. 'I suppose I should have guessed – same surname. Related, like everyone else in this bloody place.'

I stared back, eyeball to eyeball, matching her dislike. 'I have been here less than one month. My father's connections are a complete coincidence. I'm no more privy to the secrets here than you are.'

'Secrets!' she snorted. 'I've never been in a dump like this.' Her loud voice had partially hushed the bar. She was drawing some menacing stares herself from the regulars.

'Tact, Tabitha,' said Brian. 'That means you need a whole basinful of it. I've been here for months and I've broken a lot of taboos.' He went on. 'You've gotta cool it a bit, or you'll undo all my work. Come on – let's be a bit more professional, eh?'

'I suppose so,' she said glumly. 'It's weird that's all. I've never seen this before. Most places people fight to be on telly. We usually get more interviewees than we can handle.'

'Not in Duddlestone,' I said.

Tabitha spun round on me. 'Where's the money gone?'

I was flummoxed. 'What money?'

'Oh come on,' she sneered. 'It's on the record. Your father had a small fortune salted away somewhere, but when he died he left under five thousand pounds. Your mother had to sell her house so you could stay on at school. She had to take a second rate job sawing a fiddle in a palm court band. The bloody Navy did nothing for you. You've grievances, Mr Wilson. I can help you hit back.'

I was furious, although I had resolved to stay calm. 'There wasn't any money. We were hard up. Dad's business wasn't broke, but there was precious little left after the debts were settled.'

'Import-export business, so I'm told,' Tabitha sneered again.

'That's correct, so what? If you're alluding to what happened here after the war, thousands of people in the services were at it. Look at Sir… (I mentioned the name of a well-known entrepreneur). He's untouchable to this day.'

'Your mother's in South Africa?' said Tabitha.

I made no comment.

'I want to interview her. How can I find her?'

'Mind your own business.'

'That's what I'm doing. Has she got something to hide? Have you for that matter?'

Brian intervened. He could see I was close to saying something I might later regret. 'Peter's mother, Mrs Bowker, is staying in this hotel at the moment.'

'Bloody hell, Brian. You never told me that either.'

I had had enough. I looked at the cameraman and the sound recorder. They had been sitting drinking their beers and munching their crisps as if nothing unusual was happening. It seemed I had stumbled on some surreal world that I couldn't begin to understand. I left the bar and walked into the open air.

'Peter, hang on a minute.' It was Brian. He glanced back towards the pub door as if he feared being followed. 'Let's walk, I want a word.'

'What about?'

'Come on, let's put some distance between us and Tabitha.' He set off at a cracking pace along the street. Within two hundred yards the pavement ended and we were walking along the leafy, tree-lined road to the end of the village. It wasn't a walk I much fancied. A hundred yards more and we would be level with the entrance of the council estate and Laurel Close. The memory of Steve Gulley and the wretched Kylie had left a bad taste. Instead Brian turned right into the other estate. Here we were among modern privately-owned houses, all detached, with built-in garages and manicured front lawns. Instead of the pleasing local stone, these dwellings were built in garish dark brickwork and tiles, in the style of the boom years of the nineteen eighties. "Thatcherian" architecture, I had heard it called.

'Who lives here?' I asked.

'Bournemouth commuters mostly. Some of them even make it to

London. There's a few locals as well – couple of families of Stone-mans – or should that be Stonemen, plural?'

'Any Gulleys?'

'Definitely no. Come on – through here.' Brian plunged into a gap between two houses, marked by a wooden footpath sign and a plaque declaring this to be a "neighbourhood watch zone". On cue, a middle-aged woman with blue-rinse hair fixed us with a stare of icy dislike. Now, suddenly and delightfully, we were in open country again. Across the fields I could see the house and barns of Honey-critch Farm.

Brian halted, giving us both a chance to draw breath. 'You know,' he said. 'I'm beginning to wish I'd never agreed to collaborate with that Channel Nine mob.'

I said nothing.

Brian broke off an ear of barley from the cornfield edge and began to chew the grains. 'The contract agreed that we should share all information. I've done my bit, but Tabitha is being mighty chary with what she gives in return.'

'Doesn't that let you off the hook?'

'Yes, but that would be too easy. Tabitha knows something and I intend to get it out of her. The thing is, we've come at this story from different angles. My interest is in Arthur Rocastle.'

'What's the Long woman's interest?'

'She waiting for the reunion of the Double Six. She wants to know what they were up to, especially Bobby Fuller. She's hoping to butter up the old salts in the hope they'll give something away.'

'Something to discredit my father?'

'Afraid so.'

'Why does she have to do that?' I rounded on Brian. 'What good will it do? Who cares after all these years? It's my mother who'll suffer, and she's gone through hell and back already. You're parasites you people.'

'I know, I've heard it all before,' he shook his head. 'Just remem-ber; I'm here to clear the name of Arthur Rocastle and nail his killers. I deal in justice – I'm not like Tabitha and never will be.'

Brian started walking again, following the footpath around the edge of the field. 'If we take this route,' he said, 'we come out opposite the lane to "Ashwood". Come in and have a drink.'

In due course we did just that, but I declined Brian's offer to come in. I looked at my watch, it was seven o'clock. I had spent too long away from the harbour and needed to be moving. It was a good ten minutes walk by road back to the pub to collect my car.

'Peter, there's something you can do for me – a favour.' Brian looked at me intensely.

'That depends,' I was on the defensive.

'Tabitha's told her TV crew that she's meeting one of her sources in private tonight. It's so confidential she's confined the boys to the pub.'

'I don't suppose they'll find that a hardship,' I remarked. 'Any idea who this witness is?'

'No,' he sounded a mite put out. 'I thought I'd tracked down every possible source here. I can't see what pull Tabitha's got that'll make them talk to her and not me.'

'What do you want me to do?' I asked warily.

'Nothing out of your way, just keep an eye open. It's something she said. I got the impression she might be meeting her contact down at your place – the old harbour.'

I walked back to the village. Outside the pub I could see some new arrivals. Two elderly gentlemen were standing, pint glasses in hand, enjoying the evening light. Both wore blazers and ostentatious rows of jangling war medals. The first Double Six veterans were here.

The big reunion was tomorrow. I had promised Harry I would conduct the veterans round the harbour in the afternoon. I might have looked forward to this. It should have been an interesting diversion. Sadly it had lost its appeal. I was torn in two about my father. Maybe the less I knew the better. No, that was nonsense. I was committed to finding the truth about him; every last gruesome detail.

I drove back to Old Duddlestone in a thoughtful mood. The weather was on the turn. The midday forecast had warned of a low-pressure system working in from the west. The cloud had been building for a while, and the first spots of rain were falling. Lights glowed in Laura's cottage, but otherwise I could see no signs of life. The big doors of the undercliff store were firmly shut. I opened the little wicket door and peeped inside. The sub-aqua club's RIB was parked on its trailer. Presumably these boys would be back tomorrow if the wind didn't pick up too much. Everything was as it should be, and no sign of Tabitha or her mysterious "source". I guessed the rain, which by now was teeming down, must have put them off. I walked slowly back to my dinghy and rowed out to my boat. Once aboard I went below and cooked myself a meal.

I awoke to Friday morning and it was still raining. The warm front had almost passed, but with it came heavy prolonged soaking rain. Wet and windless, the combination to spoil any sailing holiday. Not that it was bad for our business. During the morning we attracted another three visiting yachts and several of those already with us put off sailing this day. The sky lightened around half past twelve and by one o'clock the rain had almost ceased. The clouds began to break, and the first rays of sunshine beamed through to hearten everyone. At two o'clock I saw the visitors I had been expecting. Two army mini-buses descended the hill and pulled up on the quay. Here were our wartime veterans, twenty-three of them: my father's shipmates.

The old men gathered on the quay while Harry introduced them to me one by one. I tried to make that leap of imagination that could place these men when they were young, some only teenagers. Youngsters caught up in horrific events, that to them seemed a great adventure. For much of the war these had been the Navy's Channel strike force, in daily confrontation with the enemy. Their expectation of life could only have been a few months. Fifty years on, older and wiser, they were still miraculously alive. I wondered how they had coped with civilian life following such an experience? I wondered how I would have measured up to their war? Thankfully, it would be something I would never know. They were a disparate bunch, these veterans. Some seemed as physically fit as I was; fitter probably. Some were visibly frail, and two were in wheel-chairs. It was moving to learn how far many had travelled for this event. From all parts of these Islands, plus a small Dutch contingent and one man from as far away as California. I asked Harry about the Germans. He explained that they would be arriving at Bournemouth airport that afternoon and would be with us for the dinner on Sunday evening. I had hoped my mother would be here. No, said Harry; she had hired a taxi that morning saying she was off by train for London. This was news to me; I was surprised.

'She said something about a visit to South Africa House,' said Harry.

'Did she say why?' I asked.

'Not really, but she was concerned about something,' Harry hesitated. 'That Doctor Hooder came in the pub last night – first time ever. He seemed to be looking for somebody. Bought himself a Martini, and then he went across and chatted to that odd little girl.'

'What little girl?' I snapped at him.

My furious reaction showed. Harry was looking at me in an odd way. 'It was that Jolene – the Australian bit.'

I relaxed, the scruffy Jolene must be at least thirty, "little girl" though she might seem from Harry's perspective.

'She hangs around the harbour,' I said. 'What were she and Hooder talking about?'

'Couldn't say. They talked, very intense, for about five minutes and then Hooder walked out. Your mother asked who he was, and when I told her she turned a bit strange. It was just after that she asked me to book a taxi for this morning.'

I left Harry to show his old comrades around. They seemed harmless; I couldn't imagine any of them deep in crime. One more happening that afternoon was remarkable but not really a surprise. As the old sailors gathered by the pontoons a voice called out: 'Here's George, where've you been hiding lad?' The rest was lost in a raucous cheer. George Dunlass had walked up the ramp. He stopped at the top and clasped both hands above his head in a gesture of mock triumph. For the first time I saw him smile.

Tommy Stoneman was back complete with mountain bike. He was leaning against the office hut watching as the two buses drove away up the hill. The tide was out, so I presumed Tommy had pushed and ridden along the stony foreshore. He seemed excited about something.

'Over there,' he pointed across the cove. 'They've found a dinosaur.'

'Oh really, you mean the university people?'

'That's right, Charlie and Babs and all them students. They're over there now.'

'That's interesting. I must go and look sometime. Where is this?'

'Down on the shoreline. Not far from the bottom of the old track.'

This was news to me. Last time I had seen the bone hunters they had been on top of the hill. I said so to Tommy.

'That's right, Charlie says they're looking lots of places, but this time they struck lucky.'

'What did you see?'

He looked a little disappointed. 'Not a lot. They were brushing the dirt off a bone and there's something Babs says is an egg.'

'Oh well, best of luck to them.'

Tommy was staring at me. 'You don't really fancy Aunt Laura?'

I sighed; oh the innocence of youth. 'Your Aunt Laura is a work colleague,' I replied firmly.

'My mum told Auntie Trish, that you liked Laura more than her. I heard 'em – mum was crying.'

'You shouldn't listen to other people's private conversations.' I stared at him severely and he wilted a little. 'Now look, I haven't been here very long. Not long enough to know you all properly, but…' I made a long pause. 'But as I say, Laura is a work colleague, but I'd like to think your mum is a friend – OK?'

He nodded solemnly. 'Can we come sailing again?'

'Any time you like, both you and your mum. Just give me a day or so's notice.' I felt an enormous sense of relief. It was as if I had just put in place the first plank of a rebuilding bridge. Tommy looked equally pleased.

'Right, young man. You'd better be going before it rains again.'

'Got wet last night,' he said. 'I was up Weavers Down on my bike. D'you know who I saw? He got wet too, poncing around in 'is best suit and carrying that bag, y'know brief case.'

'What are you on about, Tommy?'

'It was Doctor Hooder.'

'What!' I was so startled I made the boy jump. 'Are you sure?' I didn't like this. I didn't like the idea of the dubious doctor wandering around following pre-pubescent children.

'Yeah, it was 'im all right.'

'What was he doing?'

'Jus' standing in the rain getting wet. Like he was waiting for something.'

'Did he see you?'

'Not likely, I hid – don't like him much.'

CHAPTER 25

I stood on the quay and watched the sub-aqua boys power out to sea in their RIB. The wind was still a moderate breeze from the southwest, but the seas offshore were choppy and near the edge of the safe limit for diving. They seemed excited about something and had been tight-lipped, almost rude, when I had enquired as to their progress. I had been both annoyed and surprised. My remarks had been no more than polite enquiry; the equivalent of commenting on the weather. Keith had better watch his step. He needed Old Duddlestone more than we needed him. Laura was leaning out of the window telephone in hand. She made a face and waved the handset.

'For you,' she said curtly. I took the phone and answered.

'Hello, Captain, I'm Drucilla Carstairs, Doctor Hooder's secretary. The Doctor would like to see you immediately.' It was a well-bred voice resonant with authority, perfect vowels and an expensive school. In my present mood it was the red rag waved to the proverbial bull.

I bit back. 'What d'you mean immediately? I'm busy.'

'I'm sure you are, Captain Wilson,' the woman had moderated her tone without seeming the least bit fazed. 'But the Doctor would be very gratified if you could see him as soon as possible today.'

'He can come here now,' I was uncompromising.

'I'm afraid Doctor Hooder has another surgery at six o'clock. He really would be most grateful if you could come over soon.' The voice was conciliatory now, almost humble.

'All right, where am I supposed to meet him?'

She gave me the doctor's home address in Boscombe. Reluctantly I agreed to drive over there and see him within the hour. Annoyance turned to anticipation. I would give the doctor a piece of my mind.

'That Drucilla gives me the creeps,' said Laura. 'I know she was listening at the keyhole when I tackled Paul about Kylie.'

An hour later I found Prince Albert Avenue, a long sloping street of majestic Victorian houses with leafy trees and a view of the bay. Dr Hooder lived in *The Limes*, a three-storey red-brick house with a car park where once I guessed there had been the front garden. I counted eight steps to the porch. The Doctor's brass plate was fixed to one door pillar and shone vividly in the late afternoon sun. I rang the bell and watched a vague figure through the stained glass door panel.

'Captain Wilson – so good of you. I'm Drucilla, please come in.' It was the same voice, but nothing like the face and figure my imagination had invented. At first sight Drucilla Carstairs could have passed for a fairground fortune-teller. She was thin, probably in her early forties, dressed in a garish gypsy-style dress, all mauve and black, with silver embroidery and skeins of wooden beads around her neck. Her jet-black, shoulder-length hair was bound at the forehead with a red band. She was a strange apparition, although I didn't share Laura's opinion that she was creepy. I realised that I knew next to nothing about Hooder's medical practice. I did know something about his other business activities and his apparent sexual tastes. It was on these that I intended to tackle him.

'We've still nearly an hour to surgery,' said Drucilla sweetly. 'If you'll follow me? She set off up a long carpeted stairway leading to a landing above. I could hear music, deep booming orchestral music, filtering out from somewhere within the house. I thought it sounded familiar but I couldn't place it. I followed Drucilla's scented wake as she flitted silently and barefooted upwards. On reaching the landing she set off down a long gloomy corridor. Ahead of us, now loud and clear, was the music; the opening movement of Mahler's fifth symphony.

Hooder was standing in the doorway at the end of the corridor. Here on his own ground he was certainly imposing. He stood aside to let me enter the room beyond. In contrast to the darkness in the rest of the house this place was bathed in light that streamed through two west-facing windows. We were in the doctor's private study, a pleasing little room with glass fronted bookcases and a big roll topped desk. Through a second door I could see what seemed to be a scientific laboratory with wooden benches and glass retorts.

'Come in, Wilson. I'm sorry to call you away at such short notice but I needed to talk with you.' Hooder was polite, gracious almost, but I was not impressed. He had some damning charges to answer and he was not going to sweet talk me from confronting him.

'Cilla my dear – coffee?' He smiled at the woman.

'Back in two ticks,' she smiled back affectionately and bustled from the room.

'Drucilla is my personal assistant and my muse,' said the Hooder. 'She watches over me like Caesar's slave.'

He saw my puzzled look and laughed. It was the first genuine expression of humour I had heard in him. 'Oh you must have heard the old story. When a conquering commander rode in triumph through ancient Rome his favourite slave would be placed by his right ear. The slave would whisper, reminding the great man he was mortal.'

'Yes, I've read that.' I watched his face as he glanced after the departing woman as she sped down the corridor.

Laura had one thing wrong. I would have wagered a month's salary these two were having a full sexual relationship. More than that they gave every impression of being a happy convivial partnership, married or not.

'Please sit down Wilson,' he waved me to a padded swivel chair. He placed himself on another facing me. 'You know that Laura came to see me. I've no doubt you are aware that she made some wild allegations. She was not in a mood to allow me to explain, but she touched on some work of mine that is very confidential.' He looked at me, watching my reaction.

'She was acting on information from me,' I said. 'The girl Kylie told me you approached her in the street and I believed her. She is known to be an active prostitute, so obviously you are going to keep the matter secret.' I replied deliberately and coldly.

'Yes I know,' he replied. 'I become so wrapped up in my research that I lose all sense of proportion. It's Cilla who is insisting I talk to you. I can see why you put the worst possible construction on these events.'

Hooder's choice of phrase was as pompous as ever, but he seemed genuinely contrite. He didn't give me the impression of a man pleading to save his skin. The Mahler had reached another crescendo of brass, diverting me from forming a reply. The doctor walked across and turned down the volume on the stereo in the corner.

'Thanks,' I said. 'I love Mahler myself, but he does like to dominate.'

'That's me as well,' said Hooder. 'Cilla says I'm arrogant and so does Laura, although in her case I think it is pots calling kettles black. What about you, Wilson?'

'What about me?'

'You've been a ship's captain. I would say you like to dominate as well.'

That set me thinking. This conversation was taking an odd turn. 'As captain I have to meld a crew together and they in turn have to trust me, even if they don't always like me. It has to be that way – life at sea would be dangerous if it was otherwise.'

‘I’m told your late father was a most dominant personality – charismatic is the word I think.’ Hooder spoke quietly, all his pomposity had vanished.

‘He’s been dead for years, I hardly knew him.’

‘I hardly knew my father. It’s an interesting coincidence is it not?’

‘What coincidence?’

‘Your father and mine probably knew each other, socially at least. They were both privy to the events in Duddlestone.’

So now we were coming to it. ‘What relevance has this to now?’

Hooder swivelled in his chair and pointed to a large framed photograph on the wall. It was of a fair-haired man, dressed in a formal suit. He sat staring at the camera through round, wire-rimmed spectacles. ‘My father,’ said Hooder. ‘He was the world’s foremost authority on tropical medicine. He should have won the Nobel prize.’

‘My father thought he should’ve been an admiral, but it never happened.’ I replied bluntly.

I’m not sure Hooder heard me. He was staring into space, an odd expression on his face. ‘I’m going to tell you something that is not widely known,’ he said at last.

‘Has this any relevance to the girl Kylie? That’s the only thing that’s bothering me and Laura.’

‘Indirectly she has every relevance. Her grandmother worked in my father’s laboratories. She’s the only bloodlink I’ve been unable to test.’

I looked at the man with considerable cynicism. ‘OK, I’ll listen.’

‘Good, in a way it helps that your father was there at the time. Please remember that what I’m telling you is in confidence. Technically I could be in breach of the Official Secrets Act.’

‘All right,’ I agreed.

Drucilla appeared again flitting silently into the room. She placed a cup of coffee and a sweet biscuit on the table by my elbow. I wasn’t sure if I wanted either but accepted with half a smile. Drucilla placed herself in an armchair to one side of the doctor’s desk.

‘On the day in question my father was in London. He delivered a paper on his work to a top-secret seminar.’ Hooder’s demeanour had changed completely; he was almost mumbling.

I interrupted. ‘Can we establish exactly what his work was?’

‘He was researching countermeasures to germ warfare. He was an acknowledged expert on tropical viruses. He had experimented in Africa.’

‘Were the Germans in a position to use such weapons?’ I asked. I was still suspicious.

‘Not as far as we know, but our intelligence said that the Japanese were on the verge of developing a water-borne virus that would thrive in a European climate. My father had been working at the main government unit at Porton. He was given the purpose-built lab at Duddlestone especially for this research. It was top priority.’

I was alarmed. ‘Are you telling me all those people died from some tropical nasty and that’s why the place was sealed?’ Something of this sort had been bothering me ever since I came to Duddlestone.

Hooder shook his head. ‘Please hear me out. When my father tried to contact the lab there was no response on the phone extension to the underground section. When he sent a member of staff from ground level, that person never emerged. My father ordered the unit to be isolated and hurried back to Duddlestone.’ Hooder hesitated. ‘He never got to read his paper.’

‘So, he found everyone dead?’

‘In a sense, yes. It was impossible to enter the place. They sent in security men with breathing apparatus and they were lucky to come out alive. The lower levels were awash with potassium cyanide.’

‘Poison?’

‘A huge concentration of one of the deadliest substances. It was seeping out everywhere, you could smell it above ground, and it killed some sheep near one of the ventilator caps on Weavers Down.’

‘What did they use cyanide for?’

‘That’s just it, they didn’t use it. Neither cyanide, nor any related chemicals, had any part in the research. Someone took it down there for sabotage – there’s no other explanation.’

‘But they would have died as well wouldn’t they?’

‘Of course.’

‘We’re not seriously into Japanese kamikazes I hope? I don’t buy that.’

‘One theory is as good as another. We simply don’t know. The upshot was that the Government sealed the place for eternity. Then they made all concerned swear an oath of secrecy. The record is closed until July 2046, by which time…’

‘I know – none of us will be around,’ I finished his sentence for him. ‘All right,’ I continued. ‘Tell me about Kylie.’

‘Shall I tell him?’ Drucilla spoke, gently touching the doctor’s forearm. He nodded and she turned to me. Despite her odd appearance she was really quite an attractive woman. Her intense dark eyes reminded me of Carol.

'My grandfather,' she said, 'was Doctor Richard Harrington, he was deputy director of the Duddlestone project. He was one of those that died that day.'

'So you've never been able to recover his body?'

'Not my family nor any of the others.' There was a ring of bitterness in her tone.

I felt a tinge of guilt and embarrassment as I read the unhappiness in her face. My reply had been tactless to say the least.

'I never knew my grandfather of course,' she continued. 'He was my mother's father. It's so cruel, she's never been able to bury him. They're all reptiles, no compassion. We've a right to bury our dead – make a closure.'

'Who's they?' I asked.

'Officialdom, government ministers who parrot what they're told to say. "There never was an accident at the Old Duddlestone research project because there never was an Old Duddlestone research project. Why? Because we say so, and all you pathetic boring little people whinging about your loved ones can wait 'till hell freezes over or 2046, whichever comes soonest.' Drucilla ended her tirade in a crescendo and buried her face in her hands. Hooder stood up and put an arm around her as she sobbed.

I felt more uneasy than ever. 'Look,' I said. 'It can keep. Would you like me to come back tomorrow?'

'No,' Hooder was emphatic. 'You want to know about the girl and I would like to tell you.' He sat down once more facing me.

'The girl is Kylie Bones. Her grandmother was Margaret Gulley an employee at the lab.'

'I know that. She looked after the live animals?'

'Correct, but as you also know Margaret died before the incident at the lab.'

'More than that,' I reminded him. 'She was raped and murdered on the cliffs.'

'I know, but my interest lies in her descendants and the living descendants and contacts of all those who died. 'Over the last five years, a local GP colleague and I have taken blood samples from fifteen persons. The problem with the girl Bones, was that she would never co-operate. The doctor who was going to take blood samples says she's terrified of being found HIV positive.'

'Shouldn't she be made to take tests?' I asked. 'She could be carrying a multitude of sexually transmitted diseases, as well as

AIDS.'

'We in the medical profession have no powers of compulsion. You'd be surprised at the number of people who bury their heads in the sand. I decided to offer her a substantial monetary reward. Stupid of me, I should have seen the consequences.'

'Yes you should,' said Drucilla. 'If a man approaches a tart like that it's usually for one reason only.'

'Can you tell me about these blood samples?' I asked.

'My colleagues and I believe that by analysing these samples, we may detect certain factors that will tell us what organisms the workers on my father's project were in contact with.'

'Would this be hereditary?'

'We believe traces of such viruses could be found but in a harmless form. My late father tested himself and I've donated my own samples to the test pool.'

'Any results?'

'There have been certain consistencies that justify me in continuing with the next part of my work.'

'Can you explain?'

'Wilson,' he caught my eye. A manic quality in his stare made me uneasy. 'I intend to enter my father's laboratory. I believe there are papers in there whose findings could benefit humanity.'

This was a real shock. I wondered if it explained Hooder's haunting the downs above the defunct lab. 'But you said the place was awash with cyanide?'

'No, no,' he dismissed my query with an irritated wave of the hand. He was almost back to his old pomposity. 'The cyanide would have dispersed long ago. It's over fifty years, remember.'

'How do you plan to enter the place if it's sealed and the authorities won't open it?'

'I know a way, but I can't reveal too much now and it would be much better for you not to know. In that way you won't be held accountable should anything go awry.'

'What do you mean? The old lab's nowhere near the harbour. But I agree, I don't want to know a thing about it.'

Drucilla was staring at me, 'Captain Wilson, we've been very frank with you. Will you accept our word about all this?'

'If you mean about Kylie…' I paused for a second. 'Yes, you're telling the truth about her.' I was certain of that now. It was a much more plausible explanation. 'What do I tell Laura?'

Hooder spoke. 'Tell her you are satisfied with my explanation.

I'd rather you didn't say any more. If she asks questions, tell her to come to me. If she's prepared to listen, I'll explain.'

I left Hooder's house and drove straight to Old Duddlestone. I needed to talk to Laura. It was a slow, frustrating journey in the rush hour traffic. Near the hospital I had to pull over onto the pavement. A passing ambulance sped by, its lights flashing and siren screaming. I reached the harbour at last and drove down onto the quay. Laura came out of the office and sprinted towards me her long hair streaming in the wind. Something was wrong. I could see the expression on her face. Breathless she stumbled over the news.

'Peter, it's your mother – there's been an accident…' she looked wild-eyed. For a few seconds I couldn't take in her message.

'What … what accident?'

'Harry rang me from the pub. He's been trying to find you. Your mother's been taken to hospital.'

'What happened?'

'She was knocked down by a car, just outside the village, by the turning to Honeycritch. They didn't even stop. It was a hit and run.'

CHAPTER 26

In all my years I have never been in anywhere as awful as that Accident and Emergency unit. The reality eclipses anything one may see in a television drama. The medical staff were wonderful; incredibly professional, under conditions of stress that I would not care to face myself. I was among a little group of other traumatised people; the families and friends of that evening's tragedies. Inevitably we were all tossed around like flotsam on a chaotic tide. I talked to the parents of a teenager who had fallen from his motor bike and was now in intensive care. We spoke in desultory platitudes while we sipped vending machine tea. I tried not to look at the young couple, clinging together in the corner. Their four-year-old had been dragged unconscious from the sea an hour before. The nurse talking to them had been white-faced and tense.

'Mr Wilson, would you come this way.' Beside me was a sister in a dark blue uniform. 'You're Mrs Bowker's son?'

'That's right, how is she?' I almost choked on the words.

'Come this way and the doctor will explain.' She was a kindly person, plump and black, with a slight Caribbean accent.

The doctor was a dishevelled young man. He looked desperately tired and his face was lined with strain. 'Prognosis isn't too good. I think I ought to tell you that straightaway,' he said.

'Do you know what happened?' I stuttered on the words. I had to say something.

'Her injuries are consistent with being hit by a car. Broken arms, broken leg, three broken ribs, contusions to the head.'

'What are her chances? You can be frank with me. I won't hold it against you, but I must know.'

He paused and wiped his face in a towel. Suddenly I felt desperately sorry for this young man. He couldn't have been more than a year or two older than my Emma, and he looked to be near breaking point. 'Well, she's been in surgery. We've set some bones – but she's unconscious and she's lost blood. Luckily she had a medical card on her so we know her blood group. All the same…' He paused again.

'Go on,' I said. 'I'd like to know.'

'It's not really for me to say, but she's not young and we haven't done a brain scan. Evens chances. Call it fifty-fifty.'

‘Thanks,’ I patted him on the arm and managed a smile. He reminded me of the young purser who had cracked up in that typhoon. I forced myself into the present. ‘Can I see her?’

‘Just a minute,’ suddenly he looked relieved. He beckoned to a male nurse who was sorting the contents of a trolley.

The nurse took me along a short corridor and stopped outside a window; inside the room was a bed surrounded by apparatus. A vague shape lay on the bed connected to a blood bag and a number of other tubes and wires. Even through the glass I could hear the bleep of the heart monitor.

‘That’s as far as we can go at the moment,’ said the nurse. ‘Are you her son?’

‘Yes.’

‘You know she was semi-conscious when they brought her in here? She was delirious – shouting in Russian.’

‘She is Russian. How did you recognise the lingo?’

‘My granddad’s a Russian. We speak it at home.’

‘It’s a small world,’ I sighed. ‘You didn’t catch what she said, by any chance?’

‘If you put it into colloquial English it would be – “that little bastard”.’

‘Just that?’

‘Yes, over and over again, until we knocked her out with the needle.’

I almost ran out of that hospital. I needed the open air; I needed to breathe. I was confused, angry and grief stricken. The medical people might assume they were dealing with an accident. The police might assume they were looking for another drunk driver. This time I knew better. There was an awful inevitability about everything that was happening to me. I was certain that someone had tried to kill my mother. Everything that had happened to my father traced back remorselessly to Duddlestone. Mother knew something. She was planning to make revelations to this reunion. Now she was in hospital and near death. For someone this was very convenient. Yesterday I had seriously thought of washing my hands of this place; throwing in my job and walking away forever. Not now – I had a score to settle. I wanted justice. The Duddlestonians would find they had an unfamiliar and vengeful Peter Wilson in their midst.

I rang Laura on my mobile phone and told her the news. Then I set off for Duddlestone. My first call was to the De Gullait Arms and

Harry Broadenham. I found Harry in his private quarters. Sharon the barmaid had taken over the restaurant with another girl helping behind the bar. Harry was not just upset, he was distraught. He seemed to have aged another ten years; he had the look of a shrivelled gnome.

'I offered to drive her,' he muttered. 'It's all my fault.'

'No it isn't,' I said firmly. 'None of us could have foreseen this.'

'I should have.'

'Why?' I snapped the question. He lifted his head, but avoided my gaze. I thought he looked guilty. 'It was deliberate, wasn't it?' I stared at him and again he wouldn't meet my eye.

'Peter, I don't know – honestly I don't.'

'Tell me what you do know – about my mother'

'She took a taxi from the station, but instead of driving here she must have told the driver to drop her at the junction with Honeycritch Lane.'

'Where was she found?'

'Just twenty yards up the lane towards the farm.'

'Honeycritch Farm, was that where she was going?' Again I snapped the question. Harry seemed unnerved; the man appeared on the edge of tears.

'I don't know. Honestly I don't. The police won't say much. All I know is what that bloody TV woman told us.'

'Not Tabitha Long?' My disgust must have shown.

Harry nodded in sympathy. 'If I'd known all this was going to happen we wouldn't have staged this reunion.'

'That Long woman's been digging dirt about you and all the other Double Six people.'

The climax of the reunion was to be tomorrow night. Mother was to have made the keynote speech at the dinner. Suddenly I felt cold. She had been planning some dramatic revelations in that speech; she had as good as told me so. "I will put a bomb under this reunion", she had said. Mother loved drama. The theatre of the occasion would have appealed to her. Could it be that it had nearly killed her?

'What's going to happen now?' I asked.

'I was all for calling the dinner off, but the others want to go ahead unless…' Harry stumbled into silence.

'Unless what?' I quietly challenged him.

Harry looked utterly miserable. 'How bad is your mother?'

'Doctor says fifty-fifty.'

'If Elena passes away we will have a short gathering at the church and then disperse.'

I was in two minds about Harry. I believed he knew the gist of Mother's undelivered speech. I was also certain he knew nothing about the assault on her, although he may have guessed who was responsible. Like me Harry was filled with grief and, brave man though he was, my instinct told me he was frightened. I decided not to press him further. I left the pub and stood outside in the street. The sun was low in the sky, almost cresting the ridge of the downs. Once again, I could see in silhouette the sinister shape of Tollands Copse.

Around the corner of the building I could hear conversation; a woman's voice, clear-cut and confident, with a man's voice replying in a stilted mumble. I walked the few yards and saw Tabitha Long and her camera crew. Tabitha was interviewing a local, or one I assumed to be a local. He was an elderly man with unkempt hair and a dishevelled beard. Despite the heat he wore an ancient full length waterproof secured round his waist with a length of baling string. Whoever he was, he did not seem to be enjoying his five minutes of TV fame. He looked shiftily around as if he was planning an escape.

'OK, cut it there,' said Tabitha. 'Thanks a lot, I'll be in touch.' The elderly interviewee scuttled away and Tabitha turned her attention to me.

'Who was that?' I asked.

'Local shepherd – says he wasn't here in forty-six. He's lying of course – they all are.' For once Tabitha seemed uneasy. 'Captain, I'm very sorry about your mother. Please accept my condolences. Such a tragedy – she'd agreed to be interviewed by me.' It seemed churlish not to accept Tabitha's condolences. I'm sure she meant well, although I suspected the real "tragedy" was mother's failure to appear for Tabitha's interview.

'Thanks,' I said. 'What do you know about the accident?'

'You think it was an accident?' Tabitha raised an eloquent eyebrow.

'No, I don't think it was an accident. What do you say?' I stared her down. Tabitha looked startled. It must have been a change for her to be on the end of an aggressive question.

'Too much of a coincidence,' she replied. 'I think your mother knew the answers.' Tabitha glared at the distant hills. 'I think she knew the bloody lot. Now we may never find out.'

'What is it you think she knew? And don't anticipate her death. I've just come from the hospital and she's still alive.'

'Really,' Tabitha looked genuinely surprised. 'She took one hell of a knock. The car was travelling at speed. The witness estimated sixty miles an hour. Of course that could be imagination – these things generally improve with the telling.'

'There was a witness?' This was news to me. I had to know the details. 'Look Ms Long, don't hold out on me. I'm not some rival reporter – it's my mother we're talking about.'

'Sure, sure – take it easy,' she was being irritatingly soothing and it didn't suit her personality one bit. 'The whole thing was seen from the far side of the field by the road by a farmer and his wife.'

'Ian and Tricia?'

'If they are Mr and Mrs Rocastle, yes.'

'I know them. What did they see? Have you spoken to them, and how d'you know all this?'

'I haven't spoken to them, but the police took a statement and they talked, off the record, to a stringer from the local rag.'

'Well nobody's seen fit to tell me. So, what happened?'

'The taxi dropped her at the road junction. There was another car parked in a gateway. As your mother walked up the road this car caught her and mowed her down. It never stopped just speeded away past the farm. It's been found abandoned. Your local copper says it was stolen in Weymouth this morning. That's all I know – sorry.'

'Thanks,' I nodded and walked away.

Now I felt ill. I stumbled into the back yard of the De Gullait Arms. As I did so I caught the full aroma of the kitchen. It was the final straw. I staggered a few yards and vomited into a water drain.

CHAPTER 27

Half an hour later I took my car and drove to Honeycritch Farm. I had steeled myself enough to turn that corner and drive up the little narrow lane. As I rounded the first bend I saw a police accident sign. A few yards further stood a police car parked by the roadside. Two officers were taping off an area of the grass verge. I stopped in the gateway opposite and climbed out.

One of the policemen waved me away. 'Could you move along please. This is a crime scene – we don't need spectators.'

'It's my mother who's been knocked over!' I snapped. 'I've a right to know what's going.' I walked up to them. Inside the line of blue and white tape there was blood on the grass. My own flesh and blood, but I no longer felt sick and angry; just empty and purged of any emotion.

'Name?' asked the PC.

'Peter Wilson, the lady was my mother.'

'Casualty's name was Bowker.' The PC glanced at his notebook.

'Bowker's my step-father's name – second marriage. What can you tell me?'

'We can't really help you, sir,' the second PC was conciliatory. 'We're only securing the site and conducting a ground search. I suggest you contact the police station. Ask for DCI Channing.'

'Yes, I know him, I'll do that.' Suddenly I wanted out of this place. I was feeling sick again. These two young coppers were only minions doing their job. I climbed back in the car and drove on.

Honeycritch Farm was noisy with a scent of cattle and a symphony of mooing. The afternoon milking had long finished, but a herd of young cattle was corralled in the yard, jostling and stamping. Amidst this uproar I could see Ian Rocastle wandering nonchalantly among the animals examining their plastic ear tags. He saw me and came across. 'Give us half an hour and I'll tell you what I know,' he said.

Tricia appeared out of the milling throng and called. 'Go indoors, ask Carol to make you a cup of tea.'

I acknowledged and walked across the gravel to the front door. Carol was standing there. In other circumstances this could have been a tense meeting for both of us. Now I had other things on my mind. Her face looked pale and wan, far from her usual self.

'Peter, I saw you drive up just now. How is your mother?'

'The doctors give her a fifty-fifty chance, but she's in a bad way.'

'I feel awful about it – you see it's partly my fault.'

'Don't be silly, Carol, it can't possibly be your fault.'

She shook her head. 'Peter, please come in and I'll explain.' She led the way into the kitchen. There was a pleasing spicy smell of a slow-cooking dinner and strangely it no longer repelled me. It was still the same cheerful room where I'd first set eyes on her. Not even our sombre mood could change that. I sat down, and Carol began to fill a kettle. It was a mechanical response, a soothing conventional thing. I didn't prompt her further; I waited.

'I feel kind of responsible,' she said. 'You see your mother rang and arranged to meet me here. She was on her way when it happened.' Carol flopped onto a chair and the tears poured down her cheeks. I moved next to her and put my arm around her shoulders; she buried her face in my woollen jumper.

For two minutes we sat there. I had the sense to say nothing. I slowly rocked her, as one would comfort a child. I felt her relax, and I knew that the misunderstandings that had come between us were diminished. We could try and begin again.

'Of course it's not your fault,' I spoke gently. 'Do you know why she wanted to talk to you?'

'No – do you?'

'Yes I've an idea, but it'll keep for now. When did she ask you?'

'It was the day before yesterday, in the pub. Harry says she asked him to point me out.'

For a second I could almost smile. I knew very well why Mother wanted to size up Carol. 'What did she say?'

Carol looked up at me. Her dark eyes were wet with tears but she saw my expression and smiled in return. 'She was nice. I liked her.'

'What did she say?' This was embarrassing, but I needed to know.

'She just said, hello, and asked me if I remembered Granddad Rocastle.'

'Do you?'

'Not really, only a few childhood memories.'

'Did she say anything else?'

'No, she just looked at me in a funny way. Then she said she was going to London, and could we talk when she came back to Duddlestone.'

'Was that all?'

'She said she would ring me when she got home, and she did. She rang from the railway station. She said she would like to see me, but it was very important that she spoke to Ian.'

'When was this?'

'The phone call?'

'Yes.'

'Just after four o'clock. She said she would call in on her way back to the De Gullaits, but she never did.'

'Carol, do you know the exact time my mother was taken to hospital?'

'Ian says it was just after five.'

I felt cold again. I had passed that ambulance, the very same ambulance, and I hadn't known. Gently Carol eased herself from my grip. 'I'll make the tea,' she said.

Ian came into the kitchen through the back door. He had kicked off his wellingtons and was standing on the tiled floor in thick stockings. 'Trish'll be along in a minute,' he said. 'She's the one who saw what happened. How is your mother? We rang the hospital but they couldn't tell us much.' He looked awkward.

'There isn't much to tell, I'm afraid.' I explained the situation.

'I'm sorry, Peter, really I am. I apologise I kept you waiting but we had to sort those cattle, we've a ministry blood test tomorrow.'

'Don't talk to me about blood tests,' I replied. 'I've just spent the afternoon with Paul Hooder.'

'Never knew he was your GP?'

'He's not. I went to grill him about his supposed habits. Laura told you about Kylie Bones?'

'Yes, she asked me if there was a case to answer.'

'You being a magistrate?'

'For my sins. I do my best but it ain't easy. No ego trip if that's what you're thinking.'

'No I'm not.' I could say that with sincerity. Ian Rocastle was a man of infinite self-confidence, but ego no. Suddenly I remembered George Dunlass. 'There's another JP who's been visiting the harbour in his yacht.'

'Oh yes, anyone I know?' I didn't like the way he looked at me. this guy was too shrewd by half. His Dorset accent, and easy going personality, belied a clever mind. He was a match even for his sister, Laura.

'Tell me about my mother.' I said.

‘You’d better talk to Trish. She saw it. You’ll stay for supper o’course?’

I hesitated. ‘Thank you, but I’ve left the harbour unmanned and I ought to go back.’

‘The harbour’s OK,’ said Carol. ‘Laura phoned to say she’ll do your shift, and the Aussie lad’s staying to help as well.’

‘How did she know I was coming here?’

‘She didn’t, she’s been ringing around trying to trace you. It seems your mobile’s been switched off.’

Tricia Rocastle appeared in the doorway. She smiled at me. ‘Sorry to be so long. Had to have a shower – got covered in shit out there.’ She wore a full-length housecoat and her hair was still wet and in disarray. It was all at variance with her clipped vowels. The Lord-Lieutenant’s daughter married to the grandson of a farmer-fisherman made good. The farmer, whose considerable acreage had been bought with some mysterious funding from my father.

‘It was a black Volvo estate, an old one,’ said Tricia. ‘There’s lots like that around so I didn’t take much notice.’

‘It was parked up and waiting I reckon,’ said Ian.

‘What makes you think that?’ I asked.

‘He came down the Wareham road about ten minutes before and pulled into that layby where the council store gravel. He’d be out of sight there and just fifty yards short of our turning.’

‘Then the taxi came?’

‘I didn’t see that bit. I was banging in a fence post,’ said Ian.

‘I did though,’ said Tricia. ‘The taxi came down the road and the Volvo pulled out of the layby and stopped. Then the taxi stopped and your mother got out – only I didn’t know it was your mother of course.’

I sighed. ‘I wish I knew why she decided to walk that last bit. She’s got a bad hip, for God’s sake; why not ride the whole way?’

‘I know why,’ said Carol. ‘She said on the phone she would walk the last bit because she remembered the farm from the old days, from grandfather’s day, and she wanted to see it again.’

‘I wonder if she talked like that in the pub?’ I mused. ‘I’ll have to ask Harry. Somebody must have heard her.’

‘It is … I mean the police are certain it’s murder?’ asked Carol.

‘Attempted murder,’ I corrected her.

‘I’m afraid there’s not much doubt about that,’ said Tricia. ‘You see the Volvo drove past the entrance to the lane. Then it turned round and drove in like the wind.’ Tricia’s upper class cadences faltered. 'Oh God, I don't like to think about it.'

'But you saw?' I persisted.

'Sorry Peter,' she made an effort to restore her calm. 'No the bastard drove straight at her. He hit her a hell of a crack. I heard the bang and saw the body fly into the hedge like a rag doll.'

'Did you see the driver?'

'No, I was just mesmerised by the car, but I've a sort of gut feeling there was only one person, a small person, but that's all. I told the police that, but I'm not sure why.' Tricia looked at me sharply. 'Christ's sake, you don't want tea. Carol, get him a proper drink. What'll it be?'

'Thanks,' I replied gratefully. 'I'd like a scotch, and do you mind if I ring the hospital? I feel a complete idiot letting my mobile switch off. It was the only way they could reach me.'

'I'll show you.' Tricia indicated me to follow her. She led into the front hall and then into another room that was clearly the farm office. She activated a data-base on the computer and pulled out the phone number of the hospital and the Poole police. Then she left me to it.

The ward sister was helpful and confirmed that Mother's condition was stable. I gave her the Rocastle's phone number, and she promised to call me if needed. There was nothing more that I could do. As they say, no news was good news. Next I called the police. DCI Channing was off duty, but I left a message and was told to call next morning. Tricia was waiting tactfully outside. I told her what I'd heard.

'I think you'd better stay here tonight,' she said firmly. I hadn't expected this and was hesitant.

'Look,' said my hostess, 'Laura can take care of your harbour. Won't hurt her. You can have the spare room, same as last time. Then you'll be on the spot if we hear news.'

'Thanks,' I said. 'I'm grateful.' I felt an enormous surge of relief. These Rocastles were good people. I no longer felt utterly alone.

Outside we could hear a car pull up on the gravel. 'Here's Gran Gwen, my mother-in-law,' said Tricia. 'She's been at choir practice. She sings – Welsh of course.' I wasn't certain if Tricia approved of this or not.

Gwen was certainly in good voice. She had already heard the news and I was nearly overwhelmed in sympathy. 'Of course you must stay here, until we know your mother's on the mend.'

I didn't argue. Suddenly the prospect seemed more than appealing. I would have the support of a close family; something I had never experienced in my life. More important I would be near Carol.

Tommy appeared to complete the family. He had been to football practice and was suitably grubby. His mother sent him to have a bath. Tricia poured me another scotch. For the first time that day I began to relax. There was nothing more I could do. All was in the hands of fate.

I was tired. More than that I was fighting sleep. My eyes were closing and I found myself slumping forward towards the supper table. I pulled myself up and glanced around. Falling asleep would be an appalling social gaffe.

'Finish your meal and I'll show you to your room,' Carol smiled.

'These pyjamas belong to my ex-husband. Do you mind?' Carol had come into my room with an armful of towels and night attire. I didn't mind one bit and I was intrigued. This was the first time she had mentioned the husband.

'We've been using his stuff for cleaning rags,' she went on, 'but these are brand new – still in the wrapper.'

'Your ex-husband – Tommy's father?'

She laughed. 'Jim Stoneman is definitely Tommy's father. No other male involved, thank you.'

'Sorry, I didn't mean..'

She laughed again. 'You've got a daughter?'

'Yes, Emma.'

'I know, Laura says she's pretty, and clever too.'

'She certainly is. Emma's a doctor now – newly qualified, but very green of course.'

'And you don't want to talk about your wife?'

'There's nothing to talk about. She's gone and I don't miss her. What about you?'

'Jim's a Duddlestone man. We were both teachers.' Carol sat down on the end of the bed and stared at the ceiling. 'I thought I loved him, but he turned out to be … to be someone else.'

'You mean a different personality to the one you thought you'd married – same here.'

She nodded. 'I might have lived with that, except he never gave me the chance. One day he walked out and vanished. No warning, no message, no notice at his job – he just vanished.'

'Tommy said he was in Australia.'

‘He is now. He turned up there a year later with a new woman. In the meantime Tommy and I were destitute. We couldn’t pay the mortgage so they took our house away. It’s a lovely house … the little garden I made. They meant more to me than Jim.’

‘Tommy told me the Child Support Agency are on the case. I hope it was all right for him to tell me. I don’t want him in trouble for speaking out of turn.’

‘No of course not, everyone knows that.’ She paused again. It was odd but I’d forgotten tiredness. I wanted to know more, but I knew better than to push her; I waited. ‘It was history repeating itself,’ she said quietly.

‘How so?’

Carol swung round and faced me. ‘Look, I heard what you said about a JP in your harbour. You meant George and Rita didn’t you?

‘You mean George Dunlass?’ I was wide-awake now. ‘Tell me about him, because Laura won’t.’

‘He changed his name, but he’s really George Stoneman, and he’s Jim’s father.’ There was anger in her eyes. ‘I’ll tell you something else. He was one of them. He murdered Arthur.’

CHAPTER 28

The morning news from the hospital was the same. Mother was in intensive care and still unconscious. I thanked the ward sister and replaced the phone. No news is good news as they say. I felt both relief and then, seconds later, desolation. If only I had done something; but what could I have done?

For the moment I was alone at Honeycritch Farm. Carol had left for her teaching job taking Tommy with her, while Gwen Rocastle had driven off somewhere in the battered Land Rover. Across the yard, I could hear the whine of the compressor that drove the milking machines. I looked at the kitchen clock; it read seven thirty. I guessed this was mid-morning by farming standards. It was time for me to be heading for Old Duddlestone.

As I moved to the door I noticed a large brown envelope on the kitchen table, and with it a note.

Peter,
Thought you might find this stuff interesting.
Ian says you can borrow it as long as you like.
See you this evening
Love, Carol. x

I needed something to divert attention from my troubles. I opened the envelope and peeped inside. I could see some old letters and a few black and white photographs. I tipped the whole lot out on the table. The first photograph I had seen before in Brian Byrne's file. It was Ernest Rocastle with the wartime workers, including Arthur Rocastle. Arthur stared back at the camera. The boy had a pleasant open face. I wondered again, for what purpose did he carry a tin of paint? The second picture caught my interest at once: Old Duddlestone harbour from the cliff top. A harbour filled with vessels: landing craft, rafted together in every navigable corner, leaving only the central channel clear. Alongside the quay lay the MTBs; I counted eleven. Dwarfing them all was a full-size cargo freighter. Beside her on the dock, where my office now stood, was a large crane. I looked at the back of the picture. *Invasion, D-Day minus 5,* was scrawled in pencil. Two more pictures were of the same scene from different angles. Then I picked up the last photograph and I felt that strange sensation when, as they say, you feel the hairs on the back of your neck tingle. I saw the garden of Honeycritch Farm. I knew where I was because the house was unmistakable. Standing on the lawn was a group of eight people. Four of them I didn't know. In the front right was Ernest Rocastle, in his best suit, with a lady who must be Mrs Rocastle. In the centre was another couple: they were a wedding pair, the bride in white and the groom in full Navy uniform complete with dress sword. I was looking at my own parents' wedding reception. I wondered why I had never seen this one before? Lastly I examined the letters. The first one was hand-written on hotel stationery in writing that I knew to be my father's.

Royal Braemore Hotel
Wester Ross
Dear Ernest,

We are having a wonderful time here. The weather has been exemplary and today I caught my first salmon. Elena tried her hand yesterday and caught a superb fish three pounds heavier than mine. The only blight on a perfect honeymoon is that we have to come south again in three days time. I have to be in Portsmouth to give evidence in this wretched court martial. I never thought I would say this but I want nothing more to do with the blighted Navy. If all goes well I can cock a snook at that ass Sutton. Damn him and his demob pay offs.

With regard to the other forthcoming proceedings, I too am worried, but I am inclined to let the law take its course. I have faith in the civil law, even if I do not trust the fairness of the service model.

I look forward to seeing you soon. My regards to Dorothy and young Johnny. Elena sends her love.

Sincerely
James

PS. The enclosed is a photographic copy. May it bring as much cynical laughter to you as it has to us.

Norwegian Embassy
London
W1.
Dear Captain Wilson,

I am commanded by His Majesty King Haakon on behalf of the Norwegian people, to convey His Majesty's heartfelt thanks. The skill and devotion of you and those under your command undoubtedly saved the lives of Captain Anderssen and his crew.

Please convey His Majesty's good wishes to all officers and other ranks of Motor Torpedo Boat Flotilla Sixty-Six.
Carl Torkel
Navy Attaché

I reached my office at nine o'clock, uncertain if I was satisfied or slightly annoyed to find everything in good order. Clearly I had not been missed. No, I should be grateful to my colleagues who had rallied round this troubled day. Now it was time to ring the police.

'Channing,' the Inspector's voice crackled down the line. He did not sound pleased.

I reminded him who I was, and then launched into a long tirade about my mother and my suspicions of foul play.

Channing interrupted. 'Look, we're already treating this as a serious crime. Causing injury by dangerous driving and failure to report an accident. If your poor mother were to pass away it'll be death by dangerous driving, and that could lead to ten years in jail.'

'I say it's attempted murder.'

'Then you'll have to produce evidence of intent, motive and a suspect. Can you do that?'

'Not at the moment but…'

'Exactly, now why should anyone try to kill your mother?'

'She's the only one who knows all the facts about Duddlestone in 1946. She not only knows what happened fifty years ago, she was due to reveal all in a speech to the Navy reunion tonight.'

'Hmm, that's interesting. What was in this speech?'

'I don't know, she never got round to telling me.'

'Why not, you're her son when all's said?'

I had already anticipated that one. 'I think she wouldn't want me in danger.'

'If I didn't know both you and Duddlestone, I'd say you were paranoid. However, I promise I'll take what you say seriously.'

'Thanks. Any progress on the Roy Gulley front? Have you identified the other hitchhikers in that lorry?'

'We've questioned Stoneman, the driver, and he says he'd never seen them before. He fluffed on giving us proper descriptions and in my opinion he's lying.'

'Are you charging him?'

'We can't, he hasn't committed any crime. The army are charging him with a breach of their rules, but that's not our affair.'

'It's all right for you, but I was nearly drowned that night. I could be the next to have a knife in the back.'

'Mr Wilson, I can't give you official protection but if it's any comfort we shall be keeping a careful eye on both of the Duddlestones. My recommendation to you is keep a low profile and don't say anything. Could you tell me, when and where this Navy reunion?'

'It's in the De Gullaits tonight – seven thirty. Harry's got a special license to go to midnight.'

'Interesting, have they taken over the whole place?'

'No, only the Double Six room.'

'You know, I promised my wife a meal out. I think I might try the Gullaits.'

I put down the phone and it rang again within five seconds. It was Harry Broadenham. He had been trying to reach me and had begun to assume the worst.

'No, Harry, she's still in intensive care, but no worse.'

'Thank God for that. Look, Peter, I've a favour to ask. Could you stand in for your mother tonight? You know, say a few words to the lads?'

'Why me, Harry, I wasn't even born then? They would probably resent me as a young upstart.'

'No they wouldn't. You're the captain's son and you're a professsional seaman. I've asked one or two and they think it's a great idea.'

For seconds my mind raced. I had the germ of an idea if I had the balls to carry it through. 'OK, Harry, it would be an honour.'

It was Eriksen who greeted me as I edged my way self-consciously into the room. The youngest person present must have been twenty years older than me, although I am rising fifty. Eriksen at once asked me about mother. I had driven to the Gullaits straight from the hospital but I had no fresh news. Her condition was stable but she was still in a coma.

'It's such a bad business,' Eriksen commiserated. 'Many of us remember your mother, and we were looking forward to her speech.'

I bet you were, I thought. 'I know, Harry's asked me to stand in for her.'

'That's good,' he clapped me on the back. 'Very proper, it keeps the link to our captain.'

Eriksen took me through the crowded room introducing me to various characters. Some of them I had met the previous day in the harbour. They were a cross-section of every region and social class. There seemed to be no residual distinction of rank, and I noted that the ex-officers were little different from the ex-ratings. Father had been the only pukka Royal Navy man in the whole outfit. If his ghost wasn't actually present, he loomed large over these proceedings. It was gratifying to see and hear the awe in which he was held by these men. The distances some had travelled to be here amazed me: one from California, plus three Dutchmen, a Dane, a Spaniard, and a Greek. Then we came upon a little man in a Navy cap of a style that I didn't recognise. 'Meet Gunther,' said Eriksen, 'or Unter Offizier Gunther Hartmann, of Schnellboot Flotilla 12.'

So here was one of the Krauts. He was a funny-looking little chap, with a walnut brown face, wizened by years of sun and rain. This man was a professional seaman. I recognised the type instantly because he stood out from this roomful of wartime amateurs.

'Captain Wilson, I am so happy you to be meeting, and not for the first time.' He spoke reasonably intelligible English. I shook hands and smiled politely. I guessed I must have come across this guy before somewhere and he had remembered me. 'In 1966, you were on the *Ptarmigan*, I was Second Officer on the *Gretchen*,' he laughed. 'England, that week in the World Cup, had us beaten. So we rescue you English sailors and that makes us feel a little amused.'

I laughed myself now, and clasped his hand again. I had been Second Officer on that awful old rust bucket, *Ptarmigan*, when she had caught fire ten miles south of Bornholm. A German coaster ship, the *Gretchen*, had ignominiously taken us off.

'Only later did I discover you had been in that crew,' said Gunther. 'Your father was a fine man. I am remembering how many boats we lost at Portland. I was not there, but I remember.' He looked sad and a little embarrassed. 'Also I remember the time we hear your father is honoured. Our captain calls a toast; "to the heroism of the little ships of both nations".'

It was oddly moving this tribute across the years. I felt a renewed sense of pride in my late father, despite the flaws that I had begun to uncover.

There was another half-hour of introductions; blurred faces and names that I tried to remember. George Stoneman, alias Dunlass, was there. He seemed cheerful among his old shipmates and he was friendly to me, even complimenting me on the harbour. I tried to conceal my suspicions. Carol had told me that George was one of the men who had murdered Arthur. He had also been seen in the harbour the night I had been pushed in the water. The same night that Roy Gulley had died.

Harry, ringing an enormous polished ship's bell, stilled conversation. It was the one that had hung outside the flotilla offices in the wartime harbour. 'Gentlemen, dinner is served.'

The seating was arranged in the shape of an inverted U. Two long tables with a short one crossing at the head. I was invited to sit in this place of honour, along with Eriksen, Harry, and an elderly retired admiral whose name I didn't catch.

'Knew your father,' this man grunted, 'fine fellow – damn fine. Impulsive though, acted like a reservist.'

'How do you mean?' I asked.

'I mean he interpreted his orders to suit himself. Royal Navy officers don't do that – not if they want Navy careers after a war. Reservists though, they don't give a damn for admirals. Only wanted to get the war over and back to civvy-street. Lot of 'em reckoned they had more grasp on events than the regulars.'

'You say you knew my father?'

'Good heavens, yes. We were together in battle cruisers, then James volunteered for MTBs. Won him glory, of course, but it wasn't a smart move, as the Yanks would say.'

'Why not?'

'Turned him into a maverick, an adventurer.'

Before I could question further, Eriksen intervened. He tapped me on the arm and pointed. The TV film crew, complete with Tabitha, was circling the room.

'How did that lot get in?' I asked.

'It's all right, we've given them permission.'

'I don't like it. You know the Long woman is trying to dig dirt on my father?'

'Much better we co-operate, then with luck she'll go away.'

The food was arriving. The finest that the Gullait's kitchen could provide, borne by a posse of servers, recruited by Harry for the evening. Among these youngsters I recognised Kylie Bones. The scruffy nymphet of the other evening had transformed herself into a picture of sweetness and modesty.

The dinner was strictly in tradition. A thick pea soup, followed by roast beef and Yorkshire pudding and a magnificent apple tart with local clotted cream. The veterans fell on this food with a will; not a vegetarian in sight. I chose a red wine to go with my fare, as did the admiral. Most of the company chose beer, the standard mealtime tipple in the war years, but less usual in the sophistication of today. Harry called for the loyal toast which, once completed, was the signal for half of them to light up cigarettes, pipes and a few cigars. These men had lived in the wartime years when smoking was universal. I wondered how so many of them had survived with lungs intact. Harry called for silence and Eriksen climbed to his feet.

He formally welcomed us all to the reunion of the "Double Six" Association. There was scattered applause and banter. He welcomed the two Germans; polite applause.

'Now,' he said, 'our two guests of honour. First our president and patron, Rear Admiral Sir Denzil Sutton, DSC.' Loud applause. 'As you will all have heard our late Captain's lady, Elena, would have been with us tonight, had she not been involved in a bad road accident yesterday evening. We send our good wishes for her speedy recovery.' Subdued applause. 'In her place we have our Captain's son, Peter Wilson.' Warm applause. I acknowledged with a wave and a cheerful nod. 'Peter is also a captain, red ensign in his case, and he is the man in charge of our old harbour. So here you have history returning to serve the present.'

I was scanning the faces of the assembled company. George Stoneman was sitting four places down on the right hand side. He sat impassively, taking the occasional swig from his beer glass. I made a careful study of the two men on either side of George. They were brothers – more than that, they were identical twins.

The Admiral was on his feet. He gave forth a short cheerful speech on the theme of the song, "Forty years on". A bogus sentiment, he declared. He could remember the events of his youth as if they were yesterday, whereas today he would be hard put to recall the details of last week. He was warmly received, having clearly struck a chord with his listeners. He sat down amidst loud approval. Now it was my turn. I stood up and reached inside my jacket for a wad of folded A4 paper. The first sheet contained the head notes I had prepared for my actual speech. The remaining four pages were in fact a spare-parts list from a mail order firm. Making an after dinner speech holds no terrors for me. I have addressed similar functions, as well as my own ship's crews, all over the globe. This time however I was playing a game; taking a gamble that could put my life in jeopardy.

I thanked the organisers for the honour of inviting me to speak. I thanked all the assembled company for keeping the memory of my father alive. I remarked on the camaraderie that seemed so strong among the crews of the little ships, as opposed to the battleships of that period.

I paused and surveyed the rows of faces turned towards me. 'As you have heard, my mother is in hospital and unconscious. I have here in my hand the speech she was to have delivered to you tonight.' I waved my sheets of A4 for everyone to see, taking care not to show the contents. 'She tells of her time here. In particular she remembers the period immediately after the end of hostilities. All of this is new to me, but it throws much light on the mysteries that dog our life here in Duddlestone. I do not believe it is for me to repeat these things. When all is said, they are my mother's revelations, and they concern my late father. So I will not dwell on these matters on such a happy occasion as tonight.'

I stared intently at my audience. Most of them looked mildly baffled. George and his two companions sat poker faced. I saw no reaction whatever. Never mind, I had set my hare running.

I quickly rescued the remainder of my speech with some standard platitudes followed by a few seamen's blue jokes. The veterans laughed and some of the serving girls squealed in embarrassed delight. I sat down to a respectable burst of applause. I could see Tabitha and her film crew in the background. This was a bonus and I decided to exploit it.

It was a full hour before I could decently make my excuses and leave. I shook hands with the Admiral, and explained to Harry that I had to be early at the harbour in the morning. The veterans had long since lost interest in me so I quietly slipped away. Tabitha was by the door waiting to pounce. She had just finished filming a group of old-timers as they recounted their war experiences. From what I could hear these tales were alcohol-inspired and eighty per cent fantasy. I wondered if Tabitha was aware of this.

That lady had caught sight of me. I lingered in the main bar while she wound up her interview. As I expected she headed for me, the film crew trailing in her wake. 'What's in that speech?' As usual Tabitha was straight forward and to the point.

'Speech?' I stared back blandly.

'Oh don't piss about, man. You're mother knows something and she's told you – yes?'

'It's my mother's story.' I tried to look severe. Inwardly I was laughing at the expression on this ridiculous woman's face. 'I think you should discuss it with her.'

'Are you trying to wind me up?' she eyed me frostily. 'Even if she's conscious she may have amnesia. I want results now. What's your price?'

'Price, for Christ's sake – my integrity is beyond price,' I replied pompously.

'Will you talk to Brian then – he's Mister Integrity around here.'

I'd forgotten Brian Byrne. I saw him chatting with the same group that Tabitha had just finished with. I beckoned him across. 'I heard what you said in there,' he said. 'I thought your mother would know something. Told you so the other day.'

'Ms Long is about to reach for her chequebook,' I said. 'What should I do?'

'I can't match that, mate. I'm looking for the truth; if you want to accept blood money that's up to you.' Brian gave me a hard look.

I noticed the room had gone very quiet. Regulars and veterans alike were listening to our exchanges. I looked at Tabitha. 'OK,' I said. 'Come to my office tomorrow evening, say around eight o'clock and I'll talk.'

I walked outside, inhaled a deep breath and stared up at the starlit sky. I was aware that I was not alone. A small conspiratorial group was huddled together under the lighted inn sign. I recognised all four. George Dunlass, the two elderly twins and now a real surprise. The fourth person I knew, although I'd never spoken to her. It was Jolene, that disreputable looking waif: the alleged Australian journalist.

CHAPTER 29

Carol was sitting in the kitchen of Honeycritch Farm. It was eleven thirty and the house was quiet.

'Thought I'd wait up for you,' she said. 'How did it go?'

'Went well, they seemed to enjoy it.'

'Did you make your speech?'

'Yes.'

She tilted her head and stared into my face. The dark eyes glinted in the lamplight. 'You were tense this evening before you went there – I could tell.'

'Oh come on – how could you possibly tell?'

'You were pacing around muttering.' She was eyeing me now with an intense stare. I had to think quickly. Had my disquiet been so obvious?

I sat down opposite her. 'Carol, I think I should clear out of here.'

'Peter, why? We want you to stay, and what about your mother?'

I shook my head. 'I'll level with you. It's pretty obvious my mother was the victim of a deliberate attack.'

'I know Trish thinks that, and she saw it happen.' Carol muttered the words; she really had the most expressive face.

I didn't want to distress her, but I had to talk to someone. I reached across the table and took her hand. She responded with a gentle squeeze on mine.

'Carol, my mother knows what really happened here in 1946. She knows about Arthur's murder. She knows other things – things that show my father in a bad light.'

Her grip on my hand tightened. 'I thought it might be something like that.'

'Now, we all want the answers – agreed?'

'I want justice for Arthur,' she said quietly.

'I want justice for Arthur,' I sighed. 'The problem for me is my father. He died when I was ten – I hardly knew him. Everything about him is a facade that other people built for me. He was the great hero, Wilson VC. I had to model myself on him – had to live up to him. Do you understand?'

'I think so,' she sounded hesitant as she sensed the anger within me.

'No, I don't think you do – you couldn't. You see, my father killed himself. I almost saw it– I was the one who found his body…'

She clenched my hand this time, her fingernails digging into my skin. 'Peter, I didn't know– that's awful, I'm sorry.' She hesitated. 'I knew that he killed himself, but not the rest – I mean about you.'

'I know, but it happened, I've learned to live with it. I was always told he was depressed, that he couldn't adjust to peacetime civilian life. Then I came here to Old Duddlestone, and I've learned a different story.' I sat in silence for a moment. Carol had released her grip and was gently stroking my hand. Her eyes were fixed on me.

'Carol, I believe my father, my supposed role model, the great hero…' I stopped, I could hardly bring myself to say the words. 'I think he was probably a crook. He was engaged in something outside the law, and he thought he was about to be unmasked.'

Carol shook her head. 'Peter, that can't be right. Whatever could he have done?'

'I'm not sure, except that it involves Duddlestone and Arthur Rocastle and the accident in Hooder's senior's lab, which wasn't an accident by the way. Paul Hooder says it was murder and I know my mother agrees.'

Carol stood up. 'I should act surprised I suppose, but I'm not.' She walked to the sideboard. 'I think there's a bottle of Ian's special malt in here. I'm going to pour us both a slug.' She returned with two glasses.

'Ian hides this away for medical emergencies, as he calls them – he bought it in Scotland – says it's the real thing.' Carol gave me the flicker of a smile that faded instantly. 'What are you going to do?'

'I'm not prepared to leave my mother at risk. So tonight I drew the fire away from her – or I hope I did.'

She looked alarmed. 'What did you do?'

'I showed them some papers and pretended they were my mother's speech, the one she'd been proposing to give. You see, she'd made no secret of her plan. She was going to reveal everything she knew about 1946.'

'Did she tell you exactly what she knew?'

'She dropped a hint that's all. I don't know how much she knows and I don't suppose the murderer does either, but he was alarmed enough to try and kill her.'

'You've deliberately put yourself in danger?' She eyed me quizzically.

'I hope so, I want them to show themselves. I only wish to God I knew who I was fighting.'

‘Oh you silly man, why didn’t you tell me all this before? Look, I live here. Don’t underestimate these people, they’ve spent fifty years intimidating us and we’re none of us sure who they really are.’ She stood up. ‘Come with me and I’ll show you something.’

Carol led the way to the farm office. She opened a filing drawer, pulled out a sheet of paper and handed it to me. It was a crude computer graphic. It showed a drawing of a gravestone, with tufts of grass growing around its base. On it was an inscription.

Arthur Rocastle
1927 – 1946
Tom Stoneman
1987 –1997
So perish all who betray us

There was no doubt about the implied threat. Its simplicity was chilling. ‘For Christ’s sake, Carol, who sent you that?’

‘It was in an envelope on my desk at school, on Thursday.’

‘You’ve shown it to the police?’

‘Yes, they’ve kept it, this is only a photocopy. They’ve tested the original for fingerprints and they’ve asked me questions, but it’s that man Channing; he won’t take it seriously.’

‘Surely he’s got to.’ I was horrified. ‘I know he doesn’t like Duddlestone, but this isn’t a prank, not after what’s happened to my mother – he must know that.’

‘I hope so. He asked me for a list of Duddlestone kids at my school. We’ve got fifteen, but even if it’s one of them, they could have been forced to carry it. No Duddlestone child would talk to the police under those circumstances. I’m afraid it’s an ingrained part of their culture.’

‘What does your brother say?’

‘Ian thinks it’s only a bluff. He says I shouldn’t have spoken up in the pub that night.’

‘What’s your opinion?’

Carol rubbed her eyes. ‘If you must know I’m worried sick. We’re keeping Tommy under observation. He doesn’t understand why. We’ve always let him go wherever he likes in Duddlestone.’

‘Carol, who do you think’s behind this?’

She flopped on a chair. ‘It’s not just a bunch of village simpletons. That’s what Inspector Channing thinks, and he’s wrong. This sort of thing’s been going on for years.’

'Then who's behind it, what's the secret?'

'I'm sorry, I've no idea. I'm the baby of the family – they don't tell me anything.'

'Who's they?'

'Laura and Ian, they both know things that I'm not trusted with.' She sounded bitter.

I was beginning to see a chink of daylight. I remembered that time when Laura finally admitted that Arthur couldn't have been the killer of Margaret. Something she'd heard, "that Carol must never find out".

'No, they think they're protecting you.'

'How d'you know that?' She stared at me open mouthed.

'It's something Laura said, in confidence.'

'Not that night!' suddenly her anger flashed. 'Not pillow talk!'

'No, it was not that night. It was the next day. I accused her of setting me up so that Eriksen could do one of his smuggling runs. That night was a stupid mistake, probably alcohol-driven, and it will never happen again.'

'Do you give me your word on that?' She snapped the question. 'Peter, look at me. If we are to be friends, I want your word.'

'You have my word,' I said contritely.

She was standing now as she looked coldly at me for a full ten seconds. 'Come here,' she said. Obediently I walked the few steps to face her. She smiled and placed her hands on my shoulders.

'Consider yourself forgiven.' She flung her arms about my neck and pressed herself against me. I put my arms around her as I kissed her on the forehead and then on the lips. Then our tongues engaged, and we joined together as if we were a pair of fresh-faced teenagers.

Carol drew back and looked up into my face. 'What are you going to do? – don't leave us.'

I pulled her close to me again. 'No, I'm not going to run away. Your troubles may be my father's doing, and in that case I'm going to purge this place if it's the last thing I do.'

I went to bed less troubled than I might have been. In fact I felt almost serene. I had a cause now, a sense of duty, and a mission that overrode any danger. I liked to think my father would have understood that. I slept peacefully but not so deeply. Subconsciously I heard the latch on my bedroom door. There was someone moving quietly into the room. Instantly I was awake, alert and tense.

'Peter, can we talk?' It was Carol. Slowly I relaxed, but my heart was still pounding like a child's awaking from a scary nightmare. 'I had to look in on Tommy,' she said. 'I was worried and I can't sleep.'

'How's Tommy taking all this?'

'He doesn't understand the restrictions. It's difficult and the police-woman advised me not to show him that paper.'

'You really think he's in danger?'

'You know what happened to Roy and your mother?'

'Yes, but what threat could a little kid like Tommy be to anyone?' I tried to sound reassuring, and yet that nasty little cartoon had coupled the boy with Arthur and talked of betrayal.

'I don't know, but I'm nearly off my head with worry. I'm his mother, he's my life, and he's just a child. How could these people threaten a child?'

'Because they're the lowest of the low,' my own anger was beginning to burn. 'They're the sort of scum who would. It's not Tommy they're after, it's you. So they're working on you through your son. It's the most potent way to bring compliance from a mother and they know it. You'll have to be careful.'

'You too; if I'm in danger you must be even more so.' She was sitting on the bed looking at me. I could see the outline of her face in the moonlight from the window.

'I shall watch my back, you can be certain of that. After what you've said tonight, I can tell you one thing.' I paused. 'They have made an implacable enemy in me, and you've found yourself a loyal friend in trouble.' I reached out and took her hand.

'Peter,' she said hesitantly, 'I can't sleep for worry, can I come in with you? I don't mean make love or anything. I just want to be close to you.'

I was wakened by birdsong. I looked at my watch; the time was four fifteen and the dawn chorus was starting to swell with the first glimmers of light. I wondered if I would ever become accustomed to life on shore. The girl beside me was still fast asleep, her breathing soft and peaceful. It might be a hard thing to explain to an outsider, but there had been no thought on either side of sex and no physical contact between us. These things could happen in days to come but for now both of us were content. Somehow, I knew that night together was the forging of a bond. I rolled over and put an arm around her. Carol, still sleeping, muttered something and snuggled closer. I drifted once more into slumber; when I awoke it was daylight. The early morning sun was streaming through the window, and I was alone; Carol had gone. I looked at the time; it was seven thirty.

I left my bed and stared out of the window at the world. A tractor was moving in the yard, and I could see the newly-milked cows making their stately way back to pasture. I went to the bathroom, showered and dressed. No one was around; once again I had been caught out as a sluggard. As I descended the stairs I heard a car pull up in front of the house. I recognised it as Brian Byrne's. This was a surprise, and I went to the front door to let him in. I wondered what on earth could bring him here so early? I assumed it must be some repercussion from the reunion last night.

'There's been a development,' he said, 'another killing.'

CHAPTER 30

Suddenly I felt resentful. This tiresome little reporter was spoiling my morning with bad news. A morning when I had felt at ease and, dare I say it, in love.

'What's happened?'

'It's Reg Stoneman, you know the guy who gave Roy's abductors a lift to the harbour. He's our only witness. They got him yesterday afternoon. Clever too, they made it look like an accident. Took the police in for an hour or so.'

'Where was this?'

'Just down the road at Corfe Castle. His head was smashed in.'

'Sorry Brian, I can't focus at the moment. Make us both a cup of coffee while I ring the hospital.'

Mother had been on my mind from the moment I woke up. I couldn't get my head around this latest development. Byrne would have to wait.

The ward sister reported that mother was still unconscious, but her pulse rate had steadied, and she had passed a peaceful night. The doctors were considering doing a brain scan.

In the kitchen Brian handed me my cup of coffee. I told him about Mother and then asked what he intended.

'DCI Channing's at the Scene of Crime. He would like to see both of us. He says we can go there now if we like.'

'All right, but I'll have to ring Laura first. I'm overdue at work.'

Brian parked the car and we walked through the old stone archway into the outer perimeter of Corfe Castle. A police constable examined Brian's press pass and waved us through. It was a lovely summer morning, but the gaunt hilltop ruin added a sinister chill to my mood.

'Oliver Cromwell's engineers blasted this place to stop it being used.' Brian explained. 'You know the background?'

'I can't say I do.' I wasn't really in the mood for a history lesson.

Brian stopped and gazed up hill. 'It's a tale of two families. The Bankes and the De Gullaits. The Bankes family owned this place and they defended it for King Charles. They held out to the end. The castle was never taken; it was betrayed by insiders in the garrison.'

I looked up the steep bare hillside. Any attempt to storm that castle would have made the attackers sitting ducks.

‘Now hear another tale,’ said Brian. ‘Sir Roger De Gullait, of Duddlestone Manor, wouldn’t join forces with the Bankes. It seems they didn’t get on. So he defended his own place.’

‘What happened?’

‘The Roundheads captured the house and burned it to the ground. You can still see it, but it’s just a mound on the Rocastle land. Later the Commonwealth levied fines on the De Gullaits that broke them. The Bankes were cannier folk, they survived.’

‘What happened to Sir Roger?’

‘He died and his family sank steadily down the social scale till they can’t sink much lower.’

‘You mean the Gulleys?’

‘That’s them, from riches to rags, as we say where I come from.’

Half way up the slope we could see police, some in white overalls and hoods working inside a taped off area at the foot of another broken wall of masonry. Channing detached himself from the others and greeted us gloomily.

‘I could see where you were coming from with that speech last night,’ he said to me.

I was surprised, because I couldn’t recall seeing him there. ‘I want to draw the fire away from my mother. I can look after myself, she can’t. What are you doing about her, by the way?’

‘I’ve an officer stationed in the corridor outside her room at the hospital. We’ll run shifts through twenty four hours until this thing is settled.’

‘So you do take the threat seriously?’

‘See here, Mr Wilson. I always take anything to do with Duddlestone seriously, especially now we’ve two murder investigations.’

‘So this Stoneman was definitely killed deliberately?’

‘In our opinion, yes.’

‘What happened here?’ asked Byrne.

‘Yesterday afternoon, between ten past three and twenty five past, Reg Stoneman was here taking his grandchild for a walk. The little girl, she’s only three, was found wandering around crying her eyes out. The staff here searched, and they found Mr Stoneman with his skull fractured. Our police doctor says death was near instantaneous. On the face of it he climbed this wall and fell off, or at least that’s what we thought at first.’

‘You mean it was what you were meant to think,’ said Brian.

‘I can only comment on matters of fact. However, there is a piece of rock we found under the head that would be consistent with the damage, but neither our surgeon or the forensic people are wearing that.'

'Meaning he didn't fall off the rock, rather the rock fell on him?'

'I can only comment on matters of fact, but we are working to ascertain if the stone in question was the weapon used to effect the crime.'

Brian sighed audibly as he turned to me. 'That's cop speak for saying someone unknown smashed that rock over Reg's head.'

For the first time Channing had a bleak smile. 'The little girl, Tracie, we've had a specially trained WPC talk to her. The poor little mite's withdrawn into herself but she did say something. "Man upstairs…" over and over again. Off the record, Brian, we suspect the assailant was waiting, lying on top of the wall.'

'How would the murderer have known Stoneman would walk under the wall? Even if he knew his victim was coming here, it's a very public place.'

Channing looked grim. 'We understand Mr Stoneman was devoted to his granddaughter. The trip to the castle was a regular event, and they would always picnic under this wall.'

'But they could have killed the little girl.' I was horrified.

'Frankly, between you and me, they probably wouldn't care.' Channing's tone was icy. 'I think this was staged to look like an accident – very clever too.'

I looked up at the jagged wall. No elderly Duddlestonian could have shinned up there. Only a young and athletic figure could have achieved such a climb unassisted.

'Mr Channing,' I said. 'Will you accept that something is going on here?'

'Mr Wilson, you are asking me to speculate or theorise, and we don't do that. It's true there have been three violent crimes in a short space of time. They may all be connected to some criminal activity, but the nature of that activity is unknown to us at present. So, Mr Wilson, it's up to you. If you learn something, report it.'

I tried again. 'What relation is this Reg to Carol Stoneman?'

'Ex-husband's cousin, but that's nothing in Duddlestone, they're all bloody related.'

'You know someone's threatened to kill Tommy Stoneman?'

'I've seen it,' Channing grunted. 'Sadistic little drawing. Oh sure, we've some screwed up people to deal with.'

'But you will take the threat seriously. Carol's nearly out of her mind.'

'We've given Mrs Stoneman advice. We've recommended she and her family take precautions. But I can't see anyone harming the little lad – for what purpose? No, I say to Mrs Stoneman what I've said to you: listen, think and report. Report anything, even if you think it's wholly trivial – we'll be the judge.'

'We've got to be patient, Peter,' said Brian. 'This isn't a normal investigation –it's Duddlestone.'

Channing released a loud sigh. He looked skyward towards the castle summit. 'Mr Wilson, my colleagues past and present have battered our heads against Duddlestone for fifty years. If I could blow that place wide open and expose all its nasty little secrets then, I would retire a very happy man.' He gave me an oddly enigmatic look. 'Don't worry, we'll be around. Meantime, you keep an eye on Carol Stoneman and her boy and…' he paused. 'Watch your back.'

I finally reached Old Duddlestone at half past eleven. I found Laura and told her the latest news. She didn't seem particularly surprised, but then you could never tell with Laura.

'Look,' I said, 'take the rest of the day off; Mick as well. You've both done brilliantly covering for me. I'll be OK now.'

'Thanks, but not today. That Tabitha Long's been nosing around. I caught her looking in the sub-aqua boys' boat.'

'Are they out there now? Where do they get all this time off?'

'Keith told me they've special leave.' Laura looked worried. 'In fact, from what he said, this isn't a fun dive; I think it's semi-official.'

'So what, as long as they pay their dues it's no concern of ours.'

Laura said nothing but I knew something was bugging her. 'Keith and the other one are out there now,' she said. 'The bloke called Dave is in London. Keith says Dave's their wreck historian. He's spending the day in the Public Records Office in Kew.'

'They seem mighty interested in that ship, but I wouldn't call her historic. She was only a Liberty Ship, they built hundreds of them, all identical.'

'I don't know,' said Laura. She was looking at me in that inscrutable way. 'Tell you something though. She went down the day before Margaret was murdered.'

'You're not saying there's a connection?' I laughed.

She reacted angrily. 'Of course not. Margaret was raped by Arthur Rocastle and afterwards he killed her.' She glared at me.

'That's not what you told me the other day. This is plain stupid. I thought you'd given up this childish denial.' Frankly I was appalled.

'I don't know what you're talking about,' she glared at me and stalked out of the room.

It was four thirty and all was well. The sun was shining, the harbour was full of family yachts and their crews; all nice people. I had decided to move back here tonight. I would anchor *Stormgoose* in the open harbour and wait. I had my mobile phone and, as a last resort, I had my distress rockets and a powerful foghorn. I could draw attention to myself in spectacular fashion if I cared to.

I was ready to return to Honeycritch when Keith of the sub-aquas strode into the office. He was angry and this made him a formidable presence.

'Who's fucked about with our gear?' Keith banged two clenched fists down on my desk and leaned forward aggressively.

I've spent half a lifetime dealing with stroppy young men. I stared at him bleakly. 'Get your hands off my desk. Now, sit down!'

Slowly he relaxed. 'Sorry skipper, but this has just about pissed me off.'

'OK, tell me what happened and I'll see what can be done.'

Keith flopped down on one of the chairs. His hair and face were both salt encrusted as was the wet suit he was still wearing.

'That's better,' I said. 'Now tell all.'

'One of our film cassettes has been nicked.'

'For your video camera?'

'Yeah, and not a blank one. It was full of material we'd just shot.' Keith breathed audibly; he was controlling his rage with difficulty.

'Where did this happen?'

'The stuff was in a cool box in the back of our truck.'

'Didn't you lock it?' I must have sounded unsympathetic.

Keith's indignation flared. 'Of course we bloody did. Some light-fingered bastard must've had a key.'

I considered the facts while he cooled down. 'Look, I think you should report this to the police. I don't want to be heavy with you, but we do not accept responsibility for petty theft. Was there anything special about this film?'

'Too bloody right there was. Nothing we can't shoot again, but I tell you this skipper, it's what we came for and it's dynamite, in more ways than one.' This time he laughed.

Having unburdened himself Keith left in a milder temper, while I hastened in search of Laura. She was in her cottage. I came straight to the point. 'Tabitha Long's stolen a film tape from the sub-aqua lads.'

'Who told you?'

'Keith did. He stormed into the office and went ballistic. I had a job calming him.'

'Why didn't he go for the Long woman – it's nothing to do with us?'

'He doesn't know who did it and I didn't enlighten him. I told him to go to the police.'

'Fat lot of good that'll do – it's high summer, they get hundreds of lost items reported everyday.' She passed me a cup of tea.

'What exactly was Tabitha up to this morning? You said you saw her messing with Keith's things?'

'She was clambering around in their boat. You see, they've brought in a second RIB. Keith says he borrowed it from the Special Boat Squadron in Hamworthy. It's in the old tunnel now.'

This was news to me. The SBS was the Royal Marines' equivalent of the dreaded SAS. They were tough, elite and secretive. As far as I knew they wouldn't lend their equipment to anyone. I said so to Laura.

'Keith is SBS,' she said.

'The hell he is – I thought he was an ordinary marine.'

To tell the truth I hadn't really asked. I knew all the team were armed forces of some category, but the SBS was a different kettle of fish altogether. I began to regard Keith with a new respect.

'Keith says someone took the film from their car. He says it was a clean job. The lock was opened with a duplicate key and the thief knew exactly where to look. That's got to be Tabitha.'

'I don't know,' Laura frowned. 'I saw her in the tunnel. That four-by-four of theirs was parked in full view. I doubt it was Tabitha.'

'Why?'

'Tabitha Long's a national figure, a high profile TV presenter. Frankly I don't see her nicking stuff from the back of a car.'

Laura was right. Tabitha was often rude and aggressive, but she was a consummate professional. She would never sink to the level of some tabloid hack. 'Then who would do it?'

'The one person who's always hanging around up there – that Australian girl, Jolene. She was here this morning.'

That made more sense than blaming Tabitha but I still had doubts. 'Why should she take it?'

'God knows, but she had the opportunity. Mick says he's seen her with George and Rita Dunlass – thick as thieves, so he says.'

For the first time the nasty little Jolene was beginning to bug me. Up to now she'd been an elusive presence that seemed harmless enough. Apparently she had a family connection to Double Six – so why should she run away whenever I showed?

'Can I bar her from this site?'

'Yes, of course we can, but in practice there's a mile long boundary and no security guards. If she's nicking stuff you'll have to catch her at it.'

I found Carol standing in the yard at Honeycritch. With her was Tommy and another kid. The youngsters were circling the area on their mountain bikes. I stepped smartly aside as Tommy's companion took a turn too wide and narrowly avoided a painful collision. The rider was a little fair-haired girl, with pretty features, aged around ten or eleven.

'Hello Mister Wilson,' said Tommy. 'This is, Alix, she's my girl friend.'

'I acknowledged and walked across to Carol. 'I never had a girl friend at ten,' I laughed. 'We thought girls were beneath notice.'

'Times change,' she smiled. 'Alix is a nickname, spelt with an li. She's Alexia really, but she's got half-brother called Alec. Alix is the daughter of one of Tricia's posh-nob friends.' Carol really had the most mobile face and now it was troubled. 'I've just heard about Reg Stoneman. Peter, I'm scared.'

'I know, we've all got to be careful. I only wish we knew who's behind this. I feel we're fighting shadows.'

'I know,' she said. 'But half of me is pleased. If there's a shadow, we've been living in it far too long. Maybe all this will change things.'

'Can you tell me anything about Reg?'

'He's my ex-husband's cousin. I'm sorry about what happened, particularly for poor Tracie, but I never liked him much.'

'Why?'

'He was always rude or, you know, sort of gruff. His daughter is Tracie's mother. We don't know who the father was. She looked after Reg, but I know he beat her up sometimes, and her mother too when she was alive.'

'Nice people you have in this village,' I said.

'And there's no need for that sarcastic tone – we're not all bad. But Reg, he was one of them.'

'You don't mean the people who killed Arthur?'

'No, he wasn't old enough for that, but he was part of that set. He would have known who.'

'If so, he died for it.' I caught Carol's eye. 'How much do you know?'

'Practically nothing, believe me. I'm out on a limb, even with my own family, because I championed Arthur. I can make guesses, but that's all.' She replied vehemently. I reached out to her. Now we were holding hands in full view of the house.

'Come in and have a meal with us,' she said softly. 'Do you really have to go back to your boat tonight?'

''Fraid so, and it's worse than that. I've got an appointment with Tabitha Long at the harbour, eight o'clock.'

I returned to my office at seven thirty. Laura had gone home to her cottage in the street. All was quiet in the harbour and on the quay. We had twenty-two visiting yachts, their happy crews unaware of the dramas being played onshore. I motored *Stormgoose* out into the harbour, anchored her, and returned in the dinghy. There was no sign of Tabitha Long and it was nearly eight fifteen. I waited until twenty past and then, irritated, I walked into the village and knocked on Laura's door. She waved me over the threshold and offered to cook me a meal.

'No thanks, your sister made me something back at the farm – I'm all right.'

'How thoughtful of her,' Laura grinned. 'Where are you off to now?'

'I'm going to have a look in the tunnel. I'm interested in that SBS boat.'

I went outside and glanced back at the quay. There was still no sign of Tabitha. It looked as if she had changed her mind, which suited me fine. It was nearly nine o'clock on this June evening, and the sun had passed below the level of the downs, leaving the village and the undercliff in deep shadow. The glare still shone from the sea, and its reflection lit the whole scene enhancing the deep colours. I unlocked the little wicket door and walked into the cavern. I had no torch, and anyway light still filtered in from outside. Parked in front of me was the grey RIB, resting on its launching trolley. I could see nothing in the least glamorous about this craft. It was well weathered by salt and wind and had been repaired several times. Suddenly I stopped still, the boat forgotten; from somewhere not far away came a sound. It was a deep echoing "boom", followed by a metallic clang, a distinctly musical note, an *f sharp.* I was alert, standing with ears strained. Someone or something, not far away, was throwing metal objects around. I listened for a full ten seconds – but the cavern remained silent. I could hear some voices by the harbour and the beat of a helicopter, somewhere in the sky above.

Inside here all was still. 'Hi, anyone there?' I shouted. My echoes bounced around the walls and ceiling. No reply; not a sound apart from the subdued background noises of the harbour. I was not alarmed but I was puzzled. The door had been firmly padlocked when I arrived. It was impossible to lock oneself inside. If anyone was trapped in the tunnels they would surely have made a call for help. I walked around the cave, looked in the different bays, and inside the old office building; I found nothing. I shrugged, went outside, and locked the door again.

I stood for a while looking down the village street. I wondered what I had let myself in for. I had deliberately set myself up as a target. Perhaps tonight would prove if I was right. I was aware of voices, raised, angry voices. Damn, I could do without aggravation among the harbour users. Wrong, these sounds were not from the water, they were overhead, high above me at the cliff top. Then I heard it, a shout of rage that turned to a scream of pure terror. I have never before or since heard such a scream, and I profoundly hope I never will again. It sounds a cliché but my scalp did prickle and, despite the heat, I felt cold with shock. A large object, dark and sinister, seemed to flutter down from the cliff top. It hit the ground with a liquid smack, not twenty feet from where I stood.

I admit I stood transfixed, my brain could not assimilate the sight before me. The dark bundle was a human body. I forced myself to go to it. I felt as if I was in one of those slow motion nightmares, crippled by leaden boots. The body lay on its back, distorted and broken, while blood oozed from the mouth, ears and nostrils. Here at last was Tabitha Long. I knew instinctively that there was nothing I could do. She was dead beyond recall.

CHAPTER 31

It was almost dark when the ambulance came. The paramedics shook their heads sadly: no pulse, no breath and a rapidly cooling corpse.

I was surprised how quickly the police were on the scene; proof, I hoped, that Channing was keeping his word and watching Duddlestone. Two officers in a car were followed by a van with three more dressed in those bulky white overalls. Someone began to photograph the body and mark a line around it, or as far as could be done on the rough surface.

The police wanted a statement. My mind refused to function, everything was a blur. I remembered standing breathless, hammering on Laura's front door. We had called 999 and then sprinted back to the scene. I had this crazy delusion that maybe I would find it was all a dream. Tabitha was still there. We could do nothing except wait.

Laura turned her back on the scene. 'What on earth was she doing on the cliff top?' Her voice was odd and she looked tense and unwell. I had seen bloodied accident victims before, but this must be a first for her. Accident – was this an accident?

Instinctively I glanced up at the dark outline of the cliff top. 'She wasn't alone up there,' I replied. 'I heard voices yelling like there was an argument.'

'Peter, is this another one?' Laura was visibly trembling. I had never seen her like this before.

'I don't know, but I'm sure the voices came from the top. Should I go up there and look?'

'No way!' She clutched my wrist in her alarm. 'For God's sake come away from here,' she muttered. 'I think I'm going to be sick.'

'Go back indoors.' I was firm. 'Keep an eye open for the emergency services. I'll stay here and wait.'

Laura hesitated before she turned, fled a few yards and was sick by the roadside. I turned away, not wanting to intrude on her dignity. Instead I forced myself to look once more at the grotesque object. Tabitha had changed from her power suit. The body was clad in jeans and a dark blue fleece. Something glinted in the fading light. It was a gold chain with a little heart locket. It seemed out of character, but so poignant; somebody, somewhere had loved this abrasive woman. Something had rolled out of the pocket of the fleece. It looked like a can of hair spray. I edged closer and found I was wrong. It was a tin of penetrating oil; the brand called WD 40.

I had serious suspicions regarding Tabitha's fall, but it was clear the police regarded the event as an accident. So why all the uproar? I asked the man who was about to take my statement.

'Tabitha Long's a celeb,' he grumbled. 'All hell's going to break out tomorrow. We've got to cover our backs.'

'Will Chief Inspector Channing be coming?' I was feeling desperate and I wasn't certain I would be believed.

'What, the CID bloke? Shouldn't think so – unless it's foul play.'

'I think it is foul play.'

I made my statement, sitting in the passenger seat of one of the patrol cars, while the copper scribbled on the paper attached to his clip board.

'If you would read this, please, and sign it,' he handed me the paper. It was a well-written précis of my words. I had no need to correct anything. I signed.

Ignoring me he left the car and ran over to his sergeant, who was talking to the police surgeon and a forensic man dressed in white overalls.

The sergeant read my statement in the light of a torch and then came across to me. He pointed to the cliff top. 'What's the quickest way up there?'

'There isn't a quick way, you'll have to go up the chine.' I pointed them to the pathway. The man acknowledged with a wave, and took off along the shoreline, followed by two others carrying lamps.

'It'll be too late,' I told the statement copper. 'Whoever was up there will have scarpered.'

'They'll do an on-the-spot search while things are still warm.' Suddenly he groaned. 'If you're right it'll be CID's problem, but it's something we don't need.'

'Why?' It was a silly question, but there was something in his manner I couldn't quite relate to.

He glanced at me with that weary look of one dealing with impenetrable stupidity. 'Because it will be a high-profile, media-spotlight murder investigation, which is just about the last thing we want at the height of the tourist season. We're seriously undermanned as it is. I hope to God you're wrong, Mr Wilson, but if you're right – it'll be a nightmare, especially as it involves Duddlestone.'

To say that my mind was in turmoil would be an understatement. I declined Laura's offer to put me up for the night. She was no fool, and by now she must be thoroughly aware of the peril we were in. I declined the offer; I didn't want misunderstandings with Carol, and I had no intention of putting Laura into danger. Instead I motored *Stormgoose* to the very centre of the harbour and anchored where I had a maximum all round view. I spent the night hours crouched in the cabin hatch or in the cockpit. Bedside me I kept my heaviest boathook and my pack of distress rockets. Nothing happened, and when dawn began to show I fell asleep. I was too tired and too demoralised to care any more.

I was awake at seven. The sun was shining, the water sparkled, but for me the day was already dead. I could see parked cars and dark figures scurrying around near the cliff base. In the cabin I turned on my radio, not the ship-to-shore but my little transistor set. I had another nasty shock, although I suppose I should have expected it. The Radio Four "Today" programme was paying a fulsome tribute to Tabitha Long. '*A compassionate and thoughtful journalist, beloved by all her colleagues...*' waffled the reporter, a BBC local from Bournemouth. He went on to speculate as to the cause of the accident. '*Yet again death has blighted the little community of Duddlestone. The police will not say whether this tragedy is linked to the spate of murders down the years that have marked out this ill-reputed Dorset village.*'

I refused to listen to anymore. Instead I pulled out my mobile phone and rang the hospital. Mother was still in a coma, but her condition was no worse. I was told that my step-father Grant Bowker had arrived late last night and was by her bedside. This was good news, but I had better make contact with Grant and tell him all I knew. If our murderers suspected that mother had confided in him, his life could be on the line as well. Next I rang Channing. The Chief Inspector was unavailable; all I could do was relay my worries to a minion. I turned on the radio again to catch the full eight o'clock news. Incredibly, Tabitha was the lead story. I wondered how on earth the media had cornered so much detail so quickly; then I remembered Tabitha's Channel Nine film crew.

I took my dinghy across to the slipway. Mick had arrived with a package of newspapers to sell to our customers. He knew nothing about last night's horror. I explained, and I could see that the news had given him a nasty jolt. Mick was an easy going laid-back guy who lived for his sailing. For the first time in all his worldwide travels he had hit the seamier side of life. Whatever disasters came our way, I could not afford to lose him. I put this to him tentatively.

'No worries, Pete, mate. I'll stick around, it'll be something to tell the folks back home. Never thought you Poms was such a murderous lot.'

The newspapers were first editions and too early to report on Tabitha. The tabloid headlines screamed with some contrived indignation about politicians' lavish holidays. I guessed that by tomorrow the same politicians would be doubly grateful to Tabitha for drawing away the heat. One thing I did do. I went round our customers, visiting every boat as soon as I saw signs of life. I told them there had been a fatal accident on the cliffs. It had no connection with the yacht harbour, and we would do everything in our power to avoid the tragedy disrupting our services to them. We would appreciate it if children were kept away from the village until the police had gone. I breathed a mighty sigh of relief when this was over. Everyone took the news well. Some of course had already heard the story on the radio. I noticed that George and Rita Stoneman had gone, or at least their *Marietta* was no longer with us.

I went into my inner office and shut the door. I wanted to be alone. Last night's memories were vivid and they intruded into everything I did. The sight of a living human being smashed into oblivion at my feet was recorded in my mind, and it played over and over again, with no escape. At least she hadn't screamed as she fell. In stories or in films, the victims always screamed; awful cries fading into the distance. That horrible thud as the body hit the ground kept echoing inside my head. Why had she fallen? It might still be an accident. Tabitha was unfamiliar with the terrain. She could have lost her footing. Not so, she had been forced over. Seconds before the fall I had heard her. Yes, she had screamed then; not the kind of terror stricken yell of the films. It had been an odd sound; a mixture of, pain, rage and fear. Seconds before that there had been voices; two voices raised in angry confrontation. The woman's voice was Tabitha's, I knew that now. The second voice was quieter, almost muffled. I had not heard enough to recognise it, even to be certain whether it was man or woman. It could possibly have been a woman. I concentrated, trying to recall something, but it was hopeless.

Laura walked into the room. 'I've just driven back from New Duddlestone. There's a crowd of press people at the army gate trying to register for passes. The first lot are already on the way here.'

'Oh God,' I buried my face in my hands.

She continued. 'That copper Channing is up the street, and he wants to see you now.'

The Chief Inspector was standing at the spot where the body had fallen. The area had been surrounded with a taped boundary. Outside the tape I could see press people and two TV crews milling about. As I walked up the street I could see more figures standing tall in silhouette on the cliff top. A uniformed police constable, with a loud hailer, was attempting to pacify the crowd. DCI Channing, he said, would address a press conference in Poole Police Station at one-thirty. Until then the police had no comment to make. This satisfied none of them. I elbowed my way to the front of the mob. Channing saw me and waved to his people to let me through. This created further uproar and two journalists physically grabbed me demanding to know who I was. I pushed them away, only just restraining myself from throwing a punch. Two policemen intervened and I was escorted to where the DCI stood, hands behind his back, in a posture of grim professional detachment. 'What the hell've I done to deserve this?' he grumbled.

'It'll be a big plus for your career if you solve the case,' I said.

'Bugger that, I'm due to retire in the autumn. I don't need a place in history. Now I'm about to get one – same as Albert Stobart.'

'Who was he?'

'He died ten years ago. He was the DCI who fouled up the Rocastle case in 1946. Got him a public rebuke from a high court judge. It finished him for good.'

'I remember, I've read the reports.'

'I know, not that I've much sympathy for Stobart. He must have known he didn't have a case. He never said much but I always had the impression he was under threat himself.'

'How could that be?'

'There's other kinds of police in this country, Mr Wilson, and it doesn't pay to cross them.'

'You don't mean MI5?'

'I don't know what I mean. Right now I've my own problems. Come with me, Mr Wilson, and tell me what you make of all this.' I followed him into a large caravan parked among the police vehicles. It bore the sign, *Incident Room.* Channing waved me to a chair and sat down himself. Before he could speak his mobile phone jingled. The Inspector answered. 'Understood – hold please.' He put the phone down and turned to me. 'Excuse me a minute. There's a missing persons alert, I've got to divert some of my officers.'

'Who's missing?' I asked.

'Couple of kids. Happens this time of year with all the holiday-makers makers around. Probably wandered off and got lost, but we don't take chances.'

I told Channing what I suspected and then left him to get on with his job. I walked back to the quay. More cars were arriving, all containing media people. I directed them up the street to join their fellows and then escaped to the privacy of my own office. Laura was already there and so was Keith of the sub-aquas. He was sitting by my desk with a batch of colour photographs spread out before him. I greeted both of them and gave them a run down of events up the road. I wasn't feeling too good but I was pleased to see Keith. I badly needed a distraction and it seemed he was keen to provide just that.

'These are my stills of the diving site.' He picked up a photograph and passed it to me. It was an underwater shot of the usual barnacle encrusted steel hull of a sunken vessel. In the foreground a diver was pointing to some lettering; the ship's name.

'We cleaned off that part first,' said Keith. 'Confirmed the identity of the ship, but we knew that anyway.'

I studied the picture trying to pick out the letters on the encrusted plating. WILMA E..ARD, was the nearest I could make of it.

'She's the *Wilma Everard*,' said Keith. 'Standard Liberty Ship. American flag, but all European crew. Now look at these.' He handed me two more pictures and a magnifying glass.

I wished I could share his obvious delight in all this, but I am a professional seaman. I can summon no enthusiasm for wrecks and such pictures make me feel queasy. The first shot revealed an underwater hull section in a remarkable state of preservation, apart from a jagged hole that had been punched in low down.

I looked at Keith. 'That's where your mine blew I suppose?'

He grinned. 'That's the bow section, starboard side. Take a look at this one – port side stern – see the propeller?'

I picked up the second photograph and squinted through the magnifying glass. Keith was right, the heavily encrusted propeller was clearly visible, but near it was a second jagged hole similar to the one made by the mine. I was no expert, but there was something wrong here.

'Looks like two mines?' I said.

'No, two explosions, but neither was a mine.' Keith sat back with an expression of smug triumph. 'These were internal blasts, and if you want my opinion, that ship was sunk by pre-laid charges inside her.'

'Accidental or sabotage?'

'Can you think of a third possibility?'

'You tell me.'

'How say she was scuttled by her own crew?'

'Keith, that's crazy. Why on earth would anyone do that?'

'Depends on your motives,' he was wholly serious now. 'Look, we hit on that wreck purely as a training ground. There's hundreds like her all round the coast. My mate, Dave, is big on history. When we found something funny about the *Wilma Everard,* Dave began to do some checking.'

I didn't like this. A horrible yawning chasm was opening at my feet. 'What has Dave found?' I asked in as neutral voice as I could manage.

'The *Wilma Everard* sailed from the USA in May 1945, bound for Gibraltar. She had a part consignment of motor bikes and aero-engines. She discharged that lot in Gib' and then she sailed for the UK with the remaining cargo…'

'Which was?'

Now Keith laughed. 'Cigarettes and whisky and wild, wild women. Well not the women, but ten tons of US Army cigs and one thousand bottles of Southern Comfort. Value of that lot at today's money?' He looked at me questioning.

'I've no idea – you tell me.'

'One and a half a million quid at a modest estimate.'

'What's in the ship now?'

'I can't tell you about the cigarettes, they'd've rotted long ago, but there ain't no bottles in the *Wilma's* hold. If there were we'd see 'em.'

'Have you talked to the press about this?'

'No, we're an official service club. It'd probably be a breach of our remit. The only media person we've consulted is that Brian, here.'

'What does he know apart from events in Duddlestone?'

'He's a historian. He's talked to a colleague in the States on the internet. He's found out some more about the *Wilma,* and it's mega…'

'Explain please.' I was not happy and I beginning to be annoyed by Keith's self-congratulating smugness.

'The *Wilma Everard* was a standard Liberty ship in all respects but one. She had a built-in strong room next to the Captain's quarters. On that voyage she was carrying money – five hundred thousand in dollar bills. United States forces payroll.'

Something was happening on the quay. I could hear a hubbub of voices outside the window. In the circumstances I was glad to make an excuse and leave the room. I noticed Laura had already gone. The sun was burning down and I pulled on my dark glasses against the glare. To my surprise Carol was there. Laura was standing with her arms around her sister. With them were some people whom I guessed were reporters. An angry police constable was trying to push them back. With him was Babs Stent, the dinosaur girl. I ran to Carol who extracted herself from Laura and flung her arms around me. She was trembling and her face was streaked with tears.

'Peter, Tommy and Alix are missing.'

CHAPTER 32

I gently released Carol's grip on me and led her to the office door. I turned to the policeman. 'Can you keep these people away?'

'Yes, sir, no problem.'

'What exactly happened?'

'Two kids gone missing,' he pulled my elbow and led me a short distance from the others. 'I see you know this lady?'

'Yes, I do. It's her boy that's missing?'

'Two missing – Thomas Stoneman and Alexia Ford-Watts.'

'It's an abduction isn't it?' I stared the man in the eyes and he shied away.

'We don't know yet, sir, and we don't want Mrs Stoneman more alarmed than needs be.'

'Can you tell me anything, any details whatever?' My tone was sharper than I intended but I was worried. I liked Tommy and he was Carol's boy. I felt protective as if he was almost my own.

'They're probably only lost, but my chief is concerned. You see the little girl, Alexia, is the daughter of Jonathan Ford-Watts.'

That name did ring a bell. I wished I was better informed. I had been out of the country for so long I had lost track of people and events that were everyday news. I wasn't going to expose my ignorance by asking who Ford-Watts was. He didn't sound like a footballer or a pop singer. He was probably some well-heeled industrialist.

The policeman was glaring at the reporters who were trying to edge closer. 'Don't worry, sir. The odds are they've wandered off and they'll turn up OK.'

I stood still, I needed to calm down and think straight. All other problems had dwindled to nothing compared to this. I wanted to go to Carol and console her if I could. I wanted to run back up the street to Channing and urge him to action, now, this moment. The copper I had spoken to seemed to ignore Tommy. He assumed any kidnap attempt must involve the girl, Alix. The worst scenario would be forcible abduction by a paedophile. One read about such cases all the time. The very suggestion was enough to send a nasty shiver through me. Keep calm, be positive.

Laura had taken Carol inside the office. Babs was standing by the open door. 'Can you tell me anything?' I asked her.

'Peter, it's all our fault, I feel awful. I never realised...' She shook her head, she looked almost distraught. 'Tommy and Alix came to see us on their bikes around six o'clock. We didn't know they'd been told to stay at home. We'd no idea they were in danger!'

Oh God, I thought, we'd all let our guard slip. The children would resent being grounded for no reason. They must have sneaked off while adult backs were turned. I told Babs so. 'They're spirited kids, and any grownup imposition like that would be fair game.'

'I only wish we'd been told,' she sighed. 'Anyway, it seems they never went home. Carol, Ian and Tricia have been out all night searching for them.'

'Why didn't they come straight here?' I was surprised. 'I never had a phone call and Laura seems to have only just heard.'

'It's that deceitful little minx, Alix. She left a message at Honeycritch saying they were going down to the village shop. It was a lie, and it meant that Carol and the others were searching New Duddlestone knocking on doors.'

'But they weren't anywhere near New Duddlestone?'

'No they weren't; we saw them near our dig on Weaver's Down at six o'clock. Ian found their bikes there at seven this morning. That's over twelve hours…' Babs voice had a tremor as her composure broke.

'Did you see anyone else on the downs, apart from the kids?'

'The police asked us that, but honestly we were absorbed in our work and we probably wouldn't have noticed.' She was near to tears now and I didn't want to push her further. A nasty thought was intruding and it wasn't going away. The children might well have been near the scene of Tabitha's fall. They might well have witnessed something even if they hadn't seen the actual assault.

'Come on.' I said. 'I'll talk to Carol and then we'll see what we can do.'

Carol was sitting in my office chair. She had stopped crying but was ashen faced and very still. Laura was trying to coax her into drinking a cup of tea. I walked over and put an arm around her shoulders. 'I'm going to find them.' I tried to sound strong and confident. 'I'll get some people together right away and I'll gee-up the police.'

'I've been everywhere already,' she spoke quietly without expression. 'I've shouted and I've called but there was no answer – nothing.' She broke down clinging to me, sobbing.

'That's true,' said Laura, 'look at the state of her.' I could see what she meant. Carol's summer dress was the same one she'd worn yesterday. Now it was stained green from grass and torn by brambles. Her white shoes were discoloured by dirt and cow dung.

Carol spoke, 'I'm coming with you.'

'No,' I was firm. 'I don't think so. You're shattered – all in. Rest here for a bit while we take over. Fresh pairs of eyes could make all the difference. We'll start along the shoreline. I wouldn't mind betting one of the kids has twisted an ankle and the other one's stayed there waiting for help.'

'No, Peter, I can't wait here. I know the ground. You don't, nor do the police.'

I managed to assemble a twenty-strong search party. With myself were Laura, Mick and four police constables, plus six volunteers from our visiting yacht crews. In addition I recruited two press reporters and a photographer. One of these was an ebullient little man who presented his card for that brashest of tabloid papers. 'I reckon this could be a better story than Tabitha falling on her nut,' he said.

'No,' said my policeman. 'Remember there's an official block on all reporting until we're certain this isn't a kidnap.'

'I'll take a chance on it,' said the man with an irritating grin.

I fixed him with my most hostile stare. 'If you come with us, you are here to search, not harass the boy's mother – understood?'

I was just about to brief my forces when three more helpers appeared in the form of Steve Gulley and two of his mates. For once I was pleased to see them. I asked Steve to act as a guide to the six yachties. The man looked pathetically grateful. I guessed nobody had ever trusted him with responsibility before. I turned to Carol and squeezed her hand. 'Right everybody – let's go.'

In the end we covered over three miles of coastline with no result. We met a few walkers and solitary sunbathers; no one had seen a trace of the children. After two hours we stood in a demoralised group: hot, sweaty and very thirsty.

I was even more concerned for Carol. She had slumped against a rock, her speech slurred, her movements almost that of a zombie. We needed to find her a doctor. She was doing neither herself nor us any good here. I asked if anyone could help? I was in luck; we had a doctor. Actually the man was an eye surgeon, one of our visitors. A policeman agreed to help him take Carol back to the harbour. Once she was gone I felt a little better and I sat down to think.

I reminded myself that Tommy was a local boy. He had been

raised here and knew every inch of this shoreline and all the surrounding country. In this context he could be termed, "streetwise". I could not believe he would be so stupid as to be caught by a flood tide. I called a conference with Laura, Babs and the police.

'They're not here,' I said. 'We had to look, but I don't think they were ever here.'

'I think you're right,' said Laura. 'Let's ask Steve.'

'Steve Gulley?' I was dismissive.

'Yes, Steve. He's always wandering around here. He'll know what Tommy gets up to.' She jabbed a finger at me. 'Remember how he set Tommy to spy on you?'

'I'm not likely to forget. He nearly wrecked my boat.' I stood up and yelled for Steve. He wandered over to us and stood looking both nervous and truculent.

'Steve, we had to check the shoreline, but now we've got to search for real. Where would you start?'

'Weavers Down, up by the old quarry.'

'That's where they found the mountain bikes. The area's already been checked.'

'I knows that, Mister Wilson. I still says as we ought'a be starting up there.'

'All right, we will.'

As we walked back to the old village the coastguard helicopter roared overhead and began to follow the contours of the cliff top. The police with us checked by radio with their control. They confirmed that the rescue services were searching for the children, but there was still a news blackout. In the village the police provided us all with a drink of water. The temperature on the quay was Celsius thirty degrees. We were all thirsty and tired. Laura went to find her sister and reported that Carol had been taken home. She was mentally and physically exhausted.

We struggled up the slope to Weavers Down. There was now a cooling sea-breeze, thank goodness, but I was still sweating. We spread out in an extended line and combed the ground inch by inch. The police had told us to look for items of clothing and anything, however trivial, that looked recent. Even scraps of paper might provide a clue. I tripped and nearly twisted an ankle in a rabbit hole. The hillside seemed to be alive with the creatures. Once on the ridgeway I made straight for the first of the concrete mushroom vents. I walked around it and kicked the metal grilles. All was solid and secure. I followed the line, checking each one in turn without result. In the distance I could see Babs and a lone policeman by the old stone quarry. Someone shouted and pointed; another search party was spread out along the skyline moving towards us. Ten minutes later we met them. They were army lads and led by my friend Alistair Pickering.

He greeted me wearily. 'No joy – bad business.'

'This is where they found the bikes,' I told him. 'Let's have another look round.'

The bikes were still there. The two machines were leaning against a grassy bank as if the riders would return at any moment. I felt an awful sense of desolation.

'We've already checked every nook and cranny around here,' said one of the police.

'Never mind,' I replied. 'I think I'll have one more try. Let's start in here,' I pointed down the slope into the quarry.

The old stone working was a cheerless place, although I could understand its fascination for two ten-year-olds. The roadway into the quarry was made of crushed and powdered stone. The whole area was devoid of vegetation except for a few patches of thistles, ragwort and a layer of dried moss. The sides were sheer and coloured with different shades of grey. I remembered reading somewhere that the miners had to take off the stone in layers before they reached the lower levels and the valuable masonry blocks. It was a shadowy place, devoid of the breeze and even more sultry than the hillside. In front of me was the strange pict-like stone hut. I stooped and entered it, leaving time for my eyes to adjust to the darkness. The interior was bare apart from a square rock that could have done justice as the quarrymen's table. They must have been short in stature those old miners; I had to bend in order to move around. The floor was dusty and there was no sign of footmarks or anything else. I emerged again into the full glare and the heat. I was feeling increasingly depressed; I had never felt so utterly impotent.

Alistair was examining a pile of rusty junk. It had been a vehicle of some sort, the panelling had rotted away but one could still see an engine block and wheel rims. 'It's a World War Two Jeep,' he said. 'Must be from your father's time. We haven't used that model in years.'

'Looks like it was burnt out,' I said. The floor of the quarry was a mess. Remote as it was, the place seemed to be the dumping ground for old oil drums and fertiliser bags.

Laura was standing by the derelict engine shed. ‘Hi, Peter, I think they’ve been here.’

Forgetting the heat, I sprinted across to her. I had noticed this building on my first visit; the day I had encountered the palaeontology team. It was much bigger than I had realised, although its tin roof had long since decomposed. The decaying remains of some sort of conveyor projected into the quarry.

I followed Laura through the arch that still had the vestigial remains of a wooden door. The light streamed in through the rotting beams. The carcass of a steam engine occupied the centre. All that remained was a wrecked and vandalised boiler and a giant flywheel that lay detached on the floor.

‘Peter, over here,’ Laura called. She was standing in the far corner, the only part with some roof sheeting still in place.

I joined her. ‘Have you been in here before?’ I asked.

‘Not since I was a child.’ She caught my arm and pointed. We were looking at a small picnic table. In the middle of it was a large biscuit tin. ‘The police have checked in here but I don’t think they knew the significance.’

‘This is the kids’ private den?’

‘That’s about it. I’m going to rummage around.’ Laura began to examine the floor and walls. I couldn’t see the point of this, I wanted to move on and search somewhere fresh, although I didn’t know exactly where.

‘Tommy keeps his stuff in this box,’ said Laura. She levered the square lid off the biscuit tin. She picked it up and carried it across to me. It contained a pocket knife, half a pack of Mars Bars, a small hammer, a box of matches, a torch and a ball of string; exactly the kind of stuff I would have assembled at Tommy’s age. The little collection had an innocence that brought a lump to my throat.

Laura put down the box. Her hands were shaking as she faced me. ‘Tommy always took this with him in a rucksack – he always did.’ Her voice was flat and expressionless. She walked back to the table. Suddenly she stopped, reached down, and picked up a scrap of paper. ‘This was underneath the box,’ she said.

It was a single sheet of lined paper torn from one of those loose-leaf notebooks. Laura stared at it, shook her head and passed it to me.

There was a message; meaningless in any normal context, written in an untidy scrawl with a felt tip pen.

Mummy

High jump
High jump
Alix.

'Does this mean anything,' I asked.

Laura shrugged. 'I don't expect so.'

'We'd better give it to the police?'

'No, not straight away. I think I'll show it to Carol and Alix's mother.'

I didn't like this. 'You could be in trouble, withholding evidence.'

'I don't care. I told you I don't think our police realise the significance of this box. Tommy wouldn't willingly leave it here. He took it with him everywhere, and I think Alix's mother should see that paper today.'

'Laura, who is Jonathan Ford-Watts?'

She stared at me with blank astonishment. 'Peter where have you been these last few years?'

'I've been at sea, and when I haven't been there, I've been fighting a losing battle with a pack of female lawyers.'

'Don't you ever go to the cinema or watch telly?'

'So, I suppose he's some sort of actor?'

'That's rather like saying Yehudi Menhuin was a bit of a fiddle player, or that Elvis was some sort of ballad singer.'

'OK, point taken, but I'd still like to know who he is because the police seem to have forgotten Tommy completely. I'm sorry for the little girl, of course, but my loyalty is to Carol and Tommy.'

'Jonathan Ford-Watts is a super-star. Royal Shakespeare, television, Holywood, including one Oscar...'

'All right, I get the picture.'

'He's also had five spectacular divorces. Alix is the product of marriage number four. Her mother, Sara, is a mate of my sister-in-law, Tricia.'

We walked out into the quarry. A policeman, his white shirt wet with perspiration, was making his way towards us. 'Any news?' Laura called.

'Sorry, no. We're calling off the search around Old Duddlestone – there's nothing here.'

'What happens next?' I asked.

'We'll regroup and await instructions.'

I looked at Laura; my stomach felt as if it had just received a block of ice. 'What do we do?' I gestured helplessly. I was worrying about my mother now. I felt I was being torn in two. 'I must ring the hospital.'

'We'll go back to the harbour and then to Honeycritch,' she said firmly. 'Both of us.'

Channing was on the quay when we trudged back into Old Duddlestone. It took me a minute or two to catch his attention. I was desperate for news and I was determined to prise the details from him.

'Sorry,' he said, 'but it's not my investigation. Uniform are setting up an incident room at Poole and their own task force.'

'Are they keeping this secret?' I struggled for the right words. 'I mean, have the kids been abducted?'

'All possibilities are being examined, but we still think they're lost, or possibly one of them has had an accident.' He paused and I didn't need to follow his gaze. The Coastguard helicopter was sweeping an area half a mile offshore. 'As for secrecy, we've compromised. We've said the media can report two children missing but we've banned mention of names.

'That's all very well,' I said, 'but you people can only think of the Ford-Watts girl. You know Tommy Stoneman's been threatened for real.'

'Of course I do, but that's only a crude attempt to lean on his mother. But this Alexia Ford-Watts; her father's a wealthy man, he'd pay up if it was a ransom. That's why we've ask the media to play this down.'

'They'll find that difficult, there were over sixty people searching this afternoon.' I wasn't satisfied. The whole operation seemed to be grinding into a procedural tangle while each minute was vital.

Channing was every inch the policeman. To him this was a standard problem with a considered professional response. No doubt the rule book had a preordained drill.

'Look,' he said kindly. 'Supposing the worst has happened. The Ford-Watts kid is a hot property. They won't hurt her. If it's a paedophile he'd more likely only snatch one. We still think the most probable scenario is that they're lost.' He nodded and walked away.

I watched him go. I felt angry, helpless and sick with apprehension. Laura had vanished, as had most of our search team. I went to the office, stripped off my shirt, and put my head under the cold water tap.

A familiar yacht was coming alongside the outer pontoon. I ran down to help with her mooring lines. Here, once more, was my daughter Emma and her fiancé Simon. Emma jumped ashore and flung her arms around me, then she stepped back and stared. 'Dad, something's happened?'

I told her about her grandmother.

Emma reacted with anger. 'God, Dad, you say it was deliberate! Who on earth would drive a car at an old lady out for a walk?'

That of course was the point. The act was murderous and utterly callous. I was fairly sure of the attacker's motives, but I was not going to worry Emma with my suspicions.

'I don't know,' I replied. 'But we shall catch whoever did it.' I paused. 'We've other troubles here – two children have gone missing.'

'Are these local kids?'

'Yes, one of them is the son of a friend.'

'That's awful – can we do anything?'

'No, not now – it's out of our hands.' I looked at her concerned face. It was good to see her again. 'Go on, cheer me up – tell me about your cruise.'

'We've been to Devon. We sailed back across the bay yesterday.'

'I never saw you.'

'The weather was so settled, we anchored at Chapman's Pool,' said Simon.

I had never been there, but I knew Chapman's Pool to be another little nook in the coast, a few miles east of Duddlestone.

'We've had enough of marinas,' Simon continued. 'We were looking for a bit of peace and quiet – some hope.'

'What went wrong?'

'There was a bloody great helicopter buzzing overhead.'

'I know,' I explained. 'They were looking for the missing kids.'

Emma looked at me. 'Dad, we were going to ask you to join us for a meal in the De Gullait Arms tonight. That was before you told us about Gran.'

'She's stable but still unconscious. I'm allowed to call at the hospital any time, so we could all go over later.'

'OK, let's go to the Gullaits first. You need to relax a bit – you look awful.'

This caught me out. I wasn't sure I could sit down and eat a formal meal. At the same time it was good to see Emma again.

There was only one answer. 'All right. I'd be glad to. Be ready at seven o'clock and I'll drive you there.'

I said goodbye to Emma and Simon and then drove straight to Honeycritch Farm. I wanted to be with Carol, although it was with a sinking feeling that I turned into the narrow lane past the place where my mother had been brutally mown down. Outside the farmhouse were two cars. One was a police Panda car; the second was an immaculate blue Mercedes.

Tricia Rocastle met me at the front door. She looked haggard and careworn, very far from her usual self. 'Peter, thanks for coming. This is awful, and it's all my fault.' Her eyes were swollen and she clearly hadn't slept that night.

'Why?' I was appalled at the change in her.

'They said they'd gone to the village. I was busy when I should have gone looking for them.' She fell on my shoulder and sobbed.

I gently steered her into the kitchen and sat her down. 'You mustn't blame yourself. They could have got lost any time, and if professional kidnappers were after the girl they would have taken them from anywhere.'

'Not from this house they wouldn't.' Tricia's voice hardened. She nodded towards the twelve-bore gun that lay on the sideboard.

'Yes, I can believe that,' I said quietly. 'Can I see Carol?'

'I expect so, but she's sleeping at the moment. The doctor gave her a sedative.' Tricia stared at me with an eye contact that seemed to read my innermost thoughts. 'Carol's very fond of you – you know that?'

'I like her too,' I stared back.

'How would you define, "like"?' Normally I resent such superior county-type females, but there wasn't much I could hide from this one.

'Tricia, I've had one bad marriage, and so has Carol. The scars are there, inside both of us, even if we don't show them to the world.' I stopped to let the words sink in. I turned away from her and walked to the window. 'Yes, I'm very fond of Carol and I like young Tommy. I believe we could build something good between the three of us. In the meantime…' I turned back and met her eyes again. 'In the meantime let's find these kids and bring them home.'

Tricia stood up. 'Come with me,' she said.

I followed her into the living room. Two women were seated facing each other on either side of the fireplace. One was a police constable, the other was a blonde woman in her thirties. She was dressed in jeans, a floppy sweater, and riding boots. As she turned towards me I could see that she too had been crying.

‘Peter,’ said Tricia, ‘this is Sara, Alix’s mother.’

I walked across and offered my hand, which she took limply, but managed a flicker of a smile.

‘I’m sorry about your daughter,’ I said, ‘but please believe me everyone is doing everything possible to bring her home safe.’

‘I know that,’ she said, ‘and if it’s a matter of money I know her father will pay.’ She spoke perfect English, with just a scintilla of an accent, definitely Scandinavian.

I looked at the WPC. ‘Have there been any developments?’

‘Not as yet. They’ve switched the search to the army ground, and we’re making house to house calls in the villages and Swanage and Wareham.’

‘We’ve covered Old Duddlestone, but I’m going to try again.’ There was nothing else I could say. I felt trapped in this stuffy humid room. ‘Can I go to Carol?’ I asked.

‘Go upstairs, she’s in her bedroom,’ said Tricia. ‘Please take it quietly.’

Carol was asleep. She lay curled up, covered by a yellow duvet. I sat beside her on the bed and held her hand. She stirred and muttered something. I could feel her pulse and hear the steady rhythmic breathing. I made no attempt to wake her. No comfort that I could bring would help her now; her refuge lay in sleep.

I returned to Old Duddlestone. At the crest of the hill I stopped the car and again rang the hospital. Mother had had a peaceful day, she was stable, but had not yet recovered consciousness. I had been warned it might be some days yet before she began to be aware of her surroundings. I drove on down to the quay where Emma and Simon were waiting for me to drive them to the Gullaits.

That evening the De Gullaits was quiet. The media folk had mostly dispersed, leaving a scattering of reporters and TV crews to await whatever pickings they could secure from the missing children story. The police were being tight-lipped about the death of Tabitha Long. Officially her demise was still “misadventure”.

I found a corner table for three in the Double Six restaurant.

Sharon the barmaid served us. ‘I can’t hack all this trouble,’ she said dolefully. ‘Will they find those two little kids?’

‘Yes, I’m sure of it,’ I replied.

‘Not if it’s one o’ them sex fiends took them. They’ll be found dead. That’s what I think. Them sort o’ people – I’d hang ’em.’ She put down our soup plates and stumped moodily away. I felt more depressed than ever. The wretched girl had spoken the thoughts that had been in all our minds.

I turned to Simon. 'Tell me about your cruise?'

He looked relieved, glad of any excuse to change the subject. 'We crossed the bay to Brixham, then we pottered along the coast to Dartmouth and Salcombe. We came back in one hop, night passage. We anchored in Chapman's Pool at twelve forty. It was the best non-stop passage I've done.'

Something was troubling me. Something that didn't quite click. 'Simon, you said there was a helicopter?'

Simon grimaced. 'Yes, that aircraft was a pain in the rear. He was around the place, on and off, for an hour, hovering almost mast height. Suddenly he chuckled. 'We'd chosen a nice quiet anchorage on a blazing hot day. Give Emma a chance to sunbathe in the altogether. As soon as she stripped, that bloody thing zoomed overhead and she had to hide in the cabin.' He took a sip of wine. 'I thought you said they were looking for the missing kids?'

'Not yesterday, the children weren't reported missing until the evening. What type of helicopter?'

'Well,' he thought for a moment. 'It was smallish, very noisy, and I think it was painted black.'

'Then it wasn't a coastguard helicopter.'

It was a subdued dinner, though I ate more than I had anticipated. I was suddenly very hungry; I hadn't eaten a thing for over twenty-four hours. In that time I had witnessed the horror of that cliff fall, and the anxiety of today's search. We talked in a desultory fashion about nothing in particular. Nobody mentioned the possibility of abduction, and I didn't care to reveal the nature of my relationship with Carol. As we reached the coffee stage, despite myself, I found my eyes closing; fatigue had finally overtaken me. Then the mobile phone in my pocket shrilled.

'Mr Wilson?' It was a voice I didn't recognise.

'Speaking.'

'I'm Detective Inspector Righton, Dorset Police. I am the officer in charge of the Ford-Watts missing persons enquiry.'

I had a nasty queasy feeling in my guts. 'How can I help you?'

'Could you come to Police Headquarters now, sir?'

'I suppose so. What's happened?'

'There have been a number of developments. We would like to discuss them with you as soon as possible.'

CHAPTER 33

Harry offered to drive Emma and Simon to the hospital to see mother and then return them to the harbour. I walked into reception at the police station and to my surprise found Laura and Brian Byrne. These two antagonists seemed to have put aside their differences, for the moment at least. 'What's going on?' I asked.

'Doesn't look good,' said Brian. 'The police have some definite information but they're holding out on us.'

'I've left Mick at the harbour,' said Laura. 'They wanted the three of us here before anyone will talk.' I had never seen her so subdued. The blasé hard-nosed Laura had vanished. 'You know that paper we found up on the downs with Tommy's box?'

'Yes, some sort of jumping game.'

'Sara says Jonathan Ford-Watts is obsessive about kidnapping. He's taught all his kids to use the code word, *high jump*, if they think they're in trouble. Write it on paper or shout it down the phone, whatever.'

'Then that's where they were snatched,' I said. 'It was always likely and I think I know how it was done.' The other two stared at me surprised. I had my own theory but I didn't want to reveal it here. I had some investigating of my own to do.

A WPC approached us. 'Inspector Righton will see you now.' She beckoned us along a passage and into an interview room. It was a dreary featureless place, exactly like those one sees on the films. It smelt of floor polish and disinfectant.

DI Righton was young, sharp and I guessed ambitious. He came straight to the point. 'We've had a communication from kidnappers. They claim to be holding the children, Ford-Watts and Stoneman. We have analysed this communication and in our opinion it's genuine.'

'Are the kids all right?' I asked. 'Do you know for certain that they haven't hurt them?'

'I have no information one way or the other, but,' the Inspector paused, 'all our past experience tells us that the children will be unharmed. There hasn't been a demand for money yet, but there will be one soon. That makes Miss Ford-Watts a very valuable asset to these criminals, whoever they may be.'

'They might just kill them both and take the money.'

'No, Mr Wilson, they will not. If these are professional criminals they would know the consequences. Deliver the children alive and well and they might face ten years if they fail. Kill them and they would spend the whole of their natural lives behind bars. Don't worry. If we play this by the rules the kids will be fine.'

'Mr Righton,' said Brian. 'Are we to take it there's been no ransom demand?'

The Inspector pursed his lips. He eyed Brian in a none too friendly way. I knew that Byrne was a highly rated crime reporter and as such he had a special relationship with the police.

Brian pressed again. 'Can we take it that there's something unusual about this case? And why do you want us here?'

'We've had communication from unknown abductors. They've named you three as intermediaries.'

I felt as if I had taken a punch in the stomach. I heard Laura give a sharp intake of breath. I looked at Brian but he sat impassively. I thought I detected a gleam of anticipation in his eye. 'Why us?' I managed to say. 'Who are these people?'

'We don't know that, but there are unusual features. Now we've come to the point I will give you a full briefing. First, I must ask each of you if you are prepared to help?'

'I'll do whatever I can to rescue Tommy,' I was taking a step into the unknown but there was nothing else I could say.

'Me too,' said Laura.

'What about you Brian?' Righton had half a smile. 'I hear you've done something like this before?'

'That was in Liverpool, twelve years ago. Duddlestone's a different ball game.' He could no longer conceal his excitement. 'Of course I'll help you. We've all got an obligation when there's kids involved.'

'I never doubted you,' said Righton, a touch cynically I thought.

'Yes, I do have an interest,' said Brian. 'Something's about to happen in Duddlestone. I've known it for weeks, but I can't put my finger on exactly what. Tabitha Long found something that I didn't, and she had no bloody right to. I've been here for months delving and she'd been around five minutes.'

'Much good did it do her,' said Righton. 'Now, to business.' He had an air of authority this young copper. I could see why he had won early promotion. However bad things were, at least we had a competent leader. 'We know nothing for certain, but we've had a single phone call taken by Mrs Ford-Watts. It only lasted forty seconds, but we heard the recorded voices of both children. Then we had a second message with instructions.'

'They definitely said our names?'

'Correct, an unidentified adult voice named each of you. We're to await further instructions. Moreover, Mr Wilson, the two mothers have expressed their full confidence in you personally.'

'What do we have to do?' I asked. 'Where did this phone call come from?'

'We've traced the first one to a pay phone in France.'

'France?' said Laura.

'Doesn't mean a thing. If these are sophisticated criminals they could arrange to call from anywhere. We suspect the children are close by.'

'Any reason for that?' I asked.

'Yes, and this is confidential. We've had a second call. This time the cheeky sods rang here, direct into the incident room. We traced that call to another payphone, but in the Tottenham area of London.'

'That's a long way from France.'

'The next one could come anywhere, from Aberdeen to Marrakesh.'

'They're not putting pressure on the families then?' said Brian.

'No point, they know the search has been on, it's already in the papers. They said no mention of abduction and no naming of either children. I think you'd better hear the second recording for yourselves.'

Inspector Righton inserted a cassette into a tape recorder and pressed the play button. We heard the voice of the police operator. There was a background scraping noise, then a new voice. I find it hard to describe this voice. It was pre-recorded and electronically distorted. '*We hold Alexia Ford-Watts and Tom Stoneman. The youngsters are well treated. We have no wish to harm either. You will do the following. One: All police forces, uniform and plain clothes, will withdraw from a zone of three miles from the centre of New Duddlestone, including the yacht harbour. Two: The following persons will make themselves available as negotiators.*' The tape named the three of us. Then came a shock. '*Mr Wilson from the yacht harbour will not speak of anything he may have heard about past events in Old Duddlestone. He will know what we mean. If he says anything to the police or media, Tom Stoneman will lose one finger of his right hand. The three negotiators will remain in readiness to await our instructions.*' At that point the tape cut. We heard the voice of the police operator asking for a repeat of the message; thereafter, only silence.

'I'm sorry to bounce that on you, Mr Wilson. My colleague, Chief Inspector Channing, has explained your situation. I think you were a little unwise to challenge these people in that way.'

'I had to draw the heat away from my mother.' Somehow I had felt no surprise at the message I had just heard.

'Very well,' said Righton. 'The implications are clear. I can tell you officially that as from now, the Duddlestone murder and the Ford-Watts abduction investigations will merge. I will require you people to be available on call. Mr Byrne, I understand you will be at Ashwood cottage?'

Brian nodded.

'I don't need to tell you to keep away from your media colleagues. Mr Wilson, I would prefer you and Mrs Tapsell to move from the yacht harbour to somewhere more accessible.'

'We'll be at Honeycritch Farm,' said Laura. 'Can I go back to my house and collect my things?'

'Yes, but be quick.'

'Peter, I'll collect some stuff for you, and I'll fix it for Mick to camp in the office.'

'Thanks,' I replied. 'Could you ask Emma and Simon to help mind the harbour?'

Laura left followed by Brian. I was preparing to leave myself, when I was intercepted by Inspector Channing. 'A word please.' He beckoned me into another room and waved me to a seat. 'I understand you were due to meet Ms Long about the time she met her death?'

'The appointment was for eight o'clock at the harbour,' I replied. 'When she never showed I went to have a look in the old ammunition store.'

'Why should she have been there?'

'I didn't go to see her, I'd already assumed she wasn't coming. The Marines have left a RIB in there and I wanted to check it out.' I couldn't see the purpose of all this. Channing must have read my statement.

He nodded. 'You reported seeing a can of WD40 oil by the body?'

'Yes, I can tell you definitely that it wasn't there earlier. I'm certain it fell with her.'

'Yes, we're inclined to think that too. It had her fingerprints on it and those of another, almost certainly female, for whom we have no record. There was nothing else on the body to positively identify her.

She'd left her money and cards in a hotel room in Swanage.'

'I don't know what she was doing on the cliff top. She was definitely due to meet me in my office at the harbour.' I remembered something. 'I'm told she was due to meet someone in secret the day before the Navy reunion. She even confined her camera team to the hotel.'

'That's correct, but they know nothing. We've questioned them at length already. They're both genuine. They didn't like the lady, but they're pretty shaken by what happened.'

'Inspector, do you think Tommy Stoneman and the girl saw it? I mean the murder?'

'No, Mr Wilson, I've told you before. We don't speculate. Personally I would say no. If they'd recognised the killer they'd be dead by now.' His voice was chilling. I wished I'd kept my mouth shut.

'Do you want to hear the first recording, with the kids voices?'

I shook me head. 'No thanks.'

'Mr Wilson, I know how you feel, but I think you should listen to the tape. I gather you're a friend of the boy's family. Mrs Ford-Watts is the only intimate to have heard the voices and she was too badly shocked to tell us much.'

'I don't see how my listening will help. Why not ask Laura Tapsell, or the boy's mother?'

'We will do that if things don't resolve quickly, but you know the boy. You might detect something in his tone. We've voice experts working on the second tape but that one is so distorted it may be a day or so before they come up with results.'

'Very well, if you say so.' This was something I hadn't prepared for. I had seen many horrors in my life but the thought of those two frightened children hurt me. I visualised them, cooped up in some foul smelling cellar, watched over by cold hearted villains … No, I was not sure I could face this. Without glancing at me, Channing pressed the play button on the tape recorder.

'*Mummy it's me Alix. I'm all right but I've got to read this to you.*' There was a pause, a whispered voice, then silence for a couple of seconds. Clearly in the background I could hear an odd bumping sound that seemed vaguely familiar. '*Mummy, we will be looked after, and nobody will hurt us, but you must do what you are told. This is a high jump and Daddy has a picture I drew him, in his study.*' Channing pressed the stop button.

'The code, "high jump" is the family's own warning, and the bit about a picture is another authentic detail. Clever bastards, they've done this before, I wouldn't be surprised.' Again he pressed the start button.

'I'm Tom. Alix has been sick like she always is...' The boy stopped in mid sentence. There was the same whispered voice almost indistinguishable from the background noise; the same half squeak half thump. It was teasing me because I knew I had heard it before somewhere. *'Sorry, I've gotta' read what it says here. You can stop looking for us, 'cos we're safe and well. Keep the police away from Duddlestone, do what you're told and we can come home. It's all right, mum. I'll look after Alix, it's like...'* The voice cut. There was only the hissing of the blank tape.

At ten minutes short of midnight I stood in the Honeycritch Farm garden. It was a gentle warm summer evening. The light had finally died an hour ago, but my eyes had adjusted to the dark and I could see the house and the barns and the line of the downland ridge. The air smelt good with the scent of roses and night stocks. I could hear sounds, the shuffling and mooing of the cattle in the nearby field, traffic on the road into the village and the noisy shouts of some revellers making their way home from the pub. Mundane things that I would normally hardly notice now seemed very sweet. I felt cut off from this world – a prisoner looking out from my own nightmare. A figure came from the house, through the patio doors and onto the lawn. It was Laura. She joined me and we stood together.

'Oh Peter,' she sighed, 'why have we dragged you into our rotten little world?'

'Why rotten?'

She answered with a question of her own. 'If we come out of this safe – if we get Tommy back...?' she hesitated. 'Peter, I've made silly jokes about Carol and you – stupid childish wind-ups.'

'Sisterly jealousy?' Despite everything I couldn't resist a dig at her.

'No way, but Peter I'm serious now. I think you should know that our family are not exactly saints. In fact we're really rather a nasty lot.'

'Laura, that's nothing. All my life I've thought my father was a hero. Now I discover that he was a pirate. He sank a ship out there and stole her cargo.' Now at last I'd said it. Admitted the awful truth that had been staring me in the face for days. 'What could your family have done that was worse than that?'

'Supposing you had discovered by accident, that your terribly respectable, chapel-preaching grandfather, had committed a serious crime?' She grabbed my arm and shook it. Her whole body was tense; even in this half-light I could see the misery in her face.

'You don't mean your grandfather, Rocastle. He was my father's friend. Did you know that my father put up the money for him to buy this place?'

'No I didn't, but we know somebody did. Grandfather paid cash for the farm. There was never any mortgage or bank loan.'

'Laura, that money was tainted. Father and Double Six pirated half a million US dollars. People in a London gangland laundered it. You can be damned certain that was the cash, or some of it.'

She let go of my arm. 'Then my grandfather was up to his neck in it too. That's why he was on the cliff. That must have been the ship.'

'Sorry, I don't follow.'

'Oh shit, Peter. Now I've got to tell you. It's all such a bloody mess and Carol's the only one who's not been told. Ian and me, we weren't supposed to know and we both found out, and ever since we've had to put the blame on Arthur. That's what Carol doesn't understand. It's the bloody great barrier between us.'

'She told me you treated her like the family's baby. She knows something's wrong, but she doesn't know what, and that's the basis of her resentment. I think you should tell her. If you're going to tell me you'll have to tell her.'

'Oh bugger it,' she yelled into the night with all her anger and frustration. 'All right, I'm going to tell you the truth. One evening in May 1946, my father was on the cliff top. He was a randy little sixteen-year-old, and he had all his pocket money ready to pay for a ride with Margaret Gulley. He wasn't the only one to enjoy her, there were a dozen others, but that evening was his turn.

I could imagine that. The village whore would have been a standard item in a place like Duddlestone. With the addition of two or three hundred matelots, Margaret would have made a financial killing. Killing was the word. There seemed to have been a lot of killing resulting from that day, including Margaret and Arthur.

'Go on,' I said. 'You'd better spit it all out. Maybe you'll feel better.'

'Dad said there was a bloody great ship alongside the wall in Old Duddlestone harbour. The base was supposed to be empty. Most of the personnel were on leave, pending demob. Father said he and

Margaret saw that ship and there were people unloading something with the crane. They had a big crane on the dock then, and it was going like the clappers.'

'That ship was carrying whisky and cigarettes, as well as money in her strong room,' I told her. 'Jesus, they were taking one hell of a risk bringing her right into port.' It all fitted so well with father. Always the arrogant swashbuckler, he would have loved that.

'The brotherhood must have been part of the plot. They doubled as the local Home Guard,' Laura muttered. 'Grandfather was leading a patrol of them along the cliffs. I can see why now. It was to chase the locals away. He was a big man then, nobody would risk crossing him.' Laura gripped my arm again. 'Peter, I don't bloody care about your father. Whatever he did he wasn't a murderer. You call him a pirate, but he didn't massacre the ship's crew, or I assume not?'

'On the contrary, there was no walking the plank, it looks as if they were deep in the plot themselves.'

They had to be of course. The ship had been unloaded and taken back to sea. The crew had radioed a *mayday,* before exploding settling charges deep in her hull. Then a Double Six boat had taken them off. It was planned and precise; so typically like father. I glanced at Laura, apparently still deep in her private thoughts. 'You've more to tell me?' I asked.

'Yes, but only because you're involved and because of Carol. You will have to give me your word that you will never repeat any of this.'

'That's what Carol made me do – give my word.'

'Whatever for?' her solemn tone turned to surprise.

'My word, never again to go to bed with you.'

'That's a shame,' she was laughing as some of the tension eased. 'I enjoyed you, you're good. Nevertheless, I want your word of honour never to repeat what I'm telling you to anyone.'

I was about to reply when I heard a movement in the shadows to my right.

'What about me – isn't it time I was told?' Carol stepped into the light. 'It's my boy who's missing. I won't take this deceit, from either of you.' She was standing there in full view now, barefoot and dressed in a towel robe. She had arrived so quietly that neither Laura nor I had heard her, or been remotely aware of another presence.

'How long have you been there?' Laura snapped at her sister. 'You're supposed to be asleep.'

'You insensitive bitch, how the hell can I sleep at a time like this?

I can't eat, I can't sleep, and when I come for fresh air I find you telling Peter some secret I'm not allowed to know about.'

'Please, please,' I said. 'Don't quarrel, we must keep together.' I touched Laura on the arm. 'Nothing you can tell us about your family matters in the slightest compared with our troubles now, and I'm not promising to conceal anything from Carol that she has a right to know.'

'You'll have to tell me now anyway,' said Carol. 'I've been here for the last five minutes. I heard everything you said about Peter's father and our granddad, and about Dad paying Margaret for it. It wasn't Arthur who killed Margaret and you've known it all the time. So go on admit it!' All Carol's anger was now directed at her sister.

'Arthur's dead, unjustly or not, it doesn't hurt him to take the blame if it protects our family.' Laura's tone was cold.

'Laura, that's a wicked thing to say.' Carol in her turn was clearly outraged. 'Tell us who did kill her and why? Be honest for the first time in your life!'

'Margaret was killed by our grandfather.' Laura said quietly.

CHAPTER 34

'I don't suppose he meant to kill her,' said Laura. 'Dad told us grandfather was in a fit of religious outrage. Apparently he was gripping Margaret by the throat. All the time he was screaming stuff from the psalms and biblical quotations about whores of Babylon. Dad said the man was demented. He said grandfather carried Margaret to the edge of the cliff, and Dad thought he was going to throw her over. Then two Navy men came from out of nowhere. Grandfather saw them and threw Margaret to the ground. They calmed Granddad down and made him go home. Father asked them if Margaret was dead. They said if she was it was just as well, because she'd seen too much.'

'How do you know all this?' said Carol. 'Who else does and why wasn't I told?'

'You weren't there. It was when Dad died – remember? You were away in France. 'Dad was terminally ill with cancer. He died peacefully in the end, thank God. Mam didn't want him telling us. To this day she wishes the secret was in the grave with him.'

'Maybe it would be better so,' I said.

'Dad wanted to tell us. He'd been carrying this awful guilt thing all his life. I think he was holding on until he'd told us.'

'Who's us?' asked Carol.

'All of us by the bedside, Mam, Ian and me. We were horrified but somehow Dad seemed elated – almost serene.'

'I wasn't there,' said Carol. 'I've always felt bad about that. Am I being punished?'

'Oh don't be daft. You were his favourite, we all had to accept that. Daddy's little girl, "not like our Laura", as he used to say.'

'You could have told me – not left it 'till now.'

'Dad said not. We were never to tell you – so now your eavesdropping has made us break our promise .' Laura switched her gaze to me. 'Peter, take Carol indoors and upstairs. God knows what tomorrow will bring, but we really ought to try and rest.'

In the end I did sleep. Yesterday's all night vigil at anchor in *Stormgoose* had left its mark. I fell on my bed fully clothed and remembered nothing until I awoke again to the sound of the dawn chorus. For a full minute I had no idea where I was, only that I had some awesome duty wished upon me. Then, with total recall, I remembered everything. I swore silently; not for the first time I wished I was still at sea, where life had a beautiful simplicity. Ashore meant trouble, and here in supposedly civilised Southern England, I was in the biggest trouble of my life. The son reaping the consequences of a devious father.

I went downstairs to the kitchen for a cup of coffee. I found Laura already there, standing in the open door that led into the yard. I could hear engine noises. Some vehicle was moving along the farm track that led to the downs. 'Is that Ian,' I asked? I had wanted to talk to Laura's brother, but last night he and Tricia had been driving Sara Ford-Watts to meet her ex-husband off a plane at Gatwick. I'd been too dead to the world to hear them return.

'No,' she replied. 'It's Babs and Charlie on the way to their dig. The police have given them the all clear. It's odd though…'

'Why?'

'Another truck came down from the hill about two hours ago. I don't know if it was them. They wouldn't normally work at night.'

'Is Babs all right; do we trust them?'

'Of course we do. They're not Duddlestone, they're academics and I've known her for years.'

'Sorry, everything about this place gets to me.'

She looked me up and down in that officious manner of hers. 'God, you look a mess. It's about time you shaved off that terrible beard.'

My hand touched my face almost as a reflex. It was true the thing was straggly and unkempt. It was probably time it came off, but not on the instructions of this bloody woman. 'Have you seen Carol?' I asked.

'I peeped in just now. She's sleeping – the Doc gave me some knock out drops.'

'Not Hooder?'

'Paul? of course not. No, Doctor Baker, our proper doctor – he's been keeping an eye on her…'

The telephone was ringing. Both of us stiffened. Laura took a deep breath and ran from the kitchen. I followed her into the farm office where she grabbed the phone. There was a tense moment while she listened. I could hear a voice that seemed familiar. 'For you,' said Laura and handed me the phone.

'Peter it's Grant. I'm at the hospital.' I recognised the voice of my stepfather, Grant Bowker.

'Grant, hello – what's the news?' Good news or bad news; this call was unexpected.

'Peter can you come over here now, man? It's OK, better news, but we may need you.'

The policeman was still outside my mother's room in the Intensive Care section. There were other people there as well, both inside and outside the ward. I was feeling a tinge of guilt. Duddlestone's troubles had kept me away for over forty-eight hours. Grant clasped my hand. It was a while since I'd seen him but he was unchanged. A great bear of a man with immense strength and a face weathered by seventy years of sun and rain. I had never objected to mother's re-marriage. I loved this rock-steady South African farmer, almost as if he'd been my real parent. The two of them had struggled to establish their vineyard. Mother's outspoken views had not endeared them to the apartheid regime, and they had suffered ostracism and police snooping. Now they were established financially and were moderately prosperous. It was cruel that they had been visited with this tragedy.

'I should have been here before.' I told him.

'No you shouldn't. The cops told me about your local problem. Look, man, it's good you've come. We're going to try and wake your ma. We've got a little surprise for her.' His self-confidence was infectious. Suddenly I was beginning to feel better.

The consultant appeared and invited us both inside the room. It was the first time I had been past the glass screen. Mother's head was swathed in bandages, the heart monitor still bleeped, but to my unpractised ear it sounded more rhythmic and regular. Her face also seemed to have some colour despite the cuts and bruises that still disfigured it. Another little man in a suit introduced himself. He was a policeman, a detective constable. 'Just in case she says something relevant,' he explained.

'We're going to play a tape,' said the consultant. 'It's something that could shake a memory. We think she's very near to regaining consciousness and this could be the catalyst. I expect you've heard about the technique.'

'You play the voice of a soap star or a pop singer. Won't work with my Mum.' I was extremely sceptical.

The consultant grinned. 'Your mother isn't a teenager rocker. We've something much better. This came by special courier, courtesy of the Imperial War Museum.' He called for silence.

I noticed another tape player on the bedside table, similar to the model in the police station. He pressed the start button and I received a shock that nearly floored me on the spot. It was the crystal clear and perfectly modulated voice of my dead father. After all these years the voice sounded alien, the pedantic refined speech of the educated classes of the period, but there was no doubt it was Father. He was describing the Battle of Portland. "*We had fired our last fish and our ammunition was spent. The last E Boat was clearly damaged and making very little way. I had to come to a rapid decision. I could see that Lieutenant Ericksen was wounded and the coxswain was dead. I was alone at the wheel. I turned the boat forty degrees to starboard and aimed her to ram the enemy amidships. In the event we struck her abaft her port beam....*' Yes, and both boats had sunk in half a minute leaving a handful of sailors of both nations clinging to a single raft. Among them my father, Harry Broadenham, and Eriksen, apparently wounded. His survival did not entirely surprise me. Even in old age he struck me as a tough nut.

I forced myself out of my reverie and, like the rest of the company, concentrated on Mother. Could it be my imagination or was there a flicker of an eyelid? The tape finished playing. The consultant rewound and started again. 'We'll be lucky to have an immediate response,' he remarked, 'but I did detect some brain reaction.' He stood up and surveyed us. 'There's a bit of a crowd in here. I suggest that the family go to the canteen and have a rest. We'll call you if we get a result.'

I looked at Grant, and he nodded. We left the ward and wandered down to the self-service refreshment room. I was worried about time. I had cleared my visit here with Inspector Righton. If there was a development with the kidnapping he would recall me by text message on my mobile phone, which I could only operate outside the hospital. We bought two cups of the usual insipid coffee and sat in a corner out of the way. It was my first chance to brief Grant on the full story of my time in the Duddlestones. I told him everything except the darker secrets of the Rocastle family.

'Hell, man, you've had a time of it.' He shook his head. 'This Doctor Hooder, what's he look like?'

It was an odd question, but I gave him a rough description.

'Your mother was interested in him. She phoned me the night before that car hit her. You say he's South African?'

'His father was.'

'And how long has this bloke, the son, been in these parts?'

‘I don’t know, Grant, but I don’t think that long – I can check.’

‘If it’s the same guy I think, that might be an explanation for your mother being in here. That’s if he thought he’d been rumbled.’

I remembered something Harry had said. ‘I was told that Hooder came into the pub in Duddlestone. When Mum asked who he was she went a bit funny. Next day she took off for London – said she was going to South Africa House. It was when she arrived home that the car took her out.’

‘Yeah,’ said Grant. ‘That figures. Maybe this has got nothing to do with your Dad and his pirate ship.’

‘Hey, hang on a minute – explain please.’

‘I suspect that your Doctor Paul Hooder may have lost his way in the interests of science. During the civil war in Angola there was a guy, a doctor from SA, allegedly from a Christian charity would you believe. He had a clinic dispensing free medical aid – very charitable.’ Grant sipped his coffee. ‘Jeez this stuff’s foul – what’s in it?’

‘How do you know all this, Grant?’

‘Lot of rumours coming out of those parts, but this was told me by a proper doctor, a black guy, who’d been working there on war victims. He said he’d been watching this clinic. Said lots of women and kids went in there and plenty never came out except in a box. Some that died had symptoms of Lassa Fever, and there was no Lassa in that part of the country.’

‘OK, you say there was some sort of Nazi type research going on?’

‘Couldn’t prove it, but the rumours were around. You see there was no law and order, no government – nothing that we would rate as normal life.’

‘What makes you think these two men are one and the same?’

‘Because by all accounts he was an arrogant sod, and his name was Hooder. I’m not saying for certain it’s the same guy, but it’s a mighty coincidence.’

CHAPTER 35

I left the hospital after an hour. Grant remained and promised to phone me the moment Mother showed signs of recovery. I was now in limbo. At the request of the police I could do nothing and go nowhere. I did call at Ashwood cottage to talk with Brian Byrne. I found him commendably calm, even excited. It was all right for him, of course. As the one person not emotionally involved, and a journalist, he saw things differently. I found him in front of the computer engrossed in the internet. I told him about my mother, and then I told him about Grant's theory.

Brian whistled. 'Germ warfare was what Hooder's old man was about. Your step-dad could have something there.' He grinned. 'I hope not. If he's right it'll blow all my research into the weeds.'

'You think everything links to Old Duddlestone?'

'Convinced of it, and this bogus kidnap as well.'

This startled me. 'What d'you mean bogus? There's not the slightest doubt that those kids were abducted. You heard the second tape and Channing played me the first. It was Tommy Stoneman speaking.' I was annoyed now. It was as if Brian was implying the Rocastles were involved.

'All right, cool it,' said Brian. 'Somebody snatched those kids – that's real. Those coppers can't see the wood for the trees. This isn't a kidnap for ransom. Remember the conditions. All police withdraw from Duddlestone. You and me named and told to stay put and wait – it's bloody obvious.'

'Not to me.'

Brian swivelled round in his chair and faced me. 'Something is going to happen in Old Duddlestone within the next twenty four hours. I think a number of things, including your arrival here, have upset their plans and whatever it is they're up to, the date's been brought forward. That's why they've taken this gamble to clear the decks as you would say. Very effective too. Not a single police officer within miles.' He ended moodily.

Whatever Brian might suspect I was certain of my own mind. 'In that case we do nothing. I don't care what happens. Let them do whatever they like, and then we'll get the kids back.'

Brian wasn't happy but that was too bad. I knew where my priorities lay. I was on the road for Honeycritch when my mobile phone shrilled. I pulled over far too sharply and received an angry blast from the car following. It was Grant calling. Mother had regained partial consciousness.

‘Peter, why am I here?’ Mother’s eyes were open but her speech was laboured and little more than a whisper. I had to lean close in order to hear. I took her hand, the good, non bandaged hand, and squeezed it between both of mine. There was a flicker of a smile on her face mixed with pain. ‘Peter what has happened?’

‘Mum, you’ve had an accident, you’re in hospital.’

She had closed her eyes again, but I could feel warmth as she half squeezed my hand. I felt a great outpouring of relief. My mother was awake again; she would live. I could relate to nothing further ahead than that.

I had raced to the hospital and stormed through the corridors, brushing aside passers by and dodging trolleys of instruments. I had reached Mother’s room to be met by Grant who had seen me through the glass. ‘Your mother’s awake,’ he said, ‘but she’s babbling in Russian – can’t make too much of it.’

‘Grant, there’s a Russian-speaking male nurse somewhere in this place. He heard her when she first came in. Ask the nurses if he can come here.’ I remembered the young man I had spoken to. Mother had said something about, “the little bastard”. It was just about the only clue we had.

‘Mum, you’re all right now, you’re going to be fine. You’ve been in an accident but you’re going to be fine.’

I was babbling platitudes when I wanted to pour out my heart and tell her I loved her. I wanted to say all these things but I was very aware of the other people in the room. The Englishman in me called for restraint, the Russian in me demanded I shout my feelings to the world. As usual, the Englishman prevailed; the emotions remained bottled within me. I could hear voices in the corridor and another figure entered the room. It was my nurse interpreter. I squeezed my mother’s hand and kissed her on her bruised cheek. I could see that the room was overcrowded again. There was nothing more that I could do and I was impeding the medical staff. I greeted the new arrival patted him on the shoulder and left.

I stood in the corridor and watched through the glass. The Russian-speaker sat on the edge of the bed. Obviously I had no idea what he was saying, all I could do was wait. Twenty minutes later he stood up, spoke briefly to the charge nurse, and came into the corridor. 'I've got to go back on duty,' he said, 'but I've done my best.'

'Did she say anything?'

He shook his head. 'Not really. She asked where she was in English and then she did say a few Russian words but it was like she'd gone back to childhood.'

My spirits sank with this news. I had assumed Mother would recover consciousness and still be in the modern adult world. The nurse went back to his work while I cast around for someone to reassure me. None of the other nurses would give an opinion without reference to the consultant. Apparently his lordship had gone home and would not be back until four-thirty. I sat with Mother for a few more minutes. She was sleeping and I hadn't the heart to try and wake her. I left the hospital and drove back to Honeycritch Farm.

Carol was sitting on the settee in the living room. Her face was ashen, and she looked tired and ill. She had been crying. I guessed the tears had flowed until there were none left and exhaustion had overcome her. I knelt beside Carol and took her hands in mine. She responded with a wan smile. I tried to mumble a few words, but nothing I could say would have much comfort let alone reassurance. We had gone past the point where words could help. I could only imagine the awful torment that both mothers must be suffering. I looked at Carol, and then I thought of my mother, maybe mentally crippled, and inwardly my anger began to burn. I dreamed of violence and vengeance; I had a vision of myself gripping an iron bar and wreaking death on some nameless featureless, human shape. Somehow I found myself in the garden where Laura was pacing up and down the lawn. With Laura was her mother, Gwen and Tricia. I joined them and we muttered a few platitudes although Laura, for the first time that I had known her, was speechless. There had been no contact from either police or criminals. I wasn't sure if this was good or bad news. Could Brian Byrne just possibly be right? Was this an elaborate charade to keep us out of the way? I excused myself and went indoors. I phoned the police and asked for Inspector Righton. I was told he was unavailable.

I spent the next four hours waiting. I felt trapped, I could understand why prisoners spoke of "doing time": the time that seemed endless, the restless hour that turns out to have been a mere ten minutes. There was one moment of relief when the phone rang, and we all sped in a shambling race to the office. It was not the police; it was my Emma ringing from the harbour. She wanted the latest news and I told her about her grandmother. I asked her about the harbour.

'We've got a huge great yacht just moored here,' she said. 'We're not sure how much to charge them. She's so big we've had to put her alongside the quay.'

I gave her the standard fees to charge based on length. 'How long is she?'

'I don't know I'll ask, but she's gynormous, a real gin palace! They've got a great big sun deck over the whole of the aft section. Looks like an aircraft carrier.'

'Who does she belong to – some Arab?'

'I don't know, Simon dealt with the skipper.'

Despite everything I smiled. It seemed Emma was having fun. At this moment I had forgotten the harbour. It was another world and wholly trivial.

The local doctor arrived to see Carol. She was still curled up on the settee, zombie like, speech slurred. I picked her up in my arms and carried her upstairs to bed. The doctor persuaded her to drink some water and then sedated her. 'Can't keep doing this,' he said, 'it could have long-term effects.' He stood up. 'What a bloody awful business. I know what I would like to do with people who snatch kids.'

At six o'clock, Ian came in from the farm. He looked hot and tired. At least he'd had his normal work to distract him. He went upstairs for a bath while Gwen cooked a light meal. We were going to eat; whatever happened we must eat, she said. I could see her point. If we weakened mentally or physically we would play into our enemy's hands.

I asked Ian, 'Did Mrs Ford-Watts meet her husband off the plane?'

'Yes, he was there. We left Sara with him and they went off in his car.' He seemed evasive about something. Then he stood up and indicated me to follow.

He led the way to the farm office and shut the door. 'This is about Jonathan Ford-Watts, he's up to something and I don't trust the fellow.'

'How d'you mean?'

'At the airport he said something to Sara that we couldn't hear and we wouldn't pry anyway. But the effect on her was amazing – she seemed relieved – even happy. It makes me wonder if that slimy actor hasn't negotiated his own ransom deal.'

'Did he say nothing to you?'

'Not so much as a thank you kindly. The pair of them took off in his chauffeur limo.'

Unexpectedly Brian Byrne joined us. There was no hostility now. Even Laura welcomed him. He told us the latest news from the police. There had been no ultimatum regarding the missing children, and the press was making trouble over both investigations. The police were stalling over Tabitha Long. They refused to confirm either murder or accident. Sara Ford-Watts had agreed to appeal to a press conference this evening. Inspector Righton hoped that would satisfy the media and give him a breathing space.

'Ford-Watts, that's all they can think of.' I was angry. 'What about Tommy, doesn't he count for something?'

'Much better this way,' said Brian. 'Could your Carol face a press conference?'

After the meal I went upstairs and lay on my bed. Slowly I drifted in and out of sleep. I kept hearing Tommy's voice, over and over again. He had been forced to read from a prepared text, but not everything he said came from that. I was irritated and almost haunted by that odd background noise. I knew it, I had heard it before somewhere, but when, I didn't know. I rolled off the bed and stumped downstairs. Brian was watching television with the sound turned down low. I resented this; how could the man sit calmly watching a stupid game show. 'News in ten minutes,' he said.

'Brian, what did the police make of the items on Tabitha's body?'

He looked puzzled. 'I didn't know there was anything that mattered.'

It seemed the police were revealing nothing, even to a journalist of Brian's status. 'When she died, she had a can of WD40 in her pocket.'

Brian laughed. 'Sorry, Peter, but I can't imagine it. Maybe she had squeaky joints. Anything else?'

'The police say there were a second set of finger prints, besides Tabitha's: female prints they reckon.'

I left Brian looking pleased with himself. I wished he would be a bit more sensitive. He retained his detached journalist attitude while the rest of us were going through hell. I stamped out into the fresh air of the garden. Here I had a surprise. Babs and Charlie were in deep conversation with Laura. In the background stood Steve Gulley with one of his mates. They looked uneasy and decidedly shifty.

‘Hello,’ I said, ‘what’s going on?’

‘Paul Hooder’s up to something,’ said Laura. ‘You remember that truck we heard going up to the downs?’

I looked at Charlie. ‘We thought it was you people.’

‘No, it wasn’t us. We’ve been at a different site.’ Charlie glanced at Steve Gulley.

‘It were Hooder,’ said Steve. ‘Him and my Uncle Jake was up there last night, in his pickup.’

‘Explain,’ I said. ‘Who is your Uncle Jake?’

‘He’s Jake Stoneman, said Laura, ‘does odd jobs for Paul. You met him when he opened the door to the tunnels.’

I remembered the morose handyman. ‘I wonder what that’s about? Tommy told me he’d seen Hooder there.’

‘He’s always there,’ said Babs. ‘We’ve seen him pacing around as if he was measuring something.’

‘Perhaps we should tell the police?’ said Laura.

Hooder was clearly up to no good. He had a morbid interest in his father’s old laboratory, but that was a hundred feet below the Downs and its entrance was at least a quarter of a mile away.

‘Hooder has some agenda of his own,’ I said. ‘But I don’t see him as an abductor. We can tell the police, but they can’t do anything. They’ve got to keep three miles away remember? Whoever’s got the kids has us all over a barrel.’

‘Don’t matter what the Bill does,’ said Steve. ‘Nobody’s stopping us. We’ll go watch for you. I don’t like Hooder,’ he added.

‘What do you think, Peter?’ Laura looked at me.

‘Steve,’ I said. ‘Can we trust you to keep an eye on things without a confrontation and, more important, without being seen?’

‘Yeah, o’course.’

‘Have you got a mobile phone?’

‘I ain’t, but Kylie has.’

‘Uses it for her work I imagine?’ I looked coldly at him as he smirked.

‘Get it, I’ll pay the charges. Keep an eye on the top of the downs and if anything odd happens, tell me.’

‘Sure, that’s easy.’ He looked pleased. ‘Maybe we’ll catch who killed my Dad.’

‘Just keep out of trouble. Observe all you can, but no confront-ations.’

‘Don’t worry, Mister Wilson. I don’t want to go over the cliff like that Tabitha.' He turned to leave, hesitated and spoke. 'We won't let you down, Mister Wilson. Tommy's a Duddlestone boy, if they touches 'im they touches all o' us. We looks after our own.' He raised an arm and followed by his silent friend he left the farm.

Laura glanced at her watch. 'The local news'll be on in a minute.' She led the way indoors and we followed. Brian was already watching, and so were Ian, Gwen and Tricia. Brian turned up the volume. 'Main national news was all about Tabitha, we're on the local, "South Today", now.'

Within half a minute we were watching the item we were expecting. It was the police press conference. Sara Ford-Watts sat facing the cameras, flanked by Inspector Righton and an Assistant Chief Constable. She looked commendably calm as she relayed her appeal in a soft voice that finally broke only as she finished. It looked suspiciously like acting to me. Could Ian's suspicions about Ford-Watts be correct? Righton explained that no ransom demand had been received as yet, but the police were very hopeful that the children were alive and well. He made no mention of the two tape recordings. I remarked on this to the others.

'You've heard the one where Tommy spoke?' asked Ian.

'Yes, I did, and although he was meant to be reading off a text, I had a feeling he was trying to tell us something.'

'Could be,' said Gwen. 'He's a cool head on him.'

'Can you remember what he said?' asked Laura.

'I'm not likely to forget. It's been playing in my head ever since.' If I shut my eyes I could hear his voice and that odd background sound. 'He said Alix was fine but she'd been sick, "like she always is".'

Laura and Tricia were both staring at me. Laura drew in a deep breath and shook her head. 'Peter, it means they're being held on a boat. It's a family joke with Sara. Alix is always seasick. Always, even on the boating lake, or on the Isle of Wight ferry in a flat calm. As soon as she sets foot on board she's spewing up all over the decks. It was really embarrassing…'

I only half heard her, my own thoughts were racing. I knew it. I knew where I'd heard that noise. It was the sound a yacht would make as she rocked against a pontoon protected by her fenders. And I could go further; I could make a sporting guess as to the name of that yacht and her owners. George and Rita Stoneman and their *Marrieta*. It must have been so easy for an unscrupulous villain to kidnap his own grandson.

CHAPTER 36

'It took some persuading,' said Brian, 'but Righton's issued an all ports alert for the *Marietta* and George Stoneman.'

'What will be Carol's reaction?' I asked.

'All she wants is Tommy back,' said Tricia. 'She hardly knew George and her husband, Jim, was a nasty piece of work in my opinion.'

'There must have been something there, some memories,' I mused.

'Oh God,' Laura snorted. 'Don't you be jealous of Jim Stoneman. He's a creep of the first order.'

At seven o'clock I was back in the hospital. Mother was progressing. She was sitting propped up on pillows and definitely aware of the world around her. Grant was near the point of exhaustion, I don't think he had slept since he arrived. I took his place by the bedside and the nurses persuaded him to go to another room and lie down.

'Peter you are here?' she spoke slowly.

I smiled. 'I'm here, you're looking better.'

'They say I've had an accident, at Duddlestone?'

'A car hit you. The sod never even stopped.' How much did she remember?

'Did I miss the Navy reunion?'

I nodded, 'You were going to make a speech. I had to do it for you.'

'Oh yes, I remember. They were all going to be there…' She shut her eyes.

'She's doing well, much better than I ever expected.' It was the consultant; he seemed to have materialised from nowhere.

'Does she remember anything?'

'No, and she won't, they never do. It takes time. That's what I've told the police.'

I sat with her for a while, but there was no further communication. In the end I kissed her goodbye and left. My Russian speaker waylaid me in the corridor.

'Mr Wilson, have you a moment?' He jerked his head towards an empty ward office. I followed him in.

'There's something that's worried me,' he said. 'I told you that your mother was shouting in Russian.'

'She was saying, "that little bastard".'

'Correct, but I've been worried that I've misled you. You see, in English when we say the word, bastard, it's like an insult – right?' He looked at me intensely.

'Invariably, these days, anyway.' I said, wondering where this was leading.

'It's like this. Your mother was talking colloquial Russian. It's possible that what she meant was the person was illegitimate. You know – not necessarily an insult.'

I wasn't sure what to make of this but I thanked the nurse. He clearly wanted to be helpful. Whether the police would take much notice was another matter. I supposed I would have to trawl around Duddlestone for a list of bastards. I suspected that list would not be short. I drove back to Honeycritch. Indoors I found another woman police constable talking to Ian and Tricia.

'I'm Helen,' she said. 'I'm here to give support to Mrs Stoneman and her family.'

'Any news? I asked.

'Sorry,' she looked awkward. 'Inspector Righton's holding a press conference tomorrow morning. I'm afraid that's all I've been told.'

I felt sorry for this girl. She had been given a rotten job, but I was glad to see her and to have her support.

I looked into Carol's room. She was lying full length on her bed. I did not disturb her but went down to the kitchen and boiled an egg. I felt tempted to try another slug of Ian's special malt, but refrained. I had a feeling I would need all my wits about me this night. Then my mobile phone rang. I fumbled in my pocket while the others gathered round. To my surprise Brian Byrne was still with us.

'Mister Wilson, it's Daryl – Daryl Gulley.' The voice was a conspiratorial whisper but clear. 'We'm here, on Weavers Down, me and Kylie.'

I remembered Daryl, the spotty faced boat mechanic who had taken me to see Steve Gulley. 'Are you with Steve?' I asked.

'Yeah, he told me to ring you. We've just seen Doctor Hooder.'

'Well done, Daryl. What's he doing?'

'Not sure, but he's up here, with Jake and posh-toff George.'

'With who?'

'My Uncle George. I only met 'im a couple o' times. He's got too much money to mix along o' us.'

I could scarcely believe what I was hearing. ‘Daryl, this is important. Do you mean George Dunlass, the man you call George Stoneman? The man with a yacht called *Marietta?*

‘Yeah, that’s ’im.’

I felt my heart begin to pound. I strove to keep my voice steady. ‘Daryl, is the *Marietta* in the harbour now?’

‘Yeah, I see ‘er.’

‘Are you quite sure?’

‘Yeah, I knows ’er. We changed the filters on his diesel last April.’

‘Where exactly are you now?’

‘We’m by the old quarry, on the edge like. Steve’s gone on forward a bit.’

‘Thanks Daryl, good lad. Stay where you are. Is your mobile on silent call? Fine – stay in touch and don’t get seen.’

I lowered the phone; Ian was already calling the police on the emergency number we had been given. After a short delay he was put through to Inspector Righton at the latter’s home. Ian pointed me to a portable extension.

‘Trouble is, Mr Rocastle,’ said Righton, ‘that we don’t know for certain that Stoneman is holding the kids. It’s pure speculation. We’d be taking one hell of a risk if we went crashing into Old Duddlestone. We could put them in jeopardy wherever they are.’

‘But Peter Wilson is certain the kids are on a boat,’ Ian pleaded.

‘They may have been, they still may be, but even if he’s right, it doesn’t mean they’re in Old Duddlestone.’

‘But you can’t just do nothing. For God’s sake man…’

‘No, Mr Rocastle, you should know us better than that. We shall be around – trust me.’

It was unsatisfactory, but I could see Righton’s point. I was certain it was a boat sound I’d heard but there was nothing to prove it was the *Mariettta.* I said so to the others.

‘No, I think Peter’s right,’ said Brian. ‘It’s what I’ve said all along. The kidnappers have told us to stay out of Duddlestone, including the harbour. Wherever they are, a boat would be a good hiding place. It’s not like a house with nosy neighbours on the lookout. It’s the last place anyone would expect.’

‘There’s a saying,’ said Tricia. ‘It’s always darkest under the light.’

‘My point exactly.’ Brian looked at me. ‘Peter, I’m going up to Weavers Down – are you with me?’

The three of us were crammed into the tractor cab. Ian was driving with Brian and me on either side. We were taking a mild risk by using the tractor. It was too far to walk to the downs, but an ordinary road vehicle would arouse suspicion.

'I'll pull over here,' said Ian. We were in the little copse of trees, just before open country. The sun had already sunk below the hills. I could see the line of the ridge, etched black against the skyline. From now on we would walk. We all wore dark clothing and Ian had lent me a waterproof with a hood.

'Peter, you ever done anything like this?' asked Brian.

'No, never.'

'What about you, Ian?'

'I know these downs, like the back of my hand. I can take you anywhere around here.'

'And not be seen?'

'Yeah, as long as you don't talk and don't crash around like elephants.'

We walked, Ian leading, myself following and Brian bringing up the rear. We went through a narrow valley, up a sloping defile and down another steeper one. I heard a scuffling noise in the grass, but it was only rabbits. It was a sultry humid evening, although the air was full of a pleasing scent of herbs and wild flowers.

Ian stopped and pointed. 'We're going up there.' I followed his line. The slope in front looked vertical and never ending. The skyline seemed a mile above us. My life at sea had been a sedentary one, and I was breathing hard and sweating. I was feeling my years as I followed Ian up the ascent. The hillside was covered in a mat of thick grass dotted with thorn, thistles and other prickly species that embedded in my fingers. The surface was rough and littered with more rabbit holes. I found my breathing laboured, as was Brian's. Ian, who seemed unaffected, signalled us to be quieter. Then we saw clear sky in front of us. We had reached the plateau, and there, a hundred yards away, bathed in the last of the sunlight was the old stone quarry. Brian and I fell flat on the grass and lay there relieved and gasping. Ian knelt beside us and began to study the ground ahead. 'I can see 'em,' he said. 'Come on, quick – dash for it.'

We followed him across the flat open downland in a comic crouching lope. If anyone had been looking that way we would have stood out as conspicuously as gorillas on a golf course. We made it to the quarry entrance and raced down into the half-light below. We stood in a huddle uncertain of our next move. 'I saw them looking over the edge,' said Ian. 'They're in here somewhere.' He whistled softly. 'Daryl – Steve?'

A shape detached itself from the outline of the little stone hut in the centre. 'Mr Rocastle, it's me, Steve.'

Steve Gulley walked towards us. 'Daryl's over the other side,' he said, 'and Kylie's gone down to the harbour. There's something goin' on there.'

'Where's the doctor?' I asked.

He looked awkward. 'I dunno, he was around here an hour back and then he just vanished – both of 'em.'

'All right, Steve. Have you noticed anything else?'

'Yeah, there's another lot. We got a look at 'em – they're spooky.'

'Who were they?' asked Brian. 'What did they look like?'

'Sort of hit men. We didn't hang about to look.' Steve glanced shiftily around.

'Where was this?' I asked. 'Can't you be a bit more precise?'

'About half-hour back, Mister Wilson. We see three of 'em over by the chine.' Steve was clearly scared of something.

'All right,' I said. 'You go and find Daryl and we'll have a look round ourselves. If you want to go home you can.'

He shook his head. 'We'll stay.'

'Fine, now go and find Daryl, I'd like to know what he's seen.'

Steve vanished into the shadow of the far end of the quarry.

'What are we doing here?' I asked. 'Shouldn't we be down at the harbour?'

'I want to know what Hooder does,' said Brian. 'We're getting reports of him wandering about up here. He's not out for a country stroll – not his scene.'

'I want to go down to the harbour. I want to have a look inside the *Marrieta.* We're wasting time here.'

'No!' said Brian.

'Why not? I am the harbour master. I don't need the police, I'm entitled to board her…'

'No Peter,' said Ian. 'It's too risky. You've been told to keep away from here, remember.'

This was so frustrating, but Ian knew George Stoneman. I couldn't conceive of a man hurting his grandchild, but Stoneman could be a psychopath for all I knew.

Steve Gulley was returning with Daryl. ‘What’s happening?’ asked Brian.

‘Not sure,’ said Daryl ‘Jake’s pickup’s still there. I’ve been right up to it. Can’t see neither of ’em but there’s this old bird wandering around.’

‘Meaning female?’ asked Ian.

‘Yeah, she were talking to herself.’

‘Wait a minute, Daryl,’ I said. ‘Could you describe the lady, please?

‘Old biddy – she were sitting on the ground by one o’ they mushrooms. Proper wierdo – talking to ’erself like she was meditating – like them hippies.’

‘Drucilla Carstairs – it’s got to be her,’ I said.

‘Who?’ asked Brian.

‘Hooder’s fancy woman,’ said Ian. ‘I think Peter’s right.’

‘Steve,’ I said, ‘does that phone you’ve got do text?’

‘Yeah, that’s what Kylie…’

‘I don’t want to know what Kylie does, thank you. I want you two to go down to the harbour and text me back anything you think odd. You can wander around, as long as you don’t look suspicious.’ I pulled a slip of paper from my pocket and scribbled a short note. ‘Take this and find Miss Emma Wilson, she’s my daughter. Give it to her and say I want you to have a free hand to walk around. Look, listen, but don’t do anything stupid. Report back – OK?’

Steve and Daryl disappeared in the direction of the entry road. They refused to go to the harbour via the cliff chine. Something there had definitely scared them. My thoughts were still concentrated on the harbour. Hooder was a side issue. I had no idea why he should be wandering around on the hills at this time of night. His interest was his father’s lab buried deep beneath us. Hooder was an arrogant man obsessed with his work to the point where Grant Bowker suspected him of war crimes. But that was in Africa and far away. Tonight I was in Duddlestone and two children were missing. ‘I’m going to have a look over the edge at the harbour,’ I announced.

I left the quarry and walked towards the chine and the footpath to the harbour. I had no wish to look over the cliff at the point of Tabitha’s fall. The sun had set, but the long midsummer twilight was still with us with faint illumination from the new moon. The grassland was a silvery grey, and the sinister mushroom vents stood out in stark black. Beyond was the line of the sea and the land eastward already shone with the lights of the coastal towns.

The black shape came from nowhere and flattened me with the force of a charging bull. A hand gripped me around the mouth and something twisted my right arm behind me. I was in pain but I couldn't cry out. I wasn't frightened, I just lay there, trapped and uncomprehending. With my ear to the ground I could hear footsteps and a whispered conversation.

'Let's look at you,' came a soft but familiar voice. Someone had hold of my shoulders while another pair of hands gripped my ankles. I was rolled onto my back and lay gaping at the black sky. The hood was pulled back revealing my face.

There was a quiet burst of laughter. 'Look who we've got. Sorry, skipper – mistaken identity.' It was Keith.

I staggered to my feet spitting out a tuft of grass. 'Where the hell did you spring from?' I spluttered.

'Sorry, skipper, really I am,' said Keith. 'Keep your voice down. We're watching Doctor Hooder, and we're not the only ones. We thought you were one of the others.'

'What others? Will you please tell me what you're doing here?'

'Doctor Hooder and his sidekick have gone down into the old tunnel, through vent number seven, that's just short of the place where it's been bricked up. They've left a watcher at the top and there's another elderly geezer swanning around. We thought you were with him.'

Keith was busy brushing the dirt and greenery off my clothes. I felt like a small child in the hands of a nanny. 'We've been following the old fellow. Flip's watching the vents.' Flip, short for Philip I guessed, must be the third member of the sub-aquas, the saturnine guy who never spoke. This was beginning to make some sort of sense. I remembered Laura's opinion that these SBS men were on some sort of undercover business.

'How did they get down the vent?' I asked. 'I've seen those grilles, you'd never get the nuts off without a hell of a struggle.'

'I dunno,' said Keith. 'Bit of WD and some elbow grease should do it.'

'WD 40?' I asked so abruptly that Keith stared at me.

'Of course, we never go anywhere without a can – why?'

'It's no matter, it'd take too long to explain, but you've solved a puzzle.' I was alert now, mind racing. 'Look, Keith, there's a boat in the harbour belonging to a man called George Dunlass but his real name is Stoneman. We suspect he's the one that's snatched the two kids.'

Keith made a whistling noise through his teeth. 'The two we were looking for, Jono Ford-Watts' little girl? We felt sick for the boy's mother – how's she taking it?'

'Not well – what'd you expect?'

'Why d'you think this Stoneman guy is the one?'

I explained as briefly as I could. 'You see Brian Byrne thinks it's all a ploy to keep the law away from Duddlestone and the harbour.'

'And that little kid is his own grandson – that's really gross.' Keith's tone had become cold. 'Mr Wilson, I suggest you stay up here with Flip and Dave. I'll go down to the harbour and I'll have a look under this *Marietta.*'

'Under – what good will that do?'

'Because we're trained to do that. Go under unseen and undetected. I don't want to be too specific but we've got some listening gear – not ours, it's MOD equipment, but I reckon I'm justified in using it.'

Keith whispered into a phone; I guessed it must be on open line. Two minutes later, Dave reappeared out of the gloom. Once again I never saw him until he was standing beside me.

'Are those your friends, the lot hanging around the quarry?' asked Dave.

'Yes.' I gave him a list of all my party.

'God, you've brought a platoon with you,' Keith groaned. 'Whatever you do, don't frighten Hooder. We want to see what he's after.'

'He as good as told me. It's the papers from his father's lab.'

'He's never going down there for bits of paper.' Dave was dismissive.

'What else would he go there for?'

'That is the question.' Dave released a low sardonic laugh.

'What's your interest in all this? I asked.

'A result of my historical research.'

'Keith,' I asked, 'who is this other man you thought I was with?'

'Seen him before – Government man – elderly bloke, thin as a bean pole – could be a spook.'

'MI5?' I was incredulous. 'Oh come on, Dave – this is fantasy.'

'I don't know, Mr Wilson. That's why I wanted to grab him. We'd frighten the shit out of him, until he explained.'

'You can't do that!'

'Why not – they're never going to complain.' Keith gave me a friendly slap on the shoulder and vanished down the hill.

CHAPTER 37

'Follow me,' said Dave. 'Do what I do – stop when I stop and don't make a sound.'

'There's two of my friends around somewhere,' I said.

'That's what's worrying me.'

I followed my guide as ordered. I was to learn something. Dave not only moved silently, he seemed to read the ground, to pick out every little fold and use it for concealment. As we came up to the nearest vent, Dave gave a sharp hiss and pointed to a figure prone on the ground. I guessed it was the third of Keith's subaquas, and I was right.

'What's on, Flip?' said Dave in a low voice.

'Started,' Flip jerked a thumb at the vent grille. Dave dropped to the ground and placed his head against the metal. He listened intently and then beckoned me to join him.

I crawled to the vent. At least the grass was cropped short around the concrete base apart from a heap of rabbit droppings. Dave rolled away from the grille to give me room. I pressed my ear against the metal and then I heard it. Somewhere in the cavern below came the roar of a concrete breaker.

'What's going on?' I whispered.

'They're knocking down that wall. Beyond it's the old lab complex.'

That much I had already guessed. 'Dave, I must go down to the harbour.'

He shook his head. 'Wait for Keith.'

'He's gone diving, he could be hours. I need to be down there now.' I pulled out my mobile phone and found a text.

wot we do cops is ear.

I couldn't make sense of this. 'Dave I've got to go there. Find my friends and tell them.' I took the phone and texted the one word. *Wait.*

I reached the bottom of the chine and began to make my way cautiously along the foreshore. I could clearly see *Stormgoose* still anchored in the centre of the harbour, and I could see the outline of

Emma's super-yacht. She was an odd shape with this huge elevated deck; Emma's comparison with an aircraft carrier was apt. All seemed peaceful, apart from the putter of a small petrol engine.

Now I was suspicious: that stationary engine was a generator, and it was nothing to do with any yacht. It was in the village and near the cliff face. I pressed forward, determined to find out who was messing about on my domain. I reached the village; the noise was now distinct and very close. The wicket door into the ammunition store was open, and a beam of white light streamed through it. I could see the generator now. It was a standard, lightweight portable model and it stood unattended as it powered away. I was tempted to turn the thing off and cause confusion to Hooder and whoever else had invaded the tunnels. That would be premature. I would do nothing dramatic until I had located Keith. My first priority was the safety of Tommy and the girl. I skirted the tunnel entrance and set off down the street, keeping in the shadow. I hadn't realised how much loose gravel and dirt lay on the surface as I strove to move unheard. I needed to find Emma and Simon, as well as Steve Gulley.

The quay was clearly lit by the floodlight outside the harbour office and I could see three figures on the dock. To my surprise I saw uniformed police. I was alarmed now and angry. It had been a precondition, spelt out by the abductors, that no police would be in Old Duddlestone. If Channing and Righton had ordered a premature raid all could be disaster. I walked openly now determined to have an explanation.

The whole marina area seemed absurdly normal. I could hear snatches of conversation and scent alluring cooking smells. The nearest two policemen looked overweight and, I would have thought, short in stature. They didn't give the impression of youth and vitality. Maybe some local "specials" had arrived not knowing the new orders. Another copper, a sergeant, had stepped out of my office and stood in full view under the light. He looked the part, aged thirty or so, slim athletic build. I was about to call out, but instead, and to this day I don't know why, I stepped back into the shadow of the open door of the nearest dilapidated cottage. I could hear footsteps coming from the head of the street. As I stood in the gloom of that cottage I had a clear view of the man as he passed: it was George Dunlass. I moved to the door and watched him walking away from me towards the quay. The two policemen standing on the edge turned to meet him. Now I fully understood. I was looking at the twins, Tweedle Dum and Tweedle Dee, the same two old veterans who had sat with George during the reunion meal. How on earth they had hoped to fool anyone I couldn't say, although they had evidently taken in Steve and his friends. To my eyes, the twins looked as if they had stepped out of the chorus of the Pirates of Penzance. I had no idea who the bogus sergeant was, but I had seen enough. I wished to God I could make contact with Keith. By this time he would be somewhere in the harbour. I would have to be patient and watch.

'Billy!' a shrill voice yelled, almost in my ear.

This latest shock almost unnerved me, then I recollected the voice. It was Rita Dunlass. She must have followed George down the street. I could see her standing not three metres from me. 'Oi, Billy, both of you – come here.'

Obediently the two elderly twins stumped up the road to meet her.

'We're almost ready,' she said. 'Got the trolley?'

'They're unshipping her now,' said Twin One.

'What about our share?' said Twin Two.

'You'll get it,' said George. 'We're salting that away already.'

'What about the kids?' asked twin one.

'What about 'em,' said George. 'You can't touch 'em even if you had the chance.'

'Why not?'

'That's out of our hands. The big men have taken them,' said Rita, 'but I know what I'd do.'

'I hates kids,' said Twin One. 'The boy was always spying around here. That Jojo said she'd do it – no need for us to know anything about it.'

'You heard what I said,' George growled. 'We ain't got 'em – and there's Jim to think of, it's his boy.'

'Jojo's got him round her little finger – the dirty slapper,' said Rita.

It sounds a cliché, but I was literally in a cold sweat. The police were wrong if they thought this gang would release the children unharmed.

A distant whirring rumbling sound drew my attention towards the quay. An odd vehicle was winding its way slowly past the slipway and into the street; a miniature electric powered tractor towing two tiny four-wheel trolleys. It was a smaller version of the sort of rig one sees on main line train stations, and the man at the wheel was the bogus police sergeant. It passed where I was standing and went on up the street. In the distance I could hear the grating and squeaking as someone rolled back the main doors of the tunnel entrance. I took out my mobile phone. I only hoped to God I was far enough away from the cliffs to have a signal. I called the number of Honeycritch Farm. Tricia answered, her voice sounded tense.

'Tricia, ring the police and get them to Old Duddlestone fast as they can. I've no time for explanations. Get them here and if they can come into the village quietly – so much the better.'

'Your sound's breaking up. Are the kids there … is Tommy there?'

'I think so, but we're running out of time.' At that moment I lost connection.

Tricia was a sensible woman. All I could do now was hope and pray I had taken the right decision.

CHAPTER 38

I had two choices. Go down to the marina with the authority of harbour master, or stay in the shadows and watch. I wanted to march down that street and face George Dunlass. I wanted to seize hold of both him and the murderous Rita and tear their rotten little boat to pieces. Despite everything, common sense prevailed. If I was to take direct action I needed Keith and his boys. I retraced my steps and walked back along the foreshore. I glanced at my wristwatch: it was nine o'clock. With a high spring tide the water was lapping to the edge of the shoreline.

I reached the junction with the path to the cliff top. I stood looking back towards the harbour. The generator was still purring away. The floodlight on the quay illuminated the scene and I could see figures scurrying about. Whether they were villains, or innocent yachties, I had no idea. I worried about Emma and Simon. They were intelligent perceptive, youngsters; I dreaded them suspecting trouble and intervening.

I could hear a new sound coming from the water and much closer than the dock. A soft bubbling that I couldn't recognise and had me looking wildly around. 'It's all right, mate,' said a voice almost in my ear. For the second time this night I froze with shock. Very slowly I turned to find a grinning Dave standing at my shoulder.

'Christ,' I hissed at him. 'I wish you wouldn't bloody keep doing that.'

'Part of our drill,' he laughed. 'Could've slit your throat and you'd never have known it.'

'Thanks,' I replied. 'What's happening?'

'Here comes Keith,' he said. 'I've been waiting for him.'

He pointed at the water as a black object emerged and hauled itself upright. It was Keith in full diving gear. Everything else was driven from my mind. I ran down to the shoreline as he pulled off his facemask. 'Are they there?' I asked.

He shook his head. 'If they are, I can't hear them.'

'How good is this listening gear of yours?'

'Sorry skipper, can't be specific, but if they were there I'd know.'

'But they might be doped?'

'Don't think that I don't realise that – but I've done my best.'

I explained that the police were on their way. 'Keith, could you get the children out if there was trouble?' I told him about Rita and her threat.

'Christ,' he muttered. 'What kind of evil bitch would kill kids?'

'I heard her and there wasn't much doubt what she'd do given a chance.' I could scarcely believe it myself and the memory was chilling. 'Trouble is, I'm not sure they are in that boat.' I told them what I'd heard George say about handing the kids over, "to the big men". But handing over to whom – big time villains?

'I tell you,' said Keith. 'We'll get 'em out if they are there and I wouldn't recommend nobody to get in our way.'

'You say that's a helicopter pad on that ship?' I asked. 'My daughter thought it was a sun deck.'

'Wishful thinking,' Dave laughed.

'It's a bolt on heli-pad,' said Keith. 'But no chopper there.'

'That's how they were snatched,' I said.

I explained about the helicopter that had been cruising above the cliffs that evening. I had heard it overhead just before Tabitha fell. It would explain how the two children had vanished on Weavers Down, literally into thin air.

'Where are my friends?' I asked Dave.

'We persuaded the farmer to go home. I don't know where Brian's got to.'

'And the locals?'

'They're still in the old village. I think we ought to find them.'

'The police should be on the way,' I said.

'If so,' said Keith, 'things could get very confusing.'

'Cheeky sods – they've moved our bloody RIB,' Keith muttered. He was peering towards the main entrance to the tunnel. I could clearly see the boat on its launching trolley, standing in the village street. Even as Keith spoke we saw the electric powered tractor and its trailers emerge through the doors. It was difficult to identify the load. It looked like a stack of small wooden boxes. The whole outfit trundled down the street and onto the quay. This lot must have come from beyond the block wall and it didn't look like scientific papers. Where the hell were the police?

I made up my mind. 'I've got to get down to the quay.'

Keith and Dave clearly had plans of their own which they were not revealing to me. I was not going marching down the middle of the street. If all these cottages were similar to Laura's they would have garden areas behind them, enclosed by low stone walls. If I chose that route, even as unskilled a soldier as I should be able to reach the waterfront unseen. I parted from the others and scrambled over the first wall and into what had once been a garden. It was a mass of nettles and man-made rubbish. I ignored the stings, but I had to watch carefully not to make a racket by kicking the mass of old fuel drums and pieces of timber. Clearly, the Navy in their day regarded these areas as useful rubbish tips. This was the harbour side of the street, the opposite side to Laura's house. I could see that we were on the time of high water and I could hear the wash of the tide as it rippled against the shoreline. I negotiated five gardens and their surrounding walls; there was only the sixth to go. From the far wall of this one I should have a clear view of the quay and the yacht pontoons. I drew back quickly. Three persons crouched behind the wall. As I watched, one of them took a quick glance over the top before falling back again. I was relieved; it was only Steve Gulley. I slid over the wall and crossed the area as quietly as I could. Steve and his companions swung round in alarm before they in turn recognised me. As I expected, they were Steve, Daryl and the wretched waif, Kylie.

'Thank God you've come, Mister Wilson,' said Steve. 'We'm stuck here watching and we don't know what to do.'

'Did you find my daughter?'

'Yes.'

'What happened?'

'I gives her your paper and she don't believe it.' He sounded aggrieved.

'Why ever not?'

'She said as you'd told her we was a bad lot and we tried to wreck your boat.'

'Which is exactly what you did. Has she told you what's happening here?'

'That police sergeant, he told the yachties the government's moving stuff from the old tunnels, all top secret like.'

'So I imagine. Where is this top secret stuff going?'

'On the big yacht there. We see'd the first lot come down. All wooden boxes and they was heavy – made the lads on the ship sweat when they carried 'em. We reckons it's guns.'

'Let me have a look.' I risked a twenty-second peep over the top of the wall.

The ship alongside the quay was a classic luxury motor yacht and she was huge. A millionaire's showpiece; her lines suggested her to be a product of the 1930s. In old measurement, I would calculate her to have been well over one hundred feet in length – probably nearer one hundred and thirty. Her bulk would have dwarfed even Eriksen's *Persephone.* Even at this distance in the half-light, I could see dilapidation and neglect. Her hull, which should have been a gleaming white, was painted in some drab colour. The floodlight on her foredeck revealed the decaying varnish of her superstructure and the ugly helicopter pad built over her aft section was a cruel disfigurement. A yacht once fit for royalty was now a vehicle for use by some criminal conspiracy. The high tide had brought her level with the main quay, to which she was connected by a substantial gangplank. Two men stood by it looking back towards the village. I could hear, but not see, the returning electric tractor. A minute later I risked a second look. The tractor was in view as it stopped by the end of the yacht's gangway. George appeared with Rita and the tractor driver, while two other men began to move the second load of boxes. I could see that these were stout wooden containers with rope handles. I was surprised that the rope was in such good condition after fifty years, and it needed to be. The boxes were clearly heavy, incredibly heavy for their size. I had a suspicion and I didn't like it one bit. Lead-lined boxes are designed to contain dangerous chemicals or viruses. Was this the haul that Hooder had come all the way from Africa to retrieve? But why should George Dunlass and all these old Navy men be involved? What was in it for them that they should indulge in kidnapping? My speculating came to an abrupt end as the big yacht's diesels came to life. These were not the modern silenced variety; they were definitely of their period and they were noisy. I was conscious of the little girl Kylie grimacing at me and putting her hands to her ears. I was alarmed now to see that the two men on the quay were loosening the mooring lines. The ship was leaving and in my state of mind I became convinced it had the children on board. Now I began to panic. Tommy was being carried away from me on a ship with the murderous Rita. I hoped for a second that she might be staying with George, but then I saw her trip daintily up the gangplank followed more slowly by the twins. George was still on the quay with the bogus police sergeant who was disposing of his cap, jacket and tie in our wheel bin. Steve and friends were chuckling, but it was not funny to me. Even now, above the roar of these engines, I could hear police sirens and see the flash of blue lights. So much for my request that the law arrive quietly. I resolved angrily that if any harm came to Tommy as a result of this I would have Righton's guts. I scrambled over the wall and began to run towards the dock. Even as I did so the gangplank was heaved aboard. I heard the distinct bell of an engine room telegraph. The mooring lines were loosed as the ship moved astern on one back spring rope. Before I reached the edge of the dock she was away and heading for the open sea.

My fury lasted for seconds before turning to near despair. I had blundered. I had sworn to Carol that I would return her child to her. It had been the ultimate responsibility laid on me and I had failed.

I became vaguely aware that I was not alone. Police cars were parking on the dock, with policemen in uniform standing beside them. I could see Chief Inspector Channing waving his arms around issuing orders. He saw me and walked over.

'You're too late. The children are in that ship that's just leaving. They're probably already dead.' I shouted.

'You mean that ship that's just left the harbour – do you know that for certain?'

Of course I didn't know for certain, I realised that now, but I must persuade this man to action. There still might be some hope.

Channing began to call into his radio, before he turned back to me. 'All right, Mr Wilson: we've a navy, we've coastguards, we've customs patrols. One way or another we'll catch them.'

'It's no good, they'll be too late. Some of the gang want to kill the kids. And they're the one's that sailed in the ship.' I was as near to panic as I will ever be.

'All right,' said Channing firmly. 'Give me a description of the vessel as accurately as you can. We'll do our utmost.'

I did so and that part at least was easy. Every detail of the exterior of that ship was printed on my mind.

Channing finished with his radio. 'Actually we anticipated something like this. We've set the wheels in motion. The Navy are on the move. They're scrambling a *Sea King* helicopter with night vision and all the latest gadgets.'

'They'll find the ship but that won't help the kids.' It was Keith speaking; I hadn't noticed him. For that matter I hadn't heard the marines, complete with RIB, roll down the village street. Dave and Flip were launching it at that moment.

'Skipper,' said Keith, 'you got a hand-held radio, VHF – we'll need it to talk to that chopper.'

'In the office,' I said and took off at a run. I entered the building, looked on the shelf, and found what I needed – our spare hand-held ship to shore radio. I raced back to Keith and pushed it into his hands.

‘I’ll come with you,’ I said.

‘No way, mate.’ He shoved me back and then ran to join his companions. I heard the RIBs twin motors fire and watched as it roared seaward in a surge of foam.

‘Marines are they?’ asked Channing.

‘More than that – they’re SBS.’

‘Really, in that case I feel almost sorry for the personnel on that ship.’ Channing turned around to scan the village. I was more interested in the yacht pontoons. To my astonishment walking boldly up the ramp came George Dunlass.

‘Channing,’ I yelled. ‘That’s George Dunlass – he’s the leader of them – get him!’

George paused and looked at me with an air of complete astonishment. ‘Hello, harbour master. What am I a leader of?’ He favoured me with a shifty smirk.

I knew he had me beaten, for the moment at least. Nothing I could tell Channing would link George to anything criminal. He was not even one of those impersonating a police officer. Hooder might well claim that the material in the tunnels was legally his. By the time the police resumed their ponderous enquiries Tommy and the girl could be weighted corpses at the bottom of the sea. On every count I had lost.

Channing had strolled back to meet us. He greeted George with a genial smile. ‘Mr Dunlass, this is a happy co-incidence, I’d been hoping to have a little chat with you.’

George put on an ingratiating grin. ‘I’m always ready to help the police.’

‘Is that so,’ Channing reached in a pocket and produced his warrant card and a scrumpled sheet of paper. ‘You are George Henry Dunlass, formerly known as George Henry Stoneman?’

‘Yes.’ George was suddenly wary.

‘Good.’ Channing’s grin became even more genial. ‘George Henry Dunlass, I have a warrant here for your arrest.’ He waved the sheet of paper.

‘That’s rubbish,’ said George. ‘You can’t pin anything on me for those kids – prove it.’

‘Now, what would you know about any kids?’ said Channing. The geniality had gone and his voice was icy. ‘George, you interrupted me – let’s start again shall we? George Henry Dunlass, you are arrested on suspicion that on October the twenty-third 1946, you conspired with others and instigated the murder of Arthur Joseph

Rocastle. You do not have to say anything but I must warn you that it may harm your defence if you fail to reveal something that you later rely on in court.'

CHAPTER 39

George had been removed uttering threats and promising Channing that he would report him to various police complaint bodies. He put on a pompous show of his indignation and alleged importance, although he did not seem too worried. Even I could see it would be almost impossible for the police to produce a case against him. The Rocastle murder had after all been fifty years before. I guessed that Channing was using this charge as a ploy to hold George Dunlass, while the police searched for evidence to connect him with the kidnapping. Again I felt a chill like ice in my stomach. Everything, Tommy's safety, Carol and our future together, was hanging on a thread.

Channing had reappeared on the quay. 'Sorry, but we've searched the *Marietta,* the boat's clean – no persons in there. I've news for you, Mr Wilson. An hour ago I had a talk with your mother.'

I was surprised and for a moment I felt guilty. In the stress of the last two hours I had almost forgotten her. 'You're saying she's conscious enough to talk?'

'We couldn't stop her. She doesn't remember a thing about her accident, but talk – we could hardly keep up with her. She's given us the names of all the men who lynched Arthur Rocastle, including the man we've just taken into custody.'

'But will the charges stick?'

'Not on your mother's say so alone, but she's set us on a trail and I have a feeling we could succeed on this one.' He turned away to shout an instruction. 'Trouble is,' he continued, 'Dunlass will have a smart lawyer and he'll be out within a day. There's no way that we could oppose bail.'

'But you'll watch him?'

'Of course.'

He left me standing alone outside my office. I knew Brian Byrne must be around somewhere, but Steve and his friends had vanished. No doubt the sight of so many police had triggered their disappearing act.

'Dad, what's been going on?' Emma startled me as she tapped my arm.

I needed to confide in someone and I poured out the whole story.

‘Tommy’s mother’s important to you isn’t she?’ Emma was staring at me in an odd way.

‘Yes,’ I said, ‘I rather think she is.’

‘I thought so.’

At this point Brian rescued me. He arrived on the quay breathless and perspiring. ‘Hooder’s got away,’ he gasped, ‘up his rope ladder and off down the hill in that truck.’ Brian was angry, but I couldn’t really share his concern. My thoughts were with Keith and his team, somewhere out there in the night.

‘Come on, Peter, let’s get up that tunnel before the law stop us.’

‘The tunnel?’

‘Yes the tunnels, the germ lab – I want to see what all this is about.’

‘I ought to stay here.’ I wasn’t interested in the tunnels. I wanted news from that ship.

Emma pulled my arm again. ‘You won’t do any good hanging around here. Come on let’s all go and look. I’ll fetch Simon.’

Brian looked worried. ‘If we go into the lab there may be human remains still there.’

Suddenly Emma laughed; it was her old girlish laugh that I knew so well. ‘Oh come on – I’m a doctor. As a medical student I’ve been slicing up human remains for real. If these ones have been dead fifty years, I don’t think they’ll bite.’

‘I think you should have a look, Peter,’ said Brian. ‘You wanted to know what your old dad was up to. Well, chances are you’ll find out.’

I told Channing where we were going. He had one of his men guarding the entrance to the cavern, but he allowed us to go through.

In the confusion, and in my anxiety, I had failed to mention the removal of the boxes. Rightly the police were concentrating on the kidnapped children. For the moment we had the tunnels to ourselves. The portable generator was still running and appeared to have unlimited fuel. I had equipped us all with torches as a back-up.

‘We’ll have to watch the air,’ said Simon.

‘We’ll be OK as far as the point where the wall is. After that, yes, we’ll be careful.’

The long communication tunnel was brilliantly lit. The gang had replaced many of the lamps and, so long as the generator kept turning, we would see. Our footsteps echoed eerily; behind us we could hear the drumming of the engine. Within ten minutes we reached the end of the tunnel at the point where the stairs began. I shone my torch up and into the vent. The cone was a mere twenty feet above us and I could see where the grille had been removed. Hooder must have departed by some sort of rope ladder, although it, like the man himself, had vanished. I continued up the steps to the wall. An electric compressor and a pneumatic drill stood abandoned. A hole about the size of a normal door had been hacked through two layers of concrete blocks.

'This was built in a hurry,' said Brian, examining the brickwork. 'They must've done it around the time the lab was sealed.'

'There will be another tight fitting door beyond,' I replied. 'The people in the lab were poisoned with cyanide.' I explained the story that Hooder had told me.

'We'll have to be careful if we go on,' said Emma. 'The cyanide won't be there but nor will there be much safe air. Not if they sealed all the vents.'

I climbed through the opening into a square room, properly walled, not like the raw stone of the tunnel. Ten feet away on the far side was an open door and beyond it I could see another room with a table and a row of drab coats hanging from hooks. I examined the door. It was of metal construction and fitted with rubber seals all round, still in perfect preservation. It reminded me of a ship's watertight bulkhead door.

'They didn't intend the bugs to leave the lab this way,' I said. Very slowly I peered inside.

The walls were brick, covered with a coating of limewash. The floor was made of seemingly good-quality tiles although at present it was littered with sheets of cardboard and a tangle of very musty straw.

'This mess was made tonight,' said Brian. 'Look in that corner.'

He pointed to an area about ten feet square. It was filled with wooden decking, rather like that found in a contemporary garden. It looked as fresh and unstained as if it had been installed yesterday.

'That's where the loot was stacked,' said Brian.

'It was only a lot of boxes,' I said. 'All Hooder's father's stuff.'

'I don't think so,' Brian sighed. 'Just like me to arrive half an hour too late. Yes, half an hour late and this stuff was here fifty years.'

'What was it, Mr Byrne?' asked Emma.

'A monument to your own famous grandfather: a most remarkable man.'

'Panov the composer?' Emma was clearly baffled.

'No,' I snapped, 'he means Grandfather Wilson. The one who was here in the war.'

This was a sore point and we didn't need it now. Emma was a child of her generation. She had little time for war heroes, but she revered her musical great-grandfather.

'That's the one,' said Brian. 'The old pirate never lived to reclaim his buried hoard. Funny that, neither did Captain Kidd.'

'Give it a rest, Brian,' I said. 'Emma knows nothing about this.'

'Is that what you think?' Emma was laughing. 'Mr Byrne, are you telling me the great swashbuckler was a villain? Why, I've known that for years.'

'How come?' I knew I must be standing open mouthed. 'How d'you know anything about it?'

'Gran told me, just before I left for college – just after she got married to Grant.'

'Well, she never told me.'

'I think she wanted you left alone with your illusions.'

I couldn't handle any of this. I brushed it aside and, ignoring the others, I walked to the door at the far side of the room. It was an ordinary wooden door and it was firmly shut. I was feeling bloody-minded now. I turned and faced the others – sod you all, I thought. I twisted the handle and pulled the door open. The room beyond was in darkness, evidently the temporary electric link did not function here. I must be on the threshold of the actual laboratory.

'Careful, Dad,' Emma warned. 'Watch for bad air!'

I switched on my torch and shone it inside. I saw another room similar to the one we were in. It was empty apart from a trestle table and a chair. I shone my torch on the chair and felt my whole body go rigid, the spontaneous gasp gathered in my throat and emerged as a yell of nausea and disgust. I was looking at the mummified corpse of a human being. The figure in the chair was slumped over the table its hands still clasped to its head. I could see its clothing, a laboratory coat still recognisable, but the head was a skull with a covering of hair and parchment-like skin. I held the torch beam on that corpse, fascinated; unable to tear my glance away. Someone grabbed my arm, it was Emma, she was breathing hard and, for all her experience of bodies, she was clearly shaken.

'Jesus – holy Mary,' Brian muttered. 'What a sight – poor bastard whoever he is.'

'It's a woman actually,' said Emma. She had passed me and was now bending over the horrible object. 'Incredible state of preservation. This whole place must have been sealed tight – like an Egyptian tomb. I can't understand why the air is so good.'

'It means somebody's opened the ventilation'' said Brian. 'Feel the draught.'

I could feel it too; a tunnel draught, the sort of wind that sometimes gusts through a station on the London tube. My thoughts broke abruptly as Emma let fly a yell, or rather a squeal that developed into a shriek of terror. It was so shrill and unexpected that I think we all nearly turned and fled. She had moved a few feet from the table and had trodden on another mummified corpse lying where it had fallen doubled up on the floor.

Emma stepped backwards and tumbled into my arms. I could no longer help myself, as the tension broke I laughed. We all laughed, even Emma laughed as she attacked both Simon and me in turn, pounding us with her clenched fists.

'Hello, what have we here?' Brian was shining his torch on the new discovery. 'British Army uniform – corporal.'

'Security guard probably,' I said. 'Poor bugger thought he had a nice cushy number. Now he won't even have place on his local war memorial.'

'Oh God – I don't believe this.' Emma was angry now; blazing with fury.

I swung round as did the other two. Emma's torch was playing on the right hand wall. It was not in fact a wall, it was two barred cells, similar to those of an American jail. Each contained a metal bed, a table, a chair and a latrine. The gate of one was open and the cell empty. In the other the gate was shut and on the floor lay yet another mummified corpse.

'No wonder they've tried to cover up this place,' said Brian. He walked to the edge of the cage and peered in.

'He's not a Jerry POW. Probably some Army deserter – can't tell from the clothing. Only a little fellow – shorter than me.' He turned away. I could see by his face that his usual, hard-man, seen-it-all attitude had vanished.

'Like father, like son' I muttered.

'What?' said Brian.

'Experimenting on people,' I said. 'It may not be true, but my step-father says there's talk in Africa that our Doctor Hooder's done just that.'

'I don't know about you but I'm going on,' said Brian. 'I must see the rest of this dump.'

He shone his torch on each of us in turn. Nobody wanted to turn back. I had to see every corner of this vile place and I guessed the others felt the same.

In front of us we could see double doors; old style hospital doors with round windows set at head height. 'That looks like a theatre,' said Simon.

He walked to the doors and heaved on them with such force that he nearly fell headlong into the space beyond. He steadied himself and pointed his torch. 'It's a time warp,' he sounded awe-struck. 'I've got to see this.' He strode forward. 'It's all right – no stiffs in here – sorry I'm wrong, there's one over there.'

The room was an operating theatre but, as Simon had suggested, it was a museum piece. Table, anaesthetic bottles and instrument trolleys were all there, reminiscent of the wartime movie *Green For Danger*. Simon shone his torch into a corner near the far door. Yet another shrivelled body curled into a foetal position.

'Male, elderly I would say. Lab coat – wearing a bow tie.' He shrugged and swung the light around the room.

The beam shone back off a glass partition; a side office. I pushed at the door and then recoiled back. Yet another corpse was on the inside. Its emaciated fingers, frozen in time, as they scrabbled against the woodwork. In disgust I turned to the window and stared inside. A picture calendar was attached on the wall, with a monochrome photograph of the Tower of London. The month was May and the year 1946. The tear-off date read two days after the murder of Margaret Gulley. Murder? Or manslaughter, by a deranged religious delusionist?

Simon had reached the next door. He turned and looked back at us and I caught his lopsided half smile in the beam of my lamp. I drew a deep breath, the air was still good. We had to go on but I think we all dreaded what might lie beyond this place. It turned out to be a corridor cut from the rock but walled with decaying plasterboard. We passed a hospital trolley of the type Americans call a gurney. The doors at the end were propped open and the draught was fiercer. In the background, far away at the harbour, we could still hear the generator. The room we had now entered was the largest yet. This was the real laboratory with everything in place: the workbenches with glass retorts and tubing; shelves arrayed with bottles and other equipment that I couldn't identify. Against the wall were refrigerators and other chest-like fittings.

'Where's Doctor Frankenstein?' whispered Brian.

One distorted corpse lay under a bench. The laboratory had a side office similar to the one in the theatre. The door was open and a quick look revealed no dead bodies, only furniture: a table, metal cabinets, a roll-top desk and a long wooden chest of narrow filing drawers. The drawers had been pulled out and were lying on the floor. The cabinets were open and the table and desk were covered with cardboard trays and document boxes. Paper folders littered the floor along with odd pieces of paper. I picked one of these up. It was a typed requisition order for forty gallons of paraffin. The form was in triplicate interlaced with carbon paper and still unsigned.

Brian was rummaging among the litter. 'Hooder's been here,' he said. 'All this was done tonight, by somebody looking for something in a hurry.'

'His father's experiments and their conclusions. That's what he's after – he told me so himself.' I was losing interest. I didn't care about Hooder or his father. I wanted to see the rest of this evil warren and then get back to the open air and sanity. Apart from that I desperately wanted news of the missing yacht and the fate of Tommy and the little girl.

Emma and Simon seemed to be absorbed in the main lab. They were rummaging among the workbenches and opening cupboards. I walked across to a circular object about a metre in height with a lid held by securing clamps.

'Don't touch that, Dad,' Emma sounded alarmed. 'If there's any nasty viruses, they'll be in there.'

I backed off rapidly.

'If we're going on,' said Simon, 'we'd better reduce the torches to two, with two spare.'

That made sense and I agreed at once. We pressed on into the next section, a passage with proper plastered walls broken by two well-made wooden doors. Each door had a painted wooden sign. Dr P. Hooder Phd, said one. J. Carstairs MA Bsc, said the other. I opened the one marked Hooder and went inside. Another office, it had better quality furnishings and a padded chair behind the desk. The occupant's son had been in here as well. The filing cabinets had been rifled and the desk drawers pulled out. Hooder Junior must have known what he was looking for, because the only papers we could find looked wholly mundane; certainly not scientific conclusions. By chance I picked up small filing tray. It was piled with envelopes addressed and bearing vintage two-and-a-halfpenny stamps. Only one remained unstamped with the neat words, "by hand, Top Secret". It was addressed to: "Cdr J. Wilson, VC, RN. Base Commander. HMS Duddlestone". I slipped it into my pocket.

'Peter,' Brian called. 'Have a look in here?' He pointed into the other office.

It was identical to the other, with one exception. Two bodies lay on the floor. One was female, a twisted shape beside an overturned chair: I saw a wizened mummified face topped by blonde hair. I turned away in disgust. She must have had been a young girl dressed in a Wren's uniform. Brian handed me a writing pad. Its pages were lined but yellowed with age. I could just decipher a string of pencilled hieroglyphics.

'Pitman's shorthand,' said Brian. 'She was half way through taking dictation. You can still read it. *Now that the hostilities are over, I think we can secure the co-operation of Professor Yam....* That's where it stops.' He shook his head. 'She was well trained, perfectly formed words. Poor little kid – choked to death and if it was cyanide it wouldn't have been a nice way to go.' He caught my arm and shone his torch at the floor. We saw another lump concealed by a blanket. 'Whoever was in here tonight took the trouble to move this one and cover it – now why?'

'I think I can tell you that,' I said. 'The man who had this office was Carstairs, the deputy director. I guess that's him under the cover. His granddaughter is Hooder's girlfriend, Drucilla. She was seen up top earlier this evening.'

We entered another laboratory, this time without human remains. We moved quickly on into the next passage with doors to either side. One of these was a small laundry room, crowded with wicker baskets stuffed with lab coats. All appeared to be in pristine condition. In one corner it looked as if the roof had collapsed, leaving a pile of loose rock, concrete and what looked like tar and broken timber. It wasn't a roof fall; I pointed my torch upwards. The vent had been firmly sealed from the outside with a wooden plug backed by some sticky filling. Once again I wondered where the fresh air was coming from. Under the vent was a large galvanised iron trough with antique water taps. It was empty apart from the remains of three paint tins. I moved away and took one last look at the place I was in. It was dull and functional; it was time I was moving on. Perhaps in hindsight, I should have realised that I had the solution to this fifty-year-old mass murder staring me in the face.

Brian walked around the room. He muttered something that I didn't quite catch and at that moment Simon called to us. 'Come and look at this!' He had an edge to his voice that sent us scurrying out of the room to join him.

He and Emma were in the staff canteen and the staff were present, eight of them around the table, the dusty remnants of their half-consumed meals in front of them. It was a grisly tableau, a horrible freak show made even more surreal in the torchlight. The walls were covered with old posters; *Careless talk costs lives. Salute the soldier. Back them up;* time warp and all the other clichés could not properly describe how I felt. Did my father ever walk this way or share a meal with these people in this room. Very likely; but was he responsible, however indirectly, for their terrible end?

We left the canteen and pressed on. None of us would suggest turning back, although by this time even our two doctors had lost their professional detachment. We looked in the kitchen and found two bodies. I was relieved that there were only two. The cooking range was a paraffin burner; that explained the fuel order I had picked up. There were pots and pans in place and unopened bulk tins of beans and corned beef. 'These should still be good,' said Simon.

'Then help yourself, mate,' said Brian. 'I'll pass on that one.'

We walked on into another interminable corridor with more offices, and a storeroom lined with bottle-filled shelves and wooden crates of glass vessels packed in straw. At last we reached the end of the line. We were saving light by running on one torch. We knew we would soon have to turn round and go back. Although I could just hear the generator in the far distance, I couldn't know how long its fuel would last, or whether somebody would switch it off. We were in some sort of reception area. I could make out a table with a figure seated in a chair. Brian, who was carrying the light, jerked it nervously away, a sure sign that the atmosphere had finally affected him. Something was different now. The air was definitely sweeter, with scents of the hillside and grassland above this awful underworld. Then I saw the doorway to the outside, and I could see stars in a clear sky. I stood looking at that sky and the relief washed through me. The release of tension left me speechless and weak-limbed. I'm sure the others felt the same. They clustered around me, staring at that rectangle of light. Brian shone his torch back into the room and played the beam around the walls. It would have been a cheerless place at the best of times. There was a little glass cubicle that I took to be a guard post, and an antique telephone switchboard and the table with the dark shape of its chair and occupant. As the light beam touched this seated figure it moved and slowly sat upright.

'Good evening, Captain Wilson, perhaps you would introduce your friends.'

CHAPTER 40

Emma screamed, another awful blood-curdling shriek. Then all of us fled yelling, pushing and fighting to reach the doorway and through into the open air. I tripped and fell, bringing down Brian on top of me. My torch fell and shattered. I scrambled to my feet and ran through the door. I had an awful illusion, a feeling that long tentacles were stretching out, trying to catch me and drag me into some terrible abyss. I could hear the others running. I looked around desperate to see if Emma was safe. Thank God, Simon was with her dragging her by the arm. We were running on a hard surface, it was old lichen encrusted concrete. Ahead of us I could see men, dark shapes, but at least they were human and of this world. I slowed my pace; for the first time I realised I was gasping for breath and that my chest hurt. I could see that these newcomers were soldiers and that they were barring our way in an unfriendly posture. Suddenly, a blinding light destroyed my night vision. I stopped in my tracks and put my hand to my eyes trying to shade them.

'Well I never,' said a voice resonant with sarcasm. 'It's the captain what don't do his shaving.' The tone changed. 'Halt – stand still! You are trespassing on Ministry of Defence controlled property.' The light dipped and I managed a close look at the speaker. I knew his voice anyway, I remembered him from my first visit to Old Duddlestone. The Military Police corporal in command of the guard post.

'This must be an exciting day for you,' I replied. 'The first useful action your post has seen in fifty years.'

'You can shut your face, Mister,' said the corporal.

'And you can stop throwing your weight about, soldier,' said Brian. 'We're civilians and we entered the tunnels with police sanction.'

'I don't give a fucking fuck for the fucking civvy police,' said the corporal. 'You fuckers turn around and walk back – there's someone as wants a word with you.'

'And you watch your language, you foul mouthed oaf!' I favoured him with a sea captain's bellow. 'There's a lady in our group.'

'You will turn around and retrace the way what you come by, please, Sir.' The voice had authority but had modified its tone.

'Thank you,' I said, 'that's better.'

We must have made a mournful procession as we walked back up the concrete roadway towards the dark lump of hill. I still couldn't rationalise what I had seen. I had recovered enough to know that I had been the victim of a trick, an illusion of some kind, and I was not pleased. I knew now that we were walking in the above ground area of the Duddlestone laboratory. I had been here once before with Alistair Pickering for the Ministry of Defence briefing. On that day none of us had been this close to the tunnel entrance. As far as I knew it had been sealed behind a hundred tons of concrete and earth. In fact I could see the place where these works had been. Clearly we were on our way to some secondary entrance. I didn't really care, it was enough that we had escaped from that place and I had no wish to go back there. I slowed my pace and I noticed the others were doing likewise. 'Keep moving,' snarled our corporal.

We re-entered the lab through a concrete covered walkway that projected from the hill. We passed a pile of fresh earth and rubble. So that explained it; this doorway had been reopened today. A few steps and we were back in the old reception area. Now the place was lit in a blaze of electricity and I could see every detail. It was a drab room and much smaller than I had thought; no dead bodies, only one live individual still sitting behind the table. He stood up as we approached. He was a tall gangling man around fifty years old, with thin greying hair, wearing a dark suit. I had seen him once before. He was the faceless government man that Alistair had pointed out at the press briefing.

'I know you – you're Beresford,' said Brian.

'I think you are mistaken,' the man replied. 'I am a civil servant, and my name is Smith.'

Brian laughed. 'Smith in the dirty weekend sense?' His Liverpudlian speech was broader now and the tone mocking.

'Mr Byrne is it not?' asked the man. His face remained deadpan although his speech, in contrast, was precise with perfectly modulated vowels.

'Yeah, I thought you'd know me. You're Dawson Beresford – remember, Wigan, February '88.'

There was just a flicker of annoyance on Mr Beresford's – or – Smith's face. Brian was trying his patience and he, Smith, was losing the initiative.

'Mr Byrne, on that occasion you signed and agreed to the provisions of the Official Secrets Act. I would remind you that you are still bound by those provisions.'

'I know that,' said Brian. 'That's why I can't write a word about this place or the Navy in Old Duddlestone.'

'Until 2046,' a faint smile crossed Smith's face.

'But there was nothing to stop Tabitha Long from writing whatever she liked about anything.'

'I am not aware that she had signed the act – no.' Smith's refined accent was beginning to grate on my nerves. 'But the lady is hardly in a condition to write anything.'

'You can't cover up this place.' I said. 'I've seen it with my own eyes. Medical experiments on prisoners in an official government establishment?'

'Which government establishment would this be?' Smith raised an eyebrow.

'This one right here where we're standing.'

'Such a place never existed. I believe there were some caves associated with the Navy base. It seems a shame, Mr Wilson, that you should disseminate falsehoods in order to draw attention away from your late father's misdeeds.'

'Don't give me that, Beresford,' Brian was becoming dangerous. He was swaying on his feet like a boxer. Any more provocation and I would have to intervene before he did something really stupid. He was coldly angry; I suspected he was playing out some personal vendetta.

Brian dropped his fists and instead turned and looked me in the eye. 'Peter, here's a little history lesson for you. I take no credit, it was dug up in the last two weeks by that Dave from the marines.'

'Mr Byrne – be careful,' said Smith.

'What are you going to do about it? We're alone here – you've no witnesses unless you call in that dopey red-cap, and he wouldn't understand – he's got the IQ of a gorilla – less probably.'

Brian faced me again. 'Peter, after the end of the war our government, God bless them, had an embarrassing revelation. In 1941, a certain Balkan country, about to be invaded by the Germans, entrusted its gold reserves to the British forces in the Eastern Mediterranean. In 1945, our jolly Balkans asked for their gold back. Trouble was it'd vanished into thin air – yeah, vanished as if it had never existed.'

'Mr Byrne, I must protest in the strongest terms. This incident never happened. The gold was sequestered after the nation in question sank one of our ships.'

'Yes, I've heard that one as well. You see, Peter, when our people couldn't find the stuff they panicked. When one of our Navy boats hit a mine in the Adriatic they blamed the owners of the gold. Told 'em we'd keep their rotten gold until they compensated us for the ship.'

'May I ask where the gold was?' I didn't want to hear this but I had to know.

'Dave says nobody was certain. For a while our people thought it'd been lost during the evacuation of Crete. In fact we think it spent the last year of the war in Malta. At some point before that, it fell off the back of a lorry in Egypt, about the time of the battle of El Alamein, when most people's attention was elsewhere. When and how it got to Malta we're not certain. The next sighting was it being loaded on a DC3 aircraft bound for Gibraltar in November 1945.'

'Mr Byrne,' Smith had drawn himself up to his full six foot. 'That is enough.' The suave manner was gone, the man was clearly outraged.

Brian waved away the protests. 'Now, my bombshell, because this is the bit that Beresford here doesn't know. The captain of the DC3 was none other than a certain Flight Lieutenant Long.'

'Is he connected with Tabitha Long?' I asked.

'Oh yes, he's Tabitha's Daddy, and he's still alive. I got a mate of mine to search him out. He's kept quiet about it to protect himself, because he thought there was something not quite kosher about that cargo. He's kept quiet for years, but now his little girl's dead he's full of remorse. I'm sorry Beresford, but Mr Long has copies of Tabitha's notes. So have Channel Nine TV. You see, this is what Tabitha was really after, never the Rocastle affair, it was the germ lab and the loot in there.'

'That's enough – you are all under military arrest.' Smith began to call loudly for the guard.

'I wouldn't do that, Beresford.' There was a cold menace about Brian. 'Just one question for you. Did you push Tabitha, or was it one of your zombies?'

The lock-up cell in the barracks was cramped. The floor was concrete and the lone bed was a wooden board. The tiny window had bars but no glass. It must have been a freezing hell in winter, but at least a little cool air was circulating through it tonight. We had been driven a short distance in a closed Military Police van, which meant we could only be in the Duddlestone Army camp. I was worried about Emma. She had been removed immediately on our arrival and whisked away.

Our mobile phones had been taken, but not before I managed to text a message to Steve Gulley. He wouldn't have been my first choice but he alone would be on the lookout for a call from me. Actually it was Byrne who tapped out the message. It read; *monkeys got us in stir – tell bill.* It was incomprehensible but Brian said Steve would understand. Wearily, I checked my watch. I was surprised to find it was only ten o'clock. The whole traumatic experience had taken less that one hour.

'Brian,' I asked. 'How deep in shit are we?'

'By my standards hardly at all. I once got locked up for four days in Upper Volta. You could hear the firing squad hard at it in the yard outside.'

'Why is that Smith character so wound up about the war? You don't really believe he pushed Tabitha over the cliff?'

'I don't know,' Brian shook his head.

'He didn't look the type to me,' said Simon. 'More likely Tabitha would push him.'

'Having met the lady, I'm inclined to agree,' said Brian.

'Who is he anyway?' I asked. I wasn't that interested but listening to Brian would distract me. I wanted out of here; I wanted news of Tommy and Carol.

'He's Dawson Beresford, old type intelligence officer, public-school, Cambridge. I know the type. They're steeped in denial culture. Anything the slightest bit embarrassing can't have happened. Only their version of history is true. In that way they were exactly like the Soviets. He must be near retirement now – to me he just seems very sad.'

'But not a killer?'

'No, but he's obsessed with his secrecy, paranoid I would say. I wouldn't put it past him to order an accident to happen.'

'To us?' asked Simon.

Brian laughed. 'Knowing the gentleman's mind I'd say he's holding us here long enough to make you two and young Emma sign the Act.'

I was thinking. I didn't give a damn about any secrets act. I wanted to escape from this place. 'I suppose they've got to feed us sometime?'

'It's no good trying a break for it,' said Brian. 'There'll be locked gates and guards.'

'No,' I said, 'something much more subtle.' I rummaged in my pockets and found the envelope addressed to my father. I wanted to read it but not here. I found another piece of paper. It was only an old petrol receipt but it would do. I wrote a short message and folded it in my wallet next to a twenty-pound note.

Almost on cue we heard footsteps in the passage. The door opened and there stood a soldier with a tray of food, three plates of fish and chips and a bottle of mineral water. The soldier was not alone; in the background was a Military Police guard. The latter didn't deign to enter the cell but stood menacingly in the passage. I took my chance waved the twenty- pound note, put a finger to my lips, and whispered.

'Do you know Lieutenant Pickering?' This lad was not a red-cap, I guessed he was a caterer.

He looked warily at me and nodded.

I slipped him my written message and the twenty pounds. As he bent forward I whispered again. 'There's another of these for you if you deliver the message.' The soldier left the cell and the door was re-locked. The whole incident had taken less than seven seconds.

The fish and chips were remarkably tasty. Despite my worries I managed to clear the plate. We were even more thirsty, and between us we finished the water bottle in one session. The end came suddenly, twenty minutes later. The door opened and a guard called for us to follow him. We did so across a wide parade square and into a red-brick building. The guard knocked on a door and we were shown into a room, an office, with heavy furnishings and pictures on the walls: oil paintings of cavalry charges and antique World War One tanks. In front of us was a tableau, the sight of which almost made me laugh. Behind the desk was a Brigadier dressed in full evening mess kit plus medals. To one side was our Military Police corporal, standing to attention with the rigidity of a waxwork. Next to him I saw Alistair Pickering in a deferential stand-easy posture. On the other side of the desk was Emma. Her dishevelled hair, patched jeans, and cropped-top T-shirt, gave her the appearance of an eco-warrior's wild-child. To complete the picture were two police constables who looked totally bewildered.

The Brigadier narrowed his eyes and coldly examined us each in turn. Finally his gaze settled on Brian.

'Mr Byrne,' he said at last. 'Trouble seems to follow you around like nemesis. Are you responsible for this latest cock-up?'

'No Brig, we've been illegally detained by the military, without cause and without a warrant.' I wished Brian would not be so cocky. We were in enough trouble already.

'It seems you have upset Colonel Smith of Military Intelligence.'

Byrne said nothing.

The Brigadier was staring at me. 'Are you Captain Peter Wilson?'

'Yes.'

'I know you are. I sailed my own boat into your harbour a week ago.'

I remembered him now; the cheerful man with a wife and three teenage girls.

'But I assume you are not the same Captain Wilson who commanded there in 1946.'

'He was my father.'

'That is obvious, but my guest this evening, General Stootsmyer of the United States Embassy, is convinced you are the same man. He thinks you've got something of his and he wants it back.'

'What could I possibly have? I can't help him.'

'As nobody will tell me what this is about, I can't answer that.' The Brigadier sounded exasperated. 'And frankly, I'd rather not know – life is difficult enough already.'

'Brig, this bloke Smith,' said Brian. 'When I last saw him he was called Beresford, and I never knew he was a colonel.'

'He is certainly from Intelligence,' replied the Brigadier. 'But in my experience, being intelligent is not always these people's forte, and there are a lot of Smiths around.' He turned to the two constables. 'What can I do for you gentlemen?'

They looked at each other and then the oldest spoke. 'We are acting on information that the military are holding civilians.' He pointed at the corporal who was still standing statuesque.

'For God's sake, Corporal,' the Brigadier barked. 'Stand at ease, man.'

The corporal obeyed with the facility of a robot.

'That bloke,' said the constable eyeing the corporal. 'He denied you were holding civilians, and the man you call Smith ordered us to leave the camp. As we were unaware that he was Army, we declined and demanded to see you, Sir.'

'While in the meantime,' said the Brigadier, 'Mister Pickering here was dragging me away from my guests and leaving my poor wife to hold the fort with General Stootsmyer.' He turned to Pickering and whispered. 'Alistair, do you know where Smith is now?'

'I'm not sure, Sir.'

'Never mind.' The Brigadier stood up. 'I must be going. Mister Pickering, would you please escort all these people to the camp entrance.' He faced Brian. 'Mr Byrne, in future, if only for my sake, would you please get official clearance before you go poncing around in this area.' Suddenly the Brigadier grinned and gave us a cheerful wink.

It was a relief, but there was something I must know. 'Has any-one heard if they've found the missing children?'

'The Ford-Watts girl?' said one of the police. 'No news I'm afraid.'

They say no news is good news, but that is not how I felt as we journeyed back to Duddlestone in the police car. We were on our way to Honeycritch Farm. I would have to tell Carol that I hadn't found her boy. Worse, I had let the villains who had taken him slip through my fingers as I watched. I dreaded that moment more than anything I had ever faced in my life. As we drove through familiar lanes I watched the houses, trees and hedges flick past. My companions were silent. I knew their minds were on other things. They were thinking of those macabre tunnels and the time capsule that they represented. I felt in my pocket and found the letter I had picked up, the one addressed to my father. I opened it and with the light of my returned mobile phone I read it. The sheet of typewritten paper was as white and the print as clear as the day it was composed. I read it, and for a few minutes I did forget my troubles with an overwhelming feeling of relief. Suddenly fate had turned in my favour and given me a card to play. Should Smith and his kind threaten me through my father, then I would play it.

CHAPTER 41

We were gathered in the kitchen of Honeycritch Farm. With the exception of Carol, all the Rocastle clan were there – plus Brian, Emma and Simon. I felt especially guilty for having gone off on a personal jaunt into the tunnels when I should have been here at Carol's side.

'So that's where you were,' said Laura. 'You really mean you walked right through the hill and out the other side? What did you find?'

'Death,' I said shortly.

Very tentatively I asked after Carol and was told that she was mentally and physically exhausted and had finally collapsed, sleeping without medication.

'We had the Vicar with her this evening,' said Gwen. 'He's a good man, but there's nothing he could do. We've just got to wait and hope your marine boys do the business.'

I told Emma she could take my car and go and visit her grandmother in hospital. From now on I would not stir from this house until I had positive news. Nobody said anything, but I knew that we were all steeling ourselves to face the worst. Even Channing, when I spoke to him on the phone, sounded grim. In the end I made myself have a hot bath and went to bed. This time I fell instantly asleep, but it was not a restful night. I dreamed of black tunnels, where ugly lizards fed on bloated corpses. I kept seeing the face of Tabitha Long sneering superciliously, while Paul Hooder laughed. They were coming for me, I could hear them. I wanted to run but I was trapped in the classic nightmare. My feet were shod in leaden boots and my limbs were useless. I could see them all now, closing in on me: my father in the lead, his face alight with his contempt for me. With him were George Dunlass, Eriksen, Laura, Steve Gulley, Harry, the Brigadier and Sharon the barmaid in the pub. My father raised a muscular arm and struck me on the shoulder. Then he shook me until I opened my eyes and found I was once more in bed in the real world.

'Wake up, Peter,' said Ian Rocastle. 'You're wanted on the phone – we've a call from the police.'

'John Righton here, we've news. Mixture of good and bad.'

I was fully awake now. The clock on the wall said six o'clock and it was already light outside. 'Are they alive?' That was all that mattered.

'Yes, we've had another call and they spoke and this time it was live, not taped.'

'You mean the kids spoke?'

'Yes, and they seemed remarkably cheerful. So, very good news.'

'When was this?'

'A quarter of an hour ago. The abductors have named you as the go-between. They're ready to talk turkey.'

'Thank God – you know I'll do anything I can.'

'Good man, I knew we could rely on you.'

'Inspector, what happened to the marines. Did they find the ship?' Suddenly I was concerned for Keith and his boys, which was stupid of me because they could look after themselves well enough.

'They found the ship in the end. The problem was sea fog. The helicopter got locked onto another craft. Not their fault there's a lot of traffic out there. Your SBS boys found the ship in the end, floating abandoned – like the *Marie Celeste.* No crew, no passengers, no missing children. Whatever it was they removed from those caves, well that's gone too.'

'Meaning they must have transferred to another vessel. Christ, that would be one hell of an undertaking if there was any sort of sea running.'

'It seems they have the devil's own luck. There was nil wind and very little sea. The marines fancied they heard another vessel moving away at speed, just before they boarded.

'Where was all this?'

'About five miles south of the Needles. Your boys were nearly out of fuel.'

I promised Righton I would stay near a phone and said goodbye. I turned round to find a semi-circle of anxious faces. Laura, Ian and Tricia were all there. I repeated what I had been told.

'I bet George Stoneman knows where they are,' said Ian.

'Why don't the police beat hell out of him until he tells,' said Laura.

'Can't do that – anyway he's out on bail.' Said Ian.

'Did he murder Arthur?' I asked. 'That's what they've charged him with.'

'I think he was held under suspicion, but whether it could be proved…?' Ian shrugged.

'It would be nice for Carol if it could be,' I said.

The summons came at midday. I was fetched in a police car to a point on the main road outside Wareham. Here, parked in a layby was another car with Inspector Righton. I felt I was watching myself, a spectator in a bad dream.

'Good man,' he replied. 'We've sent an officer to Old Duddle-stone to collect your car. You are then required to drive to Chichester in West Sussex.'

'What's happened?'

'We've had a further phone call taken in London by Mrs Ford-Watts. We heard the recorded voices of both children and then the instructions.'

'And they've definitely said my name?'

'That's right, Captain Peter Wilson from Old Duddlestone to travel alone to Chichester and to wait at the old market-cross, at three pm today. Have you ever been there?'

'Yes, I know it.'

'Another thing, we know you have the support of the Rocastle family. Mr and Mrs Ford-Watts are insistent that they have confid-ence in you as well.'

I remembered something. 'Ian Rocastle thinks the Ford-Watts may have paid a ransom.'

'What makes him think that?' Righton seemed surprised.

I told him of Ian's impression of Mrs Ford-Watts when she met her ex-husband at Gatwick.

'We've heard nothing about ransoms – what you've said certainly seems odd. You'll have to play that one by ear. We don't encourage ransom payments.'

'That doesn't make it any easier,' I replied. 'Will you be watching?'

'We have been told to stay clear. Any police presence and the children will suffer. Our Sussex colleagues will keep a very discreet watch, but there will be absolutely no intervention. You will be on your own from that point. That's not entirely our decision. To be frank with you we're being leaned on by the Intelligence Services and we're not sure why.'

'How will the abductors know me?'

'They didn't say. I assume whoever is sent to meet you already knows what you look like.'

I was speeding along the A27 in Sussex. Across the flat countryside I could see the great spire of Chichester Cathedral. Twenty minutes later I was parking the car in the city centre. On any other day this place, with its beautiful harbour and fine buildings, would be one of my favourite places in all the world.

I left the car and walked to the appointed spot. My watch said two forty seven. Until now, I had only been concerned with reaching this point on time. Now I began to feel deeply apprehensive. I was bitter with myself for my failure yesterday. If I had sized up the situation at Old Duddlestone just five minutes earlier, we could have stopped that ship sailing and rescued both children. I was mostly worried for Tommy. I felt less sympathy for this Alix. I visualised her as a spoilt little rich kid. The police still saw her as the abductor's real target. It had been Tommy's bad luck to be in the wrong place at the wrong time; or was it? I remembered too well that nasty little cartoon that Carol had received with its implied threat.

'Your name, Wilson?' Standing in front of me was a young lad. He wore baggy jeans, T-shirt and hiking sandals. Despite a completely shaven head he seemed personable enough and not what I had expected.

'Who are you?' I asked. 'Who sent you?'

'All right, mate, no need to get uptight. I was asked to give you a message.' He looked at me inquisitively. 'You are Wilson, I suppose?'

'I am Peter Wilson. Who are you, and who sent you?'

'Me, I'm Danny, I'm a student at the college over the way. This bloke pointed you out. He said give you this and I get fifty quid.'

This was not what I had expected. If I was any judge of character I would say this boy was telling the truth. 'How does this man know you'll bother to deliver the message?'

'Said he'd be watching. Something to do with the horses isn't it? From the race course, over the way, he was hinting.'

'Ah.' I tried to look understanding. 'Yes, that explains things. What does this gentleman look like?'

'Nothing doing, mate. He warned me about that.' The boy thrust a packet into my hands. 'Here it is.' I saw him make off down North Street where he vanished into the crowds of afternoon shoppers. I scanned around all points of the compass looking for anyone remotely suspicious. I could see nothing.

I examined the packet. It was one of those heavy-duty envelopes generally described as a jiffy bag. There was something hard and round within. For a second I worried myself with thoughts of letter bombs, then I ripped it open. Inside was a standard compact disk. I walked quickly back to my car. I pushed the CD into the player and waited.

I recognised Tommy's voice at once. 'Mr Wilson, I'm safe. We've had a good time and they say I can go home with you if you do as you're told.' He sounded calm. I did not have the impression of a child under threat. There was a pause and a second voice. 'Mr Wilson, I'm Alexia, I'm OK but I'm bored with it here. I want to go home.' This was a girl's voice. She sounded amazingly self-assured, not the sound of a bewildered youngster putting on a brave face. There was a subdued muttering in the background and then Tommy spoke again. 'Mr Wilson, please go to the public car park at Harting Down, that's on the B2141 from Chichester to…' He broke off and there was more mumbling. I guessed the boy was reading from a prepared script with a third party in the background. 'It's on the road from Chichester to Peters Field. Please get there soon – I want to go home to Mum.'

I felt a lump in my throat and a burning anger as I pulled out the maps I had brought with me. The instructions obviously meant Petersfield, the Hampshire market town just over the county boundary. I checked and found Harting Down and the car park. It was a short journey northward, around ten miles.

The sun was blazing down out of the westward sky when I reached my objective. I would have liked to call for support. I had my mobile phone but the police had been specific on that point. On no account was I to try and contact anyone on the outside. I was to carry out whatever instructions I was given to the letter. If the police, or intelligence services, were around I could see no sign of them, nor would I expect to. I parked the car and climbed out. The view from this hilltop site was breathtaking. Another time I might have lingered and admired. All I needed now was for something conclusive to happen. This ordeal had gone on for too long. I wanted it over.

Only one other car was parked near me. I thought it looked empty but I walked across to have a closer look. The back seat was occupied by a young man and a girl. They were fully involved in some heavy sexual activity and oblivious of me. I shrugged and returned to my car. Another vehicle was driving in from the road. It was a white van with the logo of a local health food shop blazoned on its side. It stopped beside my car although it had half an acre of empty space to chose from. This was a development I could do without. I wondered if the kidnapper's contact would show himself while this delivery man was drinking his tea. I walked briskly back to my own vehicle. My route took me within feet of the van's rear doors. I noticed these had been opened, and as I passed I glanced inside. A figure crouched, dressed in dark overalls and a black balaclava. I stood transfixed gaping stupidly, then strong arms gripped me from behind and threw me to the ground. I tried to fight back but it was no good. I was rolled face downwards in the dirt. I felt a slight pain in my arm and then all faded into oblivion.

I was aware that I was in a vehicle. I could hear the soft drumming of a diesel engine. I was lying flat on my back and my joints ached. I didn't want to move and I lacked the energy to try. My eyes were shut and my eyelids felt as if they were glued together. With an effort I dragged them apart. I tried to focus on my surroundings. Was this an ambulance? Had I been involved in an accident? I tried to think back. I remembered this morning and the drive to Chichester. Then I remembered my mission and shut my eyes again. Could I possibly have been involved in an accident and ruined everything? I couldn't remember and I was tired and nothing seemed to matter any more.

The vehicle had stopped and the doors were open. I could now see that this was no ambulance. I could hear a roaring noise while a gust of warm air blew into the cabin and made me open my eyes again. Now I had a shock; I could see the thing that was making the deafening noise. We were parked in a grass field and in front of us, not twenty yards away, was a helicopter its engine running and its rotor turning. It was a machine painted black or rather very dark blue. Something came back into my memory, " helicopter painted black and very noisy". Who had said that to me and when, and why should it awake such reaction? A face was bending over me. No, not a face, a black balaclava with two eyes a nose and a mouth slit. The eyes were brown I noticed. Below the mask was a white shirt, and an odour of stale tobacco. I felt the stretcher under me lift, and dimly I could see the same masked figure facing me as he backed down the steps onto the ground. Suddenly I was feeling dizzy and sick. I closed my eyes, but I could hear the footsteps of the stretcher-bearers. Some sixth sense, an inner self, was warning me to lie still and pretend sleep. At that point I had no recollection of the events on Harting Down but I remembered my mission and I knew that bonefide paramedics did not wear balaclavas. I felt a sudden sense of achievement. I had come to find the two children and every indication told me that I was being taken to them.

We were directly under the helicopter rotor and the downdraft was intense. I was gently lifted into a sitting position, from whence I was carried a few feet and into the cabin of the helicopter. I deliberately lolled around although I was rapidly regaining my movements and my senses. Large hands groped around me fixing the seat belts. I opened my eyes as I felt the movement of the aircraft as a figure climbed in and sat beside the pilot in front of me. I looked around, but the side windows had been screened and I could see nothing but seat backs. The throttles opened, the engine whined, and I felt us lift and become airborne.

This was not a new sensation for me. I have flown in helicopters before, and years ago I had learned to fly light aircraft. But this trip was different. I could not see and I did not have a compass. I had no sense of direction and the flight seemed to last forever. Intermittently I think I slept, but the noise was atrocious and nobody had been inclined to fit me with ear protectors. But I remembered now. The black helicopter had flown over the cliffs on the afternoon when Tommy and the girl had been snatched. I had always suspected this was how it was done. It would have been so easy to land in a fold of ground, out of sight of spectators. Tommy would have rushed to see this exciting phenomenon, but the girl Alix had suspected something. Alix, drilled by parents obsessed with kidnapping, had written the warning message. Brave girl; Alix suddenly rose in my estimation.

The flight ended suddenly. I heard the engine note change and felt the descent and then the soft bump as we landed. Hands undid the belts and I was lifted towards the door but not before a musty smelling hood was pushed over my head. It was made of some thin gauze; I could breath but still felt stifled. I was lifted bodily and now I was in a wheel-chair, bumping over uneven ground before the running became smooth and I knew I was on tarmac or concrete. This continued for around ten minutes, the chair making occasional turns before it stopped and I felt the whole rig being lifted and carried a few feet. The bright sunlight that had filtered through the hood was gone and I was now in some cool dark place, a house presumably. Could this be the place where the children were held? Strong hands lifted me from the chair and I was carried a short distance and then up a flight of stairs. I lay motionless, acting dead or at least unconscious.

Next I was laid on a bed and I heard a door close and a lock turn.

From that moment I began to recover fast. I had a deep and penetrating headache and I felt sick, but I knew this was a passing phase. I was about to slide off the bed and try standing when I heard footsteps outside the door. 'Will this man co-operate?' It was a male voice.

'He would be well advised to. He wants to learn the truth about his father.' A different voice now: a deep bass, cultured voice that I'd heard before but in my muddled state I couldn't remember where or who.

Then a muffled reply that I could make nothing of. 'We'll have him out tonight,' said the second voice. 'Make it civilised, invite him to dinner – call on his honour, then we'll make an offer. Find out what he knows – I don't think he'll be too difficult.'

I lay still and unmoving straining to hear more but all was silent as the footsteps faded. I opened my eyes and looked at the ceiling. It was dirty, cobweb-infested and the paper was beginning to peel. I rolled over and looked blearily towards the door. I was pleased to see my shoes there placed neatly in a corner. I gripped the iron frame of the bed and pulled myself into a sitting position. This was one move too many and I collapsed in a wave of nausea and giddiness. Very slowly I tried again. This time it was easier. Next, I eased my legs off the bed. It was a basic iron frame no more than a few inches from the ground. I sat with my feet on a floor that seemed to be heaving and pitching. Very cautiously, I made the effort and stood up. I could see a door to my left and a window in front of me. The window was curtained, leaving the room in semi-darkness, but enough light filtered through the curtains to show that outside was daytime bright sunshine. Very cautiously I gripped the wall and shuffled towards the window. I still felt giddy and sick but I was improving with every second. I reached the window, steadied myself and then eased back the curtain. The light streamed into the room almost dazzling me. The sun was low in the sky but fully visible above the roofs of the opposite houses. It was on these that I concentrated. The window was covered by an iron-mesh grille but I could see through it clearly enough. The houses were all part of one long street, typical urban dwellings, late nineteenth century or early twentieth. I could be in any city anywhere in the UK. The street itself was narrow, little more than an alley, but one vehicle stood parked a little way to my right. It was a milk float and I could just make out a name: *Collins Dairies Romford.* I must be in outer London – Essex. I knew by the position of the sun that I was facing westward but that was hardly relevant. If this was the same day that I had been captured, then I must have been semiconscious for seven hours at least. It was little wonder I felt ill. I stood still listening and straining to hear something – anything. The house was silent but in the background was a continuous muffled roar. I couldn't distinguish its source but it was definitely outside. It could be a very noisy traffic thoroughfare or some industrial plant.

I was feeling better although the headache had intensified. I was also very thirsty and I craved water, not just a glass, but a whole jug full. Surely these people were not going to let me starve. Yes, people, but who were they? The second man in the passage had sounded elderly with a cultured old world accent. A voice that resonated a respectable professional background. It was all a long way from Rita and George Stoneman. Had not Carol hinted that more sophisticated forces were behind the obscurities of Duddlestone? It was then that I remembered Rita Dunlass's angry lament by the harbour. She had been forced to hand over the children to "the big men". I lay down again on the bed. I wondered where I had heard that man's voice before? I really didn't know and I was too muddled to care.

Outside the room I could hear footsteps. A key was fitted in the door and it opened. I sat up as two men entered. One was dressed in a white jacket complete with stethoscope. Apparently they had found me a doctor, which I suppose was nice of them. He was tall gangling fellow in his late twenties and he stood staring down on me as if I was some interesting animal freak.

'What are you – doctor or vet?' I rasped.

'Please, I am a doctor. You have been not well. I think I would check you.' The accent was continental – Italian, possibly Greek.

'Good evening, Captain. I must apologise for your harsh treatment, but we've brought you our doctor and we'll soon put things right.' This was the voice of the first man I'd heard. He grinned cheerfully at me. His English was immaculate but again there was a scintilla of an accent. He must have been around eighty years old with thinning grey hair and sharp blue eyes. He was expensively dressed in a fashionable dark blue suit and there was something about him that radiated power and intelligence. I knew now for certain I was at the heart of the conspiracy.

'You are holding two children. Where are they?' That was all I cared about.

'They are safe and well and have never been in any danger.' The man gestured to the doctor who started to examine my eyes.

I co-operated with bad grace. I knew it was in my own interests to find out how weakened I had become. The medic asked a few questions and probed around with his stethoscope. 'I want water,' I complained.

'I will fetch you some,' said the old man. He slipped quietly from the room and returned a few minutes later with a tray, a glass and a carafe. I seized the glass and drained the contents. I had never felt such wonderful relief in all my days. I grabbed the carafe and refilled the glass and gulped down the contents. 'Not so much,' said the Doctor, 'too fast and not so good for you.' I ignored him and drained another delicious draught before the tray was snatched away.

'What's all this about and who are you?' I asked.

'You sound exactly like your father,' the old man smiled. 'Captain, please rest. Tonight I would like you to join my friends for dinner. You will then have your explanations. In the meantime you have nothing to fear and the young people you refer to will also have nothing to fear.' He turned to follow the doctor who had already left the room. 'You are free to move around this house, but do not disappoint me by trying to leave us. That would do your cause no good and we will be watching.' Then he was gone and I could see that the door had been left open.

I resisted the temptation to run after him, not that I could run anyway. Instead I tried to pull my senses together. This old fellow was obviously another of Father's associates. He was also a foreigner, despite his fluent English. I would place him as a Dane, not that that meant a thing in relation to Flotilla Sixty Six. However twisted these old sailors had become they should have some honour left. It sounded as if they regarded me as someone they would do a deal with. Why they should think that I couldn't say, but I would have to be careful.

After a few minutes I stood up and walked to the door. I reached down unsteadily and pulled on my shoes. For some seconds I just stood listening. The roaring sound was louder and it wasn't traffic. It sounded more like a jet aircraft running an engine test. Could I be within walking distance of an airfield? The helicopter had definitely landed on grass but that could have been near the perimeter. I tried to visualise a road map of Essex, but I could think of no airfield apart from Stansted.

In front of me was a dark passage with a doors to either side. I had two choices; I could retreat back into the room, or I could investigate. I was stronger now and almost fully co-ordinated. My head still ached but the adrenaline was beginning to surge. My captors had taken my watch as well as my mobile phone, but they had left my wallet with my cash and cards untouched. I tried the door on my left;

it was locked. Softly I called the names of Tommy and Alix. I put my ear to the door and listened for a reply but none came. I walked down the passage trying each door in turn. All were locked and no voice replied to my call.

I walked to the stairs and looked. Below was a tiny entrance hall with three doors. I walked down and stood wondering about my next move. I tried the nearest door and this one opened. I found myself in a kitchen. It was a derelict place with a smashed sink and a relic of a cooker. This house had clearly been unoccupied for some time. The second door opened to reveal a front room, dusty and devoid of furniture. Slowly I opened the last door and peered inside. I was momentarily dazzled by the glare of the setting sun streaming through two full-length glass doors. These doors were open and through them I could see a garden with a mown lawn and a rose arch. On the lawn was a table with a sun parasol and comfortable cane chairs. The chairs were occupied by two men with their backs to me, and one facing my direction on the far side of the table. It was the same elderly man, the one I had taken for a Dane. As I walked out into the fresh air he looked up. 'Captain, join us, you are just in time for drinks.'

Slowly and reluctantly I walked across the lawn. As I did so the others turned round and the sight of them stopped me in my tracks. I knew them both, and my overwhelming feeling was one of deep and profound sadness. They were Eriksen and one whose voice I now remembered, my father's old shipmate from the early days, a full admiral and knight of the realm, Sir Denzil Sutton.

I am in a dream or I am mad. This cannot be happening. I do not know how long I stood gaping, probably for no more than a few seconds.

The man I called the Dane spoke. 'Captain, I understand you have a grievance with me?'

I couldn't speak; I just stared.

'Indeed, you vented your displeasure in no uncertain terms,' said Eriksen. 'This is my brother-in-law – Erik Anderssen. Erik is the chairman of our cargo carrying division.'

Now at last I found my voice. 'You fired me from my command. I was wrongfully dismissed and it's backfired on you, because now I've found my way to Duddlestone. I've a fair idea what you've been up to. What are you going to do about it?'

'What are we going to about what?' Anderssen replied. 'Captain, you still look a mite unsteady on your legs. Please come and sit down and perhaps we can have a rational discussion.'

Most of me wanted to refuse, to spit the invitation back in his face, but it wouldn't do. I would have to play it their way. Frankly I had ceased to care what they were planning. I only wanted Tommy and the little girl free and home again.

'Would you care for a drink?' asked Eriksen. 'Nothing with alcohol I'm afraid; the doctor says it would be bad for you.

'Why should you care?'

'Of course we care,' it was the admiral this time. 'You are your father's son and it's obvious you need some explanations.'

I pulled up a plastic garden chair and flopped into it. I was feeling giddy. 'I'm here to negotiate the release of the two children. That's all I care about. You can keep your explanations for the police.'

'The children have suffered no harm,' said Eriksen. 'On the contrary, they've enjoyed an exciting sea cruise. We put into port and they made no attempt to leave us. When last I saw them they seemed happy enough.'

'You mean they were on that ship that was in Duddlestone last night?'

'You mean the *Emily Hopper,* formerly the *Alexander.* A lovely ship, somewhat the worse for wear. You should have seen her in her glory days.'

The admiral grinned. 'Yes, once long ago she was the Albanian royal yacht. I saw her when I was a midshipman in the Med in '37, I think' he paused. 'Can't be sure – memory's gone.'

'That's right,' said Eriksen. 'The favourite ship of his late Majesty, King Zog. Which brings us back to the core of matters in hand.'

'I'm sorry,' I cut in, 'but were the children on that ship or not? If they were, there may be nothing to negotiate about because the chances are they're dead.'

Now I had said it. I surprised myself how easy it was to utter words I had hardly dared to think about. I looked at the others and tried to read their expressions. I saw nothing of guilt; only puzzlement.

'This is nonsense,' muttered the admiral. 'Where on earth did you conceive such an idea?'

I told them everything I'd heard at Duddlestone; about Rita Dunlass and the twins and finally: 'You've been rumbled,' I said. 'George Dunlass is in police custody, and I would guess he's spilling the beans to save his skin.'

'As I understand it Dunlass is being questioned about his part in the killing of Arthur Rocastle,' said Eriksen.

'When he was called George Stoneman?'

'He called himself that, but he was Petty Officer Dunlass in the days we knew him,' said Eriksen. 'Mrs Dunlass's little bastard the locals called him.'

'Good God!' I sat stunned. My mother's words to the nurse the other day. "The little bastard" she had shouted.

'He's the one who tried to kill my mother. She's been shouting in Russian about a bastard. We thought it was an insult but there's a Russian speaker in the hospital who thought it was literal.'

'We are inclined to agree with you and, if it is true, Mr Dunlass will be dealt with. We intended him to pay for his part in the Rocastle affair but your mother's case is personal.' The Admiral spoke quietly.

'And now, Captain,' said Anderssen, 'we have your refreshments.' He stood up and waved towards a gate in the garden hedge.

Three people appeared through the gate on cue. My heart lurched, I tried to stand but fell back into the chair giddy with shock, relief, euphoria and utter disbelief. Leading the group was a tall, rugged looking man of around forty. I had seen him before somewhere but not in real life. I'd seen his picture … politician perhaps? I gave up, because all that mattered were the two diminutive persons with him. They were Tommy and Alexia, thank God, fit and well. Tommy carried a tray with a single tall glass of orange juice. It contained a block of ice floating at a precarious angle as the tray bearer tried to steady his load. Alexia also carried a tray laden with soft drink cans and sweet biscuits.

'Hello, Mister Wilson,' said Tommy. 'Are we going home?'

I couldn't think of any reply. I reached out to touch his arm; yes, he was real.

'Mr Wilson,' said the tall newcomer. 'I'd better introduce myself – Jonathan Ford-Watts; Tom you know and I think you've already met Alix.'

I didn't reply to him and I ignored the outstretched hand. Something in my sub-conscious was telling me I was rude. 'What in hell is going on?' the words slipped out at last. Once more I remembered I was weary and very thirsty. I grabbed the glass of orange and drained it in a single gulp.

'I think,' said Eriksen, 'that the time has come to talk about your father.'

CHAPTER 43

I hardly heard him. I was staring at the two children seemingly playing happily, kicking a plastic imitation football. I could not get my head around this latest development. The kids looked unharmed, without obvious distress, and Alexia's father was with them. It was slowly dawning on me that someone was playing games with all of us: with the Rocastle family, the police, and the public at large. But for whatever crazy motive I couldn't begin to imagine.

'Captain … are you with us? I don't think you've heard a word I've been saying.'

I came back to the present. Eriksen was indicating the man, Ford-Watts. 'Are you aware that your father's great battle is to become a Hollywood feature film. Directed by Spiellmann, with Galen Martinez as Wilson VC.'

'But he's an American,' I found myself protesting, although what this irrelevant stuff had to do with…

'That's right,' said Ford-Watts. 'As far as Hollywood is concerned James Wilson was an American, as were all his men.'

'But that's preposterous – I've never heard that there was a single American in the flotilla.'

'There was one,' said Eriksen. 'However, following much lobbying and protest, Spiellmann has recast the part, with Jonathan here as your father.'

'I'd be very grateful if I could discuss the role with you,' said Ford-Watts.

I looked at the man properly for the first time. He was the right age, give or take a few years, and he might have a passing resemblance to my father – but hold on, this was crazy.

'Whatever my father did before D-Day, it's too late to cover up that he became a pirate. I can't think of any other apt description.'

'A grain of truth,' said the admiral, 'but only a grain. Your father was eccentric; he had little respect for higher command, it's true, and he was very bitter at the end, understandably. But as far as the Duddlestone gold is concerned he was obeying orders. Very reluctantly obeying orders, because he was facing a blackmail threat he could not honourably resist.'

'Explain,' I said. 'I'll listen and I'll be the judge.'

The admiral picked up a brown envelope from the table and

withdrew a monochrome photograph; he passed it to me. It was portrait of a middle-aged man with thinning hair, dressed in a dark suit of antique cut, complete with stiff collar. He sat in front of a plain white backdrop, his face without expression.

'Meet the late Sir Justinian Beresford KCMG.'

'Beresford?' I took a closer look at the picture. 'I've heard that name recently.'

'This Beresford has been dead for twenty years, but in 1945 he was a Foreign Office departmental head – Eastern Mediterranean to be exact.'

I rummaged in my pocket and found my wallet. I extracted the letter addressed to my father that I had found in the Duddlestone laboratory.

'Your father received orders, highly bizarre orders. He questioned them of course, but it made no difference. He threatened to resign his commission. It was then that the blackmail began.' The admiral was angry now. I didn't intervene; I waited.

'Yes, your father was informed that if he failed in this mission the government would be unable to protect individual members of the Duddlestone ship's company. In effect, all non-Britons serving with the flotilla would be discharged and returned to their countries of origin. These included two Spaniards, one a former officer in the Republican Navy in the civil war. Both would certainly have been shot on their day of arrival. There were a number of others whose fate could have been precarious, including Leading Wren Elena Panov, a young lady whose repatriation had been demanded by Stalin himself.' The admiral favoured me with a glassy stare. 'Now do you begin to understand.'

Weary as I felt, I found the words. 'If you are playing some sort of dubious game, then why – why put Tommy's mother through hell for nothing?'

'We're sorry for that – of course,' replied Eriksen. 'But when so much is at stake we needed reality.'

'Mr Wilson, are we going home now?' Tommy looked at me with that odd lopsided expression, so like his mother's. 'Alix has gone with her dad an hour back.'

The boy had woken me as I lay on the bed in the same room as earlier. I had staggered up there, God knew how long ago, feeling sick, giddy and utterly at sea. Apart from all the shocks of that day I was still suffering some sort of hangover from whatever drug had been stabbed into my system.

'Can you get me a glass of water?' I asked.

'Sure – back in a moment. Then will you drive me home?'

'If I was free to go and had a car, yes.'

'Your car's outside in the street. Mister Eriksen said we can go – soon as you wanted.' Tommy disappeared through the door.

I sat up. Yes, I was feeling better, considerably better compared with the sickness and giddiness of earlier. I slid off the bed, stood up and shuffled to the window. I could still see the milk float, but I didn't care about that. Another car stood parked in the road below and, wonder of wonders, it was mine. I could read the registration clearly. Tommy reappeared carrying an overfull pint glass of water which left a spilt trail across the floor. I took it and gulped the delicious stream down my dry throat.

'Can we go now?' he asked.

'What about the others?'

'They've all left – 'bout an hour ago.'

'What time is it?'

Tommy picked up a heavy envelope from the bedside table and gave it to me. It contained my mobile phone and my watch. The time read eight o'clock. I wanted to get out of this place, the sooner the better, but I wondered how, in a drug recovering state, I would cope with an overnight drive from Essex to Dorset.

'How did my car get here?' I asked.

'Dunno' but they said give you the keys.' He held out a ring with a bunch of keys – my keys.

'OK, let's go.'

One more surprise awaited me. The house was definitely empty. I walked from room to room while Tommy stamped impatiently in the background. I could still hear the same jet-engine sounds blasting somewhere outside. The noise magnified as we walked through the front door into the street. My car seemed intact and someone had topped up the petrol to a full tank. I would need this on the long run home to Duddlestone. I looked around the street. It seemed surprisingly quiet, not a light showing nor a car moving: no voices, no muffled background sound of television or radio sets; the normal things of an urban street at dusk. I turned towards this persistent noise. It couldn't be an airfield, nor was it. At the end of the street I could see the outline of a large building and behind, incredibly, open country. I could see fields and high hills. Were there such hills anywhere in Essex?

I strapped Tommy into the passenger seat and we drove out of the street into a placid rural scene. I saw a Georgian country house with outbuildings, stables and a tractor with a high-sided trailer which forced me to pull over onto a grass verge. It was loaded with freshly harvested barley, which explained my jet engine – a commonplace farm grain-dryer. I drove on down the sweeping entrance drive wondering if I could find a road sign that would tell us where the hell we were. I reached what appeared to be a main road which, judging by the sunset, ran directly north to south. I chose south but I would need to move west if I was to pick up the M25.

To the east, high above us, lay a long ridge of downland; which was a puzzle because it didn't fit with my perception of East Anglia. Five minutes later the truth became obvious. We reached a village with a sign, *Sutton Waldron – Blandford 16*. It took me a full minute to comprehend that we were in Dorset, less than thirty miles from Old Duddlestone. It had been a clever ruse by Eriksen, and it sent a shiver of disquiet through me. That street of empty farm cottages could have been in any urban setting and the milk float was placed exactly where I could read its logo. I had been abducted by disguised assailants. Their cold efficiency suggest the security services. If I had not had my father's letter with me and had failed co-operate; then someone might have had other plans for me.

I spoke to Tommy. 'Where were we – I mean whose house?'

'Fontmell Magna, Mister Eriksen's – been there once with my Dad … long time ago.'

A mile short of Blandford, I pulled over and rang Honeycritch Farm. Tricia answered.

'Tommy's safe – we'll be with you in half an hour,' I said.

I heard her intake of breath. 'Peter, the police told us he was on his way, but it's … oh, I just mean it's wonderful you're both alive.'

'We'll talk more when I'm at Honeycritch,' I told her.

Next, I rang the police and was put straight through to Inspector Righton. 'If I had my way I'd charge you all for wasting police time.' He was far from friendly.

'What d'you mean?' I was angry. 'I've put my life on the line for you – I didn't know what I was letting myself in for. I've been drugged and abducted and I'm told I can't do a thing about it.'

'All right, sir – I shouldn't take it out on you. I'm told this is all part of some bigger picture. But I don't like being made a monkey of

– nor does my chief constable.' He paused and I detected a faint chuckle. 'And you'll have your Mr Byrne to reckon with.'

I drove the last few miles to New Duddlestone in a daze. I never found out what the drug still sloshing around my system was called, although it had no lasting effect. I doubt if I would have survived a blood test had the Law decided to question my driving. At last I found the turning for Honeycritch and only then did I remember my mother, struck down at this spot and still languishing in hospital. I drove slowly up the lane and turned into the farm entrance. Tommy released his seat belt and ran from the car tripping the overhead floodlight. Tricia Rocastle had emerged through the front door and Tommy flung himself into her arms. I remained where I was. This reunion would be very personal for the family; tact would require me to wait my turn. I felt so tired and utterly drained. It had been the most amazing and disturbing thirty-six hours of my life.

I sat in a daze, I'm not sure for how long, before there was a tap on my side window. I looked up to see Ian Rocastle grinning at me.

'Come on – inside the house,' he said.

I climbed out and followed him unsteadily through the front door. The family flung themselves on me and I was hugged in turn by Tricia, Gwen and Laura.

Laura favoured me with a smacking kiss. 'You're a bloody hero – I'd never have thought it,' was her backhanded compliment. Then she smiled. 'You've worked a miracle – we'll owe you for ever.'

'Where's Carol?' I asked.

'Tommy's with her,' said Tricia, 'but she'll be OK now.' She looked at me quizzically. 'Can you tell us what happened?'

'I'm not entirely sure what's going on myself, but I'll try.' I sighed. 'If we were dealing with ordinary criminals it would almost be easier.'

How was I going to convince these people of something I couldn't get to grips with myself. How all our lives were affected by a naval covert-operation that went drastically wrong before any of us were born. That was just about comprehensible; but I did not understand how, somehow, everything sprang from the actions of Arthur Rocastle.

CHAPTER 44

'We found the ship, no problem,' said Keith. 'So we hoisted our RIB aboard and took her into Poole.'

We were standing on the dockside at Old Duddlestone. I had found Keith and his companions unloading another RIB from a road trailer. The three of them were full of questions that I couldn't answer and this did not please them.

'This morning we were hauled before our commanding officer. We've been ordered to keep our mouths shut: disciplinary action if we utter a word.' Keith's eyes narrowed. 'There's something going on, Peter, and we don't like being pissed around one little bit, mate.'

I wasn't having that. 'You haven't been completely up-front with me either,' I said. 'Laura phoned the MOD, and the civilian sub-aqua body, and nobody has heard of a Joint Services Sub-Aqua club. And you're not inter-service; you're all Marine Special Forces. I suggest you've a hidden agenda like everyone else.'

'Ve vos only obeying orders.' Keith mimicked.

'As was my late father.'

I should have felt relieved, euphoric even, but instead I was depressed and carrying a splitting headache that refused to respond to painkillers. I had left Honeycritch last night, despite protests from the family. I still felt I was intruding and truthfully I wanted my own space. To my shame I hadn't even faced a hospital visit to my mother although I phoned them. Mother was improving, I was told, and free of intensive care. Then I had driven to Old Duddlestone and staggered aboard my boat. After that I remembered nothing until I awoke this morning. I had made myself a flask of black coffee and then wandered ashore. Laura was already in the office and she pointed me to Keith.

'I'll tell you this much, skipper,' said Keith. 'We found that ship deserted, not a soul on board, and no sign of those boxes.'

'We saw another ship out there,' Dave intervened.

'The police told me that,' I said.

'She was pulling away as we closed with the RIB,' said Dave. 'I reckon I know her – I should do, I've served on her. She was *Sir Mallory.*'

'A Navy ship?'

'Fleet auxiliary – government boat anyway. Come on, skipper

straight up – what's this all about?'

Emma and Simon appeared in a battered hire-car. Emma flung her arms around me and burst into tears, which I found mildly embarrassing. Some of our visitors on the dockside were asking for news of the missing children. I was able to reassure them and then recommend they listen to the mid-day news. Fortunately no one connected me personally with these events.

Emma and Simon had come straight from the hospital. Mother was sitting up in bed and eating soft food. She remembered nothing of the accident and the nursing staff had discouraged too many questions. Well, I had a few questions of my own to ask; not about the incident, but about events long ago. I had a blurred vision of the big picture; I intended, and had a right, to bring that picture to full focus.

'Where is Hooder?' I asked.

Inspector Channing's face was deadpan. 'Doctor Hooder has been helping us in our enquiries, as has Mr George Dunlass.'

'Dunlass was the one who ran my mother down – d'you realise that?'

'We have an open mind on that but we are still pursuing our enquiries.'

'Well, you can stop pursuing – you've got your quarry banged up. I tell you it's Dunlass and I can prove it.'

'I'm listening.'

I told him about my mother's reference to, "the little bastard". 'She was speaking Russian and she meant illegitimate. George Dunlass was known as "the Dunlass bastard". The old Double Six men told me that.'

Channing shook his head. 'It's a good theory, and I wish it was as easy as that, but we can find no DNA link in the stolen car that connects with anyone we know of in Duddlestone.'

'But…' I tried to intervene.

'No, sir. What you are saying is interesting, and believe me we will take it seriously, but your gut instinct is not enough for me to bring charges. Secondly, my hands are tied, as I think you know, in respect of the other seven persons we are questioning.'

'Sorry, you've lost me.'

'We are also questioning: Rita Dunlass, James Stoneman, William Hodge and his brother, Playfair Hodge, who usually calls himself

Sid.'

'Playfair?'

'That is the name his parents gave him. Surprising choice for an East End villain, but there you go…'

'Those are the two twins, right?'

'So it would appear, but I can't comment further.'

'You said you were questioning seven.'

'Also the master of the ship, *Emily Hopper*, but we suspect he has no knowledge of the deeper complexities.'

'He deserted his ship and left her drifting in a busy channel. He should be prosecuted for that alone.'

'That is a matter for the maritime authorities.'

I was attempting to keep my temper. 'What about Tabitha Long – what progress there?'

'We are pursuing enquiries and hope for an early resolution.'

I gave up, made my excuses and left. The thing that incensed me was Channing's refusal to discuss anything that had happened yesterday. Those poor children might have been on a holiday jaunt for all the police seemed to care. And for all our grief and suffering, it seemed that they were doing just that.

I felt in my pocket and took out the envelope containing the letter I had found in the lab. The text fascinated me. The answers were all here if only I could read between the lines.

Completely irregular ... we resent the conduct of your men ... you may be following orders but I would remind you the Admiralty's writ does not run here ... I need to be convinced of the national interest...

And who would "your men" be? Good guess: the Duddlestone Fisherman's Brotherhood plus half a dozen matelots of dubious background. It seemed father was obeying orders, while simultaneously spitting back at authority. It was time I spoke to mother.

A different policeman was slumped on a chair outside mother's new room. She had been moved from intensive care into a small private ward. The Double Six veterans had rallied round and the place was full of flowers and get-well cards. Mother was sitting up in bed, still bruised, bandaged and attached to a drip, but the intrusive heart monitor was absent.

I sat beside her and asked how she was. I wished I knew the best way to proceed; I wanted information, wanted it desperately, but I would never subject her to an interrogation.

She looked at me; I could see she had one eye open again. 'So, you are going to ask questions about your father?'

This was a helpful start. 'We think somebody tried to kill you and I want to find that person and put them behind bars. It's as simple as that.'

'I don't know, son. I don't remember anything.'

'Try this, do you remember a man called George Dunlass, or he have might have been called Stoneman?'

'Stoneman, that is not a good name to have in that village.'

I tried again. 'Do you remember a man that people used to call Mrs Dunlass's bastard?'

'No, I do not remember.'

'Have the police been here?'

'Oh, yes – but I remember nothing.'

This was disappointing, but no more than I should expect. I didn't push her harder; I changed to banalities, kissed her goodbye and left. Downstairs my luck changed. As I approached the automatic doors a large man entered; it was my stepfather Grant. I reassured him about mother's improvement and steered him into the canteen. I bought him another cup of the disgusting coffee and then told him everything that had happened.

Grant looked worried. 'Peter, don't go tangling with security services. I don't know what they're like here, but Jeez, I wouldn't cross them in my country.'

'I thought your new government had got rid of them.'

'Don't you believe it. Like the old Vicar of Bray – those guys are so hard-wired into what they do; they turn their coats and work for the same people they once tried to slap down.'

I pondered on that, recalling the man Smith, or Beresford as Byrne had named him, and the suspicion that he might have had a hand in the death of Tabitha Long; I didn't like to think of that. The horrible scream and the falling body would haunt my dreams for ever.

'Well, Peter, while you were performing your rescue I've been making enquiries.' Grant looked pleased with himself.

'Don't talk to me about pursuing enquiries. That's all I get from that copper Channing.'

'These are my enquiries, man, not cop speak.' He was adamant.

'OK, what have you found?'

'I spent yesterday morning in London, at South Africa House; your mother went there on the morning of the day she was run down.'

'Do you know what it was about?'

'Sure, I do now. She was enquiring as to the antecedents of

Doctor Hooder.'

'What did you discover?'

'All conjecture, but that man has a few questions to answer.'

Grant would not be drawn further and he was anxious to be with mother.

It was past midday as I left the hospital. The sun was high overhead and the day was hot. The streets were crowded with people in their colourful summer wear; inhabitants of that trouble-free world that I had lost. It was time I called at Honeycritch Farm.

I was surprised to find half a dozen cars parked on the green verges of the lane, with an odd assortment of loiterers near the farm entrance. An angry Ian Rocastle was having an altercation with a man carrying a camera. A cheerful police constable was gently intervening. I drew level and waved.

'Press,' said Ian. 'Caught that bastard poking his lens through the hedge.'

I parked in the yard and saw Tricia who greeted me with a kiss on the cheek. 'You'll stay for lunch?'

Carol was in the garden. She sat in the sunshine cross-legged on a picnic rug. She wore shorts and a skimpy sun top, revealing her tanned skin. A transformation, were it not for the swollen eyes and the residual marks of strain on her face. She had faced the worst experience that any mother could face. It did not help that she had seemingly been the victim of a cruel deception.

'Hi, Peter, what kept you?' she smiled.

'Thought I'd let the dust settle – how's Tommy?'

'He's fine – he's indoors watching the telly as if…'

I bent down and lifted her to her feet while she clung to me, burying her face in my chest. 'Come on,' I said 'you're making my shirt wet.'

She looked up and now she was laughing and crying simultaneously. 'Oh, Peter, I can't begin to say how I feel, how grateful I am to you – you could have died…'

'But didn't.' I kissed her on the lips. 'Has Tommy told you much?'

'Only that Alix and he were on a posh yacht, but we guessed that. There was a woman police officer here earlier but I don't think he told her much.' She stood back, her face puckered. 'There's something I don't understand. Whoever took Tommy seems to have treated him well. I mean it doesn't seem to have been an ordeal.'

‘Carol, I can’t tell you too much at the moment, but Tommy and Alix were never in danger.’

‘Maybe, but Tommy doesn’t make sense. He’s normally a truthful kid, but it’s almost as if he doesn’t want those people caught.’

‘It’s a complicated business and, frankly, I’m not sure what’s happening myself. Please, trust me.’

I accepted the lunch invitation. At least this was a happier atmosphere than forty-eight hours ago. Tommy was hustled in, reluctantly, to join us. I had quietly advised the adult Rocastles not to push him too hard with questions. I had quizzed Tommy during yesterday’s journey home and had got nowhere. I particularly needed to know the identity of the vessel on which the kids were being held. He had been evasive and in the end I gave up. A posh yacht, he told his mother; and that had to be Eriksen’s, *Persephone*. Had it been the *Marietta* or that rusting hulk *Emily Hopper,* the kids would have been in the grip of the other faction in this affair. The chances were that they would now be dead.

At two o’clock that afternoon I made it back to Old Duddlestone and work. Laura and Mick had kept things in order with a little bit of help from Emma and Simon. Laura had changed; she was quieter and her abrasive manner had diminished. Understandably, her family’s trauma had affected her deeply. She followed me into the office and joined me in my inner sanctum. I gave her my news of mother and of my talk with the police. She sniffed expressively when I described Inspector Channing’s blatant stonewalling and then fixed me with an intensive stare when I recounted my impressions of Tommy and Carol.

‘Peter, sod the police, I’m not stupid even if they think we are. What is going on?’

‘A bloody great conspiracy…’

‘Orchestrated by the ghost of your father.’

She was probably right. My mind was probing again into the text of that cryptic letter. Professor Hooder’s command of the English language was accurate if pedantic.

I did not sanction use of the harbour link ... cannot compromise the integrity of our work ... will make representations at the highest level.

The professor’s long-winded whinge never reached its intended recipient. Hooder Senior must have left for his London conference shortly after he had dictated this missive; those left behind had choked to death a few hours later. Why, and for what cause? What human agency had been so desperate that they needed to wipe out a whole working community?

'Peter, are you all right – d'you want to lie down?' Laura was looking at me with real concern. I must have been day-dreaming for longer than I realised.

'Sorry, I was miles away.' I looked at her. 'Laura, do you mind if I ask you something painful – you know – personal?'

'That sounds ominous – go ahead.'

'Your father witnessed the unloading of that ship in 1946. Did he notice what they were handling?' I paused. 'I'm sorry if this is distressing, but I have good reasons for asking.'

Laura shut her eyes for a moment and stared at the ceiling. 'He was dying … he wanted a sort of absolution … unburden himself about the murder … No, whatever it was, it was heavy cargo. He said they were using the dockside crane.'

While she was talking something had alerted me. I shook my head and put a finger to my lips. Someone was in the outer office and not one of our customers. The visiting yachties had a certain noisy presence; this had been a soft furtive scraping. Very slowly I reached out an arm and pulled open the door. The person on the other side gave a gasp and scuttled backwards.

It was a woman; the same Jolene that I had seen talking to the old veterans outside the Gullaits three days ago. I'd seen her in the pub and by the harbour on my first day here and several times since, including once beside the harbour. She claimed to be a reporter, but Mick had been convinced she was a fraud and he should know.

'Can I help you?' I grated the words sarcastically.

'I dunno, you the boss man around here?' The voice was hesitant; the accent Australian.

'I am the harbour manager.'

Harry had told me this girl was a historian and frankly, even if she was a mere reporter, she was the antithesis of Tabitha. She was attired in grubby denim, her blonde hair was awry and she wore a pair of well-worn dirty trainers. I was unimpressed, and I was damn sure she'd been listening at the keyhole.

'Hi,' she said. I noticed a further hesitancy before she continued. 'I'm Jolene – most people call me Jo.'

'Right, Jo, what can we do for you?'

'I'm a journalist, Sydney Morning Herald. Tell me about those missing kids.'

That was enough for me. Laura switched on her coldest authoritarian manner and marched the luckless Jolene out of the building. She handed the woman over to Mick with instructions to see his fellow country person off the site. I sat down in my chair and swore. Taken all round this had been a bloody awful day and I was no nearer to understanding what the hell was happening to us. Somehow, I staggered through routine work for the rest of the day, then at seven o'clock I climbed aboard *Stormgoose,* poured myself a huge slug of scotch and fell asleep on my bunk, fully dressed.

The next morning I felt better. The effects of the drug had almost gone; I could face the world and be positive. I left my boat and wandered up the village street where I found the sub-aquas busy overhauling one of their engines. I noticed that the doors of the ammunition store had been shut and closer examination revealed that new locks had been installed.

'That was done by the police yesterday morning,' said Keith. 'bloody cheek, they've sealed in our spare RIB. Never gave us a chance to move it.'

'I can't say I'm sorry they've closed it,' I said. 'Have you heard what's up there at the end of the line?'

'The old research lab and a lot of stiffs. One of the army lads told us about it.'

Dave intervened. 'They've put a block on all info about it. That spook man's around – gives me the creeps.'

Presumably they meant Beresford. I walked back towards the harbour; it was another glorious morning. I could see yachts moving: two sailing boats heading for the entrance and a big one, a full size motor yacht, heading in towards us. I stopped and shaded my eyes; this had to be the swankiest craft we'd entertained so far, in fact she seemed to fill the entrance as she coasted past the quay and glided neatly against the visitor's pontoon. I watched as I saw Mick and Simon take her lines and secure her to the dock. Now I knew her: Eriksen's Omega class yacht, the *Persephone.* I felt a mixture of anxiety and anticipation. Eriksen was one man who really knew what was happening; he'd given me a cryptic half explanation and he owed me more.

I took off and ran down the street as far as Laura's house. I knew she was in there, and I might need her support. When all was said she was Carol's sister and Tommy's aunt.

I hammered on the cottage door until Laura opened it. I half expected a rebuke but her response was wholly unexpected.

'Peter, get away – phone the police…' she whispered.

She had no time for explanations before a large hand grabbed her from behind and half-pushed her to the floor. The man who emerged from behind her was familiar; I had seen him before, and recently, but I couldn't at that moment place him exactly. Apart from anything else he was a menacing figure and he carried a handgun.

He looked me in the eye. 'I've heard about you – you've been messing around with my wife.'

CHAPTER 47

I had seen Laura's anger several times and felt it myself; but never had I witnessed such white-hot fury as exploded from this woman now.

'How dare you!' she screamed.

I watched, half alarmed, half fascinated, as she hurled herself on the man scrabbling at his throat. He stumbled backwards and toppled over, dropping the gun which skidded across the polished floor. This was enough to break the spell; I raced past the grappling pair and retrieved the weapon.

'Oi, you get off him – mad bitch!' A slight figure ran through the kitchen door and hurled herself at Laura, tugging her backwards. It was Jolene.

The man was sitting up, ruefully rubbing the back of his head: the two women were on their feet screaming and tearing at each other. I left them to it while I parked the gun on top of the Welsh dresser, then I grabbed Jolene by the neck of her tacky denim jacket, picked her up and threw her across the floor. She hit the brash new skirting board with a crack that left her gasping and whimpering.

Laura was standing holding unsteadily to a chair. I could see blood on her face and neck, so vicious had been the sudden attack.

'You,' Jolene was staring straight at me. 'You're a dead man.'

'Yes, we've all heard that before.' I had moved to stand over her.

'Now, no lies, who are you?'

'She's my girl friend,' said the man climbing painfully to his feet.

'Girlfriend; you've just said you had a wife.'

'He's Jim Stoneman,' Laura almost spat the name. 'He's got a bloody nerve. He walked out on my sister without so much as a goodbye, and now he comes here and accuses Carol of cheating on him.'

'I know where I've seen him before,' I said. 'He was dressed as a fake policeman the night they loaded that ship.'

'And these two force their way in here waving this thing.' Laura had hold of the gun. It was a small modern automatic.

'Give it me,' I said.

She handed it over and I checked it. There was no live magazine in the butt – nevertheless… 'Carrying a firearm is a serious offence. I've no option but to call the police.'

‘Wait,’ said Laura. ‘Come on, Jim, what brings you back here – and, what is this thing?’ she pointed at Jolene.

The man made no reply, he was grinning as he looked at something through the window. In the street stood George Dunlass and both of the twins. Where they had sprung from I couldn’t guess; I thought all three were in police custody. I could only assume that George had found a clever lawyer and a goodly sum in bail. Two more men, unknown to me and both younger than George, appeared from further up the street shortly to be joined by the vile Rita Dunlass.

We were obviously going to be outgunned and outnumbered. I cursed myself for not calling the police at once. Maybe I could divide this gang among themselves.

‘Mr Stoneman,’ I said. ‘That woman out there wanted your son killed. I heard her say so.’

I didn’t have time to judge his reaction. George and his group were already pushing their way into the house, filling the entire space.

‘Morning, Captain,’ said George. ‘What’s been going on here?’

‘I found this man threatening Mrs Tapsell with a gun. That’s a serious offence.’

‘Quite right,’ he looked at Stoneman. ‘I thought I said no firearms.’

‘I suppose speeding cars are good enough to kill my mother.’ I squared up to him. Old man he might be but I felt tempted to grind his head to pulp against the wall.

‘I know nothing about that. Don’t even suggest that I might have sanctioned such a thing.’

Even through my red mist I detected something wrong. George Dunlass sounded genuinely affronted and he wasn’t acting.

He continued. ‘There’s not one of us would harm Captain Wilson’s lady and you’d better believe that.’

‘The police say it was deliberate and so do both the witnesses.’

‘You don’t say,’ George looked genuinely perplexed. ‘We heard it was an accident.’

He sounded so genuine, and yet mother had almost named him. I told him about the Russian speaking nurse.

‘That’s true,’ said Laura. ‘His mother was Mrs Dunlass. She was a snooty housekeeper in one of the big mansions and his father, Jack Stoneman the gardener, got her up the duff.’

‘You’ll have to do better than that,’ said Rita. ‘George wouldn’t have the old bat touched, but I would’ve topped her, first chance I got!’

'Just like you would have killed those two kids, and don't deny it because I was in the street the night you loaded that ship and I heard you say so.'

'I never had the chance; it was your friends that snatched them first.'

'That's enough,' said George. 'Mr Wilson, it happens we've work to do and we've haven't got all day.'

I shook my head. I wasn't inclined to help George in any way. Even if he had nothing to do with the attack on mother, he was one of those who had murdered Arthur Rocastle.

I hadn't finished with Rita. 'Was it you driving that car?'

'No it wasn't,' said George. 'It so happens she was with me at the time.' He looked at his watch. 'Mr Wilson, I'm sure you are curious about our actions. Do you suspect they relate to your father?' He looked at me.

This crafty bastard was deliberately whetting my appetite: well, so be it. 'All right, what are you up to?'

'Follow me.'

We walked into the sunlight which dazzled me after the gloom of the cottage. I heard a scream behind me. Jim Stoneman had hold of Laura and was manhandling her into the street. Jolene brought up the rear, and I didn't like the look on her face. She stared at Laura's back with a look of hatred and malice.

'We're not leaving her to run to the dicks – no way,' she hissed.

One more surprise; another man was in the street. It was Steve Gulley. He took one look at us and scuttled away towards the cliffs.

'What about him?' said Rita.

'It's only one of the Gulley boys,' said George.

The entire party set off up the street following the same route as Steve, and this suited me nicely. I knew Keith and the sub-aquas were there working on their main boat. I was disappointed; the RIB stood on its trailer, but neither the sub-aquas nor Steve could be seen. I could hear a vehicle driving up the street behind us; it was a four-by-four truck. George signalled it to halt and then led the way to the old chapel, the one building that I had never entered. He opened the heavy door with an ancient looking key and we all followed him. It looked a gloomy place and inside it was downright mournful. The wooden pews were still there but piled high in a corner. The whole place had a musty smell; dust was everywhere along with bat droppings. The walls had a few, very unholy, bits of graffiti just visible in the sunlight that streamed through the narrow broken windows.

George Stoneman crossed to the far end and pulled aside a tarpaulin; beneath was a stack of the same boxes that I had seen being loaded on the *Emily Hopper.*

'Right, lads, let's go.'

The two younger men seized a rope handle each and lifted the first box. It was clearly heavy and they grunted as they heaved it through the door and into the truck. The twins attempted to lift a second box but failed even to move it an inch.

'Make them help,' Jolene snapped pointing at and Laura and me.

'Why not you, love,' said Rita. 'You were strong enough to push that Tabitha Long.'

'Shut up, Rit!,' said George.

'No, she did it, and all on her own. I want that on the record. I'm not taking any rap for that nasty little psycho.'

'I never…' Jolene shouted advancing on Rita.

'You was up there when it happened, so who else?' Rita jeered.

I looked at Laura. I didn't like this development, though it made sense. There was something about Jolene that was profoundly unsettling; almost like a confrontation with a venomous and unpredictable reptile. I believed she could kill and probably had in the past. If she was the one who killed Tabitha, then we too would be in danger.

'It wasn't me,' Jolene continued. 'It was an accident – the silly bitch never looked where she was going.'

That was true. I remembered every last second before Tabitha's body hit the ground. She had been arguing, shouting at a second person, and it had been a female voice.

Three more boxes had been moved by now out of a total of eight. I was scared. Rita's outburst and Jolene's reply had put us in danger. We were learning things that could lead to our own destruction.

Jolene was eyeballing Rita face-to-face. 'I was raped once, I know what's it's like.' She spat in Rita's face and stepped back grinning.

Rita let forth a howl of outrage as she wiped away the spittle. 'What d'you mean raped – I bet you asked for it you randy little tart.'

'Did the one your husband raped ask for it?' Jolene screamed. 'Did she ask him to strangle her?'

'You're bloody raving.' Rita laughed with her awful hyena shriek.

'Shut it!,' George yelled. 'Just shut it, both of you. We've got to get this stuff moved.'

'And how much of it do I get,' Jolene jeered.

'Will you shut it. You'll get a fair divi when we get to the other end. I've told you both that a hundred times.'

'Jolene,' said Laura. She was staring at the girl. 'Who did George rape and kill?'

'Jim told me, it was years ago, some nasty little slapper up on the cliffs there. I don't give a monkey's piss about her, but I was a good time girl once way back in Oz and I was raped by a slob like him and I ain't forgot it.' She turned on George. 'We don't want to go to wherever; we want our fair share now and out of here.'

'Jim,' said Laura. 'Is this true?'

'So what,' he replied. He was trying to sound offhand but he was surely worried. 'It was years ago – who cares.'

'Arthur Rocastle might care – he took the blame and George here definitely killed him.'

'Arthur is the whole cause of this bloody mess. He's the reason we've had to come back now, fifty bloody years too late. I'd kill him again for that right now.' George was shouting. His face was red and the blue veins stood out on his forehead. If his heart stopped now it would save the state the cost of locking him up to the end of his days.

It is difficult to put into words the relief I felt. The story rang true and George Dunlass had made no attempt to deny it. Ernest Rocastle, in a fit of religious zeal, might have attacked Margaret Gulley but he hadn't killed her. That fact alone would lift an awesome shadow of guilt from his family. Now, more than ever I wanted to survive. I wanted to be the one to tell Carol that her grandfather was no murderer.

The two strong men had ignored the uproar and continued ferrying boxes into the back of their truck. But they would have one hell of a task trying to convey their loot all the way in one conspicuous vehicle.

'What are you going to do with us?' I asked.

'Mr Wilson, I don't think you're worth doing anything with,' George laughed. 'We liked your father, respected him, any of us would have followed that old sod anywhere, but he was one of our kind and your money proves it.'

'My money, I'm stony broke, man. Why d'you think I'm working in this place?'

'Don't try that one. He took his share – two hundred thousand US greenbacks, and I was there when we divided it. No, Captain, you'll keep your mouth shut about that and we'll be long away.' He turned his back on me. 'Let's get going. Behave naturally, ignore the yachties; officially we're loading wartime souvenirs – old Navy gear from the tunnels.'

It felt better to be out of that morbid place and even better when the gang, ignoring Laura and me, piled into the truck with most of them sitting on the gold boxes. The springs were groaning at the limit of their travel. One thing was certain, that vehicle would not go far on the roads before the suspension failed.

Of course I was wrong. The truck went no further than the harbour, where it stopped alongside the main visitor's pontoon. And moored to that pontoon was the *Persephone.* I had forgotten the arrival of the giant motor yacht – now the implications hit me in the face; this was Eriksen's boat, and Eriksen was supposed to be the legitimate party to this affair.

We walked down the street as far as Laura's cottage. I was disinclined to go much further; it was time we called the police. I ran inside and grabbed the phone, it was dead.

'They've cut the line,' I said. 'The bastards know our mobiles don't work properly here.'

Laura fetched a pair of binoculars and we watched in turn the activity on the dockside. I focussed on the yacht and homed in on her flying bridge and through the glass panelling of her saloon. If there was anyone aboard her they were well concealed.

We watched George climb on deck, from where he supervised the loading of the boxes.

Laura gripped my arm. 'I'm going to the cliff top,' she said. 'If we don't call the police they'll get away.'

'I don't think so, they must be crazy, that gin palace will stand out a mile…'

Laura wasn't listening, she had taken off at a loping run towards the waterline and the path to the cliff top. I watched her go and left her to it. I had ideas of my own; I remembered the derelict gardens on the other side of the street. I ran to the top of the road and climbed into the garden of the first cottage. It seemed so unreal this time; I could hear the chatter of our visitors, the sounds of an outboard motor and the washing of the sea against the shore a few feet away.

I reached the end and settled down to watch. The cheek of these people and their overbearing self-confidence staggered me. George had actually recruited two strong young yacht crews to help him, and appeared oblivious to the bystanders some of whom were photographing the yacht.

George was now standing within ten yards of me. I ducked behind the stone wall and waited.

'Go aboard and get the engines running,' he said. 'I want every last knot you can drive her.'

'Will do, but it seems a waste of a good ship,' it was the voice of one of the unknowns and he sounded disgruntled.

'Got to be – I dare say Erik will collect the insurance and buy another one.'

'Come on, George, mate, what are we waiting for?' This was Jolene speaking quietly but with a twist of anxiety.

'Well, sweetheart, we're not waiting for you, cos' you ain't going with us – see!' George's tone had changed, and his voice had lapsed into broadest Dorset.

'What d'you mean? 'course I'm coming with you – we need our share and we'll see we get it.'

'No, Jolene, I don't think so. You tell us something. Where were you last Friday afternoon, the day Mrs Wilson was struck down?'

'Minding my own business – like you should be now.' Her voice mixed anger with fear. I couldn't move, I felt my scalp tighten and the sweat on my body begin to chill despite the heat.

'You promised me no killing,' said Jim Stoneman. 'Rita says you wanted to kill my little boy.'

'She's lying. She's the one that wanted to finish both those little shits.'

'And you agreed with her – you even had ideas of how to do it,' said George.

'What about Tabitha Long?' said Jim.

'I never touched the bitch. She fell over – I know I saw it but I never did it.' Jolene's voice was becoming louder and shriller.

'Keep your voice down – you daft little psycho.' George sounded alarmed. 'You should have stayed with your missus, Jim, this one's a bloody liability. Captain Wilson's lady is another matter, you've the whole of Double Six flotilla to answer to for that, including Lieutenant Eriksen and that pompous old admiral.'

'Why the fuck are you so wound up about that old biddy?' Jolene was screaming unrestrained. 'She was in our way – she was going to grass on the lot of you – don't you understand? I had to deal with her and it's not as if she's dead. She's still in the hospital – I checked.'

'Now we're getting somewhere,' said Jim.

'Jim, darling, don't you turn on me.'

'Sorry, Jo, but this is the final straw. I've had it up to here with you. How soon before I get a knife in the back, eh? And you stink, how come you say it's Brits that never take baths, you filthy cow.'

'You bastard,' Jolene grated. 'Who killed that old bloke over there that night. Who mixed his tea for him. You did, Jim, I was there. I saw it. You killed that poor old man and then you tried to drown the old lady's son – I saw you, didn't I.'

'Will you keep your voice down,' Jim hissed.

'No I won't, you shits.' She raised her voice to a shrill scream. 'Listen all you folks – there's murderers here – look at these two – they'd cut your throat as soon as look at you.'

Most of her words were drowned by the roar of *Persephone's* twin diesel engines. I risked a peep over the wall. Jolene was sprawled on the ground while George and Jim were scrambling over the ship's rail. The twins had released the lines to the dock without recovering them, as the yacht eased away on one remaining stern line, until she pointed into the wide expanse of the harbour. So focussed had I been in the last few minutes that I failed to notice that I was no longer alone. Somebody jerked my arm and I stiffened with shock. I turned round to see Steve Gulley.

'Don't worry, Mister Wilson, they ain't going nowhere.' He grinned through his stained teeth.

'Steve, don't ever do that again,' I found myself breathing in gulps of air. 'What d'you mean – not going anywhere?'

'Wait and see,' he grinned again.

Jolene had definitely missed the boat; we watched her in morbid fascination as she performed a sort of war dance. She was gyrating on the quay while tearing her hair and bawling incoherently. Surrounding her was a knot of amused and embarrassed bystanders.

'Come on, Steve, help me.' I scrambled over the wall.

I addressed these spectators. 'I'm the harbour manager, this woman is suspected of criminal activity.'

Jolene seemed oblivious of me; she was still screaming into the wind as *Persephone* slowly motored towards the centre of the harbour.

'You, Jolene whatever your name is,' I shouted in her ear. 'Using the authority deputed to me…' I wasn't sure if this was the right format but it sounded good. 'Using that authority I am performing a citizen's arrest.'

To say that my intended prisoner was uncooperative would be an understatement. She turned on me like a wild thing, sinking her teeth into my upper arm, and drawing a long scratch across my face. Steve stood gaping and not one of the spectators seemed willing to help. I was saved by Mick who delivered a single open handed slap to the woman's face and then dragged her, literally kicking and screaming, to lock her in the gear shed. My arm was bruised and my face bleeding. Emma appeared in front of me carrying the office first aid box.

'Dad, who is that crazy…?'

'She's the one who tried to kill your grandmother.'

'Are you sure?' She began dabbing my face with cotton wool.

'She admitted it in front of witnesses.'

'We've been trying to phone the police,' she said, 'but we can't get through.'

'Line's cut – Laura's gone for help.'

I could hear another engine; it was the big outboard on the marines' RIB. Then we saw the boat speeding down from the head of the harbour with Keith at the wheel and Dave standing in the bows. It seemed *Persephone's* master had seen them. I saw the yacht turn in the centre of the harbour and heard her engines gun into full-ahead. She lifted onto a plane and swept seawards in a cloud of glittering spray. As she came level with us I estimated she must have reached thirty knots; an unwise speed in such an enclosed space and, alarmingly, it seemed she was veering out of the designated channel and towards the rocky ledge. Everyone on the quay had turned to look seaward. There was a hush now, a feeling of apprehension.

'Where the hell are they going?' It was Simon.

'They're too far over,' I replied. 'They've been in here before, they must know the channel – it's simple enough.'

Persephone's bow wave was rolling towards us and I worried at the damage it might do. To drive at full speed through our narrow entrance was irresponsible, but safe enough if they read the entry beacons and stuck to the middle, which was exactly what they were failing to do.

'Pull to starboard!' Simon shouted.

It was too late, I heard a collective gasp from our spectators and then an odd sound, a horrible grating followed by a thump as the beautiful yacht tore her bottom open on the submerged trap of the ledge. For two seconds her bows tilted down before she settled, visibly lower in the water, her motors still roaring. Worse was to come; we could see smoke followed by a tongue of flame, and then an explosive thump as the whole ship was consumed in a huge fireball. I heard Emma scream and the sound jerked me to my senses. I sprinted to my harbour dory moored to the pontoon a few yards away.

My arrival coincided with *Persephone's* bow wave; the residue of a dead ship. Its power was enough to lift the little dory, snap the bow line and then smash it against the concrete of the quay. Water poured in through a gash in the side. I found Mick standing beside me a fire extinguisher in his hands. A lot of use that would be.

'Come on,' I said, 'we'll use *Stormgoose.'*

The pontoons were still rocking, with moored yachts rising and banging against their fenders. I climbed over the rail onto my boat while Mick released the lines. Under power we headed towards the disaster. It was a seaman's instinct that made me momentarily forget the nature of *Persephone's* crew. We were needed to save life – that was the only thing that counted.

The wind was blowing from the southeast: we could not approach the wreck other than downwind. Soon we were enveloped in an evil smoke and a smattering of falling debris that blackened the decks and threatened to set fire to our furled sails. Sensible man that he was, Mick hit the button on his fire extinguisher and doused every vulnerable point aboard. We could feel the fire now, an intense, unremitting scorching heat, and with it the foul smell of burning fibreglass. Mick had pulled his shirt over his head as he gasped and choked. I felt my eyes watering, my nose running, my lungs were burning; I was dizzy and I could not breathe. I knew that we were in the grip of very dangerous toxins. I swung the tiller over and opened the throttle. If I didn't move away from this inferno now, we too would die; maybe we were already too late. I stuck my head into the cabin and gulped air. It was foul but better than the fume filled hell above. Gradually the smoke cleared. I wiped my eyes and tried to focus. Mick was lying on the deck beside me seemingly unconscious. Something, almost compulsive, made me look towards *Persephone*. Another explosion and a huge flame temporarily expelled the smoke. The yacht was burned aft almost to her waterline. I could see one figure, staggering along the foredeck, a human form blazing like a torch. It spun around and fell the short distance to the water below. Then another pall of black smoke rolled over the scene again obscuring everything. I left *Stormgoose* to her own devices, motoring away from the devastation. There was nothing I could do; I must save my own crewman. I had brought him into this danger and now I felt an awful sense of foreboding. He had rolled onto his back and I could hear his breathing above the sounds of the engine. It was like no breathing one could imagine: more like a death rattle.

I cut the motor and left the boat to drift. I knelt beside Mick and tried to remember the revival drill. Six mouth-to-mouth, then ten downward thrusts on the breast bone. I really wasn't sure. I leant over Mick and wiped his mouth with my own sleeve. I sucked in a huge gulp of clean air and fixed my face against his. This brought one last shock; one that went near to flooring me. My patient stirred, opened his eyes, and tried to sit up. He fell back heavily and then stared at me.

'Hold on, skipper,' he whispered. 'You turned poofter, or something?'

I shut my sore eyes and sagged back; for a few seconds I thought I too would pass out. 'Mick, I thought you'd bought it – dying.'

'So did I, mate; that was a bloody close call. God help those poor bastards.'

I heard a shout from close by. The marine's RIB was coming alongside. Keith was steering while Dave bent over a figure lying prone on the bottom boards.

'This one's alive,' said Dave. 'He's burnt, but I think he'll live.'

I caught the expression on Keith's face. It surprised me; he must have seen plenty of grim sights in his service career, but now he was not just upset; he was distraught.

'Christ, I only wanted to stop her leaving. I never thought they'd go like a bull at a gate. And what made her blow like that – what caused that fire?' He didn't wait for a reply. The RIB left us and powered away shorewards.

I looked once more towards the rocks and the burning ship. The tide had ebbed a foot or so and she was clear of the water; but little was left of the once proud super-yacht, she had burned to her waterline while smoke and flames still poured from her. I felt confused, I had a sick crewman who needed medical attention, I felt guilty at the thought of leaving the scene without one last attempt to save life. Mick was lying prone on the cockpit seat; he was coughing convulsively. I took a decision and motored back to the quay. The silent but still shocked spectators lined the quay.

Keith greeted me. 'Lifeboat's on her way,' he said. 'I'm going out to see they come in safe.' With that he sprinted back to his own boat and sped seawards.

Emma was waiting on the pontoon. 'Dad, are you all right?'

'I'm fine, but Mick here's in a bad way – he's had a lung full of poison. Can you do something for him?'

'We'll see to him. We're already treating a man with burns and smoke inhalation. We've had to call an ambulance through VHF to the coastguards – the telephone's still dead and my mobile keeps breaking up.'

We helped Mick over the rail. He still coughed painfully, but he could walk as we supported him on either side. I left him in the care of Emma and Simon, plus a nurse from one of our visiting yachts.

I walked to the dock edge and looked across the water. The fires were dying now; only a blackened lump remained to mark the waste of a fine ship. I caught a final taste of those evil fumes as they reached, us blown on the freshening wind. I walked away quickly to the end of the village street, and parted company with the contents of my stomach into a drain. I had seen many mishaps in my career at sea, but never had I witnessed such an inexplicable disaster as this. I turned round and forced myself to return to the dockside.

My attention was drawn to a new arrival; a *Sigma 33* class yacht that had just made fast to one of the outer berths. My head was slowly clearing. I was still the harbour master; I had better go down, greet my new visitors and try and explain. The yacht's owner was walking along the pontoon checking his lines. I explained, as best I could.

'Heard about it on the VHF,' he said. 'What made her explode?' He looked across to the wreck. 'Last time I saw anything like that was an Argentine fuel tanker in the Falklands fracas.'

I shrugged, the whole thing was insane.

'By the way,' my visitor continued. 'I think your leading beacons are a bit out – if it hadn't been for the ship on fire we would have gone very near those rocks.'

CHAPTER 46

The ambulance was here, the police had arrived, and the Swanage lifeboat was slowly combing the sea around the entrance. Everybody wanted to talk to me at once, including the coastguards on the radio, and finally Brian Byrne.

I dealt with him first. 'Sorry, Brian, you'll have to wait – I can't speak to you now.'

He was not pleased and I didn't care. To add to my problems that woman Jolene had smashed her way out through the roof of the gear store and vanished. Apart from the unidentified man on his way to hospital, the slippery Jolene was the sole survivor. The police, concerned only with the shipwreck, were uncomprehending when I tried to explain. Laura had reappeared and was also trying to catch my attention.

'Inspector Channing is on his way,' she said. 'I heard a bloody great explosion – what happened?'

I told her.

'Oh my God! How many survivors?' Laura looked both horrified and only half-comprehending.

'Just one, so far; the lifeboat radioed to say they've found four bodies – all dead.'

'That was Magnus Eriksen's boat,' she said quietly. 'Was he part of this after all – was he aboard?'

'I don't think so – have you seen Keith? He was here, then he shot off in his boat.'

'Yes, I saw him racing back up to the head of the harbour – he had Steve with him.'

Two more ambulances had arrived on the quayside and their crews had begun unloading body bags. The lifeboat had left the still-smouldering wreck and was heading our way; I left them to it. I have a strong stomach for most things, but I was not sure I could face the blackened corpses of people I had seen alive barely an hour earlier.

As it happened I had an excuse – standing by his car surveying the scene was Inspector Channing. I sped over to him.

'Mr Wilson,' said Channing. 'I would like to talk in private.'

The office was already oppressively hot despite the overhead fans, but with a uniformed policeman on the door it did offer privacy.

'I'll be perfectly straight with you,' Channing began. 'I'm under Home Office direction. I can investigate but I can't interrogate, and I must not arrest or charge anyone until the situation is cleared with the security services. I don't like it, but that's the score.'

'I don't think you've anybody much left to arrest,' I replied. 'All the bad guys seemed to have been on that burning yacht out there and the lifeboat people can find no survivors, apart from one man on his way to hospital, and a mad woman who's still on the loose somewhere.'

Channing nodded. 'Jolene Marybelle Fuller, I think you mean. I've had a fax a mile long from the Australian police about her.'

'You know she admitted to being the one who ran down my mother.'

'We surmised as much while pursuing our own enquiries. We would like to find the lady to confirm the matter.'

'Well, you'd better start looking – she can't be far away.'

The doorman appeared. 'There's a Mister Brian Byrne, sir.'

'All right, bring him in,' said Channing.

For the first time since I had known him Brian looked flustered. 'Peter, I've been trying to catch you all morning. Dawson Beresford is on his way and he's out to get you.'

'What can he possibly do to me?'

'Make you sign the Official Secrets…'

'But I don't know a bloody thing – I'm as much in the dark as ever – so what's the point?'

Brian flopped down on our only remaining chair and buried his head in his hands. 'I got this whole thing totally wrong – about your father, about the smuggling, and about the laboratory. Worst of all, I can't face Ivy Bowler and tell her the real truth about Arthur.'

I recalled something that Eriksen had said the other evening. "Everything would have been straightforward if it hadn't been for that silly boy, Arthur Rocastle".

'How come, Brian? Even Laura admits he didn't kill Margaret Gulley.' I was on tricky ground now, privy as I was to the Rocastle secrets.

'We can confirm that too,' said Channing. 'We only discovered two days ago that we still had the clothing she wore on the day that she was killed, and Mrs Bowler still had some items of her brother's. They've been DNA tested and first results definitely clear Arthur.'

'Will that help you to find the real culprit?' I asked.

'If he's still alive and we can test him – maybe.'

'Brian,' I said. 'It seems you've found something. I think you ought to tell us.'

'I'm going to talk to Ivy first. It wouldn't be right to disclose what I know to you before I've broken the news to her.'

'I want to get away from here for a bit,' I said. 'I guess this harbour's finished anyway as a commercial prospect.'

Channing spoke. 'You have your car here?'

'Of course.'

'I could offer you a lift in one of ours, but that might look as if you were in custody. But I would like you both to come to the station in Poole now.'

'Why?' In spite of what he'd said, Channing had me worried.

'All right, calm down.' He smiled. 'I only want to hear the whole story somewhere cooler and more relaxed than here.'

Channing seemed to take an eternity to brief his scene of crime officers before taking statements from the lifeboat coxswain and the skipper of the *Sigma.* Eventually we were away, up the entry road with my car leading and Brian sitting beside me. Channing followed and a marked police car brought up the rear.

I can't easily find the words to describe how I felt at that moment. I was passing once more the spot from where I had first seen Old Duddlestone harbour. How long ago; it seemed an eternity, but in fact just a few weeks. I turned away and looked up at the ridge of Downs and the line of little vent caps silhouetted against the skyline. We would need to replace the missing grille before the gap in the vent became a safety hazard. As I returned my gaze to the road I saw a lone figure running towards us. It was a woman dressed in shorts and T-shirt; some holiday jogger unaware, presumably, of the drama being played out all around her. I was wrong. As she drew closer I recognised Babs Stent, the dinosaur hunter. I slowed as she sprinted towards us waving her arms and shouting. I couldn't but admire her athleticism that seemed out of place in an academic. She stopped beside us gasping huge breaths, in between which she stumbled out her message.

'Police … help us … someone's just nicked our Land Rover. Did it pass you?'

CHAPTER 47

The Inspector seemed less than helpful. 'Madam, this team is engaged on an investigation; we cannot divert at whim.'

Babs had recovered her breath and she was not prepared to back off. 'So, you don't give a damn about a blatant theft, in broad daylight, of twenty thousand pounds worth of university equipment. What's more,' she ended triumphantly, 'I can give you a description of the person who took it.'

'Why don't you phone treble nine and report direct?'

'Because our mobile phones are in the stolen car, of course!'

'Very well,' Channing sighed wearily. 'Give me some details and I'll radio them back to the relevant officers.'

'The woman who took it – Jo something – she's been hanging around for weeks. Around five foot six, blonde hair; looks scruffy – speaks Australian…'

'Vehicle registration number!' Channing snapped as he reached for his radio.

Babs supplied the details. Channing began to relay a county-wide alert.

'There's a change of attitude,' she said to me. 'Peter, what's going on?'

'We think she's the one who pushed Tabitha Long,' I replied. I felt it better not to mention mother as well.

'I've asked for an all units alert,' said Channing. 'It seems she's a competent off-roader. She drove right over the down and onto the ranges. But we're too late to stop her at the camp – she passed through there ten minutes ago. They say she didn't take the turning for Lulworth, she's heading into New Duddlestone. With a bit of luck we'll get her there.'

'What's the drill now?' I asked.

'Our little chat will have to be postponed.' Channing looked at Babs. 'You, madam, will keep yourself available to make a statement, while you, Mr Wilson, are at liberty to return to your harbour.'

I guessed our Inspector was unused to being made a fool of in front of his own men. The humiliation was clearly painful.

'Peter,' said Babs, 'have you got time to come back up the hill – Charlie badly wants a word with you.'

I thought for a moment. I didn't want to go down to the harbour right now. Other police and emergency services were still there sorting out the aftermath of this morning's disaster. Frankly, Laura would be much better at dealing with this mess than I would ever be.

I looked at Brian. 'What d'you want to do?'

'Leave your car here,' he said. Grinning he added. 'I'll ride with the Sheriff.'

I looked at Babs. 'OK – lead on.'

Charlie met us at the top of Weavers Down. The loss of his Land Rover had done nothing for his sense of humour.

'Absolutely nowhere is secure these days. Half our equipment, exhibits, and a whole stack of my notes, stolen under our noses,' he fumed.

'I'm sorry about this, Charlie,' I replied, 'but the police know who took your truck, and believe me they mean business – she won't get far.'

'I could happily pitch her over the cliff, like Tabitha Long.' Charlie was red faced and sweating.

'Actually, the woman they are looking for is the one suspected of pushing Tabitha.'

'She certainly spent enough time up here,' said Babs.

'You know her then?'

'No,' said Charlie, 'but she's been around on and off asking questions.'

'And we saw her once with Doctor Hooder,' Babs added.

'What sort of questions?' I asked.

'Oh, only the usual stupid stuff about our work – typical tourist ignorance.'

'But I don't think she was really interested,' said Charlie. 'She was just going through the motions. I got the impression she didn't like us being around.'

That was certainly true. 'It's not for me to pry,' I said, 'but I think the police will want you to remember every detail of every person who has been hanging around for no purpose.'

'That figures,' Charlie sighed. 'This is what I wanted to talk about. Can you tell us what's been going on? Is it anything to do with that explosion in the harbour?'

'Yes, I can tell you about that – it's a hell of a mess…'

'Charlie!' Babs interrupted, 'Sorry, Peter, but listen both of you.' She pointed over the brow of the down towards the track to Honey-critch Farm.

I could hear it now; the sounds of two diesel vehicles powering across rough ground in top gear. The noise had all the hallmarks of hooligan off-roaders indulging in some stupid macho race.

'It's our Land Rover!' Charlie shouted. 'I'm sure of it.'

'There's at least two other cars,' said Babs. 'Come on let's have a look.' She took off again running towards the slope above the Honeycritch track.

Charlie and I followed as best we could. We caught up with her as she stood looking down the hill pointing excitedly. I could see the trackway and the three vehicles on it. The first was definitely the palaeontology Land Rover. Following it was another of the same, but more battered; I recognised it as Ian Rocastle's. Last, labouring on the rough terrain, was a police car.

'They've caught her,' shouted Babs. 'Who is she?'

'A nasty piece of work, and crazy with it,' I replied.

We watched the two off-road vehicles wend their way up another trackway, a route that I had never noticed, running up a shallow defile to the top of the down. The police car made two attempts to follow before it grounded on the hard ruts. Four persons disembarked: three uniformed police and one in plain clothes. The latter I knew: this was Inspector Righton, Channing's colleague and the officer running the kidnap investigation. The behaviour of these men was odd. As they caught sight of us they began shouting and gesticulating, though their words were blown away on the wind. The university Land Rover had reached the crest of the ridge and was bumping and swaying over the uneven downland grass. It came level with us and slowed; I tried to see who was driving, but the sun was in my eyes and the windows were tinted. Charlie ran towards his vehicle, but as he did so, the side window wound down and through it came a black tube, a flash, a puff of smoke and an explosive crack. Charlie stopped in his tracks, staggered a few feet, and fell, clutching his ankles. A second explosion spattered shotgun pellets into the grass a few feet to my left. The Land Rover's engine gunned and it headed away towards the line of concrete vents.

Bab's piercing scream broke the spell. She raced to where Charlie lay staring at his blood-soaked right leg. The second Land Rover had reached us and from it came Ian Rocastle with Tricia.

'That woman,' Ian gasped. 'She's snatched Tommy and she's got my gun.'

'But how?' I still could only half comprehend.

'It's all my fault,' wailed Tricia. 'They withdrew the police-woman this morning. We thought it was over and then that Land Rover drove in our yard.'

'That weird woman's been hanging around the village for weeks,' said Ian. 'We saw the truck, we thought it was Babs and Charlie. Then this woman crashes into the house just as Tom was coming out. She grabs him, then takes my gun and drives off.' Ian's usual composure had vanished. He looked wild-eyed and in shock. 'Then the police turn up, ten minutes too late.'

'We're here now,' It was Inspector Righton speaking. He looked composed, if red-faced and a little out of breath. 'Nobody will move,' he shouted. 'You will all stay where you are and do what you are told!'

'Where is the boy's mother?' I needed to know.

'We've recommended she stay at home,' said Righton. 'We've a WPC with her now.'

'You can't just sit here and do nothing.'

'No, we will be patient. This woman has a record of mental instability. Nothing will be done to excite her. We wait, and if necessary, we negotiate.'

As the Inspector ordered; we waited. An hour passed and we were joined by officers from Channing's group. The police had already called in the Coastguard helicopter and the injured Charlie had been put aboard and whisked away to hospital. His leg had absorbed several pellets but no worse damage.

'We sit tight,' said Righton. 'I'm not going to inflame the situation. We wait and see.'

The Land Rover was stopped short of the cliff top near the first ventilator cap. It stood clear against the skyline without sign of occupation. I know that I should have felt sickened, even in despair, at this turn of events. Instead, I was filled with resignation and an odd inner calm. I knew I was very near the end of my quest for my father. Something was intended to happen, I did not know what, but it involved me and it would bring a closure to this, the strangest month of my life.

With evening drawing near the police changed tactics. Righton produced a loud hailer and began to call Jolene. Would she accept food and water for the child? Would she accept another hostage in exchange? The police would like to open negotiations. Two shots from the Land Rover sent the police diving for cover.

'Won't she run out of ammunition.' I suggested.

'No,' said Ian. 'She took my cartridge belt with ten shots and a box with another twenty.' He threw up his hands. 'If only I hadn't been so stupid.'

'Inspector,' I said. 'You seem to know something about this Jolene woman.'

'Only what the Australian police have told us. Petty criminal but can be violent; she used a gun once but luckily the victim survived. Anyway, I've called for armed backup.'

'Will she harm the boy?'

'We don't know, but if she were to try the armed response unit will take her out.'

Another half-hour passed, agonisingly, without sight or sound of Righton's rapid-response team.

'They're a specialised unit,' said Righton. 'I never claimed them to be "rapid" – anything but. By the time they've been alerted collected their weapons and been briefed this could be over.'

'I want to go and talk to her,' I said.

'No, sir.'

'But she might negotiate with me. Australians have a funny attitude to the police, right from top to bottom of their society, and if she's a violent criminal it's even less likely she'll talk with you.'

'No, sir, I can't sanction that. We work by the rules.' Righton turned abruptly and walked away.

I looked at my watch; it was four o'clock. The firearms squad arrived and deployed around the site. At least they had the good sense to keep in cover. A police helicopter arrived, circling overhead, and with it an increase in tension that I found unbearable. I lay on my back in the warm grass amidst the hum of insects and watched the sky and the gulls wheeling. I heard the hum of the loud hailer and then Righton's voice appealing to Jolene to leave the Land Rover.

Then, to my surprise, he added. 'We have Mr Wilson from the harbour. He is willing to talk to you – no strings. If you are agreeable, please call to us.'

A pause followed, then a faint voice on the wind. 'All right – send him over.'

'Are you willing to undertake this for us?' asked Righton.

'Yes.'

'Very well, I will fetch you some body armour.'

'No, I don't want it.'

Righton gave me an odd look. 'Yes, you're probably right. I

suggest you walk openly but slowly, arms raised and waving a white handkerchief or similar. Have you anything?'

I groped in my pocket and found a handkerchief. It was not overly clean but would suffice.

'Thank you, Mr Wilson. All we are asking you to do is speak nicely to the abductor and ask if there is anything she wants: food, water – that sort of thing. Don't try anything on your own initiative. We're stalling, playing for time.'

'I understand.'

'We'll be covering you all the way but the last thing we need is any rough stuff.' Righton looked at me. 'Mr Rocastle says you have an interest in the boy and his mother.'

'Yes, I suppose I have.'

'Take care, for their sake as much as your own.'

I suppose I should have been frightened, apprehensive at least. I can honestly say that I felt nothing. I had not the slightest doubt that Jolene would kill Tommy without a qualm. I had heard Rita Dunlass say as much. Only I could stop that happening. I had no idea how, but it would happen. It was almost as if my task was predestined.

Once again I walked past the old quarry and onwards towards the cliff top. The Land Rover stood a few yards from the edge and not far from the spot where Tabitha fell. The passenger side window was open and I was very aware of the two-barrelled shotgun poking through the opening. I could see Joline clearly, and on the seat beside her another, smaller figure.

'That'll do, skipper. You stand still!'

I did as I was told.

'Whad'jah want, mate?'

'We're concerned for the boy. We think he should at least have a drink of water.'

She laughed. 'Is that the best you can do? The little sod can have all the drink he wants so long as he don't piss on me.' She held up a pint bottle of mineral water.

'Very well – can we talk terms?'

'That's easy,' she laughed again. 'You get the dicks off this hill and miles away for a start. Otherwise this little bastard joins his daddy.'

The implication was clear. I needed some bluff. 'There's no certainty that Jim Stoneman is dead – we're still checking and there is one unidentified survivor.'

'Oh, don't give me that shit. Old George had the ship packed with a thousand litres of gasoline. The silly old bugger wanted a big bang and he got one.' She paused. 'Why the hell did he run on the rocks – that wasn't in the script.'

'I can't tell you that. Release the boy into my care now and I will see what I can do to persuade the police to meet your terms.'

'Piss off – bludger!' She laughed. 'Go on – get moving.'

The gun went off almost in my face and I felt and heard the whine of the pellets passing over. Badly shaken and temporarily deafened, I turned and walked away with as much dignity as I could manage, though I felt my back cringe.

'No good,' I said to Channing. 'She's crazy – that laugh of hers isn't sane.'

'Never mind; it's a start – you did well. This is mind games and we've given her something to think about.' He looked me over. 'That shot had us worried – you sure you're OK?'

'She aimed into the air. If she'd meant business she couldn't miss.'

'We've been talking with our own experts – psychological profilers and head-shrinks. They think Miss Fuller is not the type of person to sit out a long siege.' Righton looked grim.

I could have told him that. I suspected the woman Jolene, if not totally mad, was slipping over the edge of insanity. I walked away and sat down in a hollow in the grass.

The helicopter still circled; I wondered about its range and fuel load and how much this police operation was costing. Wholly irrational – who cared what the cost was? They could bring in the entire Dorset force and half the army for all I cared and much good it would do. I was the only person who could resolve this. What would my father have thought? He, who had died from the blast of a shotgun, would no doubt find it an amusing irony were I to join him this day by the same route.

'She's out!' I heard a voice.

'All right,' said Righton. 'I can see her.' I heard him talking on his radio, alerting the firearms unit.

Instantly I was on my feet and peering over the top of the hollow. Jolene had Tommy outside the car and she was dragging him towards the cliff edge. In her other hand she still held the gun.

'Hold your fire,' Righton called. 'Wait!'

In retrospect I can only suppose I had some sort of spontaneous-combustion in my brain. I knew that Jolene was hell-bent on the most dramatic exit she could conjure. If I did not act, both woman and boy would go over the cliff to be dashed to bloody pieces on the rocks below. I took off and sprinted towards the pair of them. Behind me I heard shouts: Righton was bellowing through his loud hailer. Tommy saw me, as he cried out and for a couple of seconds he broke free. Jolene threw down the gun chased and caught him. She handed the boy a stinging slap to the head and started to drag him away, only stopping to pick up the gun.

'Back off, Mister,' she jeered.

'You can't aim the gun and hold on to the boy,' I heard my own voice, calm and matter-of-fact. 'Let him go and we'll talk.'

The gun fired. The barrel jerked upwards spewing shot away in the bushes to my left. Jolene was within twenty feet of the cliff and I was within a similar distance from her. Tommy was struggling harder than ever and the woman was red faced and sweaty as she fought to keep hold of his arm. I now believe some force outside myself drove me. I ran straight at her. The gun fired and this time I felt pellets lacerate my ankles. I could feel the pain and the blood that began to seep into my shoes. But Tommy was free; he broke away as Jolene reloaded the gun. He ran to me, dangerously near the cliff edge, and I staggered to gather him into my arms.

'Say, Mister; you the Catcher In The Rye now?' She held the gun and it was aimed at my head.

'Tommy, stand behind me,' I snapped at him. He never moved; only clung tighter.

I could feel pain now, excruciating burning pain, such as I had never felt in my life. I looked down and saw the little pool of blood that had pulsed from my legs onto the turf at my feet. I could see ants struggling to escape this alien liquor.

'That'a'way,' Jolene pointed the gun towards the cliff. 'We're all of us goin' over the White Cliffs of Dover,' she half-sang.

'No!' I shouted. 'Put the gun down and we'll walk back. There's been enough death today.'

She laughed again, the same crazy cackle. 'No way, skipper.'

Tommy's vice like grip had relaxed. I spoke soothingly as I released his hands and gently lowered him to the ground and pushed him behind me. Once again I had become the main target.

'Tommy,' I said. 'Get ready – when I tell you, run. Run to your mother. D'you understand?'

'Yes.'

Jolene had moved to within a metre of us. She held the shotgun in both hands and she grinned. My legs hurt less now, but I was beginning to feel sick and giddy.

'Tommy – *NOW*!' I gave him my sea captain's bellow.

I didn't wait to see his reaction. I ran at Jolene, my hands reaching out for the gun barrel. Too late; she raised the weapon, pushed it into my chest and pulled the trigger.

By all the laws of probability I should that moment have been dead: blown apart by the close range blast. Nothing happened, only a single click. In dreamlike slow-motion I remember seizing the gun and thrusting it aside a fraction before the second barrel exploded throwing its shot skyward. I fought now with a fury I never would have known was in me. I forgot my wounded legs, the sickness and dizziness. I wrestled for that gun, punching my assailant in the face and body, again and again, until finally with a sob she released the thing. With all the strength that was left to me I hurled it into the air and over the cliff. I staggered a few feet and fell to the ground. I could see the woman standing over me face twisted in malice. Then she gasped, her head jerked back, and I heard the bullets rip into her. She fell, body twitching, blood pouring from her mouth and the exit wounds in her back.

Why – why? I'd fought and won. If she died we might never know the truth. I lay in the warm sweet smelling grass. My legs hurt and flies were gathering around my ankles. It was growing dark; much too early. The ground I lay on was spinning like some vast turntable.

Then I saw him: saw that solitary figure standing black against the setting sun – my father.

CHAPTER 48

I was back in familiar territory; the general hospital. I had regained consciousness to see once again my Russian-speaking male nurse. Now I was flat on my back, legs bandaged, my system brimming with painkillers and God knew what else. My memory was a series of very blurred snapshots. The noise of the helicopter, then transfer to an ambulance. Emma, face strained with concern. Laura bending over me muttering something about "you mad sod". Brian Byrne, Ian Rocastle, Tricia and Carol. She, who had said nothing that I remembered, but had sat beside my bed holding my hand for hours.

Now I had emerged from this twilight world to be confronted by my nurse and a doctor, hardly surprising in a hospital, but this man was the same consultant who had treated my mother. I realised I had forgotten all about her. Guiltily, I struggled into a sitting position only to slump instantly on the pillows.

'Your mother is fine,' he reassured me. 'Most amazing patient I've ever had. Despite her age, the bones are knitting nicely – remarkable.'

'When can I see her?'

He laughed. 'Now, hold it, you've only just come in here and you're in none too good a way yourself.'

'What d'you mean?'

'I mean, you've a badly splintered tibia, and there's a nasty lump out of the calf of your left leg. However, the good news is we should be able to patch you up and be out of here in a week or so. After that I suggest no more Mr Action Man. You are well into middle age and you're lucky to have survived – cheated death is what the tabloids are saying.'

'Tabloids?'

'Oh yes, wonderful headlines: *Captain Courageous ... Cliff top avenger...* and there's plenty more. There's a whole posse of them camped outside. We caught one of them with a camera in the corridor here.'

'Oh, God,' I groaned. 'I don't need this.'

'I shouldn't worry. Give 'em a day or so and they'll move on to a soap star sex scandal.'

The consultant proceeded with an examination assisted by the nurse. It was painful and exhausting and ended thankfully with some medication, which sent me out like a light. It didn't prevent dreams, or hallucinations perhaps. Once more I saw the dark outline of my father standing on the cliff top. Had he come to claim me? Well, he'd been denied that pleasure. Bloody-minded fate and a dud cartridge had left me still on this earth. Cheated death, the doctor had said. If so, there must be a reason, however intangible.

Later they helped me to sit up and I managed to eat a little.

'Are you up to a visit from the police?' asked the ward sister. 'They're outside now with Mr Byrne, and a very dyspeptic looking gentleman who says his name is Smith.'

'Oh, God.'

'I'll tell them to go away if you like.'

'No, I'll talk to them.'

This delegation turned out to be Inspector Channing, Brian, and a WPC. 'Where's this Smith?' I asked.

'He's outside,' said Brian, 'and his real name is Dawson Beresford. He's waiting for us to finish and then he'll be in here getting you to sign the Official Secrets Act.'

'He can sod off.'

'You'll have to play ball if you want the full story of your father and everything that's happened to you.'

I looked at the inspector. 'How can I help you?'

'Just a few loose ends. There will be a couple of inquests to which you will be required as a witness.'

'I suppose so.'

'Firstly, the motor yacht *Persephone* was stolen from her mooring and lost in the entrance to Duddlestone Harbour. The marine accident authorities are not wholly happy with the circumstances but I as understand it they are being leaned upon by this Mr Smith. Our concern is with the six deaths.'

'Who was the survivor?'

'He's Mr Eriksen's professional skipper, the man employed to command the ship. He's the one causing problems with Marine Accident and that, Mr Wilson, involves you.' The Inspector's tone was less than friendly.

'It's nothing to do with me if he piles up on the rocks.'

'That is a matter you can discuss with them.'

I was feeling increasingly uneasy as I began to remember details of that day. Brian caught my eye and winked.

The Inspector continued. 'There will also be an inquest into the death of Jolene Marybelle Fuller, in conjunction with a police firearms enquiry. We hope that will be a formality.'

'You shot her after she'd been disarmed,' I said.

'We found a knife on her person; she could still have done you serious damage.'

Maybe, but I would never expunge the image of a living human being ripped to pieces in a hail of bullets.

'I'm glad to see you on the mend,' Channing smiled now. 'I think I will leave you in the hands of Mr Byrne and our friend Smith.'

The police left; suddenly I felt nervous and vulnerable. 'Do I have to see this Smith?'

'Yes,' said Brian, 'and don't make an issue of his bit of paper – sign it, believe me it will pay you to.' He seemed to find something funny in this.

I couldn't see it myself. 'What's the point, I don't know anything.'

'Peter, I know your father's secrets, all of them now. Sign this little bit of paper and your father's reputation will be safe, and you'll be in line for a very nice surprise, if you want it.'

Mr Smith, or Beresford, arrived and departed. The invisible man, I thought. Beresford was one of those who can enter and leave a room and still remain unnoticed. He produced two sheets of paper for me to sign, replaced them in his briefcase and left. Hardly a word was spoken on either side. My attention was slipping, I wasn't sure if I really needed to know my father's secrets; right now I wanted to sleep.

I saw Beresford once more, at the second inquest. Inquests, I had always assumed, were a formal assembling of the facts surrounding a person's violent death. They are not courts of law in the normal sense. There is no cross-examination, no element of combat, just a calm setting out of the truth: not so in either of the Duddlestone hearings. Each could have rivalled the other for a fiction prize.

I had been convalescing at Honeycritch for a month and had just begun to resume full duties at my harbour. In most ways this had been a blissful time; an emergence from darkness to joy that I knew could never last. My relationship with Carol, forged through the hell of the kidnap, was now forever. Nothing could change that and certainly not the gushing letter that my ex-wife Rhona had written to me. Rhona had been reading the inflated press reports. Like the rest of the world she had seen the enhanced footage of the film shot from the police helicopter.

Now came the summons to the inquest into the demise of Jolene. I listened, gob-smacked as Carol would say, as Jonathan Forbes-Watts testified about his daughter's alleged escape from her kidnapper's clutches. A very cagey Inspector Righton stated that, in his opinion, it was Jolene alone who had snatched the children and held Tommy at gunpoint after she had managed to lose Alix. I wondered what pressure had been put on our ambitious inspector and by whom. The coroner pronounced death by justified police action. I shut my ears to his embarrassing spiel about myself; "being prepared to sacrifice his life and only being saved the grace of God". Or by one dud shotgun cartridge, I thought.

'They were Russian – came from a box I'd bought on the cheap for pigeon shooting,' Ian had told me. 'We had six or seven misfires already – I was going to ask for my money back.'

The court had decided that the kidnapping was no more than a scam by a penniless vagrant to extract money from Ford-Watts and from Tricia Rocastle's illustrious daddy, the lord lieutenant. That wretched man had been doing his own meddling. He'd been using his hotline to the Palace and Number Ten. So just as things were beginning to assume some normality it was announced by the great and good that: *Her Majesty the Queen has been pleased to award Captain Peter Wilson, Master Mariner, the George Cross.* The citation said that I, in my *capacity of Harbour Master…had calmly…*, yes, calmly so help us, stood and invited the gun to be fired into my body… *in order that the life of Thomas Stoneman be spared...*

This produced another feeding frenzy by the media who raked up my father's wartime story. A unique father and son double, they claimed. That had got to be bullshit. Father had survived, but two hundred seamen of both nations had perished through his night of reckless lunacy. In my case the wretched Jolene had been bent on self-destruction and though I might have had half a death wish myself I had not been passive. For a few days I hid indoors from a world that had apparently gone mad.

Everybody seemed to have forgotten poor Charlie who had also taken a blast of shot in his legs. Mercifully the pellets at longer range had done him no lasting damage and he had been discharged from the hospital after a couple of days.

I had long talks with Magnus Eriksen and his brother in law Anderssen as well as Brian Byrne and Admiral Sutton. I now knew most of the story; that is if I could really believe in the huge web of deceit that these men had spun down the years, and the strange part that the slow-witted Arthur Rocastle had played.

My father had received secret orders from higher command to co-operate in the staged sinking of the Liberty ship. He was then ordered to remove the gold bullion and hide it. He refused and the pressure began. There came the warning about his career prospects, and the threat to deport my mother to certain death in Stalin's Russia. Sutton told me of other threats, subtle, nasty little blackmails, emanating from some high-placed source that could not be touched by normal law.

My father had worked his own compromise. He'd brought the Liberty ship into Duddlestone harbour but had had no hand in the discharge of her cargo. He'd deputed that to a small, carefully selected party under the direction of one Sub Lieutenant Fuller, assisted by Petty Officer Dunlass. Father had wanted nothing to do with it. He specifically told them to hide the bullion and not to tell him or anyone else where they had put it. Apart from this group, those in the flotilla not already demobbed had been sent on leave. Father had then secured the cliff tops with the aid of Ernest Rocastle and a contingent of his Home Guard – events that led directly to the murder of Margaret Gulley. Dunlass and Fuller had chosen the stores area of the laboratory and cooked up some story for the benefit of Dr Pieter Hooder. Knowing nothing of the concealed bullion, the authorities had blocked the access tunnel as a precaution following the gas attack on the secret lab. Lost, but not forgotten either by Double Six flotilla's crooked element or by the highly placed manipulators.

Magnus Eriksen had a sardonic expression. 'If your father had been a real Captain Kidd, or Long John Silver, there would have been a map with an X on it. No, he deliberately distanced himself from the whole business. The laboratory directors knew something funny was going on, but that was only hours before they were all dead.'

'They had already complained to my father. I found a letter for him in the offices underground. I've still got it if I need it.'

'Your father had already distanced himself from the higher command.'

'But why did he kill himself? For forty years I've worried about that and I'm still baffled.' And guilty, resentful and inwardly scarred.

'He may have suspected he was about to be exposed and wanted to protect your mother and yourself – that's only my conjecture, we'll probably never know.'

I remembered Tabitha's talk about hidden accounts. 'This is to do with that American payroll.'

Eriksen agreed. 'That was Captain Wilson's revenge, or opportunism more likely. After removing the gold, he'd been ordered to sink the ship with everything in it. But would you do that if you'd found half a million dollars in greenback notes?'

'So, you are saying he found these but he didn't declare them.'

'Why should he? As far as officialdom was concerned they were dissolved at the bottom of the sea.'

'It was still theft.'

'Spoils of war. Anyway the Yanks were flush with dollars. They could afford to share a few with the rest of us.'

I tried to digest this, although the story fitted everything that I'd been told. Father had bought the Rocastles their farm, presumably with this money, but surely not with dollar bills.

'Oh no,' said Magnus. 'Robert Fuller was flotilla paymaster, Captain's secretary and general dogsbody. Logistics officer he'd be called these days. He was a bank official in civvy-street, and a dishonest one at that. He knew exactly how to launder this cash. We all benefited. Anderssen and I founded our shipping line – bought our first little inter-island packet ship. Harry Broadenham bought his pub.'

'So you think my father killed himself when he believed he was rumbled?'

'He may have thought that, but even if the authorities knew about the money there was nothing they could do without exposing the whole plot.'

I was subpoenaed to be a witness at the second inquest: the death of six persons in the fireball wreck of the *Persephone*. It was explained that my testimony would be confined to what I had actually seen. I now knew that Keith, with Steve Gulley, had repeated the trick with the harbour leading marks. Keith's motive had been no more than to stop the ship leaving. Like the rest of us he was unaware that George Dunlass had packed the vessel, including the engine room, with drums of petrol. Presumably they had planned to sail with the few boxes they'd secreted away from the main hoard, effect another transfer, and finally explode their ship in a spectacular staged disaster. Eriksen had been sanguine about the loss of his yacht but he'd been incandescent with rage when he'd discovered that his professional skipper had been recruited to the gang. I could have advised him better. The man was a notorious slippery character who'd been dismissed by a ferry company for molesting female passengers.

Byrne was sitting in the public seats. He winked and jerked a thumb in the direction of Beresford. The hearing was an even bigger travesty than the last one. The lone survivor, the before-mentioned ship's captain, told a pack of lies. My God, he was a smooth talker. Those not fully in the know must have been near to tears as he described a loss of steering, a breakdown in the vessel's sophisticated hydraulics. He'd cut the ship's power, resulting in an inexplicable fire and explosion. His voice broke as he told of his personal guilt at his own survival, and his grief at the death of so many good people enjoying a happy holiday.

Now it was my turn. I was asked two questions concerning what I had seen from the shore, and that was that. Death by misadventure. I glanced to where Beresford had been sitting, but he had vanished.

'You're not going to get any more truth out of that lot,' said Brian Byrne.

We were alone in Ashwood cottage. Stanley and Ivy were away for a few days. It had been a difficult time for Ivy as she tried to come to terms with the truth about her brother Arthur.

'As I see it,' said Brian, 'George Dunlass had written off the gold. He assumed he'd never be able to access the lab. Then he had a meeting with Paul Hooder through Jake Stoneman. Hooder wanted details of the tunnel layout – he told George he intended to enter the lab and that it would be safe. One thing to be said for George is that he had some sort of thieves' honour. Robert Fuller was dead, but his granddaughter was still alive in Australia. George put his son Jim in the picture and then sent him out to Oz to find Jolene. Jolene gets Jim into her bed, which wasn't in George's plan.

'George's big mistake was to contact Magnus. Magnus wasn't a party to hiding the loot, but he'd been under pressure for years by Beresford to reveal the place.'

'But he didn't know it,' I intervened, 'nor did my father. Anyway where does Beresford come into this?'

'Beresford's father, Sir Justinian, was the man behind the original scam. I don't think it was monetary gain that drove him. He didn't want the gold to return to the new communist regime in Albania. He had a distorted view of his duty. His son wants to save his dad's reputation – much the way you want to in your case.'

'Not so, Brian. My father stole money.'

'OK, I'll deal with that in a minute.' Brian brushed my question aside. 'Magnus is mega-rich – he didn't give a damn about the gold but he needed Beresford off his back. George Dunlass was the one person alive who knew where the gold was. Magnus convinced him he was fully in support and wanted his share. Then George did something really stupid. It was probably Jolene's idea – kidnapping the two kids to keep the police out of Duddlestone – total stupidity.'

'They were never going to get away with that,' I said. 'Worse, Jolene was prepared to kill them.'

'When Magnus heard about that, 'Brian continued, 'he decided to take the kids into his own safe custody. Admiral Sutton was the link with Beresford and he cleared it with the security services. I don't know what hold they've got over poor Sutton. He's eighty-seven years old, but I suppose he must have some skeleton in his cupboard.'

'Thank God that Magnus grabbed the kids before George or Jolene had a chance,' I said.

'Magnus had his company helicopter based at his farm. All he needed was to lure the kids onto the downs. Hasn't young Tom said anything about it?'

'No, he hasn't and we haven't forced him to. But it's odd; almost as if he thinks he's protecting someone.'

'Probably young Alix. I'm not convinced that little madam wasn't in the know from the beginning. Clever little minx – telling the Rocastles she and Tom were going to the village. Instead they went straight to the downs, where she scrawled that message in a place she knew we'd find it.'

'Brian, they were in a boat. I recognised the noises in the recordings and Tommy said Alix had been seasick.'

'Magnus took them for a joyride in the *Persephone* and somewhere along the way they were joined by Jono Ford-Watts. I think the great actor had a hand in the production of this epic.'

'What does he have to do with this?'

'Probably money, and bigger roles. Magnus's son is Jono's agent. And there's Duddlestone of course. Jono's very keen on this film part; playing your father.'

I sat in thought for a moment. 'George Dunlass must have hidden what he thought was his share in the old chapel. Who got the bullion, or the bulk of it?'

'It was loaded onto that rusty old hulk that Magnus and Anderssen resurrected for the job. It was intercepted by the Navy and transferred at sea, which I imagine would be difficult.' He raised an eyebrow.

‘No problem with the right ship and equipment.’ I remembered how Keith and his boys had identified a Navy auxiliary ship. ‘But fancy the Navy, of all people, leaving that old motor yacht drifting around unmanned in the Needles Channel. That was criminal – as a seaman I rate that a bigger crime than nicking gold.’

‘Yes, but her crew reappeared in time to take the *Persephone*. I don’t think that boat was unmanned. I think the Navy ignored the crew, but when our villains recognised the SBS lads they understandably took fright and hid below decks.’

‘Brian, if the Government knew about the gold and wanted it back, why not send in the army and take it?’

‘The Government never sanctioned the hiding of the gold in the first place, and because of your father nobody knew where it was. Then George Dunlass starts taking interest in Duddlestone again just as the MOD sell it off to Hooder. The spooks were watching, they put two and two together, and for once they were spot on.

‘You see, Sir Justinian, our Beresford’s father, arranged for the bullion to be hidden here on his own say so. Remember, this was post-war, but the security services were in a world of their own. A brand new Labour government was in power and I guess Beresford senior didn’t trust them.’

‘Too many contradictions,’ I replied. ‘Where is the gold now?’

‘On its way back to Albania I would guess. The security services still don’t want the story in the public domain so they’re digging a hole for themselves by letting our incompetent friend Beresford mount this mother of all cover-ups.’

‘But why, what’s the point?’

Brian looked at me with that weary look of a teacher with an especially dumb pupil. ‘Sir Justinian Beresford was the head of a Foreign Office department. If it became common knowledge that a grandee of his standing could get himself enmeshed in a daft plot like this – well it brings them all into disrepute. In other words vox pop – hoi polloi would be wondering if they’re still at it. Imagine all the articles in *The Guardian*.’ He laughed. ‘Think about it – but for Arthur Rocastle they would have got away with it.’

Yes, we now knew the truth about Arthur. Momentarily I had a vision of that young man, face twisted in fury…

‘Brian, this is all your journalist speculation, you wouldn’t be able to prove any of it in a court of law.’

‘Sure, I concede that, but I think I’m not far out. Tabitha Long’s father has let me read her notes, all of them, and with your help I want to put one item to test.'

'Stop talking in riddles. What d'you mean by, "my help"?'

'Why do you think I was so keen for you to sign the Official Secrets Act?'

'I did wonder.'

'You see, as far as Beresford is concerned it cuts both ways. I've signed the Act so there's limits on what I can say. You sign the Act and his secret is secure. By the same token he can't touch you.' Brian paused while this news sank in.

'So what difference will it make to me?'

'Allowing for inflation and fifty years accumulated interest, your father has around a million and a half quid salted away in bank accounts in Liechtenstein. Tabitha claims that he accessed three thousand pounds of it just a week before he died.'

Across the years I remembered. 'Yes, we were going to buy a boat.'

CHAPTER 49

It was now mid September. Carol and her family had one more ordeal to face: Jim Stoneman's funeral. If this was not bad enough there was very little of Jim left to bury. The police forensic teams had recovered four identifiable bodies floating in the sea. None of these was Jim or his father. Eventually the pair of them were found, burned beyond recognition, in the wreckage. Could they, even in that awful inferno, have been trying to save one of their bullion boxes? The coroner had released the remains of George and Rita; business associates had removed them for funeral in Sussex.

I walked with Carol and her family as far as the church wall and the little lychgate that led into the graveyard. It was a gloomy morning as cloud scudded overhead and little flurries of rain dampened the grass. I stood under a tree watching the distant gathering around the grave.

Had Jim Stoneman really meant to drown me when he pushed me into the water? I would never know his motive, only that he was about to be consigned to the ground and I was still alive. I wasn't sure if I could cope with notions of forgiveness. Jolene and Jim had certainly been the killers of Roy Gulley. The police confirmed that the dried yew leaves had been found in the rooms the couple rented. They had also found a computer; stored in its drive had been that nasty little cartoon with Tommy's name printed on a tombstone. One unexplained death remained; the battering of Reg Stoneman at Corfe. It had all the marks of Jolene's work but that would never be proved.

The only good thing this morass of secrecy had yielded was that Tommy need never know the full extent of his father's crime. I did not want that boy to grow up knowing that his father might have attempted to kill his stepfather. I knew what traumatic childhood memories had inflicted on my life. I would spare Tommy that if I could.

'How are things?' A pointless question but what else could I say.

'I'm all right,' Carol replied. 'I can't explain how I feel. Sort of guilty in a way.'

'You've nothing to be guilty about – none of this was your fault.'

'No, it's not about me, it's just that I can't grieve for Jim – it's dreadful, but I feel relief. I made a fool of myself when I married that man and now he's gone for ever – it's over.'

We were standing in the garden at Honeycritch. Ian and Tricia had insisted I come home with them after the funeral. I had agreed reluctantly, although I felt I should leave the family in peace. I was conscious that, whatever the circumstances, I was the one taking the dead man's place. Ian refused to see it that way. 'You're family now – or you will be in a few week's time. Carol's told us about you plans. November 12th to be the big day, I understand.'

'If that meets with everyone's approval.'

'You bet it does – best thing that could have happened. You'll look after my little sister and the boy – they've been through one hell of a time and so have you, I guess.'

Carol put her arm around me. 'I think we should go and see your mother.'

Mother had been discharged from hospital and I had moved her to a convalescent home in the New Forest. My solicitor and bank manager had confirmed the existence of my father's dubious hidden funds. Both had confirmed that there was no legal impediment to mother accessing this money. Overnight, she had become a very rich woman.

Neither she nor Grant were overjoyed to discover this "pirate's blood money" as she termed it.

The rain had cleared and the sun was lighting the lawns and trim borders of the nursing home. Mother was limping determinedly on elbow crutches. She waved one at us in flamboyant greeting and nearly fell over. She refused all help but pointed us to a bench shaded by a hedge. I told her about this morning's funeral.

'Always those Stonemans were bad news,' she said.

'Mother, tact is not your middle name.'

'Nonsense. Carol my dear, come here.' Carol, for the first time this day smiled, bent over mother and gave her an enormous hug.

'You see,' Mother looked severely at me. 'Carol is once again a Rocastle and soon she will be a Wilson.'

'Rocastle sounds much more exotic,' I laughed. 'The phone book is stuffed with Wilsons – fewer Rocastles.'

'Have they buried the one who tried to kill me?' Mother's tone had changed.

'I think the police are still holding the body,' I said. I didn't want to think about the mad Jolene. The recollection of her distorted, jeering face was another demon to disturb future sleep.

'Well, I am still here and I still keep your father's secrets.'

‘I think I know them too,’ I said. ‘Were you really going to spill the beans at the reunion dinner?’

‘Oh yes, I thought it would be such a good thing. Let the world know about the gold, and about that silly boy Arthur.’

We said goodbye to mother and drove back to Duddlestone. Carol seemed subdued; I knew something was troubling her.

‘It’s about Arthur,’ she said. ‘It seems I was wrong about him all along.’

‘He never killed Margaret,’ I replied. ‘Laura was in a state of denial because she thought the killer was your grandfather.’

She spoke quietly. ‘The police think it was George. He rapes and kills Margaret because he believes she’s seen something she shouldn’t, then he tries to shift the blame to Arthur. Can you think of anything more wicked?’

A man prepared to kidnap his own grandson would be capable of anything. Did it tell me something about my own father that he should have put his trust in such a transparent villain as George Dunlass?

‘Peter,’ Carol broke into my thoughts. ‘Can we go for a walk on Weavers Down?’

This surprised me. ‘I’m not sure I ever want to go up there again.’

‘I know that but I still think you should … or we both of us should together – today. It’ll complete things – make a real closure.’

I knew she was right. Confront and slay the demons. ‘All right – we’ll go this evening.’

Once more we stood at the top of the chine looking down upon the village of Old Duddlestone. The harbour pontoons were crammed with visiting and permanently berthed yachts. The violent events of mid-summer were half-forgotten. I could see our new buildings and the sailing club, the brainchild of Mick Tracic, now officially installed as Deputy Harbour Master. The portakabin had vanished, to be replaced by a smart brick office where Laura presided.

We could just see the little waterside cottage that was our home. Naturally I had been anxious as to how Tommy would take my arrival in his mother’s life. The boy never seemed to regard me as an intruder. He had been shy at first, perhaps a trifle awestruck, but I could never be a hero to him for long, and to my great joy we were now firm friends. Emma, who had been a trifle suspicious of Carol, had taken to the boy in a big way. Simon and Mick had been teaching him sailing and he now had his own dinghy to play with in the confines of the harbour.

Carol nudged me. 'Come on.' She pointed towards the summit of the hill.

Slowly we climbed, picking our way over the rough turf, scattering a few rabbits as we went – descendants of those same vermin that Arthur Rocastle had been paid to control. We finally reached the flat plateau with the line of ventilators stretching before us. I paused for breath as I took in the scene. So much had happened here, so much evil in such a beautiful and tranquil place.

'Was that the one Arthur used?' Carol pointed at the nearest ventilator.

'No, it was over there the other side of the cutting to the village. I think he blundered along the line trying to find a grille that unbolted. But it's certain that it was the Navy he was working his spite on.'

'But he couldn't have seen Margaret's murder. We know he was miles away.'

'We'll never know for sure, but I guess Arthur believed George Dunlass killed Margaret and he determined on his own-pay back. I don't know if he meant to kill anyone. I guess he was in such a state of rage he didn't have a coherent thought in his head.'

But he killed the wrong people. I recalled that photograph of Arthur; in his hands the tins of cyanide powder and the stick with its spoon taped on the end. Arthur's wartime task had been rabbit control; an endless round of the downland warrens. The killing powder combined with the damp soil to make a deadly gas. Such practices would probably be illegal today but wartime Britain had other priorities. Did Arthur realise the deadly power he held in those innocuous round tins? Possibly not; anything we knew about him indicated a harmless individual, not a man who would premeditate mass murder.

I had this bleak vision. Arthur blind with rage, scarcely knowing what he did, as he limped along the line of vents desperately trying to unscrew the bolts that held the protective grilles. At last, finding one that yielded, he had poured the contents of all three of his tins down the shaft directly into the water trough below. Arthur Rocastle's mad vengeance and its consequences had remained with us to this day.

THE END

EPILOGUE:

THE YACHTING MONTHLY
Item: November 1997
Around the Coast.
Dorset.

The Harbour and Marina at Old Duddlestone is now under new management. United Marinas report that they have sold their interests to a new consortium: Dudlestone Harbour and Leisure Ltd. The freehold of the village and harbour has also been purchased from the previous owner, Dr Paul Hooder, who is believed to have left the country. The joint majority shareholders of the new consortium are: Magnus Eriksen, Chairman of Omega Yachts, and the Harbour Manager, Capt Peter Wilson GC. A half a million pounds investment in improved facilities is promised over the next two years...

South Africa.
THE CAPE ARGUS.
Item: January 1998.

Dr Paul Hooder, British expert in tropical medicine, addressed the ongoing Seminar in Capetown yesterday afternoon. Dr Hooder the son of South African scientist, Dr Pieter Hooder, told the gathering he had come by chance on technical papers based on his father's research during the Second World War. These scientific conclusions were thought to have been lost until Dr Paul Hooder discovered them among some stored effects of his late father. Dr Hooder claimed the research contained in these papers could lead to a major breakthrough in the treatment of viral and parasite infections common in many parts of Africa. Dr Hooder spoke of his excitement at the discoveries which he claimed complimented much of his own research gathered in the field in Angola...

By the same author

THE NEMESIS FILE

Fourteen days will change Steve's life.

This tense mystery-thriller moves swiftly from Sussex to Copenhagen with interludes in Portsmouth, Italy and Scotland, and ends with a sea chase in a gale
ISBN 0-9548880-0-6

Olympic sailor Cathy Foster says:
Rarely have I read such a racy book! It carries you along at pace, and holds you fast until the very end. Just then you think that maybe this is getting far-fetched, but the punch-line pulls you up short and makes you re-assess the characters and their relationship to events. Suddenly the plot hangs together again in a very satisfactory way, just as good detective stories should.

Instead of long descriptions to 'paint a picture' of all the venues and situations, the writing is succinct and carefully crafted to give the maximum impression for the minimum words. This gives the book its fast tempo, yet nothing is lost because the accurate detailing of locations and action bonds the reader into plot. As a past Olympic sailor myself, I know the sailing venues described in both Chichester Harbour and Copenhagen well, and I can reassure any future reader that the author has definitely done his research. In addition, he's right – you do build life-long bonds with other British athletes and other countries' sailors when you are part of the Olympic team representing your country. It is a pleasure and highly unusual to read a book which describes the joys of sailing and racing so well. Yet it's not a book about sailing, full of technicalities of the sport. Sailing provides the background framework for a story of murder and blackmail where the investigation chases over four countries and three generations of lives.

A thoroughly enjoyable read.